MUTINY ON THE BOUNTY

Also by John Boyne

The Thief of Time
The Congress of Rough Riders
Crippen
The Boy in the Striped Pyjamas
Next of Kin

For more information on John Boyne and
his books, see his website at
www.johnboyne.com

Mutiny on the Bounty

JOHN BOYNE

Doubleday

LONDON · TORONTO · SYDNEY · AUCKLAND · JOHANNESBURG

TRANSWORLD PUBLISHERS
61–63 Uxbridge Road, London W5 5SA
A Random House Group Company
www.rbooks.co.uk

First published in Great Britain
in 2008 by Doubleday
an imprint of Transworld Publishers

A CIP catalogue record for this book
is available from the British Library.

ISBNs 9780385611664 (cased)
9780385611671 (tpb)

Addresses for Random House Group Ltd companies outside the UK
can be found at: www.randomhouse.co.uk
The Random House Group Ltd Reg. No. 954009

The Random House Group Limited supports The Forest Stewardship
Council (FSC), the leading international forest-certification organization. All our
titles that are printed on Greenpeace-approved FSC-certified paper carry the FSC logo.
Our paper procurement policy can be found at
www.rbooks.co.uk/environment

Typeset in 11/15pt Giovanni Book by
Falcon Oast Graphic Art Ltd.

Printed and bound in Great Britain by
Clays Ltd, Bungay, Suffolk

2 4 6 8 10 9 7 5 3 1

For Con

Contents

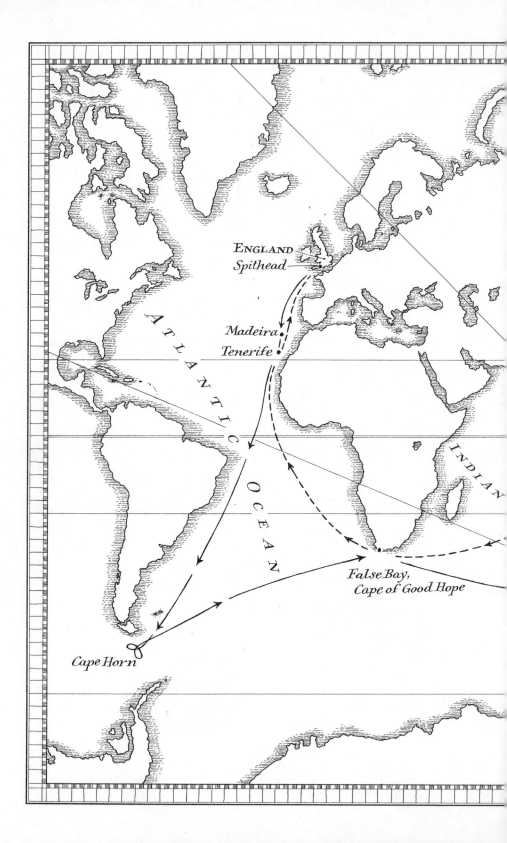

ENGLAND
Spithead

ATLANTIC

Madeira
Tenerife

OCEAN

INDIAN

False Bay,
Cape of Good Hope

Cape Horn

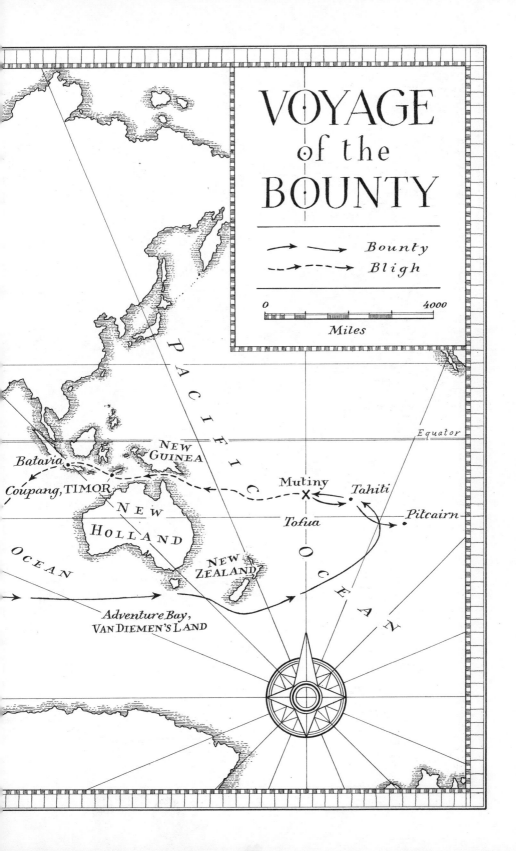

VOYAGE
of the
BOUNTY

→ → → Bounty
- - → - - → Bligh

0   4000
Miles

Equator

PACIFIC

NEW
GUINEA

Batavia

Coupang, TIMOR

NEW
HOLLAND

Mutiny
Tofua

Tahiti

Pitcairn

NEW
ZEALAND

OCEAN

OCEAN

Adventure Bay,
VAN DIEMEN'S LAND

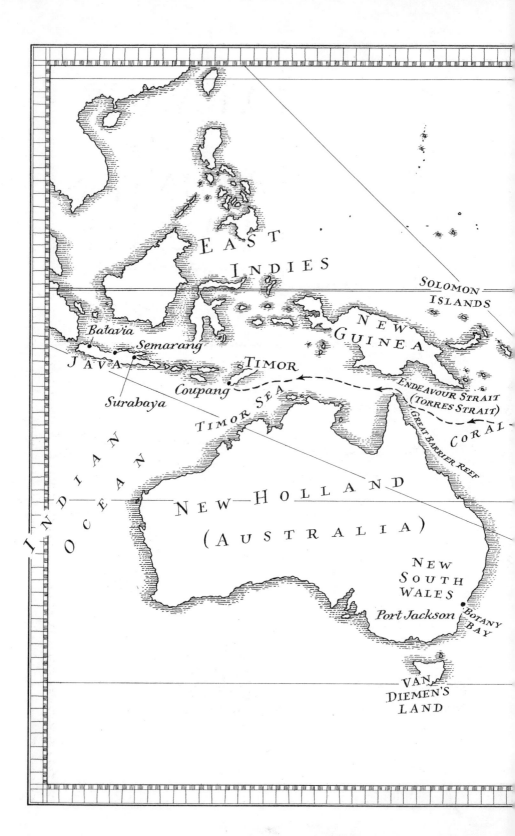

EAST

INDIES

SOLOMON
ISLANDS

NEW
GUINEA

Batavia

Semarang

JAVA

Timor

Coupang

ENDEAVOUR STRAIT
(TORRES STRAIT)

Surabaya

TIMOR SEA

GREAT BARRIER REEF

CORAL

INDIAN

OCEAN

NEW HOLLAND

(AUSTRALIA)

NEW
SOUTH
WALES

Port Jackson

*Botany
Bay*

VAN
DIEMEN'S
LAND

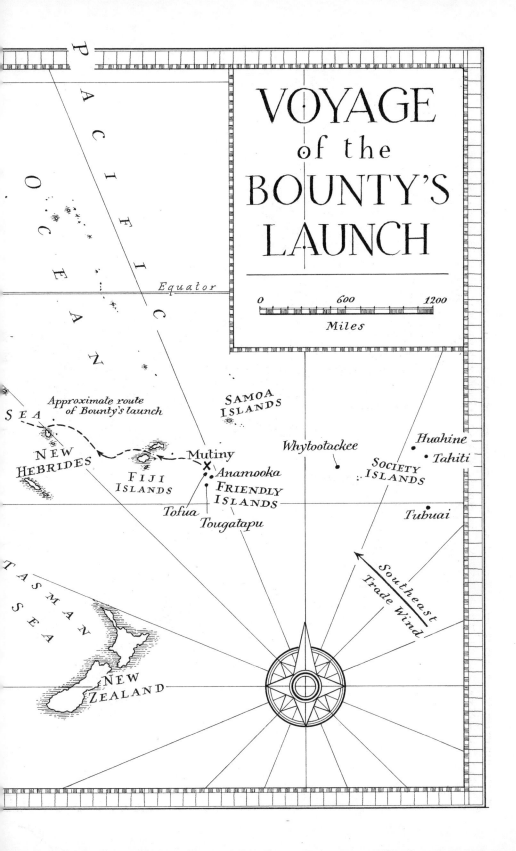

VOYAGE
of the
BOUNTY'S
LAUNCH

0   600   1200
Miles

PACIFIC

OCEAN

Equator

SAMOA
ISLANDS

SEA

Approximate route
of Bounty's launch

NEW
HEBRIDES

Mutiny
X

Anamooka

FIJI
ISLANDS

FRIENDLY
ISLANDS

Tofua

Tougatapu

Whytootackee

Huahine

Tahiti

SOCIETY
ISLANDS

Tubuai

TASMAN
SEA

NEW
ZEALAND

Southeast
Trade Wind

Part I

The Offer

PORTSMOUTH, 23 DECEMBER 1787

1

THERE WAS ONCE A GENTLEMAN, a tall fellow with an air of superiority about him, who made it his business to come down to the marketplace in Portsmouth on the first Sunday of every month in order to replenish his library.

I knew him first on account of the carriage that his man drove him in. The darkest black you ever saw, it was, but speckled at the top with a row of silver stars, as if he had an interest in a world outside our own. He always spent the best part of a morning browsing through the bookstalls that were laid out in front of the shops or running his fingers along the spines of those on the shelves indoors, pulling some out to take a look at the words inside, passing others from hand to hand as he examined the binding. I swear he came close to sniffing the ink off the pages, he got so close to some of them. Some days he'd come away with boxes of books that had to be fitted on to the top of his carriage with a length of hemp-rope so they wouldn't fall off. Other times he'd be lucky if he found a single volume that interested him. But while he was finding a way to lighten his wallet through his purchases, I was looking for a way to lighten his pockets of his belongings, as was my trade back then. Or one of them anyway. I had some handkerchiefs off him from time to time and a girl I knew, Floss Mackey, would pick out the stitching in the monogram – MZ – for a farthing so that I might sell them on to a laundress for a penny, and she in turn would find a buyer for each one at a tidy profit that would keep her in gin and pickles. Another time, he placed his hat on a cart outside a haberdashery shop and I had it too and sold it on for a bag of marbles and a feather from a crow. I tried for his wallet on occasion but he kept it close, like gentlemen do, and when I saw it emerge to pay the bookseller I could tell he was a man who liked to keep his money about him and determined that one day it would be mine.

I mention him now, right here at the start of this narrative, in order to relate a piece of business that took place on one such Sunday market morning, when the air was uncommonly warm for a Christmas week and the streets were uncommonly quiet. It was to my disappointment that there were not more gentlemen and ladies making their purchases at that time as I had my eye on a special luncheon in two days' time to mark the Saviour's birth and was in need of the shillings to pay for it. But there he was, my particular gentleman, dressed in his finery and with a whiff of cologne about him, and me hovering in the background, waiting for the moment I might make my move. Usually it would have taken a charge of elephants through the market to distract him from his perusals, but on this December morning he took a notion to look in my direction and for a moment I thought he was on to me and I was done for, even though I had yet to commit the act of felony.

'Good morning, my boy,' said he, taking his spectaculars off and peering across at me, smiling a little too, acting the hoity-toit. 'It's a fine morning, isn't it?'

'If you like sun at Christmas time, which I don't,' said I, all bluff.

The gentleman thought about this for a moment and narrowed his eyes, cocking his head a little to the side as he looked me up and down. 'Well, there's an answer,' he said, sounding as if he was unsure whether he approved of it or not. 'You'd rather it was snowing, I expect? Boys generally do.'

'Boys maybe,' I replied, pulling myself up to my full height, which was nowhere near as tall as the gent but taller than some. 'Men don't.'

He smiled a little and examined me further. 'I do apologize,' said he, and I thought I heard a trace of an accent in there somewhere. French, maybe, although he disguised it well as was only right and proper. 'I didn't mean to insult you. You are clearly of a venerable age.'

'It's perfectly all right,' said I, offering him a small bow. I'd turned fourteen two days earlier, on the night of the Solstice, and had determined that I wasn't going to be spoken down to by anyone from then on.

'I've seen you here before, haven't I?' he asked me then, and I thought about walking away without an answer as I had neither the time nor the inclination for a conversation, but I held my position for now. If he was a Frenchie as I believed, then this was my place, not his. What with me being an Englishman, I mean.

'Like as not,' said I. 'I don't live so very far away.'

'And might I enquire as to whether I've discovered a fellow connoisseur of the arts?' he continued, and I frowned as I thought about it, picking at his words like the meat on a bone and shoving my tongue into the corner of my mouth to make it bulge out in the way that makes Jenny Dunston call me deformed and bound for the knackers' yard. There's a thing about gentlemen: they never use five words where fifty will do. 'A love of literature brings you here, I assume?' he asked then, and I thought to hell with this and was about to issue a curse on his head and turn on my heel in order to go to find another squirrel, when he let this enormous laugh out of him as if I was some sort of simpleton and raised the volume he was holding in my direction. 'You like books?' he said finally, bringing it down to brass tacks. 'You enjoy reading?'

'I do,' I admitted, thinking about it. 'Although I don't often have any books to read.'

'No, I'd imagine not,' he said quietly, taking a look at my clothes, up and down, and I suppose he could tell from the motley garments I was sporting that I was not blessed with an abundance of funds at that precise moment. 'But a young boy like you should always have access to books. They enrich the mind, you see. They ask questions of the universe and help us to understand our place in it a little better.'

I nodded and looked away. It wasn't my particular habit to get into conversations with gentlemen and I was damned if I was going to start on a morning like that.

'I only ask . . .' he continued as if he was the Archbishop of Canterbury and was in the process of delivering a sermon to an audience of one but wasn't about to be put off by the lack of numbers in attendance. 'I only ask because I feel sure that I've seen you around here before. At the marketplace, I mean. And by the bookstalls in particular. And I happen to hold young readers in high regard. My own nephew, why, I can't get him to open a book to so much as the frontispiece.'

It was true that the bookstalls were my regular places of business, but only because that was a good location to trap a squirrel, that was all, for who else can afford to buy books, only them as have money? But his question, although not an accusation, gave me the resentments, so I thought I'd play along for a little while and see what a farce I could make of him.

'Well, I do love a good read,' said I then, rubbing my hands together and sounding for all the world like the well-schooled son of the Duke of Devonshire, all dickied up in his Sunday best, clean ears and polished dentals. 'Oh, yes, I do indeed. In fact, I have a mind to visit China myself one day, if I can afford the time away from my present responsibilities.'

'China?' asked the gentleman then, staring at me as if I had twenty heads. 'I beg your pardon, did you say China?'

'I most certainly did,' I replied, offering him a slight bow, imagining for a moment that maybe he would take me on as his lad and keep me in finery if he thought me educated; a change in circumstances, of course, but perhaps not a disagreeable one.

He continued to stare and I fancied that I might have got this wrong somehow, for he appeared to be entirely confused by what I had said. Truth to tell, Mr Lewis – him as took care of me in those early years and in whose establishment I had lodged for as long as I could recall – had only given me two books to read in my life and they both happened to have their stories set in that distant land. The first concerned a man who had sailed there on a rusty old tub, only to be set a multitude of tasks by the emperor himself before being allowed to marry his daughter. The second was a saucy tale with pictures in it and Mr Lewis would show it to me from time to time and ask me whether it gave me the motions.

'In fact, sir,' said I then, stepping towards him and glancing at his pockets to see whether there might be there a stray handkerchief or two springing out, seeking liberation and a new owner. 'If I may be so bold as to say so, I have a fancy to become a book-writer myself when I'm of age.'

'A book-writer,' he said, laughing, and I stopped where I was, my face like granite. Gentlemen like him, that's how they all behave. They might seem friendly when they talk to you but just you try to express a desire to make something better of yourself, maybe to be a gentleman yourself one day, and they take you for a fool.

'I apologize,' he said then, observing the disapproving look on my face. 'I wasn't making jest, I assure you. If anything, I applaud your ambition. You took me by surprise, that's all. A book-writer,' he repeated now when I said nothing, neither accepting nor rejecting his apology. 'Well, I wish you well with it, Master—?'

'Turnstile, sir,' said I, bowing a little again out of habit – and one that I was trying to break, I might add, for my back didn't need the exercise any more than gentlemen needed the adulation. 'John Jacob Turnstile.'

'Then, I wish you well with it, Master John Jacob Turnstile,' said he in what I suppose was something approaching a pleasant voice. 'For the arts are an admirable pursuit for any young man intent on bettering himself. In fact, I devote my own life to their study and support. I don't mind admitting that I've been a bibliophile from the cradle and it has enriched my life and provided my evenings with the most glorious companionship. The world needs good story-tellers and perhaps you will be one if you pursue your aims. You are familiar with your letters?' he asked me, turning his head to the side a little like a schoolteacher awaiting response.

'A, B, C,' said I in as posh a voice as I could muster. 'Followed by their compatriots D through to Z.'

'And you write with a fair hand?'

'Him as looks after me said my lettering recalls his own mother's and *she* were a wet-nurse.'

'Then, I suggest you acquire as much paper and ink as you can afford, young man,' said the gentleman. 'And take to it at once, for it is a slow art and requires much concentration and revision. You hope to make your fortune from it, of course?'

'I do, sir,' said I . . . and then the strangest thing! I found that in my head I was no longer making a farce of him at all but was thinking what a fine thing that would indeed be. For I *had* enjoyed the stories I had read of China and I *did* spend most of my time by the bookstalls in the marketplace when everyone knew that the squirrels ran wilder around the fabric shops and the public houses.

The gentleman looked to be finished with me now and replaced his spectaculars on his nose, but before he turned away I made bold enough to ask him a question.

'Sir,' said I, the nerves coming out in my voice now, which I tried to control by deepening it. 'Sir, if I may?'

'Yes?' he asked.

'If I *were* to be a book-writer,' said I, choosing my words carefully because I wanted a sensible answer from him, 'if I *were* to try such a thing, and knowing that my letters are learned and my hand is fair, where would I begin exactly?'

The gentleman laughed a little and shrugged his shoulders. 'Well, I've never had the creative touch myself, I admit it,' he replied finally. 'I'm more of a patron than an artist. But if I was to tell a story, I suppose I should try to locate the very first instance, that singular point in my tale, that set the whole business in motion. I would find that moment and begin my narrative from there.'

He nodded then, dismissing me at last, and turned back to his perusals, leaving me to my cogitations.

The very first instance. The moment *that set the whole business in motion.*

I mention this now and here because the moment that set *my* business in motion was that very meeting two mornings before Christmas Day with the French gentleman, without which I might never have known either the bright or dark days that were to follow. Indeed, had he not been there that morning in Portsmouth, and had he not allowed his pocket-watch to rest off its fob and peep too temptingly from his greatcoat, then I might never have stepped forward and transferred it from the luxurious warmth of his lining to the cold comfort of my own. And it is unlikely that I would have walked carefully away from him in the manner in which I had been trained, whistling a simple melody to illustrate the casual air of a fellow without a care in the world going about his honest business. And I most certainly would never have made my way to the entrance of the marketplace, satisfied with the knowledge that a morning's money had already been earned, Mr Lewis would be paid, and a Christmas dinner would surely be mine two days hence.

And had I never done *that*, I would have absolutely been denied the pleasure of hearing the piercing sound of a blue's whistle and seeing the sight of a crowd turning towards me with angry eyes and ready limbs, nor felt the grinding of my head as it met the cobbles beneath when some great lummox of a do-gooder jumped atop me and set me off my pins and on to the flat of the ground.

None of this might have happened and I might never had a story to tell.

But it did. And I do. And here it is.

2

WHISKED AWAY, I WAS! Whisked like an egg and beaten just as soundly. These are the moments when your life's not your own, when others grab you and take you and force you to go where you've no business going. And I should know, having suffered more than my fair share of such moments in fourteen years. But once that whistle is heard and the crowd around you turn in your direction and focus their nasty eyes on you, ready to accuse, try and judge, why, you might as well get down on your knees and pray to disappear into thin air as hope to escape without a bloodied nose or a blackened eye.

'Hold off there!' came a cry from outside the scrum, but little did I know who it was, covered as I was by the weight of four separate traders and a simpleton woman, who'd placed herself atop the rabble and was screeching with laughter and clapping her hands together as if there had been no better sport all year long. 'Hold off there! Mind, or the boy will be crushed!'

That was a rare thing to hear, a fellow taking the side of a young villain like myself, and I resolved to pass a nod of appreciation to the utterer of the lines if ever I found myself blinking in the daylight again. Knowing what indignities might be on the horizon, however, I was content to pass a few idle moments stretched out on the cobbles, the peel of an orange pressed against my nostrils, the core of a rotten apple settled by my lips, and a bloody great arse making itself friendly with my right ear.

Soon enough, however, a chink of brightness appeared through the mess of bodies above me and up they stood one by one, the weight gradually decreasing atop me, and when him with the bloody great arse took himself off my head I lay heavily on the ground for a moment longer, looking up as I tried to assess my options, only to see the hand of a blue reaching down and grabbing me, without courtesy, by the lapels.

'Let's have you up now, lad,' said he, dragging me to my feet, and to my shame I stumbled a little as I recovered my balance and the people watching made a farce of me for it.

'He's drunk,' cried one, which was a slander as I never take a drink before lunchtime.

'A young thief, is it?' asks the blue, ignoring whoever had offered the lie.

'There *was* a young thief,' said I, trying to brush myself down and wondering how far I'd get if he was to lose his grip for a moment and I was to make a run for it. 'Tried to make off with the gentleman's pocket-watch, he did, and only for I nabbed him and called for the blues he'd have had it too. A hero is what I am, only this bloody great mess leapt on me and shoddy well nearly killed me. The *thief*,' I added, pointing in a direction that made everyone turn their heads for a moment before looking back at me, 'ran yonder.'

I looked around, trying to gauge the reaction of the crowd, knowing full well that they were not stupid enough to be taken in by such a lie. But I was trying to think on my feet and this is what I came up with on the spur of the moment.

'An Irish fella, he was,' I added then, for the Irish were hated in Portsmouth on account of their dirty ways and their filthy manners and the habit they had of procreating with their sisters and so were easy to blame for anything that went on outside the straight and legal. 'Babbling away in a language I didn't understand, he was, and him with the ginger hair and the big buggy eyes as well.'

'But if that's the case,' said the blue, towering over me, standing up so tall on his toes that I thought he might take flight. 'What might this be, then?' He reached into my pocket and extracted the French gentleman's timepiece and I stared at it, the eyes fairly popping out my head now in surprise.

'The scamp,' I cried, a note of outrage racing into my tone. 'The vandal and miscreant! Oh, I am done for! He put it there, I swears it, he put it there before he ran. They do it, you see, when they know they can't escape. Try to blame another. What need have I of a watch anyway? My time's my own!'

'Save your lies,' said the blue, shaking me again for good effect and placing his hands about me in such a way that I swear I was giving him the motions. 'Let's just take a look and see what else you have secreted about your rascally person. Been thieving all the morning long, I'd warrant.'

'Not a bit of it,' I shouted. 'I am slandered. Hear me now!' I appealed to the crowd around me and what do you think happened next, only the simpleton woman came up and stuck her tongue in my ear! I leaped back out of her way, for the Saviour alone knew where that tongue had been and I didn't want a taste of her clap.

'Back there now, Nancy,' said the blue and she stepped away, sticking that same filthy tongue of hers out at me now with an air of defiance. What I wouldn't have given for a freshly sharpened knife at that moment and I might have had her tongue from her mouth in a trice.

'Wants hanging,' shouted one man, a fellow who I knew for a fact spent every penny of his earnings from his fruit stalls on the gin and had no business laying accusations at me.

'Leave him with us, sir,' shouted another, a lad who'd known a stretch or two inside himself and should have taken my side on account of it. 'Leave him with us and we'll teach him a thing or two about what's belonging to him and what's belonging to the rest of us.'

'Constable, please . . . if I may?' said a more refined voice, and then who should make his way through the gathered crowd but the French gentleman, him as had every right to condemn my soul to eternal damnation but who I now recognized as the one who had tried to stop my annihilation under the mound of stinking carcasses not five minutes before. The crowd, sensing a gentleman, parted as if he was Moses and they were the Red Sea. Even the blue loosened his grip on me a little and stared. That's what a smart voice and a fine greatcoat will do for you and I resolved at that moment to be the possessor of both one day.

'Good morning, sir,' said the blue now, bringing his voice to a posher place now, the dirty dog, trying to equal the gentleman. 'And are you the victim of this here miscreant?'

'Constable, I believe I can vouch for the boy,' he answered, sounding as if the whole mess was his fault really and not my own. 'My pocket-watch was inauspiciously placed about my person and in imminent danger of falling to the ground, where no master craftsman would have been able to repair the damage done to it. I believe the boy was merely taking it to hand it back. We had been engaged in a conversation about literature.'

There was a silence for a moment and I have to admit that I almost believed his words myself. Could it be that I was as much a victim of this unhappy circumstance as anyone? Should I be released without further assault on my character and good name and perhaps a letter of commendation from a person in a position of authority? I looked to the blue, who considered it for a moment, but the crowd, sensing an end to their sport and a denial of due course and proper punishment, took up the cudgel in his place.

'It's a sham, Constable,' shouted one, spitting the words out so hard that I had to duck to swerve away from his nasty gob. 'I saw him with my own eyes putting the watch in that there pocket of his.'

'Saw him, did you?'

'And it's not the first time either,' roared another. 'He had five apples off me not four days ago and I didn't see a penny for them.'

'I wouldn't eat your apples,' I shouted back at him, for it was a terrible lie. I'd only taken four apples and a pomegranate on the side for a pudding. 'They've weevils in them, every one.'

'Oh, don't let him say it!' shouted the woman beside him, his old hag of a wife, and her with a face on her that would send you cross-eyed. 'Ours is a going concern,' she added, appealing to the gathered masses with arms outstretched. 'A going concern!'

'That boy's a bad 'un,' called another now and they sensed blood, that was all. You don't want to get a crowd against you at a moment like that. As it happened I was almost glad the blue was there for had he not been, they might have torn me limb from limb, French gentleman or no French gentleman.

'Constable, please,' said the very same now, stepping closer and taking the watch back, I noticed, as that blue would surely have pocketed it himself in a heartbeat. 'I'm sure the boy could be released on his own recognizance. Do you regret your actions, child?' he asked me and this time I didn't bother to correct his use of the word.

'Do I regret them?' I asked. 'As God is my witness, I regret them all. I don't know what came over me in fact. The devil, no doubt. But I repent in honour of Christmas Day. I repent of all my sins and swear that I will go forth from this place and sin no more. What God has joined together, let no man tear asunder,' I added, remembering what few of the Good Words I had ever heard and joining them together to put my devotion on display to all.

'He repents, Constable,' pleaded the French gentleman, opening his hands wide now in a gesture of magnanimity.

'But he admitted the theft!' roared a man whose stomach was so big that a cat could have rested on it and got a good sleep. 'Take him away! Lock him up! Whip him soundly! He has confessed the crime!'

The blue shook his head and looked at me. Between his two front teeth were the remains of what I believed to be a stew dinner; just looking at it gave me the revulsions. 'You are apprehended,' he informed me then in a serious tone.

'And you must pay recompense for your abominable crime.'

The crowd cheered in support of their freshly crowned hero and turned as one when the sound of a carriage was heard pulling in behind the French gentleman's own fleet and, what was it, only the blue's brougham. My heart sank when I saw another blue at the reins of it and in a trice he was down from his spot and on his feet, unlocking the back doors.

'Come along, now,' said the first one in a booming voice for all to hear. 'And your judge will be waiting for you at the end of our journey, so you may start to tremble in anticipation of his magnificence.' I swear he should have been a sham-actor on the stage.

The jig was up and I knew it then but I dug my heels in firmly to the gaps between the cobbles nevertheless. For the first time I did sincerely regret my actions but not on the grounds that I had committed an error in my personal morality, such as it was. Rather, because I had committed one too many of the same in the past, and even though this particular blue didn't know me, there were others as would where I was going and I was only too aware that the punishment might not entirely fit the crime. I had but one recourse left to me.

'Sir,' I shouted, turning to the Frenchman, even as the blue started pulling me in the direction of my hearse. 'Sir, help me, please. Take pity. It was an accident, I swears it. I had too much sugar for my breakfast, that was all, and it gave me ideas.'

He looked at me and I could see that he was thinking about it. On the one hand, he must have been recalling the pleasant con-versation we had been engaged in not ten minutes before and my abundant knowledge of the land of China, not to mention my ambitions towards book-writing, of which he was wholly in approval. On the other hand, he had been robbed, plain and simple, and what's wrong is wrong.

'Constable, I decline to press the charge,' he shouted finally and I gave an almighty cheer, such as a Christian might have offered when Caligula, the dirty savage, gave him the thumbs-up in the Coliseum and let him live to fight once more.

'I am saved!' I roared, pulling myself loose from the blue for a moment, but he took me back in hand again quick enough.

'Not a bit of it,' he said. 'You were witnessed in the act and must pay or you'll be left here to rob again.'

'But, Constable,' cried the French gentleman, 'I absolve him of his crime!'

'And who are you, the Lord Jesus Christ?' asked the blue, which made the crowd erupt in laughter, and he turned in surprise at their commendation but his eyes lit up, thrilled with himself that they thought him a fine fellow and an entertainer to boot. 'He'll be taken to the magistrate and from there to the gaol, I dare say, to pay for the gruesome act, the little deviant.'

'It's monstrous—' came the retort, but the blue was having none of it.

'If you've something to say, then you can say it to the magistrate,' he offered as a parting shot, walking towards the carriage now and dragging me behind him.

I fell to the ground to make things more difficult for him, but he continued to haul me along the sodden street and I can picture the scene in my own head still, my arse going bumpity-bumpity-bump over the cobbles as I was wrenched in the direction of the carriage doors. It hurt; I didn't know why in hell I was doing it but I knew that I wouldn't stand up and make his job any easier. I'd rather have eaten a beetle.

'Help me, sir,' I cried as I was thrown inside the carriage and the doors were slammed in my face, so close that they nearly took my nose off. I gripped the bars in front of me and made the most pleading face that I could muster, a picture of innocence disbelieved. 'Help me and I'll do whatever it is you ask of me. I'll wax your boots every day for a month! I'll polish your buttons till they shine!'

'Take him off!' shouted the crowd and some of them even

dared to throw rotten vegetables in my direction, the scuts. The horses lifted their hoofs and off we went on our merry way, me in the back wondering what fate awaited me when I met the magistrate, who knew me only too well from past acquaintanceship to show any compassion.

The last thing I saw as we turned the corner was a picture of the French gentleman, stroking his chin as if thinking what to do for the best now that I was in the hands of the law. He lifted his pocket-watch to check the time . . . and what do you think happened next? It only slipped from his grip and fell to the ground below. Easy to see that the glass would smash from the force of it too. I threw up my hands in disgust and settled down to see whether I could find a bit of comfort at the very least on the journey, but there was little to be had in the back of one of those contraptions.

They're not designed for consolation.

3

SWEET JESUS AND HIS BLESSED MOTHER, if life isn't difficult enough, the blues made sure to ride the horses over every hole in the ground on the way to the magistrate's court and the carriage was up and down like a bride's nightdress from the moment we left Portsmouth. It was all right for them; they had a soft flush of cushion beneath their arses, but what did I have? Nothing but the hard metal that served as a seat for those who have been taken against their will. (And what of the falsely accused? I wondered. Made to suffer such indignities!) I buried myself deeply in the corner of the transport and tried to maintain a grip of the bars in the hope that they might hold me still, for the alternative was to be unable to sit down for the week that followed, but it was no use. They did it to taunt me, I swear they did, the scuts. And finally, when we reached the centre of Portsmouth and I thought this ordeal might be drawing to an end at last, bugger me if the carriage didn't drive on, directly past the closed doors of justice, and forward on to the lumpy road ahead.

'Here,' I cried, banging like good-oh on the ceiling of the carriage. 'Here, you up top!'

'Quiet in there or there'll be a thrashing in it for you,' shouted the second blue, the one who held the reins, not the one who seized me from my honest bit of thievery that morning.

'But you've driven too far,' I shouted back at him. 'You've gone right past the courts.'

'That familiar with them, then, are you?' he called back, laughing. 'I might have known you'd have seen the inside of the courthouse on many a past afternoon.'

'And am I not to see it today?' I asked and I wasn't too proud to admit that I started to feel a little nervous when I realized that we were leaving the town entirely. I'd heard stories about boys who had been taken off by the blues and were never seen again; all sorts happened to them. Unspeakable things. But I wasn't that bad a boy, I thought. I'd done nothing to deserve such a fate. Added to this was my knowledge that Mr Lewis would be expecting me back soon enough with the morning's spoils, and if I didn't come there'd be hell to pay.

'The Portsmouth magistrate's away for the week,' came the reply and this time he sounded friendly enough and I thought that maybe they were just driving me out of the town and were going to deposit me head-first in a ditch somewhere and encourage me to ply my trade somewhere far from their patch, a proposition I was not opposed to in principle. 'Up in London, if you can believe it. Being given an honour by the king. For services rendered to the laws of the land.'

'Mad Jack?' I asked, for I was only too familiar with that old scut of a magistrate from one or two dealings with him in the past. 'What's the king gone and done that for? Ain't there no one around who's earned a gong?'

'You hold your tongue back there,' said the blue, snapping at me. 'Or there'll be an extra charge on the list.'

I sat back then and decided to keep my own counsel for the time being. Considering the road we were taking, I imagined we were headed for Spithead; on my last-but-one apprehension a year earlier (on another charge of larceny, I'm ashamed to admit), I was taken to Spithead to pay my penance. On that occasion, I'd stood before an evil creature by the name of Mr Henderson, who had a mole in the middle of his forehead and a mouth full of rotten teeth, and he'd made remarks to me about the character of boys my age as if I was a representative for the whole shoddy lot of them. He'd sentenced me to a birching for my troubles and my arse had stung like a field of nettles for a week afterwards and I'd prayed that I would never come before him again. But looking out of the carriage I was sure that this was the very direction in which we were headed, and when it settled in my mind I took fright within and I was glad I'd allowed myself to go bumpity-bumpity-bump over the cobbles and been thrown around this carriage too as there was more than a middling chance my arse would be so numb by the time I reached the courthouse that I wouldn't feel a thing when they pulled my britches down and whipped me raw.

'Here,' I shouted, moving to the other side of the carriage now and calling out to the first blue, since we had established a relationship of sorts during the apprehension. 'Here, blue,' said I. 'We're not going to Spithead, are we? Tell me we're not.'

'How can I tell you we're not when the fact is that we are?' he asked with a bark of a laugh, as if he'd make a fine joke.

'We never are!' said I, in a quieter voice this time as I mulled over the consequences of this, but he heard me nonetheless.

'We certainly are, my young rascal, and you will be dealt with there in a manner befitting young thieves such as yourself. Are you aware that there are certain countries in the world where he who takes the possessions of another without permission has his hand lacerated at the wrist? Is this a punishment you find yourself deserving of?'

'Not here, though,' I shouted defiantly. 'Not here! Scare me, will you? That kind of thing doesn't happen here. This is a civilized country and we treat our decent, honest thieves with respect.'

'Where, then?'

'Abroad,' said I, sitting back in the carriage, deciding to have no further conversation with either one of them, the ignorant pups. 'China, for one.'

Little more was said after that, but for the rest of the journey I could hear those two halfwits cackling away like a pair of old hens on a door stoop and I'm sure I heard the sound of a vessel of beer being passed between their grubby paws, which would also account for the fact that we slowed down halfway to Spithead and one of the blues – the driver – stopped the carriage and stepped off to empty his bladder by the side of the road. No shame had he either, for he turned right in my direction in the middle of it and tried to aim his emissions through the bars at me, which made the other blue almost fall off the carriage in a hysteric. I wished he would as he might have cracked his skull into the bargain and that would have been a pretty picture.

'Get away, you filthy scut,' I shouted at him, retreating further back into the carriage, out of his line of fire, but he just laughed and finished his business before putting his whistle away and dribbling the remains down the front of his pants, so little respect did he have for himself or his uniform. Blues are a force unto themselves, everyone knows that, but they're a rum lot too. I never met one I didn't want to kick.

We got to Spithead within the hour and didn't they both take great pleasure in opening the carriage doors and wrenching me out by the arms, as if I was a baby who didn't want to take leave of his mother at birth-time. I swear the bones nearly popped out of their sockets and I don't want to think what might have happened to me then.

'Come on, lad,' said the first blue, the one who took me in the first place, ignoring my protests at their dirty violence. 'Enough of your lip now. In we go.'

The courthouse at Spithead was nowhere near as grand as the one in Portsmouth and the magistrates who worked there were a bitter lot. Every one of them wanted to come to the county capital to try the cases, as every fool knows that you get a much better class of criminal in a capital than you do in a town. In Spithead there was never much to listen to except a few cases of drunkenness or a bit of petty larceny. A year before there'd been a lot of noise about a man who'd taken a girl against her will, but the magistrate had let him go on account of him having twenty hectares and her only being from common stock. She should have been grateful for the privilege of his familiarity, the magistrate had told her, and this hadn't gone down well with her people at all and a week later, what happened, only the magistrate himself turned up dead in a ditch with a hole the size of a brick in his head (and the brick itself settled peacefully by the roadside). Everyone knew who'd done it but nothing was said and him as had the twenty hectares moved immediately to London before the same could be done to him and he sold the land to a gypsy family who could read the cards and grow potatoes in the shape of livestock.

The blue dragged me down a long corridor, one that I remembered only too well from my previous visitation, and we charged along at such a pace that I thought on several occasions I might take a fall and that would be the end of me, as the floor below was solid granite and wouldn't stand for a soft head like mine thumping against it. My feet were fairly dancing along the floor behind me as he hauled me along.

'Slow the pace,' I cried out. 'We're in no hurry, are we?'

'Slow the pace, he said,' muttered the blue, laughing and talking to himself, I supposed. 'Slow the pace! Did you ever hear the like?'

Abruptly he took a right turn and opened a door and so taken by surprise was I at the sudden change in direction that I finally lost my footing on the ground beneath and toppled over, tripping arse over tea-kettle as I spilled into the courtroom, disgracing myself in the process. And before I could right myself, the whole place fell to a hush and every head and wig in the place turned to stare in my direction.

'Make quiet that boy!' roared the magistrate on the bench – and who was it, only old Mr Henderson again, that grizzly creature, but who was so ancient, with forty or forty-five years on him, if he had a day, that he was sure to have the influenza of the mind and wouldn't remember me from the time before. I'd only been there once after all. They could hardly take me for a career criminal.

'Apologies, your honour,' said the blue, taking a seat and forcing me down on to the bench beside him. 'A late case, I'm afraid. Portsmouth is closed.'

'I am aware of that,' said Mr Henderson, making a face as if he'd just taken a bite out of an infected ferret and swallowed it whole. 'It appears that the courts there are more interested in the collection of accolades and baubles than in the proper dispensation of justice, I fear. Not like here in Spithead.'

'No, indeed,' said the blue, nodding his head in agreement so hard that I thought it might fall off entirely and his decapitation could afford me an opportunity for escape. Security at the doors, I noticed with a deal of pleasure, was not what it might have been.

'Now, to return to the case in hand,' said Mr Henderson, turning away from us and looking towards the man who was standing in front of him and who appeared very low, very low indeed; his cap was held between his hands and a look of total dismay was collected about his horse-like features. 'You, Mr Wilberforce, are a discredit to the community and I find that it would serve us all for the better if you were removed from it for a period of time.' He made sure that every word was loaded with disgust and superiority, the scut.

'Your honour, if it pleases you,' said the fellow in question, piping up and attempting to straighten himself, but perhaps his back was giving him the tractions because he appeared unable to present himself in a vertical manner. 'I was not of my true mind when the incident occurred and that's the truth of it. My dear sainted mama, her as was taken from me only a few short weeks before my error of judgement, appeared to me in a vision and told me that—'

'Enough of this nonsense!' roared Mr Henderson, banging his mallet on the bench before him. 'I swear by almighty God that if I hear another word about your dear sainted mama I shall sentence you to join her forthwith. Don't think I won't do it either!'

'For shame!' called one woman and the magistrate stared out at the collective, one eye closed, the other opened so wide that I felt sure that a clap on the back would result in the eyeball popping from its socket and rolling along the floor like a marble.

'Who said that?' he roared and even the blue beside me gave a start at the sound of it. 'Who said it? I asked,' he repeated, even louder this time but answer came there none and he simply shook his head and looked at all of us with the appearance of a man who had recently been bled by leeches and enjoyed the experience. 'Bailiff,' said he to a terrified-looking blue standing guard beside him. 'Another word from any of these *people*' – and here he uttered the word like they were the lowest of the low, which they may well have been, but all the same it's a damned discourtesy – 'another word from any of them and they are all to be charged individually with contempt. Is that understood?'

'It is,' said the bailiff, nodding quickly. 'It surely is.'

'And as for you,' continued the magistrate, looking at the poor unfortunate godforsaken shadow of a man wilting in the dock before him: 'three months in the gaol for you – and

35

may you learn a lesson there that you won't forget in a hurry.'

To his credit, the man found his dignity then and nodded as if the sentence was one he was wholly in approval with, and he was taken down immediately, where he was almost squeezed to death by a woman I guessed to be his wife, before the bailiff peeled her off him. I watched her from a distance and wouldn't have minded the squeezing myself, for she was bonny as could be, even with the tears streaking her face, and despite the seriousness of what lay ahead for me she still gave me the motions.

'Now, Bailiff,' said the magistrate, gathering his robes together and making to stand up. 'Is that it for today?'

'It was due to be,' came the reply, a nervous one, as if the bailiff was worried that he'd be sent off to the gaol himself if he detained his superior any longer, 'but for the lad that just came in, that is.'

'Oh, yes,' said the magistrate, recalling me now. He sat down again and looked in my direction. 'Come up here, boy,' he said quietly, looking as if he was pleased that he hadn't finished doling out the misery yet. 'Into the dock with you where you belong.'

I stood up and stepped away from the blue and another took me to the dock by pinching his fingers round the bone in my arm and placed me where old Henderson, the scut, could see me better. I looked at him too and thought that his mole had grown since our last interview.

'I know you, don't I?' said he quietly, but before I could answer, the blue – *my* blue, that is – was on his feet and coughing for attention and blast me if every face in the room didn't turn to look at him. I swear the man missed his calling and he should have tried out for the theatre, the nance.

'May it please the court . . .' he began, using the posh voice again that was fooling nobody. 'May it please the court that on this very morning I apprehended the miserable creature you see standing before you in the act of feloniously and illegally taking a timepiece which was not any of his business or belongings and whose ownership was in the deed of another.'

'Stealing it, you mean?' asked the magistrate, cutting through the cornfield with a scythe.

'As you say, Your Honour,' said the blue, a little downcast by the summary.

'Well?' Mr Henderson asked then, leaning forward and glaring at me. 'What say you, lad? Did you do it? Are you guilty of the abominable crime?'

'It's all a terrible misunderstanding,' I said, appealing to him. 'I had too much sugar for my breakfast, that's the fault of it.'

'Sugar?' asked the magistrate, confused now. 'Bailiff, did the boy say he was the victim of a surfeit of sugar?'

'I believe he did, Your Honour,' said the bailiff.

'Well, it's an honest answer if nothing else,' said he then, scratching his hair so that a drizzle of powder fell from his follicles to his robe, speckling them with snow. 'Sugar has no business in a boy. It gives them ideas.'

'My feelings exactly, Your Wisdomness,' said I. 'I mean to avoid it in the future and suck on a lolly of honey when the mood takes me.'

'A lolly of honey?' he cried, looking at me as if I had suggested taking a whip to the Prince of Wales to relieve the boredom of the hour. 'My boy, that's even worse. Porridge is what you need. Porridge will be the makings of you. Porridge has been the makings of many a boy turned to the wrong.'

Porridge indeed! I would have quite gladly enjoyed a bowl of porridge for my breakfast every morning if he had given me the tuppence I would have needed for it. Porridge! Magistrates like him are in ignorance of the world of people like me, if you want to know the truth. And yet they sit in judgement on us. However, no politics—

'Then porridge I will eat from now on,' I promised, bowing my head a little. 'For breakfast, lunch and supper, if I can scuttle the pennies.'

He leaned forward again and repeated an earlier question that

I hoped he might have forgotten. 'I know you, don't I?' said he.

'I don't know,' I replied, holding back my shoulders from a shrug, for the magistrates do hate it when you do that. They say it implies inferior breeding. 'Do you?'

'What's your name, boy?'

I considered giving a falsehood but the blues knew me so I told the truth, as a lie would only have damned me further. 'Turnstile,' said I. 'John Jacob Turnstile. An Englishman, late of Portsmouth.'

'Ha!' he cried, spitting on the ground, a great gob into the sawdust, the filthy swine. 'Portsmouth be damned!'

'It will be, Your Magnificence,' said I to please him. 'On the day of judgement. I have no doubt of it.'

'How old are you, boy?'

'Fourteen, sir.'

He licked his lips for a moment and I was sure that I could see some of those hideous black teeth moving around that dark canyon of a mouth, threatening to loosen themselves from their holding-gums in a bid for escape. 'You stood before me a year ago,' said he, pointing a waxy finger at me, the type you might see on an exhumed corpse. 'I recall it now. Another act of larceny, I think it was.'

'A misunderstanding,' I suggested. 'A prank gone wrong, nothing more.'

'You were birched for it, were you not? I never forget a face from my courtroom or a rump from my whipping room. Tell me the truth now and God might spare you.'

I thought about it. There's a world of meaning in the word 'might' and little of it was of use to me. But there was no advantage to be taken in lying for the records could be consulted in a trice. 'You remember correctly,' I said. 'I was chastened with twelve lashes.'

'And not one of them excessive,' said he, looking down and making a note on a sheaf of papers before him. 'I find you guilty,

John Jacob Turnstile, of the malicious act,' he said then in a quieter voice, a voice that suggested he had lost interest in me altogether then and wanted his dinner. 'Guilty as charged, you naughty boy. Take him down, Bailiff. To the gaol for a twelve-month.'

My eyes opened wide and, I confess, my heart made a jump of horror within me. The gaol for a twelvemonth? I wouldn't emerge the boy I was when I entered it, I knew that much. I turned to the blue, *my* blue, and, praise on him, he looked at me too with a frown that suggested he was regretting taking me there at all, for there was no one in the courtroom who would have thought it a fitting punishment. A birching should have been the measure of it.

'Your Honour—' said the blue, *my* blue, but Mr Henderson was gone now, stormed off to his private chambers, no doubt to receive his instructions from the lords of the underworld, and the bailiff had his hands on me and was dragging me away.

'What's done is done,' he said regretfully. 'You must be brave, lad. You must remain staunch.'

'Brave?' said I with a cry of disbelief. 'Staunch? In the gaol for a twelvemonth?'

There's a time for bravery and a time for handing a fellow a loaded pistol and allowing him to depart the world in honour, and such a time was this. My legs gave from under me and before I knew it I was being taken through the doors, to what? To a year of torment and violation? Starvation and cruelty? I hardly dared to think about it.

4

WHAT A TIME OF IT, THOUGH! I don't mind admitting that I descended the steps from the courtroom to the cells below ground with a heavy heart and low expectations. The day had begun brightly enough but had taken on such a dark complexion in only a matter of hours that I couldn't help but wonder what further torment fate had in store for me. I had managed to enjoy a breakfast of half a kipper and the yolk of an egg at Mr Lewis's establishment and had wandered to the marketplace without a care in the world. The conversation with the French gentleman had been of the intellectual variety, and I am one as likes a little intellectual discourse from time to time. And that pocket-watch of his, which came into my possession so effortlessly, might easily have been the making of me, for it was a fine piece with a solid band and a healthy hue and must have cost him a few pounds at the jeweller's; had I retained possession, I would have brought it to a one-eyed man I knew whose business is the trade of stolen items and won half a crown for it. But all was lost now. I was away to the gaol and preparing my soul for the sufferance of who-knew-how-many indignities and scourges.

Am I too proud to recall the tears that were forming in my eyes even as I sat there and waited? I am not.

The bailiff had brought me downstairs to await my transport to Hades and I found myself confined to a cold room with only the stone floor to sit upon. The blue had thrown me inside without a word of apology or excuse and who was I expected to share with, only Mr Wilberforce, him as was sentenced before me. When I entered first, the great brute was positioned on the pot, his movements creating an otherworldly stench that made me back as far away from him as possible, but the door was slammed shut behind me and I had little choice but to confront his noxiousness with fortitude. For all I knew, he might be my companion for the time hence.

'The old bastard sent you down too, did he?' he asked me, grinning away, as misery prefers company. In response, I sought out the furthest corner of the cell and sat there, my knees bent up beneath my chin, my arms surrounding them. A fortress around me. I looked down at my feet and wondered how long the shoes I was wearing would remain my own once I was transported to my new home. And I thought of Mr Lewis, and the trouble I would be in with him when he discovered what had happened to me; I had seen him beat boys half to death for less.

'He did,' I admitted. 'And unjustly too.'

'What did he have you for, then?'

'I stole a watch,' I said, unable to look at him now, for he had stood up and was examining the contents of the pot like a medic or an old apothecary. 'But him as I stole it from retrieved it, so no harm was done. Where's the crime then, I ask you?'

'You told the old bastard that, did you?' asked Mr Wilberforce, and I shook my head. 'How long did you get?' he followed with.

'A twelvemonth,' said I.

He whistled through his teeth and shook his head. 'That's a stretch,' he said. 'Oh me, oh my, that's a stretch and no two ways about it. How many years have you, lad, anyway?'

'Fourteen,' said I.

'You'll be older than your years when you emerge a year from now,' he told me with a deal of pleasure – a wonderful piece of positive news for me to be getting on with. 'I were in there myself when I were no more than a year or two older than you are now and I don't want to tell you the things that happened to me. You wouldn't sleep if I did.'

'Then, don't,' I said, glaring across at him. 'Keep your counsel and mind your business, you old sot.'

He stared at me then and curled his lip. If we were to be transported together and housed together, I knew that I must begin our acquaintance with a surly attitude in order to have him appraised of the fact that I was not one of those boys who would be made a servant of on account of my tender years.

'Call me a drunk, will you, you wee scut?' he asked, standing up and placing his hands on his hips as if he was posing for a statue of himself to be placed in Pall Mall. 'That's a slander if ever I heard one.'

'I heard old Henderson say much the same thing,' I told him then, warming to my topic. 'He sent you to the gaol for three months on account of it. And her as was outside, crying her eyes out, your wife, was she?'

'Aye, my wife,' said he, his eyes narrowing as I took her name in vain. 'What of her?'

'Cosying up to another lad, she was, when I was being taken down. Cooing in his ear enough to turn your stomach and giving him the eyes that let him know that she wasn't about to go wanting even if you were.'

'Why, you little bastard,' said he, advancing on me then, and I took a notion that I might have made a mistake in provoking him, for as he came closer I could see that he was a bigger man than I took him for originally and those hams of his had curled into fists and looked ready to do me a serious mischief. Luckily for me, just as he reached down and pulled me from my place of rest upon the stony floor, a key was turned in the door and it was wrenched open and who was back to see us, only the bailiff. He took a quick look at the pair of us in our unfortunate positions, me being held off the ground by my throat, my feet dangling an inch or two from the ground, while the man's fist stood poised to strike me down.

'Another moment and he'd have had you,' said the bailiff in a casual voice, as if he couldn't have cared less what happened to any of us and was perfectly prepared to stand by and watch the assault take place.

'Out with you, blue, and let me finish the job, then,' said Mr Wilberforce. 'He issued a slander against my wife and I'll take my satisfaction or be damned.'

'Be damned, then,' said the bailiff, stepping forward and pushing him out of the way; the hand of my attacker was loosened from my neck and I tumbled to the ground, and not for the first time that day either. My fingers ran to my voice box, wondering whether my pipes were still intact and I would ever sing again. The thought went through my head that my body, underneath my clothes, must have been a rainbow of blacks and blues with the indignities I had suffered over the previous few hours.

'On your feet, lad,' said the bailiff, nodding towards me, and I dragged myself up slowly.

'I can't stand,' I replied in a weakened voice. 'I am beaten.'

'On your feet,' he repeated, but this time more severely, and he took a step towards me with such venom that I found my balance again and placed myself in the vertical.

'Are we for the gaol already?' I asked him, because although I did not relish the idea of any more time spent there with my violent companion, I was even less enamoured with the concept of my lengthy incarceration. 'Are there no more trials that can be heard first before we go? Is Spithead cleansed of sinners?'

'You're to come with me,' said the bailiff, taking me by the arm and pulling me out of the cell. 'And you stay where you are for now,' he added to Mr Wilberforce. 'I'll be along for you presently when the carriage is here.'

'You're never letting him go?' cried my erstwhile chum, seeing me being taken unexpectedly away from his grasp. 'That lad's a menace to society, I swear he is. If there's only room for one of us in the gaol, then by rights it should be him as he has a twelvemonth to pay and I have no more than a quarter of that.'

'Rest your tongue,' said the bailiff, pulling the door shut. 'He'll be paying for his crime all right, I promise you that.'

'I'll remember you to the missus,' I shouted back at him as the door of the cell closed and a moment later I could hear Mr Wilberforce running against it and pounding the frame with his fists.

'What's next for me then, blue?' I asked as he turned and started marching down the corridor and I chased along behind; he was the first fellow today who hadn't felt the need to drag me behind him like a dog on a leash.

'Just follow me, lad, and less of your questions,' he said. 'Mr Henderson desires an audience.'

My heart sank when he said that. I wondered whether the old man had consulted further with the Portsmouth constabulary and decided that I was a bad 'un through and through and a twelve-month was not sentence enough. Perhaps I would be sent there for longer, or receive a flogging first.

'What's it about, though?' I asked, desperate to know so that I could prepare my argument on the journey.

'The Lord above knows,' he answered with a shrug. 'Do you think he confides in the likes of me?'

'No,' I admitted. 'You're not high enough.'

He stopped and glared at me, but then shook his head and continued along. I got the impression he was not as quick to anger as some around there. 'Just come along, lad,' he told me. 'And no dawdling, if you know what's good for you.'

I did know what was good for me and would have liked to tell him so. What was good for me would have been my immediate release on to the streets of Spithead with naught but a telling-off and a promise on my part to devote my life henceforth to aiding the poor and crippled and never more to rest my eyes on those things that were not my own. But I said nothing. Instead I did his bidding and followed him until we reached a large oak door. He knocked soundly upon it and it crossed my mind that behind those doors lay either my salvation or my condemnation. I breathed deeply and prepared for the worst.

'Enter!' came a cry from within and the bailiff opened the door and stepped out of my way so that I might go inside. No surprise that the magistrate's room was a shoddy sight nicer than any of the other rooms that I'd seen so far in the courthouse. A fire was burning in the hearth and a tray of meats were laid out on the table beside a bowl of soup for the old scut's dinner. Mr Henderson was sitting behind the table, a bib tucked into his collar, and he was making short work of the food. Seeing it, my stomach awakened and asserted its rights; I recalled that I hadn't eaten since morning time and had suffered enormously since.

'The very boy,' said Mr Henderson, looking up at me. 'Come in, come in, you knave, and stand tall when I talk to you. Thank you, Bailiff,' he added, in a louder voice, looking across at the blue. 'That will be all for now. You may close the door.'

He did as he was bid and the magistrate took another long slurp of soup before wiping his mouth with the bib and removing it from his collar. He sat back then and narrowed his eyes, making a steeple of his fingertips, and stared at me, licking his lips. I wondered whether I was to be next on his menu.

'John Jacob Turnstile,' he said after a long pause, sounding out every syllable as if my own name was a piece of poetry. 'What a rascal you are.'

I was about to answer the allegation with a steadfast denial, but a chill descended on my body such as you feel when a ghost hovers in the room or your grave has been trod upon, and I sensed another presence nearby. Quick as a flash I turned my head and who did I see sitting in an armchair behind me, quite out of sight from me when I had first entered the room, but the French gentleman, him as I had the timepiece off earlier in the day. Surprised to see him there, I uttered an oath and he smiled and shook his head, but Mr Henderson was having none of that kind of language in his private chambers.

'You'll keep a civil tongue in your head, lad,' he shouted, and I turned back to him and let my gaze drop to the floor

'I heartily apologize, Your Holiness,' said I. 'I meant no disrespect; the words were out of my mouth before I could shake off the bad ones.'

'This is a place of law,' he said then. 'The king's law. And I won't have it sullied by the filthy tongue of one such as you.'

I nodded but said nothing. The room was silent again and I wondered whether the French gentleman would speak, but he said nothing for the time being and it was left to Mr Henderson to initiate the conversation.

'Master Turnstile,' he said to me eventually. 'You are familiar with the gentleman seated behind you?'

I turned to look at him again, to make sure that my eyes had not deceived me, and then looked back at the magistrate, nodding my head in shame. 'To my eternal dishonour, I am,' I told him. 'He is the very fine gentleman before whom I disgraced myself this very morning. I stand before you an infamous fellow.'

'Infamy is too small a word for it, Master Turnstile,' said the magistrate. 'Too small a word indeed. You behaved like a monster, a rascally knave, no better than a pickpocket of the lower orders.'

It went through my head that I should point out that that was exactly what I was, that it was the world in which I had been reared, having never known the succour of either mother or father, but sense asserted its virtues and I buttoned my lip, knowing that these were not the words he wanted to hear.

'I am most apologetic for my actions,' I said instead and then, turning to the French gentleman, I spoke with something approaching honesty. 'You were kind to me earlier, sir,' I told him. 'And spoke to me in a way that made me feel like more than I am. I apologize for letting you down. If I could amend my actions, I would.'

The gentleman nodded his head and I thought that my words

46

had touched him and, to my surprise, I found that I had meant them too. He *had* been thoughtful to me when our conversation had begun. And he *had* spoken to me as if there was more than just a mash of cobwebs between my ears, which was a rare treat for me.

'What say you, Mr Zulu,' said the magistrate then, looking at the Frenchman. 'Is he a likely lad?'

'It's Zéla,' said the gentleman in a tired voice, and I guessed that he had corrected the mispronunciation on more than one occasion since coming into the room before me. 'I am not of African descent, Mr Henderson. My birthplace was Paris.'

'I do apologize, sir,' said the magistrate.

I could tell by his tone that he couldn't care any less and simply wanted this interview to reach a happy conclusion as swiftly as possible. I looked at the gentleman and wondered who he could be to hold such sway over a rabid dog like Mr Henderson.

'He seems just the ticket, though,' said Mr Zéla then. 'How tall are you, boy?' he asked me.

'A little over five feet, sir,' I told him, my face flushing slightly, for there are those who said that I was on the small side and it was a burden that I had borne my whole life.

'And your age, it is fourteen years, am I correct?'

'Fourteen years precisely,' said I. 'And two days,' I added.

'A perfect age,' he said, standing up now and stepping towards me. He was a fine figure of a man, I'll give him that. Tall and thin, with an elegant look to him but a touch of generosity about the eyes, as if he wasn't the type to make a fellow's life troublesome. 'I wonder, would you mind opening your mouth for me?' he asked.

'Would he mind?' roared Mr Henderson with a laugh. 'Does it matter whether he minds or not? Open your mouth, boy, and do as the gentleman bids you!'

I ignored the screeching from my left and decided to focus my attention on the French gentleman instead. He can help me, I thought. He wants to help me. I opened my mouth and he cupped my jaw with one hand – it held it entirely – and peered inside at my teeth. I felt like a horse.

'Very healthy,' he pronounced after a moment. 'How does a lad like you keep his dentals in such a fine state?'

'I eat apples,' I announced in a confident voice. 'As many as I can find. They're uncommon good for the gnashers, or so I've always been told.'

'Well, they've done the trick, that's for sure,' he said, smiling a little at me. 'Hold out your arms, boy.'

I stretched them out before me and he pressed his hands to my sides and then to my chest, but he did it in the way that a doctor might and not to give himself the motions. He didn't seem that type at all.

'You're a healthy lad, I think,' he said. 'Well positioned, with good bones. A little on the short side but that's no harm.'

'Thank you, sir,' I told him, choosing to ignore the last remark. 'Very generous of you to say so.'

Mr Zéla gave a nod and looked towards Mr Henderson. 'I think he might do,' he said cheerfully. 'I think he might do very well.'

Do for what? For immediate release? I looked from man to man and wondered what lay in store.

'Then you're a lucky lad,' said Mr Henderson, picking up a bone from his plate now and sucking on it in such a fashion that it gave me the revulsions. 'How would you care to avoid a twelvemonth in the gaol, then, eh?'

'I should like it very much,' I told him. 'I have repented of my sins, I swear I have.'

'It's neither one thing nor the other whether you have or you haven't,' he said, selecting another cut and examining it for the choicer parts first. 'Mr Zéla, would you care to let the lad know what lies in store for him?'

The French gentleman returned to his seat and looked me up

and down for a moment, appeared to be considering something, and then nodded his head as if his mind was fully made up. 'Yes, I am decided,' he said, more to himself than anyone else. 'Have you ever been to sea, lad?' he asked me.

'Sea?' I said with a laugh. 'Not I.'

'And would you care for it, do you think?'

I considered the idea for a moment. 'I might care for it, sir,' I told him carefully. 'In what capacity exactly?'

'There's a ship anchored not far from here,' he told me then. 'A ship with a most particular mission of great importance to His Majesty.'

'Do you know the king, sir?' I asked, my eyes opening wide to be in the presence of one who might have been in the presence of royalty.

'I have had the very great pleasure,' he replied quietly, but not in a way that made you think he wanted you to think him a fine fellow for it.

I uttered an oath in astonishment and Mr Henderson banged the table and offered one of his own in reply.

'This ship,' continued Mr Zéla, ignoring us both, 'is due to set off on its mission today and a small problem has presented itself, but one that we think you, Master Turnstile, can be of assistance to us with.'

I nodded and tried to rush his story along in my brain in order to understand what might be required of me.

'A young lad,' he continued, 'a lad your age, as it goes, who had a place on board the ship as the captain's servant, was making his way down the gangway yesterday afternoon at a pace not commensurate with wet and slimy woodwork and the long and the short of it is that he has cracked his legs and will not be fit for walking, let along for sailing. There is a suggestion that he had taken drink, but that's neither here nor there for the purposes of our conversation. A replacement needs to be found, but quick-smart, as the ship has been delayed by the weather long enough and must set forth today. What say you, Master Turnstile: are you prepared for an adventure?'

I thought about it. A ship. A captain's servant. I should say I was.

'And the gaol?' I asked. 'Shall I be excused it?'

'If you give a good account of yourself on board,' said Mr Henderson, the ignorant old elephant. 'If not, you shall serve your sentence on your return, threefold.'

I frowned. That was a carve-up if ever I had heard one. 'And the voyage,' I asked Mr Zéla. 'Might I ask how long it is to be?'

'Two years, I should think,' he replied with a shrug, as if such time was a pittance to him. 'You have heard of Otaheite?' he asked me. I thought about it and shook my head. 'Tahiti, then?' he continued. 'It is often known by that name.' Again, I shook my head. 'Well, never mind. Your ignorance will soon enough be rectified. The ship's destination is Otaheite,' he told me. 'For a most particular mission. And when that mission is over, the ship will return to England. You shall receive wages on your return of six shillings for every week that you were away and be absolved of your crime in addition to this. How does that sound, my fine fellow? Are we of a mind?'

I tried out the numbers in my head in order to discover how much six shillings every week for two years might be but I hadn't the wit for it; I only knew that I should be rich. I could have embraced the French gentleman, despite his heritage.

'I should be very grateful,' I told him, the words stumbling out of my mouth quickly, so anxious was I for the offer not to be withdrawn. 'I should be very grateful to accept the offer you put to me, and I assure you that my service will be of the very highest standard at all times.'

'Then it's settled,' said he with a smile, standing up and placing a hand on my shoulder. 'But I'm afraid there's no time to waste. The ship sets sails at four o'clock.' He reached into his pocket and withdrew his watch but frowned when his eyes landed on the smashed glass and broken hands. He glanced at me for a moment before returning it to its home without comment. 'Mr Henderson?' he asked then. 'Do you have the o'clock?'

'A quarter after three,' replied the magistrate, who had grown bored of both of us now and was concentrating solely on his victuals.

'Then, we must make haste,' said Mr Zéla. 'I may take the lad, sir?'

'Take him, take him,' came the reply. 'And make sure I don't see you before me again, you young rascal, do you hear? Or you'll be the worse for it.'

'Of course, Your Excellency. And thank you for your generosity,' I added, following Mr Zéla through the door and forward out to my new life. Naturally, he made his way through the corridors with as much speed as every one else did and I was forced to run along behind him. Finally, though, we were outside, where his carriage awaited. I climbed in after him and my heart danced to breathe freedom and fresh air again. I was to leave England and have an adventure. If there had ever been a luckier boy alive, I knew not his name nor his circumstances.

'Begging your pardon, sir,' I said as we drove off, 'but might I enquire after the name of the ship and the captain, him as I am to serve, that is?'

'Did I not mention it?' he asked, sounding surprised. 'The ship is His Majesty's frigate the *Bounty* and it is being led by a most able fellow and a particular friend of mine, Lieutenant William Bligh.'

I nodded and recorded the names on my memory; they did, as he had suggested, mean nothing to me then. We turned a corner and headed towards the sea front and I never glanced back once, never looked round to have a final memory of the streets I knew so well, never took a moment to stare once more at the cobbles where I had robbed and thieved for a decade or more, didn't even give a thought to the establishment in which I had been reared and where my innocence had been stolen from me on a hundred occasions. Instead I looked to the future and the thrills and the escapades that awaited me.

Oh, foolish lad; what little I knew then of what lay ahead.

Part II

The Voyage

23 DECEMBER 1787 – 26 OCTOBER 1788

1

N^O SOONER HAD I SET FOOT on the deck of the *Bounty* than the weather took a turn for the worse and the rain started; it was almost as if the Saviour himself had taken one look at the ship in the harbour and the souls on board, decided he didn't much care for any man-jack of us, and thought it would be fine sport to torment us all from the start, the donkey.

Mr Zéla had bid me goodbye on shore and I don't mind admitting that I felt a rush of the nerves inside me as I looked up at what was to be my home for the next eighteen months, perhaps even two years, of my life. The thought of this alone was enough to give me the squits.

'Are you not sailing too?' I asked hopefully, for I had grown to think of him as something of a benefactor and even a friend during our short acquaintance as he had helped me already on three separate occasions that day.

'Me?' he asked, laughing a little and shaking his head. 'No, no, my boy. I'm afraid I have more than my share of responsibilities to take care of here in England at the moment. Attractive though the idea of life as an adventurer seems to me, I'm afraid I must defer the pleasure of this particular voyage and wish you adieu and *bonne chance*.'

I don't know why he had to talk like that. Had that barrel of fruity chatter sprung from anyone else's lips it would have given me the revulsions, but it seemed as if simpler phrases lived in a different country than he did. I tried to think of something equally clever to say in reply, but he was off again with his prattle before my brain could catch up with my lips. Gentlemen like him usually are. They take silence to be a call from the audience for another song.

'She's not the grandest ship I've ever seen,' he said doubtfully, stroking his whiskers and frowning a little. 'But she's keen, I'll say that for her. And she'll get you there safely. Sir Joseph has seen to her sturdiness, I can promise you that.'

'As long as she don't sink, that's all I'm concerned for,' I told him, neither knowing nor caring who this Sir Joseph was that he spoke of.

At this he fixed me a beady stare and shook his head quickly. 'My boy, you mustn't speak like that on board,' he said in a serious tone. 'Sailors are a curious breed. They have more superstitions than the ancients in Rome and Greece combined and I dare say you'll see the innards of more than a few fallen albatrosses as they're examined for a weather forecast during your voyage. A comment such as that might make strange enemies of your new fellows. Think on it and be wise.'

I nodded but could only consider what a rum lot they must be if they couldn't hear a lad speak his mind without thinking the whole shoddy world was coming to an end. Still, I was smart enough to realize that Mr Zéla knew a damn sight more about the ways of the world than I did, so I took note of what he said and resolved to have a care with my language during the voyage ahead.

We stood there for a few more moments and my gaze became fixed upon the end of the stretch of wood that acted as a gangway and the groups of men who were marching quickly about the deck as if their arses were on fire, pulling at ropes and tightening I-knew-not-what, and wondered for a moment whether or not I should make a run for it right there and then, simply slip out of the French gentleman's grasp and aim for one of the side streets where I was sure to lose him should he give chase (which I doubted anyway). I looked to the left and to the right, saw my opportunity and was about to make a sprint of it, when – almost as if he could read my mind – Mr Zéla's hand was pinched on the bone of my shoulder and he began to steer me in the direction of my destiny.

'Time to board, Master Turnstile,' said he and that great booming voice of his cut through my plans like a scaldy-knife through butter. 'The ship will depart soon; it's already been delayed for several days. You see that chap standing at the top of the steps, waving at us?'

I looked in the direction he had indicated and, sure enough, standing on the deck without an ounce of shame was an abominable-looking creature with the face of a weasel – all points and angles and sucked-in cheeks – flapping his arms in the air as if he had just found escape from a home for the bewildered. 'Aye,' said I. 'I see him. A pitiful sight, that's for sure.'

'That's Mr Samuel,' he told me then. 'The captain's clerk. He's expecting you and will direct you to your duties. A sound man,' he added after a moment, but I didn't believe a word of it from the tone of him; it sounded as if he was just saying that to make me feel more comfortable. I turned my head and looked behind me once more to where freedom lay but dismissed the thought of it and shook my head. For here I was, fourteen years of age, a master at some things – picking pockets, knavery of a sort – and an innocent at others. Certainly, I could make my way to the capital, I had the wit to do it, and with a little luck on my side I would doubtless make a living there, but here in front of me was something different. A chance for adventure and money-making. Unlike the sailors on board, I wasn't one to waste breath or thought on superstition, but nonetheless I couldn't help but wonder whether fate had brought me to this moment and to this ship for a reason.

And there was something else I did not want to consider. Mr Lewis. Him as what brought me up. The life I would be leaving behind. The lengths he might go to recapture me. I shivered at the thought of it and looked towards the ship again.

'Right,' said I, nodding my head. 'I'll say fare thee well and thank you once again for saving me.' I extended my hand and shook his vigorously; he seemed amused by the gesture, the donkey. 'You've done me a great service and perhaps someday I will be able to repay you.'

'Repay me by making a fine captain's servant,' he told me, placing a hand on my shoulder as if I was his own lad and not just some scamp he'd collected off the streets. 'Be honest and loyal, John Jacob Turnstile, and I will know that I did not make a mistake in choosing you today and sparing you from the gaol.'

'I will,' said I, before bidding him farewell once again and heading up the gangway towards the bedlamite, slowly at first and then a little faster, as if my confidence was growing with every step.

'You're the servant-lad?' asked the weasel at the top in a voice that would have made glass crack. It sounded like his words were bypassing his vocal chords entirely and making their utterances through his nasal cavities instead.

'John Jacob Turnstile,' said I, extending a hand to him in the hope that we might get our acquaintance off to a happy start. 'Pleased to meet you, I'm sure.'

He stared down at my hand as if I had just offered him the rotting carcass of a maggot-infested house-cat and invited him to make kiss with it. 'I'm Mr Samuel, the captain's clerk,' he said, looking at me as though I had just crawled out from under the boat to stand in front of him now, covered in barnacles and sea-slime, stinking of the putrid waters beneath us. 'And I'm above you.'

I nodded. I knew little of sea life, other than what I had heard from the sailors arriving and departing from my own small world in Portsmouth, but I was canny enough to know that every man on board the *Bounty* knew his place entirely in the chain of things and that there was a strong possibility that I lay at the very bottom of that sequence.

'Then, I shall take great pleasure in looking up at you from my vantage point beneath and glorying in your magnificence,' I told him as he started to lead me away.

He stopped then and looked back at me with a glare that would have frightened a Chinaman. 'What's that?' he asked, his face contorting even more now, and I regretted saying the words because the longer we stood there the more wet we were both becoming, what with the blasted weather getting worse by the moment. 'What's that you say, boy?'

'I said I hope to learn from you,' I replied in a more innocent tone. 'I wasn't supposed to be here, you know. Another lad had the place but he lost it.'

'I know all about that,' said he with a scowl. 'I know more of it than you do too, so don't pretend otherwise or you'll be caught out. And you're not to believe what you hear from any other on account of there's no truth in anything the men say here. Young Smith, the servant as was, fell by his own mischance and I had ne'er a hand in it.'

I said nothing in reply to this but made a note in my mind to steady my feet on deck whenever Mr Samuel was near me. Perhaps clerks and servants did not have a natural affection for each other; for all I knew, that was the way of things at sea. But I had little enough time to think of this now, for away we were, halfway along the deck, and him with his head plunged down as he burrowed his way through the ranks of men who stared at me as I passed but made no comments. They were older than me, almost every one, a range from fifteen to forty, I should have said, but I didn't slow down. I could make my introductions later. Truth to tell, I felt nervous of them; they were bigger than me, every one, and looked me up and down in the way that Mr Lewis did whenever he had the motions, and that was a class of behaviour I wanted no more of now that I was an independent fellow, reliant on none but myself.

'Lift your feet and walk, lad,' shouted Mr Samuel at me, despite the fact that I was keeping pace with him. 'I haven't the time to be wasting on you. You're late as it is.'

Before I could form an answer and point out that my time-keeping that day had been entirely in the hands of others, he lifted up a hatch in the floor to reveal a staircase running beneath us to the deck below, and down he went in a moment without so much as a word to me; my own feet took longer to grow accustomed to the unfamiliar steps and I descended slowly, gripping the sides carefully with nervous hands.

'Hurry up, lad,' screeched the weasel and I started to run so that the tips of my toes were almost touching the heels of his feet as I followed him along a corridor to the end of the boat, whereupon he threw open a door to reveal a large room, surrounded by windows on either side, narrowing together as the ship tapered to a point. It was a glorious space, bright and airy and dry, and I wondered for a moment whether it might be mine. I had slept in a lot worse places, that was for sure. It was curiously empty of furniture, however, and lined up along the walls on either side were many dozens of long crates and – more mysterious to my eyes – hundreds upon hundreds of green earthenware pots, empty then, every one of them, and neatly slotted into each other so they stood, some thirty or forty tall, along each of the walls. The crates had circular holes cut in their bases, some twenty by half a dozen in width, and slats cut into the sides whereby they might stand atop each other while giving breath to whatever was stored within and below.

'In the name of buggery, what are all the pots for?' I asked in surprise, making the mistake of assuming that a civilized conver-sation between two members of His Majesty's navy would not be too much to hope for, but this foolishness was quashed when the weasel spun round and wagged a finger in my face like the old washerwoman he was.

'None of your questions, lad,' he screeched at me, his spittle flecking left and right and him not a bit ashamed of his behaviour at all. 'You're not brought here to be a question-master, do you hear me? You're brought here to be a servant boy. Let the matter start and end there.'

'Beggin' your most humble apology, sir,' said I, bowing low to him then, bending right over so that my arse was fairly in the air behind me. 'I withdraw the question without rancour. How dare I presume to have asked such a thing?'

'Mind your manners, that's my advice to you,' said he, walking through another door now and bringing us into a smaller area, a corridor with two doors on either side and a cloth curtain pulled fast at the end.

'That door there,' said he, pointing his gnarly finger towards one of them. 'That belongs to Mr Fryer, the master.'

'The door does?' I asked, all innocence.

'The cabin behind the door, you damned ignoramus,' he shouted then. 'Second only to the captain is Mr Fryer. You'll listen to what he says and obey him at all times or know the consequences.'

'I will, sir,' said I. 'Do what I'm told, I mean.'

'And behind that curtain there are the officers' berths. Young Mr Hallett and Mr Heywood. Then there's Mr Stewart and Mr Tinkler and Mr Young. They're the midshipmen and they're above you. And then there's the master's mates, Mr Elphinstone and Mr Christian.'

'Am I above them?' I asked.

'They're very far above you,' he snapped at me like an old crocodile about to take the head off a lesser creature. 'Very far above you indeed. You're not to have much to do with them, though. Your responsibilities are towards the captain, so remember that. His cabin is through here.' He stepped over towards the other door and tapped on it quickly, a noisy rat-tat-tat that would have woken the dead, before placing his ear against the frame. No answer was heard and he opened it then and stepped aside so that I might look around me. I felt as if I was on a sightseeing turn and he would tell me not to touch anything in case I sullied the surfaces with my grubby paws.

'The captain's quarters,' he told me then. 'Smaller than standard, of course, but that's on account of the ship needing so much space in there for the plants.' He nodded in the direction of the larger area through which we had just walked, the one that housed the pots and crates.

'Plants?' I asked, frowning at the thought of it. 'Is that what the pots are for, then?'

'No questions, I told you!' he shouted, looming over me like an animal about to pounce. 'Just do as you're told, that's all, and you'll come to no harm.'

As he said this, the officers' door opened and a man stepped out, hesitating for a moment as he saw us standing there. Tall, he was, and red of face, and not a pick of meat on him. A nose you'd notice too. Mr Samuel fell quiet immediately and took his cap off, bowing his head several times, as if the Emperor of Japan has just appeared before him demanding his supper.

'So much noise out here,' said the officer, and he was wearing the bright blue uniform with gilt buttons that I'd seen around Portsmouth on many's the occasion. 'And just as we're about to set sail too.' He had a strange tone about him, as if he was pretending that it didn't matter really, that he was only making conversation, but that if the noise continued he'd have our hides nonetheless.

'I do apologize, Mr Fryer,' said Mr Samuel. 'The lad here will make me shout but he'll learn yet. He's only young and he'll learn, I'll see to that.'

'Who is the lad anyway?' asked the officer, looking at me with a frown, as if surprised to see a stranger on the ship at all, and I stepped forward all bravado, a hand outstretched once again, and he stared at it with a look of amusement on his face, as if he didn't understand the gesture, before smiling a little and taking it like a gentleman.

'John Jacob Turnstile,' said I. 'Newly employed.'

'Newly employed where?' he asked me. 'Here? On the *Bounty*?'

'If it pleases you, Mr Fryer,' said Mr Samuel, squeezing in between us and blocking our sight of each other so much that I was forced to bend my body to the right a little to spy Mr Fryer once again, whereupon I gave him one of my special grins, all teeth and lips. 'Master Smith took a tumble and cracked his legs. A replacement servant for the captain was needed.'

'Ah,' said Mr Fryer, nodding his head. 'I see. And you, Master Turnstile, are – I assume – he.'

'I am,' said I.

'Excellent,' said he. 'Well, you are very welcome, then. You'll find the captain and officers to be a fair lot if you give good service.'

'Which is my aim,' I told him, for it occurred to me then that there might be larks in this yet and why not try to do the job as befitted me and have Mr Zéla know that I hadn't let him down?

'Good enough,' he said, stepping away. 'For what more could any of us ask of you than that?' And with that he was away up the ladder and gone.

Mr Samuel turned to me then and his face was on fire; he didn't like the fact that Mr Fryer was friendly towards me at all. 'You scut,' he said. 'Playing up to him like a nance.'

'I was mannerly, that's all,' I protested. 'Ain't that what I'm supposed to be?'

'You'll not last long here with that attitude, I promise you,' he told me, before pointing to a bunk slung low in the corner just outside the captain's cabin. 'And this here is where you'll sleep,' he said, and I stared at the place in amazement, for it was naught but a corner where anyone might pass me by, day or night, and tread on my head.

'There?' I asked. 'Don't I get a cabin of my own?'

He laughed out loud then, the donkey, and shook his head, before gripping me by the arm and leading me back to the captain's cabin, pulling me along the way they all do. 'You see those cases?' he asked me, directing my gaze to four solid oak boxes scattered around the floor, each one a little smaller than the one next to it.

'I do,' said I.

'The captain's clothes and belongings,' he told me. 'They want emptying, every one of them. Their contents placed in the wardrobes and shelves. *Neatly*, mind. And then the boxes stored within the next one up and put out of his way. Can you follow those instructions, lad, or are you too soft in the head to understand me?'

'I believe I can,' I replied with a roll of the eyes. 'Complicated as they are.'

'Then, carry on with it, and don't let me see you back on deck until the job is done.'

I looked at the boxes and noted that each one was locked, so I turned back to ask the weasel whether he was in possession of the keys, but he was already gone. I heard him scurrying away outside and now that I was alone and without other distractions I couldn't help but notice the rocking of the ship back and forth, from left to right, and I recalled the stories I had heard of fellows who were ill at sea until they became accustomed to its movements. Weak fools, I had always assumed, for my stomach was solid. I stepped back into the cabin and closed the door behind me.

I didn't need any key to let me into the cases, Mr Lewis had trained me far better than that. The captain had any number of items already laid out on his desk that I could use as a lock-pick and I selected a fine feather quill with a pointed tip and inserted it gently into the mechanism, listening at the clasp for the sound of the spring and then giving it that familiar jolt to trip the lock and open the case.

His belongings contained nothing more than I would have expected to find there. A few different uniforms, some fancier than others, which I presumed to be for when we ended up wherever we ended up and he had to face the savages in his finery. After that there were some lighter garments and underthings which were a lot fancier than any underthings I'd worn in my life and I dare say a lot more comfortable too. Almost as soft as the ladies wore, I thought. There was some as would get enjoyment out of going through another man's vestments, but not I, so I went about my task quickly, placing everything I found in their new homes as carefully as possible, trying not to crease his clothes, or dirty them, for this after all was my new job and I had determined to make a success of it.

In the smallest of the four boxes I found a number of books – poetry mostly and an edition of *The Tragedyes* by Mr Shakespeare – and a parcel of letters, bound together with a red silk ribbon, and these I placed at the back of the captain's desk top. And then, finally, I extracted three framed portraits. The first was of a gentleman with a white wig and a sharp red nose. His eyes were buried deep in his skull and he stared at the portrait artist with a look approaching murderous contempt; I would not have wanted to have a difference of opinion with him. The second, however, was a lot more to my taste. A young lady, fancy curls and a button nose, her eyes looking upwards in a warm fashion, and I supposed her to be the captain's wife or sweetheart and my heart skipped a little as I looked at her on account of her giving me the motions. The third was of a lad, a boy of about eight or nine, and I knew not who he might be. Minutes passed before I stepped over to the desk and placed them on either side, so that they might be seen by the captain when he was completing his log, and at the moment I was about to step away the boat gave an unexpected lunge and it was all I could do to stop myself from falling over by throwing a hand out to grasp on to the corner of the desk for support.

I hesitated for a moment, then righted myself and stood erect. There was only one tiny window in the cabin and the rain was beating down on it relentlessly. I staggered over and wiped it clear, but I could see little through it, and when I stepped away again the boat lunged in the opposite direction and this time I did fall over and narrowly avoided thrashing my skull against the corner of one of the captain's cases.

After a few moments equilibrium was restored and I resolved to place the cases within each other, as instructed, and out of harm's way in case I should slip again, and when this task was completed I made for the door, my arms outstretched as I held on to anything that might help to keep me vertical.

The corridor outside was empty of men now and I stepped through the great room with the earthenware pots, walking in the direction of the stairs beyond, when another lunge of the ship sent me in one direction and my stomach in another and I felt a great pressure building deep inside me that was unlike any sickness I had known. I took a moment to gather my thoughts and after a little concentration let loose a stream of gas from my mouth that made even me recoil with its unexpected violence and all I could think of was getting up the stairs to the air beyond.

I had decided now that a sailor's life was not for me after all and determined to make my excuses to Mr Zéla and return whence I had come – gaol or no gaol – but when I emerged at the top of the steps I looked around and land was no longer visible. We were at sea already! I opened my mouth to cry out to some of the men rushing back and forth, but no words emerged, and the sound of the waves and the violence of the rain and wind was enough that I didn't think a soul would hear me anyway.

Trying to wipe the rain off my face, I was sure that I could see Mr Fryer in the distance, standing with another man, who appeared to be issuing orders and pointing things out left, right and centre; he grabbed a sailor as he passed, pointed towards something else, and the man nodded and ran in that direction. I resolved to go over and ask them to turn the ship round and let me return home, but as I stepped on to the deck another great lunge sent me back off my feet and I tripped backwards down the stairs, falling on my already injured arse at the base. Again my stomach turned and I was glad I had not eaten since morning time, as surely now I would be unable to vomit, but, looking up, the distance back to the deck defeated me and I retreated whence I had come, collapsing into the small bunk outside the captain's cabin, where I turned on my side, faced the wall, clasped my stomach tightly and willed the ship or my stomach to stop turning, whichever might be the more solicitous.

All seemed well for a moment then, my body appeared to relax, but a moment later I knew that all was lost and I rotated at great speed, grabbing a pot from beside the canvas and vomiting in a most excellent fashion into it, a process that continued for some time, until my stomach was entirely emptied and only air escaped me as my stomach retched.

And how did my day end? This day unlike any I had known before and which had brought so much trouble to me? I know not. I drifted in and out of sleep, my body swaying to the rhythms of that demon ship, my head slipping over the side intermittently to barf into the pot once again, before I fell into a stupor. At one moment I was sure I felt a presence beside me, removing the pot and replacing it with a clean one and then returning a few moments later with a dampened cloth, which this unknown stranger placed across my forehead.

'This will pass, my fine fellow,' said the presence of who-knew-what-person in a low and kindly voice. 'Allow your body to accustom itself to the heft and flow and soon this, like all things, will pass.'

.I tried to focus on my generous protector, but the mist that covered my eyes would not give up his face and I turned away, burrowing my body in on itself even as I groaned and wept, and then a great silence, a sleep without dreams, and I awakened again, to daylight, to steadiness, to a foul taste about my lips and tongue and a hunger inside me unlike any I had known before that day but would know again, and for a longer time before my adventures had ended.

2

To MY GREAT SURPRISE we had been at sea for two full days before my body was restored to its former condition and I was once again able to walk the decks without fear of collapse. Of course I remained a little unsteady on my trotters at first and my bowels were not to be depended on for any length of time, but the constant vomiting had finally come to an end – and for that, if nothing else, I was grateful.

The low bunk in which I lay throughout those rotten days and nights had proved surprisingly comfortable, but looking at it anew from a position of standing I could only recall the endless hours of tossing and turning that had caused me such distress. I had heard men walk past me as I lay in my sick-bed, their boots making firm sounds on the wood and copper flooring below, and they conversed merrily with one another as they went about their business, paying no heed at all to the poor unfortunate creature who lay in a pit of agony by their feet, the selfish scuts. In fact, the only person who had shown me any kindness since I had come aboard was the mysterious stranger who had emptied my vomit-pot on that first evening (and again on several occasions since) and who had placed the cold compress across my perspiring fore-head to keep the ague from torturing me any further. I determined to discover the name of this good-hearted fellow at the earliest opportunity and make some show of appreciation.

On the afternoon that I was restored to good health, I ventured some careful movements away from that corner of the ship in which I had lain for too long, noting the motion of the vessel and attempting to keep my footsteps in line with it, finally deciding that my body had grown accustomed to the changes in equilibrium now and all would be well. I walked through the great cabin where the pots and crates were stored and made for the stairway at the end, when who should come running down it towards me, only the weasel himself, Mr Samuel.

'You're about again, are you?' he shouted at me, stopping for a moment and glaring at me with such disgust in his eyes that you'd think I had just whispered an obscenity in his mother's ear.

'I was ill,' I replied quietly, for despite my restoration I was not yet ready to engage in any verbal jousting with the likes of him. 'I think I am better now, though.'

'Well, isn't that wonderful,' said he, all bitter with his crooked smile. 'Perhaps we should stop the ship and fire a six-gun salute in appreciation.'

'Not necessary,' I told him, shaking my head. 'And it would be a great shame to waste the artillery. The doctor helped me, I think,' I added. 'Is he about that I might offer my thanks?'

'The doctor?' laughed Mr Samuel, looking at me as if I was an idiot-boy. 'Dr Huggan came nowhere near you. Sure, you're nothing at all: you think a man of his responsibilities would care whether you live or die?'

'Well, someone did,' I protested. 'I assumed—'

'We see less of the doctor than we do of you,' he muttered, interrupting me. 'He's been in his cups since boarding. Don't flatter yourself that there's a soul on this ship who looked after you; they're all above you, even the least of them, so don't think it, because not a one of them gives a shiny shite for your well-being.'

I sighed. He was a fellow with but one mode of discourse. 'I could manage a little food,' I said after a moment. 'If any is to be found.'

He rolled his eyes and took a step towards me, looking me up and down as his lip twisted in disgust. 'And what am I?' he asked.

'Your butler? You'll eat later. For now you're to change. You stink to holy heaven. You smell like a dog who died and was left out in the sun to fester.'

I looked down at myself and, sure enough, I was clothed in the same outfit that I had been wearing a few days before in Portsmouth. And a few days of tossing and turning in my bunk, perspiring like a horse and vomiting like a bairn, had done them no good either.

'I don't have any other clothes with me, though,' I told him. 'I came on board without warning.'

'Of course you don't, you wee scut,' he replied. 'Do you think this is a place for you to bring luggage on to? You're not a gentleman and don't think you are on account of you sleeping between the gentlemen's quarters. I have a uniform for you, the uniform of an AB.'

'An AB?' I asked.

'Yes, and don't tell me you don't know what that is or I'll have you thrown overboard for ignorance. You'll wear it at all times, Turnip, except when you're asleep. Is that understood?'

'It's Turnstile,' I told him, not thinking for a moment that he wasn't aware of my proper name. 'John Jacob Turnstile.'

'You think I give a whore's kiss? Follow me, lad.'

He marched us both quick and lively down a corridor that I hadn't seen before and withdrew a large bunch of keys from his apron, searched for one and then opened a door, stepping inside a dark room for a moment before emerging again a moment later to look me up and down, spin me round like a top, and mumble a few obscenities under his breath. He disappeared inside again then and a few moments later he was back, this time carrying a pair of long, baggy trousers, a pale tunic and a dark-blue jacket and slippers.

'Down there you'll find a washroom,' he said, pointing to a door at the end of the corridor. 'Do what you can to take the stink off your body and then put these on. Don't stand around to play

70

with yourself neither. You're to serve the captain at table tonight and you must look presentable.'

'But I haven't met him yet,' I said. 'How shall I know him?'

Mr Samuel barked a laugh. 'You'll know him right enough,' he told me. 'Mr Hall, the cook, will be along presently and give you your instructions. Now, not another word in the meantime. Wash and dress, them's your orders, and I'm above you so heed me.'

I nodded and went towards the door as indicated, only to find a pair of enormous caskets inside, each filled with water and a crate beside them to let you step up to them. I frowned. I'm no tinker and many's the time I've used the public baths in Portsmouth – Mr Lewis was always saying I was a right nance on account of how often I liked to wash myself, tip to toe, twice a year without fail – but I didn't know how many sailors had already used the water contained within and the thought of it gave me the revulsions. But, still, I could smell the rankness of my own filth about me, not to mention the vomit that streaked my shirt and pestered my nostrils, so I had little choice but to strip down to the altogether and throw myself inside. The water was cold – freezing cold, to the point where I expelled a sudden scream of shock – and I was glad the room was dark, for I didn't want to know what might be floating inside it and not seeing was half the battle. My feet only just reached the bottom, so that I was forced to hold my chin up a little to prevent myself from dis-appearing altogether and suffering a drowning, but I did this carefully as I had no desire to allow my eyes or mouth to make contact with the noxious liquid anyway. I stayed there for no more than a minute or two before emerging, flapping my arms and legs around on the floor until I was dry before donning the new uniform. I wished for a glass in order to see my reflection, but there were no such niceties to be found and so I stepped out into the corridor instead and made my way back whence I had come in search of food.

3

THERE WAS PRECIOUS LITTLE SERVING involved in waiting at the captain's table and for that I was happy as a pig in muck, since I'd never stood servant to any man at his dinner before, let alone someone who could throw me overboard if I didn't do a good job of it, and I didn't know where I should start. I'd never held down a job for a day in my life. Mr Lewis, him what brought me up, taught me to do certain things to earn my keep – pickpocketing and the like, good honest thievery and other jobs besides – but I'd never held a position where there was a wage involved, and expectations.

One of my brothers back at Mr Lewis's establishment, a lad name of Bill Holby, got a job once and when he came home to announce it all hell broke loose. He'd been offered a position at a victualler's in Portsmouth town and when Mr Lewis heard of it he said wasn't that a sign of gratitude altogether: he brings a lad up and teaches him a trade, only for that lad to come home one day and say he wants no part of it any more and seeks nothing more from life than an honest day's work for an honest day's pay. I was only a child at the time and hid in a corner out of fright when Mr Lewis advanced on him with the poker, but Bill, who was strong and taller than most of us, wrestled it off him and threatened him with it on account of the things that Mr Lewis had forced him to do over the years. *I'm finished with all of this*, I remember him shouting, and the look in his eye was enough that it would have scared an Italian. *If I could find a way to save these boys from you* . . . I thought for a moment that Bill was going to murder him, he was in that much of a rage, and I was scared at the notion of it, but finally he threw the poker away with a terrible scream, as if he loathed himself more than anyone else, before looking around at the rest of us and telling us that we should get out and make our escape before Mr Lewis corrupted us the way he had corrupted him.

At the time I considered Bill terrible ungrateful, for didn't Mr Lewis give us bed and food and warmth from the rain? Now I think differently. But then I was only about five or six years old and Bill had already gone through what lay in store for me.

I came out of the captain's cabin, where I'd been stretching out his bed sheets in an attempt to make them look fresh, when the ship's cook stepped out of the galley, took one look at me and let a shout out of him as if I was a stowaway, recently unearthed and discovered stealing from the most confidential area of the vessel.

'Who the blazes are you?' he roared, and me all dickied out in my fine new uniform, which might have given him some sort of an idea had he been in possession of even half a wit.

'The new servant-lad,' I said quickly, for he was a fine big fellow with a pair of hams on him that would have made short work of me if he'd had a mind to use them; obviously the news of my employment had not been deemed of sufficient interest to people that it should be known by all.

'The captain's servant? Don't lie to me, lad. That's John Smith and I know him 'cause he's under me.'

Mother of Lucifer, was every man on board struck by no other fancy than their position on the eternal ladder?

'Cracked his legs,' said I, stepping back a little. 'An accident on the gangway. I have his place.'

He narrowed his eyes and leaned forward a little, sniffing at me as if I was a piece of meat and he wanted to make sure I was fresh before bothering to slice me up. 'I seen you, lad, haven't I?' he asked quietly, poking a finger into the gaps between my ribs. 'All curled up in that corner over there, retching to hell and back.'

'Aye, that was me,' I admitted. 'I've not been well.' It occurred to me that he might have been my unknown benefactor, the one who had helped me through my illness. 'Did you put the compress on me?' I asked.

'Did I what?'

'And take away my pot?' I offered, and, truly, he looked like he would thump me now and send me downwards into the sea below.

'I haven't a mind to listen to your nonsense,' he said finally, simmering slowly like a pot taken off the boil. 'John Smith were a useless great lump anyway and you can't be any worse than him, so I dare say you'll do for now. You know what your duties are, do you?'

'Well, no,' I said, shaking my head. 'No one's said much to me so far. On account of me being so sick these last few days, I suppose, and then when I did awaken I—'

'Friend,' said the cook, raising a hand to silence me and giving me what he might have termed a smile. 'I don't give a bollix.'

That shut me up right quick, I don't mind telling you, and I closed my mouth and studied him up and down. Mr Hall was a middle-aged man with a rough beard on him and a gleam of constant perspiration, and the stink emerging from the kitchen where he worked did nothing to stimulate the appetite. Still, I liked him and knew not why.

'What's your name, then, anyways?' he asked me.

'John Jacob Turnstile,' said I. 'At your service.'

'At the captain's service, more like,' he muttered. 'Not that we have one, of course.'

'What's that?' I asked him and he just gave a laugh.

'Don't you know?' he said to me. 'That the *Bounty* is a ship without a captain? Now, there's a fine omen for you.'

I frowned. This didn't make a blind bit of sense to me, for after all Mr Zéla had referred to Captain Bligh as being a particular friend of his and Mr Samuel, the weasely little scut, had remarked upon the fact of it several times.

'The food's all ready anyway and they're waiting on it in there, so step lively,' he continued, leading me into the galley and indicating a line of silver plates all covered with lids. 'All you have to do is bring them into the captain's pantry and lay them down on the table, then take a seat on the floor in the corner of the cabin in case anyone has need of you. Serve Mr Bligh first, mind; he'll be at the head of the table. You can refill the officers' glasses if you see them running low, but keep your mouth shut through-out, you understand? No one cares what you might have to say and you're not there to offer conversation, so don't imagine it's of interest to anyone.'

'Right,' said I, picking up the first of the platters and going through the door. I didn't know what to expect when I reached the pantry, which stood immediately behind the captain's own cabin, as I hadn't so much as peeped through the keyhole of that door yet. As I passed through it now I noticed that two of the three picture frames I had placed on the desk earlier had been reversed in their positions – the lady's and boy's portraits were moved to the right hand of the sitter, the old man with the scowl to his left – and the bundle of letters with the red ribbon had dis-appeared from the desk top; I suspected they were of a private nature and he'd hidden them away from prying eyes. Through the door beyond I could hear the sound of conversation and, as luck would have it, Mr Fryer appeared behind me as I attempted to make my presence known and enter.

'All better now, young Turnstile?' he asked me, opening the door to let me through, and I nodded quickly and gave him a 'yes, sir, thank you, sir' for good measure as in we went, the two of us.

There were four men already inside the cabin, seated around the long table, and Mr Fryer made a fifth. At the head sat a man I judged to be of no more than thirty-three years and I knew immediately that he was the one I had been brought on board to serve.

'Ah, there you are, Mr Fryer,' he cried, looking above my head and offering a cheery smile to my fellow entrant. 'We feared you were gone man overboard.'

'My apologies, sir,' replied the ship's master with a half-nod as he sat down. 'I was engaged in a conversation about our course with one of the men on deck and he took a fit of coughing, would you believe, and I stayed with him till it passed.'

'Good God,' said the captain, barely stifling a laugh. 'Nothing serious, I hope, so soon into our voyage?'

Mr Fryer shook his head and stated that all was well now. He poured himself a glass of wine as I placed the platter down and removed the lid, revealing a clutch of roasted chickens beneath that made my mouth water.

'And who have we here?' the captain asked then, peering across at me. 'My whiskers, I believe the dead has arisen and is serving at table. Recovered now, are you, lad? Ready to do your duty?'

I'll tell you now that I've never been a fellow to get easily in-timidated by anyone, not even by those in uniforms or positions of power, but being in the presence of the captain – for I pre-sumed that it was he who was addressing me – gave me the trepidations inside, and without warning or expectation I realized that I had a curious desire to impress him.

'Yes, sir,' I replied, deepening my voice so that he might think me more mature than my years. 'It pleasures me to report that my health is fully restored.'

'His health is fully restored, gentlemen,' cried the captain with a cheer, raising a glass of wine to his fellows. 'Well, I think that deserves a toast, don't you? I give you the continued prosperity of the lad, young Turnstile!'

'Young Turnstile!' they all roared, clinking their glasses together, and I confess that although I was proud he already knew my name my face took on the reddenings out of shame, so that I couldn't get out of the room quick enough. When I returned a few minutes later, potatoes and vegetables in hand, they had already begun on the meat, the filthy savages.

'. . . but nevertheless I remain confident in the charts,' the captain was saying to one of the officers on his left as I reappeared, and him paying no attention to me now at all. 'It's true I have considered a number of contingency plans – it would be remiss of me not to have done so – but others have passed around the Horn successfully, so I fail to see why the *Bounty* cannot.'

'Others have not attempted it in the heart of winter, sir,' replied the younger man. 'It will be difficult, that is all I am saying. Not impossible, but difficult, and we should be aware of this as we progress.'

'Tish-tosh, you are being a pessimist, sir,' cried the captain jovially. 'And I'll not have a pessimist on board my ship. I'd rather have the scurvy. What say you, Master Turnstile?' he shouted, turning to me now so suddenly that I came close to spilling the flagon of wine. 'Do you share Mr Christian's downheartedness?'

I stared at him and opened and closed my mouth several times in the fashion of a caught fish with the hook in his lip, not having any knowledge of what they were talking about. 'Begging your pardon, sir,' said I, trying to add an air of education to my tone. 'I was engaged about my duties and am ignorant of the subject matter of which you speak.'

'What's that, lad?' he asked, frowning as if he couldn't understand me, which only unsettled me even more.

'I wasn't listening, sir,' said I. 'I was about my duties.'

There was silence for a moment from around the table and the captain gave me an enquiring class of a look before licking his lips and continuing. 'Mr Christian here,' he announced, nodding towards the gentleman on his left, a young man of about twenty-one or twenty-two years of age, I should say. 'He doesn't believe that ships such as ours are built to weather the storms at the Horn. I call him a naysayer. What say you?'

I hesitated; in truth I found it hard to imagine that he really wanted the opinion of one so inexperienced as I and wondered whether he was just making a farce of me. But the assembly was staring in my direction and I had no choice but to answer. 'I'm sure I couldn't say, sir,' I replied finally, for I was entirely ignorant of the Horn, having failed to consult a map of our voyage before we set out. 'Would that be the direction we're headed in?'

'It most certainly would,' said he. 'And I swear to you all now that we shall do it and in a record time too. Captain Cook managed it, and so shall we.'

Now, this was a different matter entirely. Show me the lad who did not know of or look up to the late Captain James Cook and I'll show you a lad without eyes, ears or sense.

'We're following in the captain's footsteps?' I asked, all goggle-eyed and ears a-twitchin'.

'Well, his path anyway,' said the captain. 'You're an admirer, then, I take it?'

'His most ardent,' said I in delight. 'And if he did it, then I should say we could give it a go.'

'You see, Fletcher?' shouted the captain triumphantly, slapping his hand down hard on the table before him. 'Even the lad here thinks we can do it, and he's been dribbling his innards down his chin for the past forty-eight hours like a suckling bairn. You could learn a lesson in fortitude from the boy, I think.'

I didn't look in the direction of Mr Christian; the captain's words and the atmosphere at the table that succeeded them made me think I should avoid his gaze.

'You must tell us more of your voyages with Captain Cook, sir,' said another officer after a lengthy pause, and this gentleman was in truth a lad not much older than I; he couldn't have seen more than fifteen summers, if that. 'They're of especial interest to me on account of my father, sir, who shook the captain's hand once at Blenheim Palace. Refill my glass, boy, will you?' he added, looking across at me, and I swear if we'd been back in Portsmouth, or upstairs in Mr Lewis's establishment, I would have taken that for a challenge and boxed his ears.

'Your father was a fortunate man, then, Mr Heywood,' said the captain, naming the cove for me. 'For a braver, wiser man never walked the earth than Captain Cook and I thank the Saviour every morning that I had the opportunity to serve under him. However, I think we do right to consider some of the difficulties that we face on our voyage. It would be remiss of us to do otherwise. Mr Christian, you are quite sensible when you say that . . .'

He hesitated for a moment and narrowed his eyes then, putting his fork down by the side of his plate and looking across at me as I finished pouring the wine for Mr Heywood.

'I think that will be all for now, Master Turnstile,' he said to me, lowering his tone a little. 'You may wait in the hallway beyond.'

'But Mr Hall said I should stay here in case you might need something,' said I, perhaps a little too anxiously, for who turned around to me then only that young Heywood again and him shouting at me like I'm a cur he could kick down an alleyway.

'You heard what the captain said,' he roared and the big pustules on his face were pulsing red with anger, the ugly bollix. 'You do what Mr Bligh tells you to do, boy, or I'll know the reason why.'

'I'd like to see you try, you wee scut,' said I, going over and pulling his nose, slapping his cheeks and unsettling his dinner over his britches, causing wild cheers of appreciation from the other fellows gathered there. But no! Only in my head did I say that and only in my imagination did I do it, for I might not have been on board the *Bounty* for long but I knew enough about sea life to know that I shouldn't answer back to anyone wearing a white uniform, even if he was no older than me and a damn sight more ugly to boot.

'Yes, sir,' said I, standing up and opening the door. 'Begging your most humble apology, sir. I'll be within spitting distance if you needs anything, though.'

'Spitting distance!' said Mr Christian then, laughing, and a smile crossed the captain's face too. 'Hark at him!' He exchanged a look of complicity with the lad Heywood and I could see I was off to a rough start with that pair of ruffians.

Off I went then all the same and made my way back to the hall-way, where I paced up and down, imagining the things I might have said or done, and while I was there who should come out of the galley, only the cook, Mr Hall, who looked at me more out of pity than anger.

'What did I tell you earlier?' he asked me. 'Didn't I say to stay within in case they had need of you?'

'I was sent out,' said I. 'Against my will. I'd have gladly held my ground.'

'Did you misbehave?'

'Not a bit of it,' I replied defensively. 'I answered a question that was put to me and filled the glasses and then the captain asked me to wait outside.'

Mr Hall thought about it for a moment and shrugged his shoulders, apparently satisfied with my response. 'Well, 'appen they wanted to discuss matters not fit for your ears yet. You are the junior after all.'

'I know,' said I, exhausted by this. 'And you're all above me. Even the mice in the woodwork are above me. I have it now.'

He smiled a little, but only for a moment, and then seemed to think better of his moment of humanity. 'Come in here, then, my brave fellow,' he said. 'I dare say you could do with a bowl of something hot inside you?'

He was right and I could and I was grateful for it. And, to my surprise, while I was eating the stew he laid out for me, what did he go and say only, 'Not a bad Christmas dinner for you, all things considered.' Well, didn't that make me stop eating for a moment and remember the day it was, a day I'd forgotten, a day – now that I thought of it – on which I should have been spend-ing my ill-gotten gains in the Twisty Piglet, on a fine meal to celebrate the Saviour's birth, and not here, on a ship in the middle of the sea without a friend or brother in sight.

I said no prayers, as Mr Lewis didn't allow them in his establishment, and so it was my habit not to offer thanks for all the glories that had come my way; Mr Lewis said that praying was for papists and sodomites; looking back, I find that a rich statement to have come from his blistered lips.

'What did you mean earlier?' I asked Mr Hall after a moment, looking up from my bowl. 'When you said the ship had no captain. She does, don't she? In Captain Bligh, I mean. I just served him a roast chicken.'

'Ah, well, that's the riddle of it, ain't it?' said Mr Hall, lifting a pot and scraping the slime from the bottom of it into a bowl for later use. Our lunch the following day, perhaps. 'Mr Bligh's in charge all right, only Mr Bligh ain't *Captain* Bligh, he's *Lieutenant* Bligh. The *Bounty* ain't a navy ship, you see. You've seen the size of her: less than ninety feet long, she is. She's only a cutter. No more 'n that. I been on navy ships in my time. And this ain't one.'

'A cutter,' I repeated quietly, trying to rescue a tasty piece of gristle that was escaping down my chin; I knew enough already not to waste food. 'And what's a cutter when she's at home? Ain't that the same as a navy ship?'

'Less than,' he said. 'We got three masts and a bowsprit – ain't you seen her?' I shook my head and he laughed in my face, but not making a farce of me, just out of surprise. 'Don't you know nothing about the sea?' he asked. 'We're only a cutter, and a hired one at that, and on account of that she don't have a captain, she has a lieutenant in charge. On a lieutenant's pay too, which is more than yours or mine but less than he'd like. Oh, we all call him Captain of course, but that's more of a courtesy than anything else. Sir Joseph would have us all call him that. But he's just a lieutenant, like Mr Fryer. Although Mr Bligh is above him, of course. He's above us all.'

4

LATER THAT NIGHT, when the dinner was over and the officers had long since gone back to their duties, I returned to the dining table under Mr Hall's instructions and brought the plates and glasses back to the galley, where I washed them carefully before replacing them in a chest in the captain's pantry. These weren't just any old plates and cutlery that the officers had eaten off, they were Captain Bligh's own personal supply, a gift from his lady wife at the start of our voyage, and were taken from their cubby-hole and press-ganged into service whenever he entertained those men immediately below him for dinner. I was unaccustomed to this kind of work, though, and it took me longer than I had imagined it would to complete the business, for washing and dry-ing is a terrible slow headache when the water isn't hot enough and the rags aren't dry enough to perform their duties. Still, I kept at it until the job was done, for I wanted to leave the pantry in as clean a condition as possible in order that the ship's cook would maintain a good impression of me for the future. Mr Hall, after all, was in charge of every man's meal, so I thought it a sensible thing to make an ally of him.

When I closed the door to pass back through the captain's cabin I was taken by a great surprise, for there, seated behind the desk in his nightshirt, was the captain himself, illuminated only by a candle on his desk, so he offered an appearance more spectre than man. I jumped and almost let go of a shout but managed to stop myself in time from looking a nance in front of him.

'I startled you,' came a quiet voice from behind the woodwork and he moved the candle a little further forward now so that I could see him better. I noticed that the portrait of the lady and the boy were even closer to him now and he was engaged in writing a letter; a sheaf of papers lay before him and the quill and ink-pot were close at hand. I suspected that he had been alternating his glance between the words on the page and the faces in the pictures. 'My apologies,' he added, his voice sounding low and sorrowful.

'No, sir, Captain, sir,' said I quickly, shaking my head as my heartbeat returned to its regular pattern. 'It was my own fault. I should have known you would be there. I was just cleaning your pantry, that's all.'

'And I thank you for it,' he said, looking down and returning to his writing. I watched him for a moment and took him in. He was neither a tall man nor a short one, neither fat nor thin, too pretty to be called ugly and too plain to be called handsome. All in all, a nondescript sort of a fellow but with a look of intelligence about the eyes, though, as I suppose gentlemen acquire after they've been schooled.

'Goodnight then, Captain,' I said, making for the door.

'Turnstile,' he said quickly and I spun round, wondering whether perhaps I had performed badly in my work earlier and I was to be reprehended for it. 'Step a little closer, will you?' I moved a few inches towards him and he shifted the candle again, so that it was settled at the edge of the desk between us. 'Closer,' he whispered then in a sort of singsong voice and forward I came again until there was no more than three or four feet separating us. I wondered whether I had given him the motions, but in truth I didn't take him for that sort of fellow at all. 'Hold out your hands,' he said. I stretched my arms out and bit my lip, thinking that perhaps I was about to receive a thrashing for some unknown crime. They reached out before me for a moment while the captain put his quill down and then he took one hand in each of his own, turned them over and examined them carefully. 'Quite filthy,' he said, looking up at me in disappointment.

'I had a plunge only this morning,' I told him, quick as you like. 'Honest I did.'

'You may have taken a plunge but your hands . . . your finger-nails . . .' He shook his head in disgust. 'You must take of yourself on board, lad. All the men must. Cleanliness and hygiene are the keys to a successful sea voyage. If we all remain healthy, we can stretch ourselves further. Then our ship will be a happier vessel and we shall reach our destination speedily and without incident. The result? We shall return home all the sooner to our loved ones and achieve our mission, for the king's glory. You understand me?'

'Yes, sir,' I said, nodding my head and vowing to scrub my nails every few weeks from then on if it would make him happy. I hesitated, wondering if I dared ask him what had been on my mind since the dinner conversation earlier. 'Captain,' I said finally, 'did you really serve with Captain Cook?' I was aware of the insolence of my remark but cared little for it; I wanted to know, that was all.

'I did, my boy,' said he, smiling a little. 'I was little more than a lad at the time. Twenty-one years of age when I joined the *Resolution*, as master. Mr Fryer's position here, although he is much older now than I was then. Captain Cook called me a prodigy. I suspect it was my skill with chart-drawing that secured me the post, but I made a study of it, my boy, I made a fine study of it. I served with him for many years and learnt my craft by observing him.' He reached forward and took the frame of the angry gentleman from its place on the desk and stared at it for a moment and I recalled where I had seen that face before: of course, it belonged to Captain Cook. I astonished myself that I had not recognized it before, but then all the portraits I had seen of the great man did not present him in quite such a state of fury. I wondered why the captain had chosen it as his keepsake. 'I was with him at the end, don't you know. When he was killed—' he began, but, foolish me, I interrupted the flow of his story.

'When he was murdered?' I asked breathlessly, my eyes opening wide. 'You were there? You saw it?'

Captain Bligh stared at me and frowned; he could see the hunger within me for information but perhaps distrusted my motives – and he was right to, for the salacious details of Captain Cook's death fascinated me as they did any boy. I had heard conflicting reports from sailors over the years, them as were stationed in Portsmouth or them as came to visit us lads at Mr Lewis's establishment, but they differed from each other considerably and were always sourced from a friend or a brother or a cousin who had known a fellow who had sailed with Captain Cook right to the end. I had never known a man who had been there, who had seen the events of that terrible afternoon with his own eyes. Not until now. And I was damned if I wasn't going to try to earn the report.

'Get to your sleep now, lad,' said the captain then, turning away and dismissing me. 'A long and busy day awaits you; you have much time to make up after your illness.'

I nodded, disappointed, and cursed myself inside for interrupting him. But as I made for the door to leave the dark cabin a sight took my eye; on a shelf inside the door lay a white cloth, the very same cold compress that had been placed about my forehead during my illness by my unknown and gentle benefactor, the same one as had emptied my pot during my ruptions. I stared at it and looked back at the captain, who saw where my eyes had taken me and frowned, as if he would have preferred me not to have seen it.

'I trust I won't need to use that again on this voyage,' he said finally.

'Captain—' I began, astonished by my discovery, for I swear that I thought I was for the grave during those first terrible days, but he turned away from me now and waved a hand in the air to dismiss me.

'Go to sleep, lad,' he said and in response I did something that I determined to do from that day forward, for as long as our voyage lasted, in both good times and bad.

I obeyed his orders.

5

THOSE EARLY DAYS ON BOARD THE *BOUNTY* passed by without incident. Although the weather was inclement over Christmas, it stilled finally and the ship chartered a course for the furthermost tip of South America with the intention of rounding Cape Horn. I made it my business to do all that I could to provide good service for the captain, whose initial friendliness towards me following my restoration to good health appeared to melt into indifference as the weeks went by. I cleaned his cabin, served him his breakfast, lunch, dinner and supper, prepared his bunk, washed his undercrackers, all the time hoping that he would indulge my taste for more stories about Captain Cook, but I'll be cobbled if he ever did. Most of his waking hours were spent on the deck of the ship, where the men appreciated his guidance and advice, and the time that he did pass in his cabin was devoted to maintaining his log and writing his letters. For my part, I made it my particular duty to get to know as many of the men on board as possible, as I quickly developed a fierce sense of isolation and loneliness, but I was quick to discover that this was no easy feat. Most of them seemed unwilling to exchange so much as a pleasantry or even engage in a simple conversation with such a lowly member of the ship's complement as I and I found that my time was spent mostly below deck in a triangle of opportunity between the great cabin, where the pots and crates were stored, the galley where Mr Hall prepared the crew's meals, and the captain's own cabin and pantry, enjoying no man's company but my own. That being the case, I saw a lot of the officers during those days as they were housed together in bunked cabins near the rear of the corridor that I called mine own, except for Mr Fryer, who, as master, existed in a tiny cabin with a population of one. But they never bothered to engage me in conversation either.

We made good progress through January in fairly calm waters but then one evening, without warning, the storms and gales whipped themselves up into an almighty fury and within an hour the ship was being tossed around on the seas like a rag doll and all hands were brought to the deck to aid the ship's safe passage through the storm. Happily, my stomach had learned to live with the movements of the tides and I was no longer in fear of mortal collapse, but so violent was the weather and the conditions that we faced that I found myself afeared that we would be lifted from the waves, every man jack of us, and turned upside down.

I made the mistake of stepping on deck when the storms were at their worst and the moment my head emerged into the mêlée, I could feel the full force of rain, hail and sleet attacking my pretty features with such violence that I thought they would draw blood. Around me, men were rushing back and forth, pulling on ropes and changing the direction of the sails, calling out to one another with short, pithy phrases as they each undertook their duty, none of which made any sense to me in my ignorance of sea-faring ways. I turned back to rediscover the hatch from which I had emerged but could barely open my eyes wide enough to locate it and at that moment I heard a great cry from above and looked up just in time to observe William McCoy – an AB, or able seaman as I had finally discovered those letters to mean – tumbling from the fore-topgallant sail, that section of the ship's mast immediately below the fore-royal, and narrowly avoiding slipping further down the fore-topsail and foresail itself on to the deck, below where he would surely have cracked his skull open and left his brains in a mess like a dropped watermelon. Fortunately for him he managed to grab a hold of a stay just in time and cling on to it with one hand, swinging back and forth like a punished convict, until his feet could make purchase with a line and he could haul himself back upwards to safety. The sight of it gave me an awful turn, though.

I had grown familiar with the design of the ship over the previous days by studying the design-chart affixed to Captain Bligh's cabin wall. The *Bounty* was a cutter of three masts, the fore and main masts holding four sails apiece, a royal, a topgallant, a topsail and a sail. At the rear of the ship, the mizzen mast held all but a sail. At the front sat two sails before each other, the jib and the fore-topmast sail, and the aft was served by a spanker, which was there to propel us through the waters and to balance the helm. Of course I had not yet learned how each of these might be manipulated to steer the ship and guide us through troubled waters such as we were currently locked in combat with, but I vowed to study further as the voyage continued and prove a more able seaman than my present occupation expected.

'Turnstile,' roared Captain Bligh to me, returning to his cabin at the height of the hurricane, his uniform so wet through that I wondered whether he might not catch the influenza as a result. (A lad at Mr Lewis's establishment had caught it once and, rather than infect every one of us, he'd been turned out on to the street without ceremony. He was a particular friend of mine – we slept alongside each other for a year or more – but I never saw him again after that. I heard he'd passed to his reward but I've no proof of it.) The captain's hands were pressed to either side of the corridor walls to steady himself as he walked along, while the *Bounty* continued to be tossed upwards and downwards, left to right, with such force that I swore I could feel the lining of my stomach separating from the rest of my body and striking out for a life and career of its own. 'What the blazes are you about now?'

'Captain,' said I, jumping to my feet, for I had positioned myself on the floor in a corner near my own bunk, where my toes could find purchase with the floor below and my hands could press against the walls. 'What's happening to us? Are we all lost?'

'Don't be an ass, lad,' he snapped, marching towards his cabin. 'I've known worse nights than this. This is calm, for pity's sake. Stand yourself up and show a bit of courage before I put a dress on you and call you Mary.'

I returned to the vertical, anxious not to be seen as a coward by the captain, and tried to follow him into his cabin, but the rocking of the boat and the sounds of dismayed shouting from up above held me back.

'Jesus Suffering Christ,' shouted I, forgetting my station for a moment in my trepidations. 'What's happening up there? What's wrong with the men?'

'The men?' he asked, turning round and frowning. 'There's nothing wrong with the men, lad, and I'll thank you not to take the Saviour's name in this cabin. Why would you ask such a question?'

'But the screaming,' I said, my face no doubt taking on a look of abject terror as I spoke to him. 'Can't you hear it? Perhaps they're falling over the sides and we'll have no one left to steer the ship. Shouldn't we help them? Or send someone up to help them anyway?'

As I spoke, a great sheet of water hit the window of the cabin with such force that I almost fell over again in a faint. The captain merely glanced towards it as if it was an irritant, a fly that he might sweep out of his presence with a flick of his hand. 'That's not the men screaming, you damned fool,' he said. 'Good Lord, lad, don't you recognize the pipe of the wind yet? It's sweeping across the decks, challenging us, daring us to go further. The screams are its battle-cry! The roar its strength! Know you nothing of the sea yet?' He shook his head and stared at me as if I was a terrible fool and he was a martyr to have to suffer me. 'As if the men on this ship,' he continued then, 'on *my* ship, would scream in panic. They are kept busy about their tasks. As you should be about yours, so go on about your duties, lad, before I give you something to scream about. I need boiling water for tea, this minute.'

'Yes, Captain,' said I, watching him for a moment as he pulled his maps and charts out from their storage place upon the shelves and unfurled them, placing weights on their corners to keep them flat.

'Now, Turnstile!' he roared at me. 'Enough for three, if you please.'

I ran into the galley and looked around for Mr Hall, but he was not to be found; at moments like this I had discovered that almost every man of the ship's complement was to be found on deck, assisting in the attempts to keep us afloat. Only a few remained below. I was one of that number for the moment as I was neither use nor ornament to anyone. Another who steered clear of the hard work, I noticed, was the ship's surgeon, Dr Huggan, who I had only eyeballed on two occasions to date and who appeared to be permanently in his cups and confined to his quarters. A third was young Mr Heywood, who never seemed to be on deck in times of trouble and always perceived a matter of urgency that needed attending to in a safer part of the ship, the cowardly scut.

When I returned with the kettle and the tea, I found the captain examining charts and maps with an eyeglass while the master, Mr Fryer, and the master's mate, Mr Christian, looked on. They were a study, the two of them, that was for sure, the first with his red face and anxious expression, his every word striving to be heard, the second looking as if he had recently taken a plunge and attended to his coiffure and scarcely appearing to think we were in any danger at all. In fact at the moment I entered the cabin he was examining his nails for dirt. He was a pretty fellow, I'll give him that.

'Captain, we can't continue to compete against this storm for much longer,' Mr Fryer was insisting as I entered. 'The waves are coming at us in great sheets; the deck is near drowned in sea water as it is. We must lie a-try.'

'Lie a-try?' cried Mr Bligh, looking up from the map and

shaking his head. 'Lie a-try?' he roared. 'Unthinkable, sir! The *Bounty* does not lie a-try, not while I am her commander! We scud ahead!'

'Without a drogue, sir?' asked Mr Fryer, his eyes widening. 'Is that wise?'

I knew little then of how much use a drogue could be to prevent a ship from being pooped by the waves, but it sounded important and I regretted the fact that we had none.

'Yes, Mr Fryer,' insisted the captain. 'Without a drogue.'

'But, sir, if we trim the sails and helm a-lee, we stand some chance at least of maintaining our position.'

'What a bore to maintain one's position, though,' sighed Mr Christian in a distracted voice, as if the matter was of little consequence to him one way or the other and he would be perfectly happy to return to his bunk until the matter could be brought to a satisfactory conclusion. 'Personally I would rather advance. We have a schedule to keep to after all, do we not? And lying a-try would be a waste of all our time. I didn't board the *Bounty* for that.'

'Mr Christian, you are not best placed to discuss this matter, I fear,' replied Mr Fryer, turning on him with a look of fury in his eyes. 'And if I may say so, your place is on deck at this time with Mr Elphinstone. This is a matter for the captain and me.'

'And I tell you, Mr Fryer, it's a matter for the captain who he invites into his cabin and who he does not,' shouted Mr Bligh, standing up to his full height and glaring at the ship's master with a fury in his eyes. 'It was I who invited Fletcher into this conversation and it'll be I who dismisses him, not you, Mr Fryer. Not you. Is that understood?'

There was a silence for a moment as the victim of this assault glared from one man to the other, his face growing ever redder by the moment, before he looked directly at the captain and nodded his head.

'Now, Mr Christian,' said the captain, pulling on his jacket tails

91

tight as he attempted to compose himself while he turned back to the master's mate, and I swear I had not seen him grow as angry as this since I had first made his acquaintance. 'What say you? You believe we should scud ahead?'

Mr Christian hesitated for a moment, gave a quick glance to Mr Fryer, before shrugging his shoulders and replying in that same bored, disaffected voice of his. 'My feeling is that the *Bounty* can do it,' he said. 'The storms are dreadful, as Mr Fryer says, I don't dispute that, but are they to rule o'er the seas or are we? We are Englishmen, after all. And let us not forget that Captain Cook managed it, did he not?'

The magic words, I knew, had just been uttered – Mr Christian was nobody's fool – and the captain turned back to Mr Fryer with a look of triumph on his face. 'Well?' he said. 'What say you to that, John Fryer?'

'Captain, you are in charge of this vessel and I will of course follow your orders,' he replied, defeated.

'You damn well will,' replied the captain, and I thought it short of him at the time, as Mr Fryer's answer had been a gracious one. I couldn't help but note the look of amusement on Mr Christian's face, though, and wondered about it. 'Both of you,' said the captain then, wiping a line of perspiration from his forehead and marching over to open the ship's log. 'Atop with you both. Give the order to scud ahead, Mr Fryer. We shall force our way through the storm throughout the night and the next night, and the night after that if needs be, aye, even if we are to drown in the attempt. I want every man on deck with the ship perfectly balanced from port to starboard, tack to clew, and we cut through, *we cut through*, I say, until we are clear of these conditions. We have a mission to complete, gentlemen, and with the grace of God we shall achieve it. Do I make myself clear?'

The two men nodded and took their leave of the cabin and I poured tea for the captain – there would be no need for the other two cups now – before placing it on the table beside him. He neither looked up at me nor offered his thanks but continued to make notes in the log, his pen digging sharply and with such ferocity that I feared the paper might be torn asunder; whenever he reached back for the ink-pot he did it in a fury and spots of blue ink spat out on the desk, leaving marks for me to wipe clean later before they settled in. I opened my mouth to say something to him, thought better of it and turned to leave, closing the door quietly behind me.

6

THAT NIGHT WAS A DARK ONE. I lay in my bunk, unable to sleep, not knowing whether every lift of the ship would see us overturned with every man jack of us drowned. I couldn't help but think back to that late December morning in Portsmouth when I had been wandering the streets without a care in the world, looking forward to my Christmas dinner, little knowing what fate had in store for me. I even thought of Mr Lewis, him as took care of me since I was a nipper, and wondered whether he had discovered the truth of my whereabouts since my disappearance. I hoped not. He'd have been expecting me back around dinner-time with my earnings, or at least the part I handed to him, and when I failed to appear he would have started to grow angry. And when the night-work began he'd have become furious, for I had grown popular with his clientele over the previous twelve months, more popular than I wished to be. Strange to recall, and to my eternal shame, I'd never planned on leaving him, despite the participations at his establishment, and even if I had tried to forge a plan from my wits it probably would have failed and I would have found myself in even worse trouble than I was now. He was probably hopping with anger, the monster, that I had managed to get away from him. I could imagine him at the courthouse, demanding compensation for my kidnapping and being refused it, for what rights had he over me anyway? He wasn't my father, and what did I do for him only steal and con. And the other things.

Still, I knew that if he caught up with me upon my return, there wouldn't be a whisper in it for me. He'd slit my throat from ear to ear and call it justice.

7

THE NEXT MORNING BROKE FRESH and clear and I opened my eyes, surprised that I had found sleep at all, to an almighty roar from the captain that rattled through my head and sent my eyeballs a-spinning in their sockets.

'Turnstile!' he shouted. 'Where in blazes are you, lad?'

I jumped from my bunk and pulled my clothes on before running towards his cabin door, knocking quickly and stepping inside as if I'd been engaged in a series of important duties and not just asleep in my pit, dreaming of a molly back home. The captain was poring over the charts again with Mr Christian by his side, smoking a pipe.

'There you are at last,' he said irritably, glancing up at me. 'What the devil kept you, boy? Come when you're called, will you?'

'Begging your apologies, Captain,' said I, offering him a quick bow. 'How can I be of service?'

'More hot water,' he answered quickly, his answer to everything, it seemed. 'And tea. This is a good morning, Turnstile,' he added loudly and cheerfully. 'A jolly good morning to be alive and at sea and in the king's fine employ!'

I nodded and ran for the galley, filled a pot of water from the stove and brought it back to his cabin, where I placed it down before the two men. I was surprised that Mr Fryer wasn't here with them, for after all he was second-in-command on board the ship and therefore above Mr Christian, but he was nowhere to be seen.

'Excellent,' said the captain, clapping his hands together. 'No, no, Fletcher, allow me,' he added when the latter tried to pour. I glanced in Captain Bligh's direction; his uniform was dark and sullied with the energies he must have expended the night before returning us to safety and calm waters. His eyes looked tired and his whiskers wanted shaving. Mr Christian, on the other hand, appeared before us like the very model of a handsome naval officer, such as might be displayed in the windows of a tailor's premises in London. He had the manner of one who had slept in a clean bed in a Parisian whorehouse the night before and managed eight hours' sleep after doing the unspeakables not once, not twice, but thrice. I was convinced that there was an air of perfume about him too, and the Saviour only knew where that had come from. 'Turnstile,' said the captain then, turning towards me, and for a moment I was foolish enough to think that I was to be included in their company and consultations. 'The book-shelves over there, and my papers. Everything has become dislodged during the storm. Tidy them up, will you? I can't abide a mess. It puts me out of sorts.'

'Yes, Captain,' said I, happy to do a job that might allow me to remain in their presence a little longer and imagine myself a master of the sea alongside them.

'I must commend you, Captain,' said Mr Christian, who I could tell was completely disinterested in my presence, 'There were moments last night when I began to fear for our safety. You never doubted it once, did you?'

'Not for a moment, Fletcher,' replied the captain vehemently, sitting forward in his chair as if to emphasize the point. 'Not for a moment. If I've learned anything from my years at sea, it's that you can tell the keenness of a ship from the moment you step aboard her. And, do you know, the moment I laid eyes on the *Bounty* at Deptford harbour I knew exactly what she was capable of. I said as much to Sir Joseph that morning. I told him that she was a ship that would bring us through harsh waters and safely out the other side – and I was right, wasn't I? By God, I was right!'

There was mention of that Sir Joseph again. I knew not who he was or whether he was on board, but if he was I had yet to lay eyes on him.

'Still,' said the younger man, examining his nails to ensure that they hadn't been blackened since the last time he'd checked a few moments before, 'it takes great character to scud ahead as you did. The men have always admired you, sir, you know that. But this morning I swear that they are ready to cast a golden image in your likeness.'

Mr Bligh burst out laughing and shook his head. 'Oh, dear me, no,' he said, but I could tell he was pleased by the news nonetheless. 'There's no need for anything like that. That's the job of a ship's commander, as you'll discover someday yourself, Fletcher, when you have command of a ship of your own. You see, I have a particular goal in mind that I have confided in no man. Perhaps you would care to be taken into my confidence?'

'I should be honoured, sir,' he replied, a touch more eagerness creeping into his tone than usual. I perked up a little myself in interest.

'The thing is, Fletcher,' continued the captain, 'I don't just intend to complete our mission as per our orders, although I shall of course adhere to them as if they were the very Bible. But I also intend to return our crew to Spithead without casualty or punishment. How's that for an ambition, sir?'

Mr Christian's forehead wrinkled slightly at the words and he considered them for a moment before saying something.

'We can but pray there will be no casualties,' he replied cautiously and he sounded like a man who wanted to take great care with the words he used, as he always was. 'But without punishment? Without a single one? Is that a likely outcome?'

'Oh, it may be something of a vain hope, I'll concede that to you,' said the captain, waving a hand in the air dismissively. 'But can you recall a mission like ours, covering such a great distance over such a lengthy time, wherein the crew returned with ne'er a flogging and ne'er a lashing?'

'Never, Captain,' said Mr Christian, shaking his head. 'It's unheard of.'

'But wouldn't it be quite the thing?' continued the captain, warming to his theme now. 'A peaceful voyage? Wouldn't that make the admirals back in London sit up and take notice of us all? A crew working together harmoniously will never give cause for the boson's lash to make an appearance. And I believe we can do it, Fletcher. I truly believe we can do it.'

My thoughts raced ahead of me as I carried on with my gathering and cleaning. Lashing? Flogging? Of course I knew from the chatter of the sailors berthed in Portsmouth that these were regular features of any sea voyage, even in modern times such as ours, but I hadn't thought of them taking place on board the *Bounty*.

'Then, I wish you success with it, sir,' said Mr Christian, raising his mug in salute. 'And the deuce knows that after your achievements last night the men will not want to let you down.' He hesitated for a moment and looked away a little as he spoke his next sentence. 'I dare say Mr Fryer is pleased that he was wrong.'

'Hmm?' asked the captain, looking up, his smile fading only slightly. 'What's that you say, Fletcher?'

'Mr Fryer,' he repeated. 'I was considering that we all make mistakes and he must be pleased this morning, as we are settled in these fine waters and making such speed with the headwind, that his desire to lie to last night was not accepted by you.'

Bligh thought about it for a moment. 'Well, he was right to suggest it,' he said quietly after a moment, a hint of conciliation in his tone. 'We must consider all possibilities in these situations. It would be remiss of us not to.'

'Of course, of course,' said Mr Christian quickly. 'Please don't misunderstand me, Captain. I'm not implying for a moment that it was a cowardly suggestion on his part.'

'A cowardly . . . ?' Bligh considered this for a moment and then shook his head, but without too much conviction, I felt. Mr Christian's words were settling in his mind. 'Had we lain a-try, we would have remained in those waters and never advanced at all,' he said finally. 'I couldn't see any alternative but to scud ahead. And I knew we could do it, Fletcher. I *knew* it.'

'As did I, Captain,' said Mr Christian cheerfully, as if it had been his idea all along. 'Now, if I may be excused, Captain, I am needed on deck.'

'Of course, of course,' replied Mr Bligh, who appeared to be lost in thought; if the brain gave off sounds as it calculated its thoughts, I suspected that I would have been deafened by what was going through his head at that moment.

'Oh, Fletcher,' he said suddenly, just as Mr Christian was leaving his cabin. 'As the day progresses, I want fires lit to dry the men's clothing. They shouldn't be expected to work in sodden garb. It's unhealthy and unhygienic.'

'Of course, sir: I'll see to it.'

'And give an extra ration of tobacco and rum to each man today in recognition of their labours last night.'

'We have lost some provisions in the storms, Captain,' said Mr Christian cautiously. 'Is it wise to give the men these bonuses at this point?'

'They must know how much I value their good service,' replied the captain with determination. 'And it's good for morale after so much hardship. See to it, Fletcher, will you?'

'Of course,' said Mr Christian. 'It's very generous of you.'

'Oh, and one last thing . . .' said the captain, standing up and walking towards him slowly, an expression on his face that suggested he was mightily perplexed. He hesitated for some time before speaking, as if he was unsure of his words or plans. 'Mr Fryer . . . he is on deck, I assume?'

'I believe so, Captain,' came the reply. 'Although I admit I haven't seen him myself this morning. Shall I send the lad to find him?' he asked, cocking a thumb in my direction.

'Yes,' said the captain slowly, stroking his chin as he said so and then shaking his head quickly as if he had thought better of it. 'No,' he said then. 'No, it doesn't matter. I'll . . .' He considered it for a moment longer before shaking his head again. 'It's of no consequence. We're safe and we move forward, that's what matters now. Let us say no more about it. That'll be all, Mr Christian.'

The master's mate nodded quickly and left for the deck above, no doubt to stir up more trouble along the way.

I attended to a few more duties around the cabin and pantry as the captain consulted his charts again and returned to his log and it wasn't long after that that a great cry went up on deck. Land had been spotted. Our first port of call where we might replenish the ship's provisions and repair some of her beaten sails.

Santa Cruz.

8

AFTER NEARLY A MONTH AT SEA I was a happy sparrow at the idea of stepping off the *Bounty* and on to dry land. I had found my 'sea-legs', as Captain Bligh put it, and was able to eat and drink my ration of food without feeling that I had swallowed a ladleful of laxatives. However, I knew little of the port of Santa Cruz – it was a name I had never even heard before our voyage – and had no notion whether this place would offer a chance for either. Indeed, I only discovered that it was on the Portuguese coast when Dr Huggan, our ship's surgeon, came waddling past me that very morning, extolling the virtues of Portuguese brandy and making for the gangway faster than I thought possible for a man with such a top-heavy build.

I hoped to follow him, of course, and waited to be asked to join one of the groups of ABs who were being sent ashore by the captain to replenish our ship's stocks, but to my great disappointment I was not invited to be of that party. I was deeply unhappy at this as it had seemed like a good opportunity for me to make an investigation of a new city for myself; my feet had never touched foreign soil and I wondered whether there was any chance of anyone noticing my disappearance, for I was not part of any of the officers' details, only the captain's, and he was already ashore and had failed to take me with him. I'm not ashamed to admit that the idea crossed my mind that perhaps I could continue alone from Santa Cruz and move towards Spain, if I had my geography correct, to begin a new life under the name of Pablo Moriente there where Mr Lewis would never discover me. I knew only too well that the penalty for desertion was hanging, but I considered myself light on my feet and thought I could manage a successful escape. Unfortunately, before I could consider my plan further, I was discovered and summoned to duty by none other than that young scut Mr Heywood.

'You, Turnip,' said he to me, poking his head round the door of the captain's cabin and discovering me in the act of studying the geographical charts, the better to plan my escape. 'What in blazes are you doing down here?'

'If it pleases you, sir,' said I, making a low bow to him, as if he was the Prince of Wales and I was a footman from Liverpool, in order to make a farce of him. He was no more than a year older than I was, the donkey, and neither as tall nor as pretty either, I might add. 'I thought I might venture to continue the occupation

100

for which I am put on board this here vessel and tidy the captain's quarters.'

'You were looking at the charts.'

'The better to understand the difference between longitude and latitude, sir, which has never been explained to me in a sensible way and, as you know, I am fierce ignorant of sea-faring ways, not having had your education.'

He narrowed his eyes and glared at me, trying to find a word or two in there that might be construed as insubordination. 'There'll be plenty of time for you to increase your knowledge of whatever you please when we're back at sea,' said he, looking around quickly, for he wasn't often invited into the inner sanctum and I could see that he had the resentments towards me for the fact that I spent half my waking hours there. 'Get you on deck at once.'

'I'm afraid I can't do that, sir,' said I, shaking my head. 'The captain will have my guts for garters if I don't see to my duties.'

'Your *duties*,' said he, spitting the word out, 'are exactly what I or any other officer of His Majesty's navy tell you that your duties are and I say that you are to go on deck and help the men with the swabbing down and you will do so, if you please. Immediately.'

I rolled the charts up slowly, hoping against hope itself that he might step outside in the meantime, assuming that I would obey him, and forget about me, but no such luck was with me.

'Hurry along with that,' he snapped, holding his ground and speaking as if we were all in a terrible great hurry and the world was likely to come to an end if I didn't do exactly as he said and sharpish. 'The ship won't clean itself.'

I'd known lads like Mr Heywood all my life and had never got along with any of them. During my years at Mr Lewis's establishment, most of my brothers – for brothers is what I considered them – were boys I had grown up with, lads who had drifted towards his business when they had no other means of survival, youthful fellows who had heard that there was a man nearby, a man who took young rascals in and gave them work and fed and clothed them, not much knowing what that work might entail, nor how they would be forced to pay for their bed and board. As we had known one another since we were infants, most of us boys rubbed along quite well for the most part, but on occasion an older boy would arrive, a chap who had been deliberately brought there by Mr Lewis on account of his being particularly taken with him, and, oh my, but the trouble a lad like that would cause. He might look around and quickly realize that he had competition there for Mr Lewis's affections – little did he know, the donkey – and think that if he didn't assert himself quick-spit then those of us who were of an age with him would push him out and send him off to make his living elsewhere. Such boys were trouble and I will admit that I was one of those who planned small extravagances whereby they might leave us all in peace; I take shame in the memory of it. Mr Heywood reminded me very much of such lads. I suspected that he was treated poorly by the officers on account of his youth, his inexperience and his grubby appearance – for to look at him was no great pleasure with his greasy dark hair and the pustules upon his face, which threatened to explode like the volcano at Pompeii at any moment – not to mention the fact that his phizzy wore a constant look of one who had been surprised in his sleep and forced to dress and labour before he could even grasp what time of day it was. And the sounds that came from his bunk in the night! I don't like to write it down on account of the vulgarity of it, but here was a lad who spent half his waking life with the motions and the other half at tug, it seemed to me.

About a third of the ship's complement were on deck on that bright morning at Santa Cruz, some in the rigging, repairing the sails, others on the decks on their hands and knees with pails of water and scrubbing brushes, and yet more coming back from the town with provisions for our onward voyage. The scut Mr Heywood looked around and pointed towards two men who were kneeling by the drumhead, cleaning the decks.

'Over there, Turnip,' said he.

'It's Turnstile,' said I, ready to hit him a slap for his insolence.

'I care not,' he replied, just as quick. 'You're to work with Quintal and Sumner. I want to be able to eat my dinner off this deck later, is that understood?'

'Absolutely, sir,' said I as he turned away from me. 'And I'll be glad to serve it to you there.'

'What's that?' he asked, spinning round.

'I'm to clean the deck, sir. Right you are.'

'As you know, the captain values hygiene above all thing—'

'Oh, I know he do, sir,' said I, playing the braggart. 'I know he do. Why, only the other night we were in his cabin together, the two of us, and he turned to me and "Master Turnstile," he said, "Master Turnstile, if there's one thing I've learned during my career on His Majesty's—"'

'I don't have time for your foolish narratives,' Mr Heywood shouted – barked, more like, considering the dog he was – and I could tell that I'd got one over on him then, for he didn't like the idea of the captain and me sharing a confidence in this way. The truth of it was that we did, though, for over the previous few weeks I had found that the captain did speak to me for minutes at a time whenever I was in his presence and talked about things that he might never have discussed with the men or the officers. I suspect it was because he didn't consider me one of them at all, but his own man, privy to his own particular thoughts, such as a physician might be considered, and he was right, for I liked to think of myself as a loyal chap – except when I was planning my escape from King George's clutches, that is. I did feel bad that I hadn't been allowed to go ashore and make merry, though; I thought that a fierce cruel blow. 'The captain desires that the ship is washed and scrubbed from clew to tack while we replenish the stores and make some repairs,' continued Mr Heywood, giving his nethers a healthy scratch for good measure while he addressed me, the filthy pig. 'So attend to your work immediately.'

I nodded and walked as ordered towards the two men, who in turn looked up from their work and gave each other a quick glance and a smile as I approached them. I hadn't spent much time on deck since leaving Spithead in December and, truth to tell, some of the sailors on board gave me the trepidations. I'd known many rough types in my time – Mr Lewis's friends were as unsavoury a group of ruffians as anyone might hope to meet in a month of Tuesdays – but the men on board looked as if they might kill you as soon as offer you the time of day. Grizzly, they were. And stinky. And always chewing their gums or pulling who-knew-what out of their wiry hair. The first of the two men who awaited me now was Matthew Quintal, a broad chap in his twenty-fifth year or there-abouts, and with muscles on him like a labouring ox, while the second, John Sumner, was a little older perhaps and not as strongly built, but clearly in his master's shadow.

'Good morning,' said I, and the words were barely out of my mouth when I regretted them, for didn't they make me sound like the nance of all time. I should have said naught and just got on with my work.

'Why, good morning to you too,' said Quintal, and the big broad smile on him made me feel immediately nervous. 'Don't tell me that our little lord of the under-decks is condescending to climb the stairs and join the working men?'

I shrugged and took a scrubbing brush from their pail and knelt down on the deck to begin the infernal scraping. 'Don't think I want to do it,' said I, looking him full square in the eye then. 'I'd much rather be lying in my bunk, counting my fingers and scratching my bollix, than up here on my hands and knees with you. But that filthy swine Mr Heywood, he insisted. So here I am.'

Quintal narrowed his eyes for a moment, surprised by my reply perhaps, but then gave a laugh and shook his head. 'Well, it's an honest answer,' said he, returning to his scrubbing, which gave Sumner the nod that he might return to it too. 'There's not many of us wouldn't prefer to have a little time to ourselves right now, is there?' he added, glancing towards the shore, and I followed the direction of his eyes to discover three young mollies who were standing on the cold stone beyond, looking in the direction of the *Bounty* and giggling and pointing at the men who were working in the rigging. 'My, oh my,' said Quintal, whistling through his dentals. 'What I wouldn't give for ten minutes alone with one or two or three of them.'

'You'd show them what's what, I dare say, Matthew,' said Sumner, and I could tell immediately who was the slave in that relationship. 'You'd teach them a thing or two about a thing or two, what?'

'I would that,' said Quintal, reaching between his legs then and giving himself a squeeze about the unmentionable. 'A month is too long for any man to be without a woman. What say you, lad?' he asked me with a nasty smile. 'Here,' he cried then, 'I don't even know your name, do I?'

'It's Turnstile,' said I. 'John Jacob Turnstile. Pleased to meet you, I'm sure.'

'They call him Turnip,' said the donkey Sumner with a laugh, opening his mouth and revealing a mouth containing an incomplete set of brown gnashers that I would have had no difficulty in dismantling, had I a mind to do so.

'Who do?' asked Quintal.

'The officers,' said he, trying to make a laugh of me. 'Mr Heywood, for one.'

Quintal frowned. 'The lad says his name's Turnstile,' he replied. 'So that's what we'll call him,' and I couldn't help but smile at Sumner.

'What goes on here?' came a voice from above us then, and who was it only Mr Heywood, back to haunt us. 'There's too much chatter going on here, you men. Get back to your work or I'll know the reason why.'

The three of us got back down to it then and said nothing for a few minutes, until the filthy scut had wandered off to play with himself, no doubt, and then Quintal – who, despite defending me against Sumner, still gave me the trepidations – shook his head and threw his brush down in the bucket, splashing me in the face with the force of it and causing me to wipe the suds from my eyes. 'Look over there,' said he, and I turned to see four other men – I know their names now as Skinner, Valentine, McCoy and Burkett – stepping back on to the deck of the *Bounty* laden with baskets of fruit, their mouths stained red from eating strawberries on the way, and one of them, Burkett, walking a little lively on account of the drink he must have taken. 'I could have been with them, only for the captain giving me the manual work. Lucky lads!' he added, shaking his head. 'And that Heywood, the bollix, he's mad on account of staying on board too. Wanted to be with his friend, didn't he? Wanted to play with Mr Christian?'

'Mr Christian's on shore?' I asked, doing my best to clear a stain of blood from the decking that showed no sign of wanting to be dislodged.

'It was to be Mr Fryer,' said Sumner. 'By rights, it should have been him gone to pay his respects to the governor with the captain.'

'Mr Fryer is below decks,' I mentioned, for I had seen him in his cabin when Mr Heywood was escorting me from the ease of below-decks to the labours of above.

'Aye, and not happy about it,' said Quintal. 'The captain announced that he was to go ashore for a few hours and invited Mr Christian to join him. "Captain," says Mr Fryer – I was no more than six steps away from him at the time – "Captain, shouldn't I accompany you, as ship's master?" Well, the captain looked at him and seemed about to change his mind, but then didn't he notice me watching – and he didn't want to be seen to make an alteration, I imagine, so he tells Mr Fryer that he's leaving him in charge of the ship and that Mr Christian will join him instead. Well, as you can imagine, Mr Christian was away in a hop, skip and a jump, and as he went young Mr Heywood, who's as much in love with Mr Christian as it's possible for a man to be with another, he saw his chance to go too but he was quickly slapped down and shown his place. That's what's got him so angry this morning, I warrant.'

I nodded. I couldn't help but wonder why the captain showed so much favour towards Mr Christian; I'd observed more than one instance of such partiality below decks since our voyage had begun and it seemed to me that the master's mate encouraged Mr Bligh in his dislike of Mr Fryer, which, to my eyes, stemmed from nothing more than a personal animosity between the two men. For my part, I had formed no great opinion of either officer, other than to notice that the latter worked hard and knew his craft and the former was the dandy of the ship and wore more pomade in his hair than I considered healthy. But Mr Christian had one other quality that confused me: he was the only man on board who never stank. Whether that was through a surfeit of washing or a dearth of labour, I knew not.

'*Bom dia*, lads!' came a shout from the shore then and we three looked across to see the mollies waving in our direction and blowing kisses. 'Catch these, will you?' they called. 'Store them somewhere warm.'

'I'll store them somewhere you can find them if you've a mind to,' shouted Quintal, and the three of them dissolved into laughter as if this was a fine joke, which it wasn't to my mind. 'Oh, they make me ache in the trousers, they fair do,' said he then in a quieter voice and Sumner laughed and I found myself growing red in the face as matters like this have never sat well with me.

'What's the matter with you, Turnstile?' he asked me then, catching sight of my reddening phizzy. 'Not afraid of the ladies, are you?'

'Not I,' said I, quick as you like, for reputations are everything on board a ship and I knew enough to defend mine.

'Known a few, then, have you?' he asked, leaning forward and sticking his tongue out at me before shaking it up and down in

107

such a vile manner that I took a fit of the revulsions. 'Had your way with a few of the Portsmouth whores, have you? Licked 'em up and down and in and out?'

'I've known my share,' I replied, getting on with my scrubbing and not looking him in the face lest he saw the truth of it. 'And his share too,' I added, nodding in Sumner's direction, and I could see he wanted to hit me a slap when I said it but he couldn't, on account of Quintal warming to me.

'Have you indeed?' said he, real quiet then, before repeating the words more quietly, and I could feel his eyes boring into me then, but I didn't want to give him the satisfaction of looking up, for I knew that if I did he'd see the answers written clear on my face and know full well that I had known no ladies at that time and that the business I had experienced in that department had been of no pleasure to me, no pleasure at all.

And then before any more could be said on that subject, a tidal wave came and hit us without warning out of what had appeared to be a calm sea and I blinked and gasped in surprise, spitting water through my lips, certain that I was about to be drowned, and when I reopened my eyes and looked to my left, who did I see standing there but the scut himself Mr Heywood, holding a large pail of water in his clammy hands, the contents of which he had just thrown in our direction, half drenching the three of us.

'That'll wash the decks down and quieten your tongues,' said he, walking away then, and what I wouldn't have given for the chance to chase him down and box his ears, but perhaps naval life was starting to have an effect on me, for I did nothing, just returned to my work with a sting in my temper, and felt satisfied that at least the conversation I had been having with Quintal and Sumner appeared to be forgotten then and I could keep my ignorance of the ladies and the truth of my past to myself for the time being.

9

THE STORES WERE REPLENISHED, the ship was repaired and we were
back at sea before I even knew it, but there was a right to-do
just as we were about to set sail that left the captain in a dark mood
for days afterwards. I was clearing away the plate and cup he'd used
for his lunch – which usually consisted of only a piece of fish and a
potato, as he never ate much in the middle of the day – when he
looked up from writing in his log, and at first he was full of life and
cheer, so pleased was he that we were setting sail again.

'Well, Master Turnstile,' said he to me, 'what did you make of
Santa Cruz, then?'

'I can't rightly say, sir,' I replied, quick as you like. 'On account
of only seeing it from a distance and never having set foot on dry
land throughout our stay. However, I must admit that it looked
pretty as a picture from the deck of the *Bounty*.'

The captain placed his quill down on the desk for a moment
and looked across at me with the hint of a smile across his lips,
and he narrowed his eyes as he stared, which caused my face to
take on the reddenings so bad that I looked away and started
to tidy things close to hand so that he wouldn't notice.

'Was that sauce?' he asked me after a moment. 'Were you
saucing me, Master Turnstile?'

'Not I, sir,' said I, shaking my head. 'Begging your pardon, sir, if
my words escaped me with a little more harshness than I had
intended. I only meant that I find myself in the position of being
unable to answer your original query on account of my having no
first-hand experience of the place itself. Mr Fryer and Mr Christian
and Mr Heywood, on the other hand—'

'Are all officers in His Majesty's navy,' he interrupted me, a cooler tone creeping into his voice now. 'And as such have certain rights and duties to perform during a stay in port. You'd do well to remember that if you aspire to higher office yourself. It's what you might call the benefit of hard work and promotion.'

His words took me aback a little, for I confess that I had never considered such a notion. If I was honest with myself, which was something I always tried to be, I was rather enjoying my time as the captain's servant – there were many and varied responsibilities associated with the position and, in truth, none were too onerous in comparison with the tasks of the ABs – and it gave me a certain standing among the crew, with whom I was beginning to mix with greater confidence and success. But aspirations towards a life as an officer? I wasn't sure if that was something that was in the destiny of John Jacob Turnstile. After all, it had only been a couple of days since I had been considering making my escape from the ship entirely and setting off for the life of a deserter in Spain – a fine existence, I felt. Filled with adventure and romance. The truth was that when it came to a face-off of loyalty between the king's expectations and my own selfish desires, I rather thought that old George didn't stand a virgin's chance in a whorehouse.

'Yes, sir,' said I, collecting some of his uniforms from where he had cast them aside and separating them into two piles: those I would need to launder, a thankless job, and those that could manage another tour of duty.

'It really was a very fine place,' he continued, returning to his log. 'Unspoiled is how I am describing it here. I rather think that Mrs Bligh would enjoy a sojourn there; perhaps I might return with her as a private man in later life.'

I nodded. The captain spoke of his wife from time to time and wrote to her frequently in the hope that we might pass a frigate returning to England who could take our messages with her. The small pile of letters that had sat in the drawer of his desk for weeks had vanished now, left in the safe hands of the Santa Cruz authorities, no doubt, and it looked to me as if he was about to begin a new collection immediately.

'Mrs Bligh is in London, sir?' I asked in a respectful tone, taking care not to step over the invisible line that existed between the two of us, but he nodded his head quickly and seemed pleased to talk of her.

'Aye, that she is,' he said. 'My own Betsey. A fine woman, Turnstile. It was a fortunate day in my life when she agreed to plight her troth to mine. She awaits my return along with our boy, William, and our daughters. A fine fellow, is he not?' He turned the portrait of the boy in my direction and it was true, he seemed a likely chap, and I told him so. 'A few years younger than you, of course,' he added, 'but I suspect you would make good friends if you were in his acquaintance.'

I said nothing to that on account of it being unlikely that a fellow from my society could ever be friends with a fellow from his, but the captain was behaving in such a pleasant fashion towards me that I thought it would be churlish of me to say as much. Instead I turned for one final look around the cabin to make sure that everything was in order, at which time I was surprised to notice by the small window a number of pots, which had been taken from the great cabin next door and were sitting there now on full view, filled to the brim with earth and with small seedlings starting to peep through the soil.

'I see you are observing my garden,' said the captain cheerfully, standing up from behind his desk and stepping across the cabin to look down at them. 'Quite a sight they make, do they not?'

'Are these plants the focus of our mission, sir?' asked I in my ignorance, and the words were barely out of my mouth when I realized how stupid they sounded, for there were many hundreds of pots empty next door still, and if this was all that was needed what a waste of time and energy the whole voyage would have been.

'No, no,' said he. 'Don't be ridiculous, Turnstile. These are a few mere trifles I discovered in the hills yesterday when Mr Nelson and I went a-botanizing.'

Mr Nelson was a figure who came and went from the captain's cabin with regularity but who, at first, had appeared to me to have no official responsibilities. I had recently learned from Mr Fryer, however, that he was the ship's gardener and that his duties would commence properly when we had achieved the first part of our mission, of which I was still in virtual ignorance.

'I thought to plant a few seeds,' said the captain, fingering the damp soil in the pots carefully, 'just to see whether they might flourish on board. In this first pot I've placed a bellflower, an exotic creature which produces edible berries when ripe. Are you familiar with it?'

'No, sir,' said I, for I knew as much about plant life as I did about the mating habits of dormice.

'It has a beautiful flower,' said he then, turning it ever so slightly towards the porthole. 'Yellow as the sun. You never saw such luminescence. In this second is an orobal. Have you made any study of exotic flora at all, Turnstile?'

'No, sir,' said I again, looking at the tiny seedling planted there and wondering what might shoot from it.

'You might know the orobal as ginseng,' he replied, and I shook my head again and he looked puzzled. 'Honestly,' he said then with a shake of his head, sounding for all the world as if this was a matter of enormous surprise to him. 'What do they teach you in the schools these days? The education system is in the doldrums, sir. I tell you, the very doldrums!'

I opened my mouth to inform him that I had never seen the inside of a classroom, but held my counsel for fear that it may be considered sauce again.

'The orobal is a wonderful plant to cultivate,' he told me then. 'It is a diuretic, you see, which is of course of great use on a voyage like ours.'

'A what?' I asked, unfamiliar with the word.

'A diuretic,' he repeated. 'Really, Turnstile, must I explain everything? It has pain-relieving properties and can induce sleep in a poorly man. I think it might prosper too, if attended to correctly.'

'Shall I be watering these plants for you, then, sir?' asked I.

'Oh, no,' said he, shaking his head quickly. 'No, you may leave them as they are. It's not that I don't trust you, you understand; on the contrary, you are proving a very fine servant' – there was that word again, one I did not enjoy – 'but I think I would rather enjoy tending to them myself and nurturing them to growth. It gives me a hobby, you see. Don't you have hobbies, Turnstile? Back home with your family in Portsmouth, didn't you have entertainments of your own? Frivolities that passed your time?'

I stared at him, surprised by his own *naïveté*, and shook my head. This was the first time that the captain had asked me about my life back in England, or my family, and I realized immediately that he was under the false impression that I was in possession of one. Of course, he had not conversed with his friend Mr Zéla before my appearance on board the *Bounty* – I had merely been sent on board at the last moment to step into the shoes of the slippery donkey who had cracked his legs – and if he had, perhaps he would have known a little more about my situation. As it was, he assumed that all lads had a similar upbringing to his own, and in this he was sadly mistaken. The rich always consider lads like me to be ignorant, but they display just as much ignorance at times, albeit of a very different type.

The notion of family was a strange one to me. I had known no such joy myself. I could recall neither father nor mother; my earliest memories were of a washerwoman in Westingham Street who let me sleep on her floor and eat from her table if I brought home fruit from the stalls for her supper, but she sold me to Mr Lewis when I was nine years old and told me as I was dragged away from her that I would be happy and well looked after at his establishment. There was no family back home for me. There was love, of course, of a sort. But no family.

'Now, this might interest you, Turnstile,' the captain was saying to me, and I blinked back into the here-and-now; he was touching the leaves of a small plant in the third pot with care. 'The artemisia. When it prospers, it is a great help to the digestive system of any man who finds himself in difficulties, as I recall you were when we first set sail. It could be of great use if—'

The lesson was interrupted at that moment by a sharp rap on the cabin door and we turned round to see Mr Christian standing there. He gave a brief nod to the captain and ignored me altogether, as was his wont. I think he considered me to be of slightly less interest than the wood panelling on the walls or the panes of glass in the windows. 'The ship is setting sail, sir,' he said. 'You wanted to be informed.'

'Excellent news,' said the captain. 'Excellent news! And what a worthwhile stay it was, Fletcher. I hope you thanked the governor for all his kindnesses?'

'Of course, sir.'

'Very good. Then, you may sound the gun salute at your convenience.' The captain turned back to his plants, but, realizing that Mr Christian had not stepped away, he turned round again. 'Yes, Fletcher?' he asked. 'Was there something else?'

Mr Christian's face bore the look of a man who had a secret to impart and little wanted to be the messenger of it. 'The gun salute,' he said finally. 'Perhaps we should keep our powder dry for now?'

'Nonsense, Fletcher!' said the captain with a laugh. 'Our hosts have been of great assistance to us. We cannot part without a gesture of respect; how would such a thing look? You've seen it done before, of course. A mutual salute, ours to offer thanks, theirs to send us on our way with Godspeed.'

There was a noticeable hesitancy on Mr Christian's part, one that I'm sure both the captain and I were aware of, and it hovered in the air like a bad smell from a pestilent duck until the master's mate opened a window to clear it. 'I'm afraid there won't be a return of salute, sir,' he said finally, looking away.

'No return?' asked the captain, frowning and stepping towards him. 'I don't understand. You and Mr Fryer gave the governor our parting gifts?'

'Yes, sir, we did,' he replied. 'And of course Mr Fryer, as ship's master, discussed the matter of the salute with the governor, that being his place as the officer of rank. Shall I fetch him and have him explain?'

'Damn and blast it, Fletcher, I care not whose place it is,' snapped the captain, whose voice was growing more and more testy as the minutes passed; he did not like to be kept in the dark about matters that were taking place around him, particularly when he perceived a slight. 'I simply ask you why the salute shall not be returned when I have just given orders that—'

'It *was* to be returned,' said Mr Christian, interrupting him. 'Six shots apiece, as is standard. Unfortunately Mr Fryer was forced to reveal the fact that . . . due to the circumstances of our ship and your own ranking . . .'

'*My* own ranking?' Bligh asked slowly, as if he was trying to rush forward in the conversation himself to discover where it might be leading. 'I don't . . . ?'

'As lieutenant, I mean,' explained Mr Christian. 'Rather than captain. The fact of the ship's size not meriting a—'

'Yes, yes,' said Mr Bligh, turning away now so that neither of us could observe his phizzy, his voice growing gloomier by the minute. 'I understand fully.' He coughed several times and closed his eyes for a moment as he held a hand across his mouth. When he spoke again, his tone was low and depressive. 'Of course, Fletcher. The governor will not return a salute to one of lesser rank than he.'

'I'm afraid that's rather the long and the short of it,' said Mr Christian quietly.

'Well, Mr Fryer spoke correctly in informing the governor,' said the captain, although he did not sound as though he believed a word of it. 'It would have been highly inappropriate and if he had discovered the truth subsequently, then it might have damaged his relations with the crown.'

'For what it's worth, sir—' began Mr Christian, but the captain held a hand up to silence him.

'Thank you, Mr Christian,' he said. 'You may go on deck now. Mr Fryer is up there, I presume?'

'Yes, sir.'

'Then, he may stay there, damn his boots, for the time being. Set the pace, Mr Christian. See that the men are keen.'

'Aye, sir,' he replied, turning then and leaving the cabin.

I stood there awkwardly, shuffling from foot to foot. I could see that the captain felt humiliated by what had transpired but was trying not to show any such emotion on his face. The issue of his own status was one that clearly rankled him, particularly as the fact of it was common currency among the men. I tried to think of what to say to make matters better but could think of nothing at all until I happened to look to my left again and saw salvation there.

'And this pot, Captain,' said I, pointing to the fourth and final pot on the mantel. 'What does this contain?'

He turned his head slowly and stared at me, as if he had for-gotten my presence entirely, before looking towards the pot that I had indicated and shaking his head. 'Thank you, Turnstile,' he said in a deep and troubled voice. 'You may leave now.'

I opened my mouth to say more but thought better of it. As I left, and closed the cabin door behind me, I could feel the ship setting off quite smoothly into the sea again and caught a final vision of the captain sitting down behind his desk and not retriev-ing his quill, but, rather, reaching across for the portrait of his wife, and running his finger gently along her face. I shut the door firmly and resolved to go on deck and keep my eyes focused on the land as it disappeared behind us, for the devil only knew when I might catch sight of it again.

10

SOON AFTER THAT, THE DANCING BEGAN.
For weeks we sailed on, steering the *Bounty* ever closer to the Equator, making keen progress through twenty-five degrees, twenty degrees, fifteen degrees latitude. I followed our progress daily on the charts that Captain Bligh kept in his cabin, many of which (he told me) he had drawn himself from his previous voyages with Captain Cook. I begged him to tell me more about their travels together, but he always found a reason to put the tales off and I was left to imagine the adventures they had undertaken and dramatize their heroism in my imagination. In the meantime, the storms grew and subsided, the winds blustered and waned, and the mood on the ship seemed to be inextricably linked to the weather, with days of great humour interspersed with others in which the atmosphere was fraught with tension. At this time, the feeling between the captain and the officers, and the captain and the men, was generally positive and I saw no reason why it should not continue to be so. Of course, it was clear that Mr Fryer would never be a favourite of the captain's in the way that Mr Christian was, but neither man seemed troubled by this fact and as far as I could see the ship's master went about his duties without rancour or complaint.

I began to spend more time on deck during those weeks and would often pass the evening sitting on my haunches with three or four of the midshipmen as they smoked their pipes and drank their rations of ale, telling one another stories of the wives and sweethearts they had left behind. On most evenings, one man would find himself the butt of the others' jokes and from time to time a fight would break out if one fellow accused another's wife of playing the strumpet while he was at sea. On one occasion I stood by while John Millward beat three shades of shite out of Richard Skinner on a trifling complaint and I looked to Mr Christian and Mr Elphinstone, the officers on deck, to step in and spare us the bloodshed that followed, but to my surprise they turned their backs on the fighting and walked away. Later that same evening, Mr Christian surprised me in my sleep when he was going to his cabin, the toe of his boot kicking upwards into my bunk, unsettling me and spilling me over on to the floor below, which collided in a painful fashion with my head.

'Damn and blast it!' I roared in surprise, disturbed as I was in the middle of a happy dream wherein I found myself a man of wealth and property, much beloved by the impoverished but happy servants who worked my farms and gave me comfort on the long, dark evenings. 'What the—?' I didn't have to finish my question, however, for looking up from my horizontal position, there was the master's mate standing above me, looking down and shaking his head contemptuously.

'Still your tongue, Turnip, you young brat,' he said, reaching down and offering me his hand. 'I meant merely to waken you, not upset you out of the bunk altogether. Are you of a nervous nature? I never saw a fellow jump so.'

'No, Mr Christian,' said I, attempting to regain my dignity as I found my feet again. 'I am not a victim to my nerves. However, I am not accustomed to being kicked in the arse in the middle of the night either.'

The words were out of my mouth before I could think on their wisdom and my regret began to surface almost immediately as I saw the smile fade away from his face and his eyes narrow. I looked down at my feet and wondered whether he would continue the act and kick me all the way overboard. The only thing that might prevent him from doing so, I decided, was the fact that it could give him the perspirations and that in turn would un-settle his features and unpart his hair, a thing beyond all others that Mr Christian would detest.

'In the first place, it is not the middle of the night, Turnstile, it is late evening,' he said finally, visibly trying to control his temper. 'And when the captain is about, so should his servant lad be, and the captain is currently on deck. And in the second place, shall I take it that you have momentarily forgotten yourself in the shock of the awakening and knew not who it was you were addressing?'

I nodded my head, chastened; when I looked up there was a trace of a smile back on his face and I felt relieved that I was not to be locked in irons for the remainder of our voyage.

'Very well,' said he. 'I think you were upset by the disagreement earlier, were you not?'

'The disagreement?' said I, considering it. 'If you mean the fight between Millward and Skinner, aye, I was, for Skinner'll not walk straight for a week after that.'

'And I expect you wonder why neither I nor Mr Elphinstone stepped in to separate the two men?'

I said nothing to this; of course that was what I was thinking, and he knew it too, but it was not my place to suggest such a thing. So I played the sensible game and kept my lip buttoned.

'You haven't been at sea before, have you, Turnip?' he asked and I shook my head. 'You learn certain things when you spend some time on the oceans. And one of them is to allow the men to exercise themselves when they need to. They wouldn't thank an officer for stepping into a moment like that. If anything, they would resent it. Even Skinner, the poor fool, would be unhappy about it, despite the beating he took. It's the nature of men. There are no women about for them to exert themselves on, so they must find release with one another. I suspect *you* understand a little of that, yes?'

I looked up at him and my face took on the reddenings as never before. How could I help but wonder what he might have meant by that? I had spoken to no one on board about my life before the *Bounty*; could Mr Christian read things in my face that I thought were hidden? He continued to look at me as if he could see right through to my very soul and – I knew not why – I felt a sting of tears prickling away behind my eyes.

'Anyway,' he said finally. 'Enough of this chatter. Up on deck with you, Turnip. The captain wishes to address the crew.'

I went through the great cabin, followed by Mr Christian, aware at all times of his eyes boring into my back and for the first time since we had left Spithead I began to feel how small the ship truly was. Of course, I was accustomed to confined spaces; Mr Lewis's establishment contained barely enough room to swing a cat. But now, walking towards the deck followed by the master's mate, I wished for nothing more than to be left alone, to answer to no one, to have a room I could call my own where no one might lay eyes on me. I wished in vain. Such delights were not the lot of lads like me.

On deck, the captain seemed to be in one of his moods. He was pacing back and forth as the men gathered, shouting at them to get into line and sharpish. The light was starting to fade and the waters were reasonably calm as he addressed us.

'Men,' said he, 'we've been at sea for a month now and, as you know, there's still a long way to go before our mission is even half begun. You've all been at sea before—'

'Except young Turnstile,' said Mr Christian, pushing me forward into the middle of the deck as he used my proper name at last, and the captain turned to look at me.

'*Almost* all of you have been at sea before,' said he, correcting himself. 'And, as you are only too aware, men's spirits can get low and the body can begin to disintegrate if it is not exercised regularly. I've noticed that several of you have a lethargic look to you and a pale complexion and I have decided on two courses of action to improve our conditions from now on.'

There was a general murmur of approval from the men, who

looked at one another and muttered suggestions about increased rations and more ale, but they were quickly silenced by Mr Elphinstone, who shouted at them to be silent and to pay attention to their captain.

'All goes well here so far,' continued the captain, and I fancied that he was a little nervous in his words as he addressed us forty men and lads. 'We haven't lost any men to ill health, thank the Saviour, and I dare say we may have set a new record in His Majesty's navy for the greatest number of days without a single disciplinary action taking place.'

'Hurrah!' cried the men in unison and Captain Bligh looked rightly pleased when they did so.

'To reward your fine service and to keep each man as healthy as he can possibly be, I propose to change the schedule of the ship's watches from tomorrow. Instead of two shifts of twelve hours apiece, there will be three shifts of eight hours each, thus ensuring that every man has the benefit of eight hours in his own berth to rest his eyes and catch up on his sleep. I think you'll agree that this will lead to a stronger and more alert crew for the difficult waters ahead.'

Again, there was more mutterings of approval from the men and I could see that the captain's mood was improving as he was delighted with their response, breaking into a broad smile when they gave him a hearty cheer. Just at that moment, however, Mr Fryer stepped forward a foot or two to shatter his good humour. I couldn't help but wonder why he always took it upon himself to act as he did.

'Captain,' said he, 'do you think that's wise considering the—'

'Dammit, man!' roared the captain immediately, in such a voice that made every man turn immediately silent, and I confess that even I jumped in fright at the sound of it and might have leapt overboard had the notion taken me. 'Can't you understand an order when you hear it, Mr Fryer? I'm captain of the *Bounty* and if I say there are to be three watches of eight hours apiece, then there are to be three watches of eight hours apiece – not two, not four, but three – and I'll not stand to hear questions on it. Do you understand me, Mr Fryer?'

I looked – we all looked – in Mr Fryer's direction and if the captain's face had gone suddenly scarlet with fury, then Mr Fryer's had immediately become pale in bewilderment. The captain's anger had appeared out of nowhere and the master stood there now with his mouth wide open as if in preparation for the sentence he had planned on finishing. No words came from him now, however, and after a few moments he closed his mouth again and stepped back in place silently, staring down at the deck. The look on his face would have curdled milk. I glanced in Mr Christian's direction and was sure that I could see a hint of a smile there.

'Does anyone else have a comment to make?' shouted the captain now and he stared about him with darting eyes. I don't mind admitting that I was surprised by how quickly the atmosphere on deck had changed from good humour to tension, and was unsure whether I should blame Mr Fryer or the captain for it. It seemed to me that Mr Fryer could do no good whatsoever in the captain's eyes and I knew not why.

'Right, that's the first matter,' said the captain then, wiping his brow with his 'kerchief. 'The second concerns the matter of exercise. Every man on board – *every* man – shall devote an hour a day to exercise in the form of dancing.'

The mutters started again and we all looked at one another, sure that we had misheard him.

'I beg your pardon, sir,' said Mr Christian cautiously, choosing his words carefully so as not to suffer the same fate as Mr Fryer, 'but did you say *dancing*?'

'Yes, Mr Christian, you heard me right, I said dancing,' replied the captain forcefully. 'When serving on board the *Endeavour*, I myself was a regular dancer, as were the men, under the orders of Captain Cook, who recognized the health benefits of the constant movement undertaken when one is dancing. That is why Mr Byrn is aboard. To provide us with music. Step forward, if you please, Mr Byrn.'

From the very back of the ranks of men appeared the elderly figure of Byrn – with whom I had exchanged only one conversation during our voyage and that was of the relative merits of the apple over the strawberry – carrying his fiddle.

'There he is,' said the captain. 'Mr Byrn will entertain us with an hour's music every day between four and five of the clock and I will expect to see every man taking to the deck to dance. Is that understood?' The men nodded and said 'aye' and I could see they were tickled by the idea. 'Good,' said the captain. 'Mr Hall,' he said then, nodding at the ship's cook, 'step forward.' Mr Hall, who had been kind to me when I first set foot on board, hesitated only a moment before obeying. The captain looked around and his eyes locked on mine. 'Master Turnstile,' added he. 'As we have identified you as the only person on board who has never sailed before . . .'

My heart plunged so deep and so quick in my chest that I thought it might bounce back up inside me and pop directly out of my mouth. I closed my eyes for a moment and imagined the humiliation that I was about to suffer. I would be forced to dance with Mr Hall in front of the men. I would have no choice. In the darkness of my closed eyes, a picture of Mr Lewis appeared in my head, smiling, mocking me, as the door opened and the gentlemen stepped into the room, smiling at my brothers and me while they took their seats for Evening Selection.

'You may have the honour of choosing a partner for Mr Hall,' said the captain.

I opened my eyes again and blinked. Had I heard him correctly? I hardly dared to believe it. 'I beg your pardon, sir?' said I.

'Come on, lad,' said the captain impatiently. 'Choose a partner for Mr Hall to begin the dancing and then Mr Byrn can start the music.'

I looked around at the men and every one of them looked

away. Not a single one of them wanted to catch my eye for fear that I might select him and he would be subject to the same humiliation I had just envisioned for myself.

'Anyone, sir?' said I, looking around at the men again, imagining the punishment each might inflict on me at a later date should I choose him.

'Anyone, Turnstile, anyone,' he roared cheerfully. 'There's not a man on board who couldn't do with the exercise. You're a flabby lot at the best of times.'

At that moment the ship tilted slightly to starboard and I felt the spit of water on my face and was taken back a week, to when a bucket of water had been unceremoniously thrown over my innocent person, and immediately my selection was decided upon.

'I choose Mr Heywood, sir,' said I, and despite the noise of the winds and waves it wasn't hard to recognize the sound of indrawn breaths from around the deck.

'What's that you say?' asked the captain, turning to look at me in some surprise.

'He said Mr Heywood,' called out one of the men.

The captain threw that man a look before staring back at me and narrowing his eyes, considering it. I had chosen an officer; he had not expected that of me. He had assumed that I would select a midshipman or an AB. But then he had invited me to choose anyone in front of all the crew and he could hardly take that bidding back now and retain his dignity.

I looked around and there, standing at the very edges of the men, his face like thunder, the pustules on his face seething with righteous anger, was the scut himself, glaring at me with such venom in his eyes that I wondered whether I had just made the worst mistake of my life.

'Mr Heywood it is, then,' said the captain finally and looked towards the officer.

'Captain, I object . . .' began the young officer quickly, but Mr Bligh was having none of it.

'Come along, Mr Heywood, no objections, I pray of you. Every man must take exercise and a young chap like yourself should revel in it. Step forward this instant. Mr Byrn, do you know "Nancy o' the Gales"?'

'I do, sir,' said Mr Byrn, grinning wildly. 'And I knew her mother too.'

'Then, strike her up,' said the captain, ignoring the remark. 'Come on, Mr Heywood, sir, no dawdling!' he roared, his voice attempting to sound humorous while teetering on the edge of the same anger he had displayed towards Mr Fryer not five minutes before.

As the fiddle began to strike up, the captain clapped his hands together loudly in time with the music and in no time the men were clapping along with him, while Mr Heywood and Mr Hall stood facing each other hesitantly. Then, with great courtesy, Mr Hall took a step back and delivered himself of a deep bow, taking his cap off and offering it low, thus establishing himself as the gentleman in the equation and winning a huge round of applause and laughter from his fellows for his efforts.

'Mr Heywood's the strumpet!' cried one, and the officer turned in fury, ready to lash out, but the captain was quick to intervene.

'Dance, Mr Heywood,' he shouted. 'Smile and you might just enjoy yourself too.'

Mr Hall was dancing as if his life depended on it, his hands in the air, his feet bouncing up and down in an Irish jig as he grinned madly, reasoning that if he was to look a fool in front of the men the best he could do of it was to win them on side and save himself from their mocking afterwards. Mr Heywood, on the other hand, danced hesitantly, looking more and more embarrassed by the moment, and it was only when the captain ordered every other man to begin dancing alongside them that he was surrounded by the crowd and lost to me, although I had hardly dared to catch his eye since selecting him.

'Do you think that was wise?' asked Mr Christian, stepping up behind me and speaking directly into my ear, making me jump a little with the nerves, but when I turned to face him with a reply he had disappeared too and the captain was taking my arm and throwing me into the mêlée, urging me to join in the dancing.

Hands slapped my back in appreciation, for I had made a selection that delighted them all and managed to make a farce of an officer – one they particularly disliked – into the bargain, but I couldn't help but wonder whether the choice I had made had been the most foolish of all my choices since deciding to pick the pocket of the French gentleman two days before Christmas.

I had paid for that with my liberty; I suspected Mr Heywood would hope to exact a harsher payment yet.

11

IT WAS NOT LONG before he took his revenge on me, and when that moment came I felt sure that I was going to pay for my insolence with my life. In recalling the events of that dreadful morning, I still find myself trembling with rage and feeling such despairing fear for my existence that I wish I were in that creature's company once again in order to make him feel the same level of terror and panic that I suffered. I confess that in starting this part of my story I have had to walk three times round my parlour and take a glass or two of spirits, such is the pain of recollection.

Two weeks had passed since I had been chosen by Captain Bligh to select Mr Hall's dancing partner and my standing on board had risen considerably in the meantime. When I was on deck, the men would occasionally call me 'Master Turnstile' rather than 'Turnip'; they would speak to me with a newly discovered sense of equality between us all and I began to feel that I could converse with the ABs more confidently than I had when I had first set foot on the *Bounty* a few months before. Even the toughest of the sailors failed to give me the intimidations as much as they once had and while I took my share of ribbing during the evening dancing sessions – for they did point out that I was as pretty as some of the mollies they had known in their time – I made sure to give back as good as I got. In short, I felt as if I was becoming one of the men.

Anyone who knew me when I was a lad would have cheerfully offered evidence to the fact that I was terrible fond of my sleep. Even the relative discomfort of a low-slung bunk outside the captain's cabin could never have kept me from my slumbers for long, but I had discovered that since setting sail my dreams had become far more vivid than they had ever been when I was sharing a bed with my brothers at Mr Lewis's establishment. Whether it was the rocking of the ship or the effects of the despicable mess that Mr Hall had the good humour to call dinner, I knew not, but my reveries were filled with mysterious creatures and strange lands, populated by beautiful maidens who beckoned me to their chambers and escapades of such a nature that they gave me the motions on an almost nightly basis. Such dreams had ceased to scare me as they once did and I had grown so accustomed to them that it did not come as an immediate shock to open my eyes in the dim light of this particular early morning to see a colourful beast standing over me, its teeth bared, its eyes wild, a finger pointing directly at my heart, hissing a word over and over in a venomous manner. 'Pollywog,' the creature was saying, the syllables whispered aggressively beneath its deep voice and repeated again and again. 'Pollywog, pollywog, slimy pollywog.'

I stared back at this vision for a few seconds, blinking my eyes furiously, and wondered why I was not awakening from this curious dream – for a dream it surely was – and returning to the relative banality of my shipboard home. After a moment, the

127

picture failing to dissolve before me, I put a hand to my face and retreated a little in my bunk as my consciousness returned, pulling away from the hideous creature as I realized with growing horror that this was in fact no trance, no concoction of rum and cheese taken too soon before sleep, but real life. My own waking life. The creature that stood before me was flesh and blood, but both masked and painted. I gasped in surprise and, as I did so, I considered whether it would be sensible to jump from the bunk and run as fast as possible through the great cabin and out on to the deck, where the men would surely come to my defence, such was my new heroic status. However, before I could do so, a handful of similarly attired figures emerged from behind the creature and each one was offering that awful hissing sound as an echo of its master's voice. 'Pollywog,' they shrilled repeatedly. 'Pollywog, pollywog, slimy pollywog.'

'What is this?' I cried, lost somewhere between fear and disbelief, for now that my eyes were fully opened I could see that the creature and his five slaves were no mythical beasts summoned from the depths to torment me, but the midshipmen, dressed in outlandish garb that they had found I-knew-not-where, their faces painted, their attitudes those of stage-players in a farce. 'What do you want with me?' I asked, but before another word could be said, two of the slaves – who I recognized beneath their paint to be midshipman Isaac Martin and the carpenter's mate Thomas McIntosh – rushed towards me and hoisted me aloft between them; each had one hand under my shoulder and another beneath the joint of my knee, and they raised me in the air to a cheer from the others before their leader, the cooper Henry Hilbrant, led the procession through the great cabin and towards the stairs that led to the deck.

'Put me down,' I roared, torn between defiance and despair, but my voice was lost within myself, so astonished was I by this sudden and unexpected turn of events. I knew now what possible purpose it could serve. The men who held me were among those

I had formed pleasant alliances with over the previous weeks; they had shown no sign of wanting to assault me before now. I could think of no insult that I had offered their way; their reasons for collecting me from my sleep, not to mention the nature of their curious vestments, made no sense to me at all. A part of me was afraid, but I confess that I also felt a modicum of bemusement, wondering where I was being taken and for what purpose.

Daylight was breaking when we emerged on to the deck and the men who were gathered there were each bathed in the pale yellow, cloudy light that surrounded us, while a light rain drizzled down about our heads. To my surprise the full complement of the *Bounty*'s crew seemed to be waiting for me on deck, with the exception of the captain and the majority of the officers – Mr Fryer, Mr Christian and Mr Elphinstone were all absent – but I could see my nemesis, Mr Heywood, standing away from the men, watching events from a distance and smiling, as if he could barely wait to enjoy the delights of what was to come, which was understanding enough that I was not to receive my congratulations for that earlier sequence of events. I only glanced at him for a moment, though, for the sight that confronted me in the opposite direction was enough to hold my gaze still and take my very breath away.

I had noticed in the past that whenever Captain Bligh assembled the men on deck to address them, they shuffled forward and jostled with one another for position, stepping from foot to foot throughout his speech and holding no proper lines or order, a fact that did not seem to trouble our commander. This morning, however, disorder or unruliness was not on display. The men were stood in single rows of about a five-man depth with half a dozen lines across. As those men who had carried me set me back on my feet they gripped me strongly by the shoulders to prevent me from running away and I confess that the tightness of their fists about my person began to worry my young heart and I wished that I could escape from whatever hideous event was about to take place.

But what was the most fearsome aspect of this? Was it the fact that they had taken me without warning from my sleep, or the strange clothes they wore, or the fact of their presence on deck when some should have been snoozing in their berths and others should have been tending the watch? No, it was none of these things. It was the silence. No man spoke and the only sound I could hear was the splash of the waves on the sides of the boat as we made our slow progress through the water.

'What's this, then?' I shouted, trying to sound hearty, as if none of it mattered a jot to me and it had been my own choice to appear on deck at that particular time on that particular morning in that particular fashion. 'What goes on here?'

Instantly the lines parted down the centre and revealed a chair which had been elaborately painted a bright yellow and placed at the fore of the deck. John Williams, another of the midshipmen, and one who was regularly to be found in conversation with Mr Christian and his toady, Mr Heywood, was seated on the chair, his face painted red and a garland placed above his forehead. He raised a finger and pointed at me.

'This is the pollywog?' he cried in a deep, booming voice, which he was affecting for the sham. 'This the slimy pollywog?'

'This is he, Your Majesty,' replied the two sailors who were holding me. 'John Jacob Turnstile.'

Your Majesty? thought I, wondering what game this was, for if John Williams was royalty then I was a scaly lizard.

'Bring him to me,' said Williams.

I would have been happy to have stayed where I was, my feet rooted to the deck, but my two guards pushed me forward between them and, as they did so, the men circled around me until I was standing before this ridiculous fellow while the sailors watched on, their eyes aflame with a mixture of violence, lust and the demon himself.

'John Jacob Turnstile,' said he then. 'You know why you are brought before King Neptune's court?'

I stared at him and knew not whether I should laugh in his face or fall to my knees and beg for mercy. 'King Neptune?' I asked. 'Who's he when he's at home, then?' I tried to keep the nerves out of my voice but even I could hear them and cursed myself for my cowardice.

'Before you is King Neptune,' said one of the sailors around me and I frowned and shook my head. 'Tremble in his presence, slimy pollywog, tremble!'

'He never is,' said I. 'He's John Williams, him as looks after the mizzen-sail.'

'Silence!' cried Williams. 'Answer the question which is put of you. Do you know why you are brought here before this court?'

'No,' said I, shaking my head. 'If it's a game, no one's told me the rules, so—'

'You stand accused of being a pollywog,' said Williams. 'A slimy pollywog. How say you?'

I thought about it and looked around, wishing that I could return downstairs to the comfort and safety of my bunk, but the looks on the men's faces were enough to make me think that any attempt on my part to run would only end in tears. 'I don't know what that is,' I confessed finally. 'So I don't think I can be one.'

Williams stretched his arms out and surveyed the men. 'This morning we finally pass that magnificent central line that divides the globe in two,' he announced in a booming, theatrical voice, 'north from south, hemisphere from hemisphere, that mark we call the Great Equator, and, having done so, King Neptune demands his sacrifice. One pollywog. A person on board who has never passed through the equatorial contour before.'

I opened my mouth, but words came there none. I started to recall stories I had heard about the rituals of what happened when ships crossed the Equator, the things that were done to virgin sailors who had never sailed across that line before, but I could not recall the exact details. I knew, however, that it was not good.

'Please,' said I. 'I have to attend to the captain's breakfast soon. Can't I return to my—'

'Silence, pollywog!' shouted King Neptune and I jumped in surprise. 'Servants,' he said then, looking to the men to my left and right, 'display the pollywog.'

They let go of me then for a moment, but as they did so one stood behind me and held me while the shirt was ripped from my body. A great cheer went up from the sailors and I shouted at them to let me be, but more hands were about me then, about my britches, and kick and thrust as I might, they were pulled from me, and then my undercrackers were quickly dispatched and within a few dark moments I found myself standing in the centre of the deck, naked as the day I was born, with naught but my hands to protect my modesty. I looked up as the sun came out from behind a cloud and it dazzled my eyes for a moment and the effect of it, coupled with my fear of standing there with my privacy on display, not to mention apprehension for what might happen next, made my head dizzy and my limbs weak and I felt my mind returning to moments of the past that I had tried to forget. Moments when my humiliation was equally brutal.

. . . he's a fine lad Mr Lewis a fine lad indeed and where are you from my pretty fellow is it Portsmouth perhaps you know a particular friend of mine there a boy no older than you I would warrant name of George Masters do you know George you don't how extraordinary I was under the impression that fellows such as yourself pretty fellows I mean make a company of each other do you not . . .

'We have received reports of your crimes, primary of which is the news that you have impersonated an Irishman,' continued the king, and I shook my head to concentrate on his words while staring at him in amazement.

'I never have,' I said, appalled by the suggestion. 'I wouldn't

132

even know how. The only Irishman I ever knew was Skibbereen born and bred, hanged for a thief from Execution Dock.'

'How do you find the pollywog, men?' shouted the king and a great cry of 'Guilty!' went up all around me and he smiled at me with a brutal sneer. 'The punishment for impersonating an Irishman is to eat of an Irish apple,' he said then.

I nodded slowly. If this humiliation was to stand naked before the ship's complement and eat a piece of fruit for them . . . well, I thought I had suffered worse indignities in my life, aye, and would again, no doubt. I saw Mr Heywood step forward then with something in his hand and I wondered whether he might have spat on the apple first, or worse. There was little I would have put past that donkey. He might have rubbed it against his un-mentionables, for all the dignity he had, the scut. When he handed it to me, though, I stared at in wonder, for it was no apple at all, Irish or otherwise.

'But that's an onion,' I said, looking up.

'Eat, pollywog!' cried the king, and I shook my head, for there was no way on the Saviour's green earth or the devil's blue water that I was going to do such a thing, and at that moment one of the men's boots kicked me hard in the rump, sending me sprawling on the deck with a bruise to my arse that I knew I would feel for a week yet. 'Eat it!' he screamed.

Seeing no alternative to the proposition, I put the foul thing to my mouth and tried to bite through its layers.

'You must swallow it all,' said Neptune.

'But I'll be sick,' I pleaded, and would have said more, only Mr Heywood advanced on me again with such a murderous intent on his face that I took the onion back before forcing it into my mouth; I had no choice but to try to open my jaw wider and wider and bite on the article to free room for breathing, but the essence of the bulb fair took my breath away and left me gasping for air with tears rolling down my cheeks. 'Please,' said I again then, turning to my side now, the better to stop them staring at me in my

133

nakedness, although my whistle was shrinking in fright at the assault that might be planned on it. 'I don't know what you want me to do but—'

'Pollywog, you further stand accused of a plot to set fire to Westminster Cathedral,' roared Neptune and this time I could just shake my head at the lunacy of the idea and protest my innocence. 'How do you find the pollywog, men?' he asked again and there came another loud cry of 'Guilty!' followed by a wild stamping of feet. 'Then he must kiss the gunner's daughter,' announced King Neptune.

Another cheer was heard now as I was dragged bodily along the deck to one of the cannons and stretched across it, one man holding me from the front, another by the ankles. A pain shot through my body when I crashed against the cold metal too fast at the front and my knees buckled beneath me. I thought I knew what was to come next and struggled and cried, but, no, I had it wrong, for one of the midshipmen appeared instead with a bucket of paint and a brush and to my humiliation my rump was painted red all over and then I was turned around and my whistle was painted too, and then, without warning, I was wrenched off the cannon and brought back to where I had started and the king raised his hands and shouted 'Proceed!'

The men advanced on me as one and I noticed how many of them held boards now and items to thrash me with and they slapped out, aiming for my rump and whistle, but beating me soundly about all of my person without conscience or inhibition. I held my hands out to fight them off, but what could I do, there were so many of them and only one of me, and my body started to feel as if it was suffering one long constant pain rather than a series of blows as they thumped and thrashed and broke my skin and I thought I might lose consciousness in the uproar.

. . . there are certain things that I like to do and Mr Lewis informs me that there are none so keen as you to be of assistance is this

true I hope it is for there will be a sixpence in it for you if you give me pleasure you are a good boy for giving pleasure are you not perhaps you can suggest ways to me that you might give me pleasure can you think of any . . .

I know not how long the thrashing went on for, but eventually, without warning, the men parted and there was no need for anyone to keep me held aloft to prevent my running away, for I collapsed on to the deck immediately, one of my eyes half-shut and swollen, pain searing through my every fibre. I fell to my back and cared nothing for hiding myself, for my shame was as nothing compared with the suffering my body was enduring. Through my one good eye I looked up and the sun continued to dazzle me, but a figure stepped into the light for a moment and who was it only Mr Heywood again, come to finish the job.

'Sir,' I cried, spitting blood from my mouth, my teeth feeling as if they were not mine at all, a foul taste stenching my tongue. 'Help me, sir,' I attempted to say, but I could barely hear the words, so inaudibly did they emerge from my weakened voice.

'A further punishment, pollywog,' he said quietly, and I watched as he undid his trousers, took his own whistle out and proceeded to empty his bladder upon me. The steam of his piss burned into my skin but I could scarcely escape it, so broken was my body by now. He must have been saving it up, for it felt as if the humiliation continued for an eternity; when he finally finished and dressed himself he walked away and informed the men that I needed to be washed clean after that and another cheer immediately went up.

This time I was plucked from the deck by a fresh pair of hands and brought to the side of the ship, where many hands touched me and I knew not what they were doing, and only a few moments later when there was the great sound of a heavy rope being pulled and tied did I realize that around my waist the tether had been struck. Although I could barely stand erect I pressed my hands to it, attempting desperately to untie it from my body, but the rope was too heavy and too tight. *I am to be hanged*, I thought, my mind filling with horror and fear. I had seen two men hanged in my life, both murderers, one of whom was no older than me, and he had pissed himself on the gallows as the rope was tied round his neck, and I saw my own fate as his as my bladder loosened inside me and threatened to spill over in fright.

'Help me,' I cried. 'Help me someone. Please. Whatever you want, I'll do it.'

. . . anything I want is it I have some ideas of course and you shall not say no shall you or Mr Lewis will know the reason why now don't look so shocked don't tell me you have not been asked for such practices in the past a pretty boy like you has tricks he can share has he not on your knees boy now that's it . . .

Hands gripped me and pushed me up until I was seated on the side of the ship. I placed my own hands on either side to keep me steady, sure that I was being placed there to answer some further charge that eluded me, and then who did I see emerging from below decks but Mr Christian, who, upon seeing me perched there, beaten raw, naked as a bairn, broke into a wide smile and clapped his hands loudly.

'Mr Christian,' I tried to shout but the words barely travelled a foot or two beyond me, so dishevelled was I. 'Mr Christian . . . help me, sir . . . I am to be murdered . . .'

Murdered! The last word I spoke before the great foot of King Neptune kicked me in my stomach, sending me falling backwards over the side of the boat and into the great Atlantic Ocean below. The rope tightened against my chest and I gasped in horror as I plunged deep down into the water below, my mouth filled with the sea, my breath taken from me in surprise, my only thought being that I was to be drowned for reason or reasons unknown. At speed my body was hauled through the waves alongside the ship and I was dragged towards it at such a rate that I felt that death was surely upon me. I gasped for air one last time as my body flung itself upwards for a moment as the rope was hoisted before plunging deep down again, and after that . . . after that . . . the rest is silence.

It began not long after my eleventh birthday. I had been living with Mr Lewis for nearly two years and during that time I had found him to be a strange mixture of kindness and cruelty, a man who looked after all the young boys in his care but who, when roused by the elder ones, could lash out and cause a scene of violence and horror that would give my youthful head the night terrors.

'You like it here, John Jacob, do you not?' he asked me from time to time during those early years; he always seemed particularly fond of me and treated me with unusual generosity. 'And you've learned a lot from me, haven't you?'

'Oh, yes,' I would say, nodding my head quickly, and why shouldn't I have been grateful to him after all? Wasn't he the one who gave me food and water and provided me with a bed every night when otherwise I might have been passing the late hours in a gutter by the side of the road? Wasn't his establishment the only one I had ever felt truly at home in and weren't there other lads there my own age to converse with? 'I'm most grateful to you, Mr Lewis, you know that.'

'Aye, I should think so too. You're a good lad, John Jacob, one of the better ones.'

From the start he had taught me the fine art of pickpocketing, which was the main occupation of everyone in that house, and I had taken to it like a duck to water. I know not whether it was in my blood or in my nature, but I seemed to have an uncommon swift hand, and it stood to me whenever I sauntered around the streets of Portsmouth, claiming the things I wanted and he needed. Indeed, of all my brothers there, I was well known for bringing home the greatest crop at the end of the day: wallets, handkerchiefs, coins, ladies' purses – anything that I could get my hands on. Sometimes a boy would get nabbed by a blue in the act of stealing, but there was never a one who gave Mr Lewis up. Sometimes I got nabbed myself but I kept my counsel. He had a hold on us, every one. Where it came from, I know not. Perhaps it was loneliness or the security of familiar ways. Perhaps it was the fact that none of us had ever known anything different in our lives. Perhaps it was the fear of being cast out.

There were never fewer than a dozen lads living there and never more than eighteen. Most were younger than twelve, but there were always four or five aged between twelve and sixteen, and it was they who were the most difficult. I recall many lads who were friends of mine and looked out for me but then turned that age and grew sullen and withdrawn. I knew that Mr Lewis had different jobs for each of us as we grew older, but knew little of what they were. But still, every night when the sun had gone down and the moon had come up, those older boys were sat down in front of a glass with a bowl of water placed before them and told to wash their faces and comb their hair and then they were whisked away to the uppermost floor of the house for what was known as Evening Selection, where they would stay for a number of hours. None of the rest of us was allowed to leave our beds during that time, but we would hear the heavy footsteps of gentlemen ascending the steps to the top floor and coming down again a few hours later, but we knew nothing of what took place up there. And, in our ignorance, we thought little of it too.

But the numbers of the upstairs lads had to be replenished as the boys grew older and were then expelled from the house by Mr Lewis, and shortly after my eleventh birthday Mr Lewis came to sit on my bed one evening and put an arm around my shoulders.

'Now, John Jacob, my fine fellow, do you think you're still a baby or are you ready to take on a most important job that I have in mind for you?'

I knew that I was being summoned to join the upstairs room and felt proud of the fact that I was being plucked from among the little 'uns for this role. I told him I was ready and he helped me wash my face and comb my hair before standing back and looking at me with pride on his face.

'Oh, yes,' he said. 'Oh, yes, indeedy. A fine lad you are too. So pretty. What a popular lad you'll prove yourself to be. You'll make my fortune, I swear you will.'

'Thank you, sir,' said I, little understanding what he meant by these words.

'Now, as it's your first night, everything will be a little gentle on you. We won't have any of the other boys coming upstairs. It'll all be for you – do you like that idea?'

I told him I did and he seemed even more pleased than before, but then he grew suddenly serious and knelt down on the floor so we were looking at each other eye to eye.

'But tell me this,' he said with an air of suspicion: 'I can trust you, can I not?'

'Of course, sir,' said I.

'And you're grateful to me for giving you a home and friends of your own age? You wouldn't let me down?'

'No, sir,' said I. 'I'd never do such a thing.'

'Well, that's good to hear. I'm very glad to hear you say it, John Jacob. Very glad indeed. And you'll do what you're told, won't you? And cause no trouble?'

I nodded, feeling a little more nervous now, but he seemed pleased by my responses, and soon after we were making our way up the stairs, just the two of us, to the upstairs floor, where I had never set foot since arriving at his establishment a few years before. I had often wondered what it would look like and assumed it would have the same sparse furnishings and drab atmosphere as the rooms we lived in downstairs but to my surprise the door opened out on to a fine living room with a comfortable sofa and a number of plush armchairs. Two doors led from the room at the end on either side and within each one I could see a plain bed and a bowl for water.

'Well, John Jacob,' asked Mr Lewis. 'What do you think of it here?'

'I think it is very fine, sir,' said I. 'Very fine indeed.'

'Aye, it is. I try to keep it comfortable. But now that you've seen it, you understand that there's a job of work that I need you to do and it's most important for the well-being of our happy household.'

I swallowed and nodded slowly. My confidence was decreasing by the minute and, even though he seemed to think it a great compliment that I had been brought here alone, I wished that some of my older brothers were with me for companionship and security. I was about to say something to that effect, when I heard footsteps on the stair outside, followed a moment later by a rap on the door.

'Just do as you're told, lad, and you'll come to no harm,' said Mr Lewis as he opened the door.

I stepped back as it opened to reveal a middle-aged man in a heavy overcoat and a tall hat. I didn't recognize him, but he was a toff, there was no doubt of that. Any fool could smell it off him.

'Good evening, Mr Lewis,' he said, handing him a cane and stepping inside.

'Good evening, sir,' replied Mr Lewis, bowing a little, something I had never seen him do before. 'I'm delighted you could return to see us again.'

'Well, I promised I would, didn't I, if you had something new to offer me and . . .' He hesitated as he saw me standing in the corner of the room, a position I had somehow wheedled my way into, and his eyebrows raised in surprise. 'Oh, my, Mr Lewis,' he added then, 'you have excelled yourself.'

The door was closed and the gentleman came towards me with a hand outstretched. 'Good evening, young man,' he said. 'I'm delighted to make your acquaintance.'

'Good evening, sir,' said I, my voice coming out as a whisper as I shook his hand.

He laughed as I did so and turned round to Mr Lewis again. 'You said you had something special,' he said in surprise. 'But I never imagined . . . Where on earth did you find him?'

'Oh, he's been with me a number of years, has John Jacob,' said Mr Lewis. 'Only, he hasn't been put to use yet. This is his first night.'

'You swear it?'

'You only have to look at him, sir.'

The gentleman turned and stared at me, not smiling now, and put a hand to my face. I recoiled slightly as his fingers touched my cheek, knowing not what he wanted of me, and he nodded slowly and smiled.

'You tell the truth,' he said, standing up and taking something from his pocket, which he handed to Mr Lewis. 'There's a little extra in there, you'll find. For your generosity in inviting me to partake.'

'Why, thank you, sir,' said Mr Lewis. 'Shall I leave you both to it, then?'

'If you would,' he said. 'But Mr Lewis,' he added, as he was about to leave the room. 'You may leave the cane here.'

'As you please, sir,' he replied and a moment later we two were alone.

That evening took place more than three years before my arrival on board the Bounty, but almost every evening over that time would find me on the top floor of Mr Lewis's establishment with three or four of my brothers, servicing the needs and desires of gentlemen who paid for their pleasures. I recall none of their faces. I recall little of what they did. I learned to remove my thoughts from the experience and be Turnstile downstairs and John Jacob above. It started to matter little to me what I did. More often than not it would take no more than a half-hour of the clock. I didn't care. I didn't feel alive at all.

And then one afternoon, two days before Christmas Day, I stole Mr Zéla's pocket-watch and by the end of the day I had been taken away from all that.

I woke with a start, my eyes riveted to the ceiling above me. Something had happened to me, what was it? What day was it? Monday, please the Saviour, let it be Monday, for Mr Lewis does not bring his gentlemen here on a Monday; it is our day of rest, a day after His own.

No. Not Mr Lewis's establishment.

I was on a ship.

The *Bounty*!

My body jumped in fright as the memories flooded back – the kidnapping, the stripping, the beating, the painting, the thrashing, the tieing, the kicking, the drowning – and as it did it gave up a great cry of pain and I swear that I thought I had been left to roast in hell. I tried to look down, but my body was covered by a rough blanket and I dared not lift it to investigate what traumas lay beneath.

'You are awake, then,' came a voice from beside me and I tried to turn my head to look at Captain Bligh as he crouched down.

'The men . . .' I whispered to him. 'The men . . . Mr Heywood . . . Mr Christian . . .'

'Hush now, Master Turnstile,' he said. 'You must rest a little further. You will be fine. I've seen worse effects for pollywogs than what happened to you. Sea-faring is a superstitious business, my young friend, and the men are more gullible than a bunch of old crones. Were they not to have their way, well, heaven knows what they might have done. As the ship passes the Equator, King Neptune must have his sacrifice. Others have endured it. I endured it myself many years ago. And I hear that you accepted your duty with great fortitude. You are a shellback now with barnacles on your back and must have your gift.'

He stepped away and entered his cabin, returning a few

moments later with a piece of parchment, which he unscrolled ceremoniously. 'The men left this for you,' he said. 'Shall I read it to you?'

I stared at him, neither answering 'yes' nor 'no', but he seemed to take my silence for consent, as he stretched it out and peered at the words on top.

'A proclamation,' he announced in a severe voice that reminded me of the monster on deck who had inflicted this torture on me. 'Whereas by our Royal Choice, the brave John Jacob Turnstile, slimy pollywog of old, has this day entered our domain. We do hereby declare that it is our Royal Will to confer upon said fellow the Freedom of the Seas. Should he fall overboard, we do command that all *Sharks*, *Dolphins*, *Whales*, *Mermaids* and other dwellers in the Deep are to abstain from maltreating his person. And we do further direct that all *Sailors*, *Soldiers* and others who have not crossed Our Royal Domain to treat him with due respect and courtesy. Given under our hand at Our Court on board HMS *Bounty* on the Equator in Longitude on this eighth day of February, in the year of our Lord 1788. Signed, Cancer, High Clerk to the court of Neptune, Rex.'

He rolled up the parchment and smiled at me. 'It's a fine old text, isn't it?' he asked. 'You should be proud of yourself, my boy. You are stronger than you realize. You might have cause to recall that some day.'

I closed my eyes and attempted to swallow, but my throat was so sore that it felt like chewing on gravel. I knew not what offended me more, the misery and violence I had suffered at the men's hands, or the disappointment I felt in knowing that the captain not only approved of such things, but had known of what was taking place on deck and had not stepped in to save me.

And I swore something as I lay on my bunk, a battered shell of who I had been when I had entered it to sleep the night before. I swore that if the moment ever came when I could turn on this ship and make my escape from it for ever, I would do so. If my chance would ever come, I would leave the *Bounty* and never return either to the ship, to Mr Lewis or to England.

I swore it with the Saviour as my witness.

12

BEFORE MY ADVENTURES on board the *Bounty* began, and back in the days when I was an inmate at Mr Lewis's establishment in Portsmouth, had I been asked for my impressions of a sea-going man, I should have said it was an existence filled with adventure, excitement and bravery. Hard work, no doubt, but each sunny morning would offer some fresh challenge.

As the months wore on, however, I realized how wrong I had been in my perceptions about life on the waves, for, in truth, the days ran into each other in the most tiresome fashion and it was rare that anything of interest happened to mark any spectacular difference between the one you were enduring and the one that came before it or the one that would follow immediately after. So it is that as I recount my tale it is those strange moments which separated the days from one another and offered something of little interest to me that I choose to relate. But trapped between each one was little more than long, dull days and nights of scudding forward, sometimes in good weather, sometimes in bad, with indifferent food to eat and company that failed to excite the imagination or intellect. Easy, then, to realize why any change to our routine could bring great excitement to the men. And one sunny morning, perhaps ten days after my cruel debasement as we crossed the equatorial line, something took place that offered a little relief from the humdrum passing of the hours.

I was in the ship's galley at the time with Mr Hall, preparing the captain's lunch, and, for all his decent manners, the cook was keeping a close eye on me to make sure that none of the finer food that was kept aside for the captain and the officers found its way into my own stomach as I prepared the plate.

'You've grown thin, young Turnip,' said he, looking me up and down while using that nickname which had become common currency now among the men and which I had given up correcting them on. 'Aren't you eating?'

'I'm eating as well as some and not as well as others,' said I in reply, not looking at him, for I was suffering a fit of the depressions that morning, bored as I was, and was little interested in pursuing a conversation.

'Well, that's the way it is at sea, lad,' he muttered. 'The morning you came aboard, I said to Mr Fryer, I said there's a lad who's eaten a few fine meals in his life. Should we face disaster at sea we could always pop an apple in his mouth, roast him in the oven, and have sustenance for a month.'

I put my knife down and turned to look at him, narrowing my eyes. The idea that I was a well-fed boy when I was taken from the streets of Portsmouth to the courthouse of Spithead, and from there on to the deck of the *Bounty*, was a ridiculous one, for I had never known a fine meal in any of my days. It was true that a dinner of sorts was in the pot at Mr Lewis's every evening at seven o'clock, before his late-night gentlemen came to call, but there was always an almighty fight among my brothers and me to find the choicest cuts within the stew, and this was no easy feat as it was nearly all stock and gristle.

'The man who tries to eat me will find a knife implanted in his belly,' said I then, lowering my voice and doing all that I could to sound as if I meant it and that I was not a fellow to be challenged. 'I'm no sailor's dinner.'

'Now, now, Turnip, take a jest in good humour when you hear it,' said Mr Hall irritably. 'What's the matter with you these days anyway? You're as quiet as a church mouse and wander around with an expression on your face that suggests you'd rather be hung on a cross than live on a ship.'

'I wonder that you might ask,' said I with a sniff, for Mr Hall had been one of those who had cheered on while the rope had been gathered around me and I had been sent southwards to what I thought was to be my watery grave.

There was silence for a moment then and I continued to chop the carrots that were to form part of Captain Bligh's lunch, but there was something in the silence that lingered between us and which made me wonder whether Mr Hall was angry with me for what I had said. My body tensed slightly as I waited to see whether he might attack me, but then I heard him reaching for a pan of boiling water and I relaxed, sure that he had not understood the sarcasm in my words.

'You'd do well to put your anger behind you,' he said. 'There's nothing has happened to you on board here that has not happened to every man of the company at one time or another. You have an easy life of it here compared with some and have to accept such moments and carry on without rancour. That's what makes a sea-faring man.'

I said nothing in reply, although the words that floated through my mind concerned the fact that I had never asked to be a sea-faring man, had no desire to be a sea-faring man, and planned on stopping being a sea-faring man at the earliest possible opportunity, but I kept them to myself for the time being. A bubble boiled inside me, though, and as the knife chopped up and down before me I considered how easy it would be to turn it on myself and end the boredom and anger of these days. Such ideas surprised even me, for I had endured worse in my life, aye, and done it with a smile on my face, but the thought of many more long months aboard this ship, suffering the-Saviour-knew-what indignities, was enough to turn me. I lifted the knife and stared at the blade; it had been sharpened that very morning and was keen,

146

but before any more madness could invest my thoughts a roar went up from the deck above and Mr Hall and I looked at each other in surprise.

'Go along up,' said he, as if I needed his permission to do as I pleased. 'See what it is if you want. I'll finish that for you.'

I nodded and wondered whether there wasn't some part of him that regretted his part in the events of before, but I dismissed this from my mind as I went on deck in the blistering sunshine to see the men all standing by the side, staring across at a sail on the horizon. Regrets and apologies are all very well, but there's things that happen in a person's life that are so scorched in the memory and burned into the heart that there's no forgetting them. They're like brands.

'Back to your stations, men,' cried Mr Fryer, marching between the sailors, and they dispersed quickly but kept one eye focused westward, for such was the excitement of a break in routine that the recollection of it could fill our conversations for days afterwards.

'I thought we might see her,' said Captain Bligh, stepping forward now to join Mr Fryer and taking the glass from him to look closer. 'The British Queen: a whaler, I believe. I had thought our paths might cross some days ago and when she failed to appear I thought our chance had gone. Send a signal, Mr Fryer. She travels to the Cape of Good Hope. We shall send a jolly boat across with a message. Where the devil's Turnstile?' he asked, looking around then, and as I had been walking towards him at that moment he almost collided with me as he turned. 'Ah, there you are, lad. Good, good. Step down to my cabin, will you? There are four or five letters in the top drawer of my desk. Bring them to me and we can send them across for delivery.'

'Aye, sir,' said I, and ran back downstairs at great speed, as if a failure to secure the letters quickly would destroy the great excitement ahead of us. I knew from my study of Captain Bligh's charts that the Cape of Good Hope was at the southernmost tip of the

African continent, a different direction from ours entirely, as we aimed towards Cape Horn at the southern tip of the Americas, but the whaler could deliver any parcels to the authorities there and have them delivered – slowly – onwards to their recipients in England. For the first time it occurred to me that it would be nice to have someone to write to, but were I to take up quill and paper, what would I say, and to whom? I could not possibly write to Mr Lewis, who would have no interest in my adventures but only desire my return as quickly as possible to face his wrath. One of my brothers perhaps; although they would trade the intelligence for favours from their captor. There was no one. It was a foolish thought.

I retrieved the parcel of letters from where they lay and turned for the door, but as I did so I realized that the captain had failed to seal the top missive and it was available for anyone's eyes to peruse. I glanced towards the door, but there was no one there and outside was silence, for most of the crew were on deck now watching the sail of the *British Queen*. What made me read the letter, I do not know. Possibly the fact that the opportunity was there and that I thought it would give me some insight into the captain's mind, which was a curiosity of sorts to me. Possibly because in my fancy and vanity I thought he might have written some words about me and, if so, I wanted to know what he had said, whether he approved of me or thought me a scourge. Anyway, whatever my reasons, I stepped further back from the door, placed the sealed letters down on a chair beside me, opened the top one and began to read. I quote from memory and many of the words may be wrong but the sense is there, I think.

My dearest Betsey,

it began and, oh, didn't I laugh to think of the captain addressing anyone as his dearest anything, the nance. Still and all, the portrait of his wife that stood on his desk showed a handsome woman who might give any man the motions, so he was not be mocked for it.

We make good time on our little vessel and I believe that we shall round the Horn by Resurrection Day. The weather has been in our favour so far . . .

I could scarce believe he said this, for had we not suffered unspeakable trials in the early weeks of our voyage? No one on board seemed to recall how difficult it had been, but I did.

Do I dare to believe that we could reach Otaheite before our schedule suggests? I can but pray for such an outcome for our time there might be longer than expected and who knows what I can expect on our return voyage but if every day brings me closer to YOU, won't my heart be filled with happiness?

I hesitated then, torn between embarrassment and a feeling that I should not be reading a letter written by a man for his lady-wife, but I had gone too far along and there was no stopping me now.

The men all work hard and I have improved the standing orders to such an extent that allows them time for SLEEP, time for WORK, and time for RECREATION. The result is a happy crew and I am proud to report that I have had no cause to punish a single man as yet. Has there ever been a ship in HM's Navy that has spent so many weeks at sea with ne'er a flogging? I think not and hope the men appreciate it.
My aim is to arrive at Otaheite with cobwebs on

the cat-o'-nine-tails and believe I can do so too! I have introduced dancing in the evenings, following the late Captain's routine on the Endeavour, and though it met with some facetiousness at first, and a measure of farce that I tolerated well, I believe the men now enjoy the exercise and take it all in good spirits. It puts me in my mind of that last evening we spent at Sir Joseph's, on the occasion of the well-wishes for the trip, when I took you in my arms and we danced among the others and it felt like gliding across the floor. The dance reminded me of that Christmas Eve before our happy wedding when we skated together on the frozen lake of Hyde Park, side by side, my arm around your pretty waist when I knew myself to be the luckiest of men and a fine fellow.

And so my thoughts turn to you, my dearest one, and our son, and our pretty daughters, and I confess that I find my eyes a-water when I think of you seated by our cheerful fireplace, your needlework in hand, and I recall our happy evenings together in . . .

'Turnip.'

I confess that I have never jumped so high in all my life as I did at that moment when my reading was interrupted by a low, quiet voice. So lost had I been in the captain's words that I had failed to hear the footsteps approaching along the corridor or notice as the door opened a little wider and I did not know how long I had been standing there, reading the letter, before he had spoken.

'Mr Christian,' said I, my face taking on the reddenings immediately as I gathered all the letters together and pretended that I had not been engaged in this act of indiscretion.

'The captain sent me down to get his letters. There's a ship—'

'And did he tell you to read them before delivering them to him?' he asked quietly.

'No, sir,' said I, attempting to look outraged at the suggestion but knowing only too well that it would be difficult for me to feign innocence; the evidence was plain to see. 'And I never did! I—'

'Perhaps he wanted you to check that his spellings were fine, with your vast education, I mean? Is the lettering elegant, the prose efficient?'

'Mr Christian,' said I, stepping forward and shaking my head, knowing already that the only way out of this commotion was to throw myself on his mercy. 'I didn't mean it, sir, honest I didn't. It fell open before me. I only read a line or two and was about to go on deck . . .'

He wasn't listening to me, though, for he had opened the letter himself now and was scanning it quickly, his dark pupils bouncing back and forth as he took the contents in. A quick reader, he was too, for he turned it over to the rear side quicker than I had managed.

'Will you be informing the captain, sir?' I asked, wondering whether Mr Bligh's pride at not flogging any man on board was about to be ruined and I was to be his first unfortunate victim.

Mr Christian breathed heavily through his nose and considered it. 'How old are you, Turnip?' he asked me.

'Fourteen years, sir,' said I, looking down now in shame, the better that he might take pity on me.

'When I was fourteen, I took a bushel of apples from the house next door to my father's. I ate them in a sitting, little knowing that they had been kept aside for the pigs, for they had turned to the bad a day or two earlier. For the best part of a week I lay in bed, torn between the sickness of the stomach and the sickness of the rump, and in all that time my father never chastised me, never remonstrated with me, but nursed me back to health. And when

I was on my feet again, and fully restored, he brought me to his study and thrashed me so badly that, even now, when I see an apple I feel ill inside at the memory of it. But I never stole another one, I promise you that, Turnip. I never even thought of it.'

I nodded but held my tongue. It sounded to me like one of those speeches that were not intended for reply.

'Bring the letters up on deck,' he told me after a moment. 'I will say nothing about this incident to the captain, for if I recall my old days as a lad I know how easy it is to make a mistake.'

I breathed a heavy sigh of relief, for as much as I didn't want to be flogged, I knew that I didn't want the men to think me a snooper either or for the captain to think badly of me. 'Thank you, Mr Christian,' said I. 'I'll not do it again, I swear I won't.'

'Yes, yes,' he replied, waving me away. 'On deck with you now. And who knows, Turnip, maybe someday I will call on you for a favour and you will not turn me away?'

He said this very quietly and I hesitated at the door. 'You, sir?' said I. 'But what could I possibly do for you? You're an officer and I'm just—'

'Yes, I know,' he said, shaking his head. 'The idea is pre-posterous. Still, let's keep it in mind, shall we? Just in case.'

I had no choice but to nod my head and run to the deck, where I could hear Captain Bligh shouting for me, ready to lose his return, so great was my delay. And here I am, talking about how any change in routine can be of great interest and break up the normal dull days of life at sea, but the rest of that day I spent in the jolly boat with Mr Fryer, sailing towards the *British Queen*, where we delivered our letters and paid our respects, and then sailing back to the *Bounty* again, and yet during all that time and all that voyage, do I recall anything that was said or done? I do not. For through it all I could think of nothing but my gratitude to Mr Christian for saving me and I determined that if he did call on me at some time – which I could not imagine he would – I would do whatever I could to repay my debt.

I was an ignorant lad, back then. I knew nothing of the world, truly, or the ways of men.

13

WHEN I LIVED IN PORTSMOUTH at Mr Lewis's establishment, I never gave much thought to the sea, which was such a familiar neighbour that none of us ever so much as acknowledged its presence, but my mornings and afternoons were filled with the noise of the sailors who strolled around the town, flirting with the women, drinking in the public houses, causing the Saviour only knew how much trouble when they came to port after months, maybe years, at sea with only one thing on their mind. But when their filthy needs had been satisfied, these men, who had spent so much time together that anyone would have thought they might have liked a little time apart, drank together and from the window that my brothers and I shared above the Twisty Piglet we could hear them talking.

'He were a tartar,' one might say of his then former captain. 'If I live to be a hundred years old, I'll refuse to serve on board with him again. I swear an oath on it.'

'If I saw him walking up this street now,' another might reply, 'I would stand up and spit in his face and say, "Begging your pardon, sir, I regret to say that I was unaware you were stood before me".'

And then there was always one, a third man, seated at his table with less drink than his comrades, who would shake his head and say in such a quiet voice that I had to poke my head out of the window and strain my ears in order to hear him, 'If I saw Captain Such-and-Such now, the stinking bastard,' he would say, 'and believe me, my lads, his path and mine will cross again one day soon, I would split him from belly to throat with my knife and cut out his tongue. And when I left him bleeding in the gutter, I would hang the cat-o'-nine-tails from his mouth.'

Such talk was greatly exciting to a lad like me and I had it in my head that every captain on His Majesty's frigates was a monster of sorts, violent in the extreme and one who instilled such hatred in the men serving under him that it was a wonder he ever managed to spend years at sea and return without them killing him first. It was why I had, at first, feared Captain William Bligh, for what knew I of men like him except that which I had overheard from drunken sots and unhappy sailors? As the months passed, of course, I found that he was not what I had expected at all and I wondered whether I had just been lucky enough to find the one kind captain in the navy or whether the men were wrong in the first place and they were all like this. Perhaps, I wondered, it was the men who were bad. Either way, I had grown to like and respect the captain, although I still held my humiliation at the Equator against him, and thought that when the day came for our paths to part – for part they surely would, as nothing would persuade me to return to England – I would be sorry to say good-bye to him.

His attention to hygiene on board the ship, however, was a thing to behold, for never in the history of Christendom had there been a man so attentive to the cleanliness of the flesh. Time and again he would line the men up and examine their fingernails for fear that they were dirty and any man who did not come up to scratch would find himself scrubbing his fingers clean in a pail of water until they were red raw in the noonday sun. The men's knees – aye, and mine too from time to time – were blistered from the time we spent upon them with brushes in hand as we scrubbed the decks clean, but the captain insisted that an unsoiled ship would keep us all in good health and lead to a successful voyage, which was his one true aim. And on an evening when Mr Elphinstone enquired of the captain over dinner whether it was true that Captain Cook had disinfected the decks with vinegar, our own captain roared that it was just so and looked as if he had the mortifications for forgetting to do so himself and demanded that it be carried out before the hour was passed. But if there was one thing above all others in which the captain took pride – and the letter that, to my disgrace, I had read to his wife bore this out – it was the fact that no man on board had been disciplined during our months away from home. Certainly, there were moments of tension on the ship and on most days an officer could be heard telling a man to look lively or he'd know the reason why, but there had been ne'er a flogging and ne'er a beating since we sailed from Spithead before Christmas and I knew only too well that the captain hoped to keep this record intact until we – they – returned to England once again, whenever that date might be.

And so I was not surprised to note the look of unhappiness and disappointment on his face on the afternoon that we passed through the 47th degree latitude, when every member of the crew was summoned on deck for the trial of Matthew Quintal.

Now the Saviour knows that I am not, and never have been, a violent lad. For sure, I ended up in my fair share of scraps with my brothers over the years but they were small things – name-calling that would lead to a punch being thrown, then a wrestle on the ground with legs and arms a-flailing – but we would soon bring these moments to an end when we saw how much pleasure they were giving Mr Lewis. He would take his seat by the fireplace and watch us with his demented eyes, cackling like an old hag, crying, 'That's right, Turnstile, have at 'im', or 'Show him no mercy, Michael Jones, pull his nose and tweak his ears!' We brothers fought, of course we did, but we did it for ourselves, not for his amusement, and when he became involved we would separate and shake hands and declare each other fine fellows as we strolled off, an arm around the other's shoulder. And I was glad that they ended so, for I do not like the fight and take no joy in watching the suffering of others.

But Matthew Quintal? Oh me, oh my, it was a difficult thing not to take pleasure in the sight of him, brought before the men to answer the charges for which I knew he could have no reply, for of all the sailors on board the *Bounty* he was the man I liked the least and feared the most. Why was that? Because I had known him before, that was why.

There's a twist in the tale, I'd warrant. That I have gone this many pages and not told of my prior acquaintance with one of my fellows on board our merry boat? Well, I have not been quite so dishonest as you might think, for when I say I knew him I mean I knew his type, and could see from the look in his eye and the way that he watched me that the moment would come when he would want from me what I had been forced to surrender before but did not want ever to have to give again.

Wherever I went, I could feel his eyes on me. While I was on the deck of the ship, scrubbing it clean perhaps or learning (as I was) the ways of the sails and the manner of our navigation, I could sense his eyes on my back, burning through me. Below deck on stormy nights, if I was in the men's bunk-cabin listening to the fiddle play, I could rely on him to find his way to a spot beside me, where he would force me to sing a song, which I hated to do, for my singing voice has always been low on my list of talents and would make a crow fall from the sky with a conniption if raised too loud.

'Oh, stop it!' Quintal would cry, putting his hands to his ears and shaking his head as if a banshee herself were singing to him, despite him being the one who insisted on my performance in the first place. 'Stop it this instance, Turnip, or condemn us all to deafness. That a voice so dreadful could emerge from a boy so pretty . . . which of us would have thought it, eh, lads?' And the men would laugh, of course, and hold me down to silence me and the weight of their bodies above me put me in the trepidations, for it reminded me of home and I was trying all that I could not to remember that place or the things I had done there and been forced to do. And whenever something like this happened, I could be assured that it was Quintal who had brought matters to a head and Quintal who would bring them to a close.

'You don't much care for me, Turnip, do you?' he asked me once, and I shrugged my shoulders, unable to look him in the eyes.

'I don't like or dislike any man on board,' said I. 'I'm not a man of opinions.'

'But do you think you could grow to like me?' he asked then, leaning forward and sneering at me with such danger in his eyes that what could I do but run away from him and seek sanctuary in my bunk outside the captain's cabin, and I don't mind admitting that I thanked the Saviour on more than one occasion for its lucky position.

The seas had grown calmer on the afternoon that we were all brought on deck. The crime for which he was charged had actually taken place two days earlier, but until we were through the storms – whose number was increasing almost every day at this time; in fact it was such a rare treat to be in still waters that it seemed a shame to waste them on matters such as this – it had been impossible for the indictment to be read. The captain stood on the deck with the men gathered round and Mr Quintal was before him, his head hanging low.

'Mr Elphinstone,' cried Captain Bligh in what I thought was something of a theatrical voice; the men at the stern could hear him, that was for sure. 'List the charges, sir!'

Mr Elphinstone stepped forward and looked Quintal up and down with contempt in his eyes; behind him Mr Christian and Mr Heywood stood together as ever – for those two were like a pair of peas in a pod, the one so perfectly set out with his hair pomaded and his uniform starched, and the other looking as if he'd been keel-hauled six times before breakfast for playing with his pimples – and Mr Fryer was behind them, looking even more troubled than usual, the lanky streak of piss that he was.

'Matthew Quintal,' said Mr Elphinstone, 'you stand before us today accused of the crime of theft. I say that you stole a cheese and then, when challenged on it, were insubordinate to an officer.'

'Are the charges fair, Mr Quintal?' asked the captain, his fingers in his lapels. 'What say you to them?'

'Aye, they're true,' said Quintal, nodding his head. 'I took the cheese; I can't say otherwise and keep a clean conscience. I were hungry and it took my eye and, though I don't recall the crime, I can't forget how good the dairy felt inside me.'

The men let out a roar of appreciation and the captain glared at them before shouting them down to silence.

'And the second charge,' said he. 'Of an insubordination. Who was it against anyway, Mr Elphinstone?'

'Mr Fryer, sir,' he replied.

The captain frowned at the name and looked around him. 'And where is Mr Fryer?' asked he, for from his position of standing the ship's master was blocked to his sight by the door to the galley. 'Damn it anyway,' shouted the captain, growing red about the gills. 'Didn't I give orders that every man, sailor and officer alike were to attend on deck—'

'I'm here, sir,' said Mr Fryer, stepping forward, and Captain Bligh spun round to stare at him and for a moment I thought that he was almost disappointed to see him there, for had he failed to report to the deck there was always the possibility that he could be found guilty of an insubordination too.

'Well, don't hide in the shadows like a mouse afeared of a cat, man,' shouted Mr Bligh. 'Step forward into the sunlight and let me take a look at you.'

A low murmur went up among the men and I could see them taking sideways glances at one another; the fact that the captain and the master did not get along well had escaped no one's notice, but it was a rare thing to hear him being spoken to in such a contemptuous fashion in front of the men. Mr Fryer's face was scarlet when he stepped closer to the captain, knowing as he did that we were all watching him for a sign of weakness.

'This man here, if you were listening,' continued the captain, and I couldn't help but wonder whether his anger was as much about the fact of losing his perfect disciplinary record as anything else, 'is accused of an act of insubordination towards you. Is it true?'

'He was not respectful, sir,' said Mr Fryer. 'I'd say that much. But I think insubordination might be overstating the case rather.'

Captain Bligh stared at him in surprise. '*Overstating the case rather?*' he asked, twisting his voice in a manner so that he sounded almost as posh as Mr Fryer, which led to a general titter among the men. 'Is that an answer, sir? None of your linguistic machinations now, if you please. Was he insubordinate or wasn't he?'

'Sir, I discovered the missing cheese,' said Mr Fryer, 'and had a notion that Quintal had taken it, for I had observed him hovering around the stores earlier and had sent him on his way for an indolent. I sought him out on deck immediately afterwards and challenged him on the theft and he told me . . .' He hesitated now and looked at Quintal, who grinned back at him as if the whole thing was a terrific farce, before staring down at the wood beneath his feet and frowning, as if he wanted as little a part as possible in what was to come next.

'Well, spit it out, man,' shouted the captain. 'He told you what? What did he say?'

'I'd rather not speak the words, sir,' said Mr Fryer.

'Rather not speak the words?' asked the captain, laughing for a moment and looking around him in surprise. 'Did you hear that, Mr Elphinstone?' he asked. 'Mr Christian? Mr Fryer would rather not speak the words! And why, might I ask?' he continued, pushing up the poshness even further. 'Why would you rather not speak the words?'

'Because, sir, if I may, I think it inappropriate for public consumption.'

'And I think that when your captain asks you a question, you will answer it or face a charge of insubordination yourself!' shouted Captain Bligh. I drew in my breath in surprise. Glancing over at Mr Christian, I could see that even he was a little shocked by such a line emerging in front of the men. 'So I ask you again, Mr Fryer – and I won't ask a third time, Mr Fryer, and stand idly by – what did Mr Quintal say to you when you challenged him on the theft of the cheese?'

'Sir, his exact words were that he was sorry for stealing the vittles,' replied Mr Fryer, loudly and firmly now, and without a moment's hesitation. 'But he was happy to confess to doing so and it had tasted as good to his lips as the titty of the captain's old ma.'

My mouth fell open in shock – no exaggeration either; it literally fell open – and I swear I thought that the very seas had come to a standstill in amazement at Mr Fryer's words. I believed I could hear the sea-birds hesitating in their flight overhead and looking at one another as if even they couldn't credit the phrase. I was sure that the earth hesitated in its rotation while the Saviour did a double-take and looked down at us for clarification of the sentence. Not only were his words unexpected, but Mr Fryer himself was known to be a man of God and never uttered so much as a 'blast it' or a 'damn his boots', let alone made reference to a lady's titty. Time passed slowly in those moments after he spoke and no one uttered a word. In my mind, I started to recall a bawdy poem that one of my brothers had taught me a year or so before – it referred to a poor little girl in the city, on whom no one had ever took pity – and recited it again and again in my head, counting the times I reached the final line (it was three) before Captain Bligh's voice was heard again.

160

'I beg your pardon, sir,' said he, sounding as stunned as he might have been had Mr Fryer pulled a sea trout from his back pocket and slapped him about the face with it, three times and hard. 'I think I must have misheard you, Mr Fryer. Repeat, please.'

'I said that Quintal admitted stealing the cheese but he stated that it had tasted as good on his lips as the—'

'Silence, man, I heard you the first time!' roared the captain, which I thought a little unfair, considering he had asked for the repetition. 'Quintal,' said he then, looking towards the man with fury in his eyes, 'what manner of dog are you anyway?'

'A bad 'un,' said Quintal, still jesting, knowing that he would get the cheers of his fellows for it later and there was no point trying to find his way out of the situation at hand, for the lashing was there to be taken. 'A bad dog, that's for sure, with an unhappy strain in me. There's no taming a cur like me.'

'We shall see about that, sir,' said the captain. 'We shall certainly see about that and before the hour is out too. Mr Morrison, where are you, sir?' From the rear of the crowd, the boatswain, Mr Morrison, stepped forward, the cat-o'-nine-tails already flexed in his hand. The poor man had spent months waiting for his debut and was delighted by the chance. I half expected him to clear his throat and wait for a little early applause. 'Two dozen lashes for Mr Quintal, if you please,' he shouted then. 'We shall soon find out whether this dog can be tamed or whether he is past redemption.'

Quintal was taken forth then, the shirt stripped from his back as he was tied to a deck-grating before all the men, his arms and legs stretched out on either side. We watched, each one of us, in horror and excitement, for here again was a break to our daily routine, and as no such incident had taken place over the previous few months we were each, in our shame and blood thirst, eager to see what would happen next.

The cat-o'-nine-tails – a piece of rope, about eighteen inches in length, with nine lengths of cord emerging from its tip, and three knots tied in each – did not look quite so fearsome a creature to me as I had expected and, indeed, for the first couple of lashes Quintal gave off nothing but a quiet yelp, such as one might do if one was kicked in one's sleep by an unknown assailant. But by the third, he was grimacing. By the fourth, he let out a shout. And by the fifth, each lash was followed by a cry of pain that made my stomach ill inside, even though I did not like the man. His back erupted in red lines from the thrashing, and before the numbers reached double figures blood was spurting from them. We counted the lashes in our heads, each one of us, and at thirteen, fourteen, fifteen, I felt sure the captain would call a halt, for Quintal appeared to have fallen unconscious beneath them – his body had gone lax, his back was a map of pain and weeping sores – but word came there none and the boatswain continued to the assigned twenty-four, before turning to look at Captain Bligh and raising an eyebrow.

'Take him down,' said the captain then, and the straps were immediately loosened and Quintal slumped to the deck. He was immediately picked up by four of his fellows, for it was common practice to lash a man and then send him to the surgeon to have his wounds tended – the great irony of the sea, I thought – but there was life in him yet, for as he was dragged past me, leaving a trail of blood in his wake, he looked up at me and barked. I swear it to you, he barked like the dog he claimed to be. It made me jump too, the donkey.

'Wash down the decks, please,' said the captain, turning away now. 'And disinfect them with vinegar. All officers, please to report to my cabin immediately.'

He went down the steps then, followed by Mr Christian, Mr Heywood, Mr Fryer and Mr Elphinstone. I followed too, in case they wanted tea. The pails came out as I descended and I looked back towards the men, who were grumbling among themselves at the damage inflicted on one of their number, ignoring the fact that he was a thief and a foul-mouth.

'It had to be happen sooner or later, sir,' Mr Christian was saying as they gathered in the captain's cabin and I stationed myself outside to prevent the intrusion of others and, aye, to listen to their conversation myself. I'm ashamed of naught. 'Don't be disheartened. It does the men good to see a little discipline meted out from time to time. Reminds them of their place.'

'I'm not disappointed, Mr Christian,' said the captain, whose voice was still bubbling over with anger. 'And I'm not afraid to let them know who is in charge of this here vessel and who is not. Do you doubt that, sir?'

'No, Captain,' said Mr Christian. 'No, of course not. I merely meant that—'

'And you, Mr Fryer,' continued the rant as he stepped closer to the ship's master, 'you took great pleasure in the scene that just played out before us, I'd measure?'

'I, sir?' he asked in astonishment. 'Why should I—?'

'You logged the incident, did you not, sir? Two days ago, if I'm not mistaken, sir?'

'Yes, I informed you at the time and you quite correctly stated that punishment would have to wait until we were in calmer waters—'

'Quite correct, was I, Mr Fryer? Quite correct? I'm so happy that I have your approval, sir. Does the captain of a ship need approval from its master? Is that a new regulation of naval law of which I have not been appraised?'

'I meant no insult, sir.'

'Damn you, man,' roared the captain then, so loudly that I swear the hesitant sea-birds must have scattered above our heads at the sound of it. 'Damn you to hell and back! You had two full days to tell me the cause of the infraction and what did you do, you mentioned something about a stolen cheese and an act of insubordination—'

'Sir, you never asked me—'

'Don't speak to me while I'm talking, sir! Don't speak to me!'

163

He stepped so close to Mr Fryer now that he could have kissed him in a moment had he felt an inclination to do so, but his words were as close to screams as I'd ever heard emerge from this cabin. 'Damn your boots, sir, you'll not speak when a superior officer is addressing you! Do you hear me, sir? Do you?'

'Yes, Captain,' said Mr Fryer quietly.

'You had two full days before now, Mr Fryer. Two full days to tell me the level of the insult, and when do I hear it first? On deck. Before the punishment. In front of all the officers and all the men. You don't think you might have mentioned it before then?'

Mr Fryer hesitated, no doubt wanting to ensure that the captain had finished his tirade before offering an answer or explanation.

'I tried to tell you yesterday morning, sir,' insisted Mr Fryer slowly and carefully. 'I said he had made a lewd remark that should not be repeated in front of the men and you—'

'You said no such a thing, sir!' shouted the captain, storming around the cabin now, tossing papers hither and thither for me to tidy later. 'You said no such a thing!'

'I did, Captain,' replied Mr Fryer firmly. 'I stood in this very spot and—'

'Are you calling me a liar now, Mr Fryer, is that it?' he asked, stepping over to him again. 'Speak clearly, now. Are you calling me a liar? Mr Christian, you'll witness the remark.'

There was a long silence. I wanted nothing more than to poke my head around the door to get a better look at Mr Fryer's face, or for that matter the faces of the other officers, for they had never been subjected to such a tirade in all their months at sea so far, but I feared that if I did so the captain, in his fury, would lop it off.

'I must be mistaken, sir,' said Mr Fryer finally.

'Aye! Mistaken!' shouted the captain, vindicated. 'You heard him, gentlemen, he was mistaken. I wonder that I don't have you flogged as well.'

'Sir,' said Mr Elphinstone, unwisely entering into the

conversation. 'Mr Fryer is a warrant officer. He can't be flogged.'

'Quiet, Mr Elphinstone,' said Mr Christian immediately, who at least had the sense to know that the captain was making an idle remark and not a threat.

The interruption of the two men seemed to catch the captain off guard, for he looked around then, searching for his anger again, before looking towards the door, where I was too slow to jump out of his sightline and he caught me a-hovering. 'Turnstile!' he roared and the heart crossed sideways in me, for he was in no condition to be reasoned with and if he wanted another flogging, well, there was only one of us present who was not warranted. 'Get your blasted skinny rump in here this instant!'

I stepped carefully inside, anxious to keep my distance from all. I looked from man to man. Mr Fryer was pale, but he did not seem angry. Mr Christian and Mr Elphinstone looked anxious, while young Mr Heywood, the scut, looked as if he was enjoying the drama enormously and hadn't had as much fun since he'd last popped a pimple.

'Captain?' said I, ready to apologize for anything that needed apologizing for, regardless of whether I was guilty or not.

'Turnstile, you're to draw up a note for me,' said the captain. 'Dated today. Fletcher Christian promoted to lieutenant and ship's master. John Fryer to retain his standing and assist Mr Christian in all duties as might be required of him.'

'Sir, I must protest—' began Mr Fryer, but the captain spun around, his face red with fury.

'Protest, do you?' he shouted. 'Protest at me? Damn your boots, you landed . . . Damn your boots! Insult me and my kin on the deck of the ship and think that I'll stand for the treason, do you? At school, maybe, sir, when the likes of you were in charge. As a sailor, aye, as was my duty. But not here, sir! Not on the *Bounty*! I am captain, no matter where I come from, and you are my subordinate, no matter your father's title. And you'll take my orders, sir! Won't you, sir? You'll do as I say, sir, you understand me?'

Mr Fryer glared at him and I swear his nostrils were flaring like a horse in heat.

'Do you understand me, sir?' roared the captain again, and finally Mr Fryer nodded his head slowly.

'You are, as you say, Captain,' he said.

'Aye, I am,' said Mr Bligh, tugging at his jacket and trying to calm himself down. 'Captain of all, from officers to midshipmen to cabin boys, and none to forget it either. Mr Christian, you're happy with the promotion?'

'Aye, sir,' said Mr Christian, and I could see that he was trying hard not to smile too much or puff his chest out any further than it needed to go. And as for his sidekick, the warted toady, he looked ready to explode with pleasure.

'Good, then you're dismissed,' said the captain. 'Get out, the whole blasted lot of you.'

The officers marched out of the cabin, one by one, but I hesitated and was left alone there with the captain, who sat down in his chair out of sight of the corridor before putting his head in his hands for a moment and then looking up at me. 'Turnstile,' he said quietly, looking so sad and devastated that my heart broke for him, despite his anger. 'You may go too.'

'Some tea, sir?' says I. 'Or a cordial? A glass of brandy, perhaps?'

'You may go,' he repeated quietly, and I hesitated for only a moment before nodding my head and leaving.

One final observation. In the corridor as I emerged, the triumvirate of Mr Christian, Mr Heywood and Mr Fryer standing there, two facing one, and Mr Christian's hand on Mr Fryer's arm.

'*Don't*, Fletcher,' said he sharply. 'You got what you wanted.'

'John . . .' began Mr Christian and the master laughed.

'Oh, it's "John" now, is it?' he asked. 'An hour ago it was "sir".'

They stared at each other and finally Mr Christian shrugged his shoulders and walked away, followed, of course, by the scut, who deserves no name.

Mr Fryer turned round, caught my eye, stared at me for a moment and then turned and entered his tiny cabin, closing the door quietly behind him.

14

LOOKING BACK, there were many difficult times during that voyage on the *Bounty* – days when we were hungry, days when we were exhausted, days when the expanse of water around us made us sea-blind or half-crazed with the deliriums – but none were quite so terrible as the twenty-five days that we spent attempting to round the Horn; almost a month wasted from each of our lives as we fought against nature, foolish creatures that we were, and were allowed to progress no further than a few hopeless leagues in the attempt.

The ship had changed a little since the twin dramas of Matthew Quintal's flogging and Mr Christian's promotion. The men worked harder and were quieter with it and I believed that perhaps the new lieutenant was right when he said that the men liked to see a little discipline meted out from time to time; it kept them lively. The officers appeared to be divided into two camps, with the captain, Mr Christian and Mr Heywood, the pustulant prick, on one side and Mr Fryer on the other, with Mr Elphinstone stuck in the middle trying to keep peace between them all. By the nature of my position, I spent more time among them than any other man or lad aboard, but I kept my head down, as was my habit, and tried to get on with my work.

The sea changed suddenly and dramatically as we sailed through the 50th parallel, as if it had been keeping a wary eye on our small craft for weeks and had decided that enough was enough, we were brave fellows but it was time for us to be sent back whence we had come. And so the winds blew until my eyes could scarcely keep open when on deck, so forceful were they in sweeping each of us from our feet. And the rain fell until it turned into sleet and landed upon our heads like stones from the heavens or one of the plagues of ancient Egypt. Then the tides grew so heavy that they would roar and rage and sink deep before rising up before us, sweeping across our bows, roaring like a roused lion, the vicious mouth ready to swallow each and every one of us should we lose our footing for even a moment, although to my surprise she claimed no victims yet. There was no time for personal dramas or skirmishes on board now as each man did all he could to keep us afloat and alive. Even the dancing was temporarily suspended, as the notion of us turning jigs or hornpipes while the hurricanoes spouted around us was enough to make madmen of us all. At times it felt as if there was to be no end to the tempest and my duties were extended to include keep-ing the area below decks free of water, from the great cabin where the pots were stored, to my own bunk and the doors leading to the captain's, Mr Fryer's and the other officers' cabins. And blast me if this wasn't a more difficult task than it sounded, as every time an officer appeared before me he was shaking off his great-coat and the deck was sodden again with what seemed like half the ocean's capacity. Time and again I ran up the steps to batten down the hatch, only to find it reopened by the time I returned to my post. The sound of the wind was like a whistling in my ears that never failed and it gave me a sick headache, and as the days passed the first suggestion was made – by that unlucky fellow Mr Fryer – that the Horn was impassable.

'Impassable, Mr Fryer?' asked the captain in a thoughtful voice as they sat with Mr Christian one evening, a week, perhaps ten days, into this dreadful weather. 'Did Mr Hicks say as much to Captain Cook when they attempted to round the Horn?'

'No, sir,' he replied, trying to keep his voice reasonable so as not to arouse Mr Bligh's terrible temper. 'But it was a different time of year and, with respect, Zachary Hicks was cautious about their prospects at the time. I see no end to these storms. It's been weeks now since they began.'

'What of the sails?' asked the captain. 'What condition are they in?'

'They're holding,' admitted the ship's master. 'For now anyway. I dread to think what would happen should one of our masts crack in two. We would be lost, I fear.'

The captain nodded and sipped his tea. Relations between the two men had become more civil since the weather had come upon us. For my part, I had begun to respect Mr Fryer, for he had taken the promotion of Mr Christian without further complaint and appeared to have nothing but the best interests of the ship and our mission at heart. His comments no longer seemed to irk the captain as much as they had before, but then the captain was not in an unpleasant humour, for I rather fancied that there was nothing he enjoyed more than a challenge such as the one we faced.

'The winds may blow and the sea may storm but we shall scud on,' he said finally, placing a hand firmly down on the table before him as if to suggest that that was an end to the matter. 'We shall scud on, my fine fellows, and emerge unblemished on the other side of the beast, like Captain Cook did before us, and before any of you have a chance to thank the Saviour for the blessing of it, we'll be sailing north by northwest towards Otaheite and opening our telescopes to spy land.'

No one said anything for a moment. Surely he was a confident man, our brawny captain. And a foolish one at times.

'There is the issue of the men, sir,' suggested Mr Christian finally.

'The men?' asked the captain, looking across at him. 'What of the men? They work hard, don't they?'

'Valiantly,' he replied. 'They are English sailors, every one. But their hopes are flagging. They don't see how we can get through

169

it. We've made such little progress over the past week and now several of the men are down with colds and the tremors.'

'They don't have to *see*, Mr Christian,' replied the captain testily. 'They have to obey.'

'They're afeared, sir,' said Mr Heywood then, sitting forward, and I swear it was the first time I'd ever heard him offer an opinion at a meeting like this; I suspect it was the first time he ever had, for the other men turned to look at him, each one, and his face took on the reddenings even worse than usual, and I feared his pimples would have a violent eruption and kill him altogether, which would have been no poor thing.

'Are they?' asked the captain quietly, stroking his chin for a moment and considering it. 'Are they indeed? Well, they have nothing to fear, for I shall deliver them from this storm and they shall thank me for it and be proud of their own actions. Still and all, let us increase their rations for now,' he concluded. 'An extra portion of soup and rum for every man once a day. That will give them energy, will it not?'

'Very good sir,' said Mr Christian.

An uneasy peace rested between the officers and captain and I must admit that my own relationship with Mr Christian had grown increasingly tense. Many was the occasion that I found him waiting for the captain in his cabin – which no officer was supposed to do – and helping himself to Mr Bligh's brandy as he sat there. Whenever I entered and found him thus, he would raise his glass to me defiantly and toast my good health, and what could I do only thank him for the honour of it and be on my way.

A few nights later I found myself on deck in near darkness, when the raging seas had calmed slightly and the moon overhead, which was full, appeared in the sky like a giant florin which I could pocket as easily as any I ever had before. Some instinct took me to the side of the boat and I looked up towards it, closing one eye and reaching my hand out, capturing the sphere between thumb and forefinger, and I must have looked a fright to anyone who observed me, but the men were too busy keeping the ship afloat and those who were not on duty were already in their bunks, hoping for an hour or two's sleep, so my actions were of concern to no man. I closed my eyes then for a moment and imagined that the noise had faded away and all was peace around me, all was solitude and happiness on this strange moving platform that had become my home.

'Strange to see you up here, Turnip,' said a voice behind me and I jumped so high in surprise that it was a wonder I did not fall overboard, where no man could have saved me.

'Mr Christian, sir,' said I, putting a hand to my chest to feel the heavy thumping of my heart and stop it from leaping through my skin. 'You startled me.'

'And you surprised me,' he replied. 'I saw a miserable lad standing by the bow, looking out to sea, and thought that's never young Turnip! He's always to be found in the safety and security of below decks, not up here among hard-working sailing men.'

I hesitated for a moment, weighing up the level of the insult, for he was surely calling me a coward and if there was one thing that I did not believe myself to be it was that. I had fought every brother in Mr Lewis's establishment at one time or another and had seen off a few men, too, who had taken more liberties than their payments to my benefactor extended to them and had never once shirked from the confrontation.

'My duties are below decks, sir,' said I proudly, unwilling to acknowledge his slur. 'I have to be on hand for the captain whenever he has need of me.'

'Of course you do, Turnip,' said he cheerfully. 'Of course you do! Why, how else could you eavesdrop into every conversation on board if you were not lingering by doorways, with your ear to the keyholes? Why, if only we had a chimney on board, I swear you'd spend half your time hiding in it.'

I opened my mouth and shut it again in annoyance before shaking my head angrily. 'There's a thing to say, Mr Christian,' I

171

replied finally, falling short of calling him a dirty liar, for to say such a thing to an officer, especially such a favourite of the captain's, was a sure road back to the gunner's daughter, and I had sworn that I would never make kiss with her filthy lips again. 'I can't help it if my bunk is next to the officers' cabins, now, can I?'

'Oh, don't get all twisted into knots, lad,' he said, laughing as he placed his hands firmly on the railing of the ship and breathing in the air deeply through his nose. 'I've always said that there is no greater source of information on board one of His Majesty's frigates than the captain's servant boy. You hear everything, you miss nothing. You are the heart of the house.'

I nodded. 'Well, that's true enough, sir, I suppose.'

'And you have an opinion on everyone around you too, I dare say?'

I shook my head. 'Not my place to hold an opinion, sir,' said I. 'The captain doesn't seek my counsel, if that's what you're getting at.'

Mr Christian burst into laughter at that and shook his head. 'Oh, you poor fool,' said he. 'You don't for a moment think that I thought he did, do you? What are you, after all, but an ill-educated boy of no family and no education. Why would a man like Mr Bligh look to you for anything other than a hot cup of tea and to turn his sheets down at night?'

My eyes narrowed when he said that, for it was a lie of the worst nature, a calumny that it was hard to let go by without a swipe at it. To deal with the second count first, I had all the education I needed. I could say my letters and count to a hundred and beyond and knew the capital cities of half of Europe besides, on account of a volume entitled *A Book of Useful & Pertinent Information for the Modern Young Gentleman* that Mr Lewis kept on his shelves, alongside the penny picture books that his own gentlemen liked to leaf through when they arrived in the evening times for their drink and sport. I could boil an egg, sing the king's anthem, and bid a lady good morning in French, and there were few lads back in Portsmouth who could say as much.

And to deal with the first count second – the charge of having no family – well, what knew he of that? It was true that I had few memories of my life before being taken in by Mr Lewis, but my brothers at his establishment, tough creatures as they were, were my brothers still and I would have laid down my life for each and every one of them had there been the need.

'I am not so stupid as you might think, sir,' said I finally, all bravery now as the winds picked up again and the sea rose, spitting water in our faces, but we held our places, neither of us wanting to be the first to move.

'Oh, indeed not,' he said with a smile. 'No, you're wise enough to read the captain's correspondence so as you might learn any information that he might not pass on to the rest of us.' I declined to answer the charge, but looked away, and I could feel my face taking on the reddenings, even now in the night-time, with the darkness around us to hide my betrayal. 'You've gone very silent now, Turnip,' said he then. 'Hit a nerve, have I?'

'That was a mistake on my part,' I replied. 'A misjudgement, such as any one of us might make.'

'And do you think the captain would see it that way?' he asked me then. 'Do you think he'd clap you on the back and call you a fine fellow for making such a mistake, or would he hang you by the ankles from the top foresail, shake the life from your body and then leave you for the wind and the sleet to finish off?'

I bit my tongue, for there was a stream of names I wanted to call Mr Christian, but I had no one but myself to blame for getting myself into this trouble in the first place. Finally, I turned round and made to go back below decks, but as I did so he took hold of my arm, his thumb and finger pinching the bone in it, and pulled me close to him.

'Don't walk away from me, you young pup,' he hissed, and I could smell the stink of the beef broth from his breath. 'Forget not who I am. I'll have your respect or know the reason why.'

'I must return to the captain, sir,' said I, anxious to get away from him, for he had a look of violence in his eyes that I wanted to escape.

'And how long is he to keep us at this madness?' he asked me then and I frowned, unsure that I understood his meaning.

'What madness?' I asked. 'Who are you talking of?'

'The captain, ignoramus,' he hissed. 'How long is he going to keep us trying to round the Horn before accepting defeat?'

'A lifetime, I'd warrant, and another day on top of that,' I replied, standing to my full height to defend the captain's honour. 'He'll never accept defeat, you may count on it.'

'I may count on every man jack of us perishing in Davy Jones's Locker is what I may count on if this lunacy doesn't come to an end soon,' he said. 'You're to tell him, do you hear me? Tell him that enough is enough. We must turn around!'

Now it was my turn to laugh. 'I can tell him no such thing, sir,' I cried. 'You said it yourself, he doesn't listen to me. I'm there to tidy his cabin and keep his uniforms washed and pressed, nothing more. He doesn't ask my advice on the moorings.'

'Then, let him know there is dissatisfaction among the men. If he asks you, say they are sinking beneath the weight of it. You have his ear and it's a valuable commodity on board a tub as small as ours. Let him know the feeling. Let him know they think he is leading them to their doom. I have promised the men that we will turn about and—'

'*You* have promised them, sir?' I asked, surprised now, for while I knew that Mr Christian did everything in his power to keep in with the men he was a terrible two-face behind their backs, insulting each and every one to the captain whenever the mood took him.

'Someone needs to maintain sanity around here, Turnip,' he said then. 'And someone needs to recognize that we have a mission to accomplish, not a dead man to emulate.' I said nothing to this; I knew to whom he was referring and didn't want to acknowledge that he might have been speaking sense. 'And if it falls to me—'

I pulled free of his grip then and stood staring at him for a moment before stepping back a pace or two. 'If it falls to you . . . what?' I asked, narrowing my eyes, unsure of what he meant.

Mr Christian bit his lip a little and looked as if he would enjoy nothing more than taking both his hands and throttling me where I stood. 'Just see that he understands,' he hissed, standing so close to me that his spittle was hitting my face.

'I must go below,' I said, panting as the storms roared about me and my clothes stuck to my skin, so soaked were they by the sleet.

'Then, think on what I say,' he shouted at me as I left, turning away now so that I could barely hear his words.

I ran back towards the stairs and below decks to find that all the work I had done earlier had been wasted, for the floor there was as sodden as I had ever seen it. I ran for my mops and went back to work before the captain might emerge from his cabin, but when I reached in and peeped my head inside he was not there and his greatcoat was gone and I realized that he was on deck too, helping at the worst of times, a captain among his sailors, a man among his own men, and I admired him all the more for it.

Another week passed and still nothing changed. The weather got worse; the men grew more and more exhausted. The boat was tossed around the seas with such little regard that I wondered on a hundred, a thousand, occasions whether tonight was to be the last night that I drew breath and whether my lungs would not be filled with sea water before daylight broke. The captain had changed the shifts again so the men were on deck for no more than a few hours at a time, but the result of it was that they came back to their bunks glassy-eyed, half-blinded and shivering, confused from the lashing they had received in the storms, lost in their timings and insufficiently rested to battle the storms better on their next trip above decks.

We came close to the 60th parallel and needed only another few degrees of longitude before lieing to and turning the boat around the Horn, but it became more and more clear that such a thing was not going to happen. Each morning the captain recorded our position on his chart and in the log-book and by the following morning we had barely advanced at all; some mornings, in fact, we had been routed backwards and had lost an entire day in the attempt.

Finally, the officers gathered in Captain Bligh's cabin as per his instructions and I poured each of them a mug of hot water with a little port in it, for the taste and comfort, as they awaited his presence. When he appeared, he was wet from head to foot and seemed a little surprised to see them there, even though it was he who had issued their summons, through me, not an hour beforehand.

'Good evening, gentlemen,' said he in a depressed tone, accepting my offer of his own mug with an exhausted nod of the head. 'Bad news, I'm afraid. We have barely advanced in eight days now.'

'Sir, no man could have run through this sea,' said Mr Fryer quietly. 'Not with these storms.'

The captain said nothing for a moment, but finally sighed deeply, a heavy inhalation and exhalation of breath, and I could see that he had finally been defeated. 'I really thought we could do it,' he muttered after a moment, looking up and offering them each a faint smile. 'I remember . . . I remember when I was on the *Endeavour* and we struggled with such a moment and one of the officers – I forget his name – said to the captain that we could never triumph over nature and he simply shook his head and said his name was Captain James Cook and King George himself had issued his orders, so nature must be tamed, it must obey the king. And tame it he did. Sadly, I don't appear to have his abilities.'

There was an embarrassed silence in the room. It was true that he had not managed to do what his great hero had done, but, still, the mission was there and we could not be without a captain for the remainder of it. For an awful moment I thought that he was about to resign his commission and place Mr Christian in charge of us all, but instead he stood up and ran a finger along his chart, coughed to clear his throat, and then announced to no one in particular: 'We shall turn round.'

'We shall turn round,' he repeated then in a louder voice, as if he had needed to hear himself say it again to believe that it would be so. 'We shall turn the ship and head eastwards, rounding the Cape of Good Hope at the southernmost tip of Africa, and then continue on towards Tasmania, beneath New Zealand and along north towards Otaheite. It will add ten thousand miles to our voyage, I'm afraid, but I see no alternative. Any who do, speak now.'

The silence continued. There was relief that the decision had finally been made, for none of us could imagine staying in these storms for very much longer without losing our minds entirely, if not our lives, but the idea of adding such an extension to the length of our trip sunk our hearts.

'It's the right decision, sir,' said Mr Fryer finally, to break the silence, and the captain looked up and smiled a little; I had never seen him so downhearted.

'When we turn, Mr Fryer, and when we reach calmer waters, I want all the men's clothing washed and dried and extra rations provided for all. We shall let them rest and all officers will take on whatever extra duties are necessary. I shall take them on myself if need be. We can secure ship's provisions and replenishments when we reach Africa.'

'Of course,' he replied. 'Shall I give Mr Linkletter the order?' Linkletter was the quartermaster, and the man responsible for the ship's steering during that shift.

The captain nodded and Mr Fryer left the cabin, followed in turn by the other officers when it became clear that there was no more to be said on the matter.

'Well, Master Turnstile?' said the captain when they were gone, turning to look at me with a half-smile about his face. 'What do you think of that? Are you disappointed in your old captain?'

'Proud of him, sir,' said I fiercely. 'I swear that if I'd been forced to stay in these storms another day I would have surrendered myself to them entirely. The men will be grateful to you too, you know. They were at their wits' ends.'

'They are good men,' he replied, nodding his head. 'They have worked hard. Still, the voyage ahead will not be easy. They realize that?'

'Aye, sir,' said I.

'And *you* realize it, Turnstile? We still have a long way to go before we reach our destination. You are ready for it?'

'Aye, sir,' I repeated, and for the first time I felt that I was, for now that I saw an end to our voyage in sight I had become even more determined not to go through all this torment any longer than necessary and instead to find a way off the *Bounty* and avoid the journey home. My fate, I knew, was in my own hands.

15

THERE WAS A CURIOUS ATMOSPHERE on board the *Bounty* in the days following Captain Bligh's decision. There wasn't a man on the ship who didn't feel relieved that we were no longer trying to round the Horn, but the notion of adding such an extra distance to our journey brought a gloom on all our heads that even the captain's offer of extra rations did little to dispel. We were a rum bunch during that week, I can tell you, dancing together on the deck in the evening time for exercise with scowls on our faces and boredom in our hearts. Still, the captain would have been right to ask us what we would have had him do, as it was the men themselves who believed we could never follow our original route; I believe he would have spent years stuck in the one spot trying to go round the Horn had the men been behind him on it.

I had taken to eating my meals with Thomas Ellison, a lad of my own age, who had been mustered as an able seaman and seemed at times to be one of the most unhappy fellows I had ever come across, on account of how he had been put on to the ship by his father, an officer in the navy, despite the fact that he had no aptitude for or interest in the sea. Sweet mother of divine Jesus, he didn't half like to complain. If the sun wasn't too hot, the winds were too chilly. If his bunk wasn't too hard, his sheet was too heavy. Still, for all that, we had age in common and spent a few passable hours together, even if he did like to lord it over me a little owing to his position as an AB and mine as naught but a servant boy. The distinction didn't mean pennies to me. If anything, my work was easier.

'I hoped to be back home by the summer time,' Ellison told me one afternoon as we ate, staring out at the sea ahead that would bring us to Africa, and the face on him would have curdled milk. 'My local cricket team will feel the loss of me, that's for sure.'

I couldn't help but give a snort of laughter when he said that. The local cricket team indeed! It was a long way from local cricket teams that I had been raised.

'Cricket, is it?' said I. 'I've never played the game myself. Never took an interest.'

'Never played cricket?' he asked me then, looking up from whatever muck Mr Hall had prepared for us and staring at me as if I had a second head growing out of my left shoulder. 'What kind of Englishman has never played cricket?'

'Listen here, Tommy,' said I. 'There's them as has things like that in their background and there's them as don't. And I'm one of them as don't.'

'It's *Mr* Ellison, Turnip,' said he, quick as you like, because although he suffered the indignity of talking to me on account of the fact that no one else much talked to him, he liked me to remember my place too, which was a thing I noticed on board ship just as much as on land. Them as have confidence in themselves never need to remind you of their superior social status, whereas those as don't have to ram it down your throat twenty times a day. 'I'm an able seaman, remember, and you're just a servant.'

'You're quite right, Tommy,' I replied, bowing my head in adoration. 'Mr Ellison, I mean. I do forget the difference, spending so much time with the captain and officers, I mean, on account of my position, while you lads are up here scrubbing the deck. I quite forget myself in my deliriums.'

He narrowed his eyes and glared at me for a moment, but then shook his head and looked out to sea, giving a long, dramatic sigh, such as he might have offered if he'd been the lead actress in a bawdy play on the stage.

'Of course, it's not just the cricket I miss,' said he, fishing for me to ask more.

'Oh, no?'

'Not *just* that, no. There are other . . . delights of my home town that I would like to revisit.'

I nodded, ran a finger round my bowl and licked it clean, for no matter how poor our food on board the *Bounty* it was a foolish cove who didn't finish it entirely. It was tasteless, certainly. And it rarely satisfied the appetite, that was for sure. But it was well cooked and healthy and didn't give you the squits, and that counted for something even if nothing else did.

'Right enough,' said I after a moment, for this was one of those times when I knew he wanted to tell me something but I wasn't sure I wanted to listen. Either way, I wasn't going to encourage him by asking questions that he would answer whether I asked them or not.

'I mean more personal delights, of course,' he added then.

180

'You get some good fruit trees down your way?' I asked him. 'Is it the season for them now? When the fellows are out on the crease? Strawberries, maybe, or gooseberries?'

Ellison looked around then and, seeing no one nearby, leaned forward in a conspiratorial fashion. I pulled back but he took me by the shoulder and pulled me closer to him; for a moment I was worried I was giving him the motions.

'There's a particular young lady,' he told me then. 'A Miss Flora-Jane Richardson. Daughter of Alfred Richardson, the victualler. You've doubtless heard of him? He's very well known in Kent.'

'I know him very well,' said I, who had never heard the name in my life and didn't give a tuppence for it. 'And a more decent fellow never squeezed a sausage or sliced a chop from Land's End to John O'Groats.'

'You're not wrong there. He's an excellent fellow. But his daughter, Flora-Jane, and I have an understanding,' he told me then, giggling like a schoolgirl and taking the reddenings a little. 'She says she'll wait for me to return and the night before I left for Portsmouth, which I didn't want to do but my father forced it upon me, she gave me her hand for a kiss and, do you know what, I did it too.'

'You saucy creature,' said I, leaning back and opening my mouth as if he had just told me the most astonishing secret, a detail of the most salacious scandal as had ever been heard by man or beast. 'You nimble thief! You pressed your lips to her hand, did you? My, oh my, you're practically married to her, then. Have you thought of names for the little 'uns yet?'

I could tell immediately that he was unhappy with my response, for he leaned back and took the reddenings even more and pursed his lips in irritation.

'You're poking fun,' said he, wagging a finger at me.

'Not in this world!' I cried, appalled by the calumny.

'You're jealous, Turnip, that's all it is. I bet you've never known

181

a Miss Flora-Jane Richardson in your life. You've probably never even been kissed.'

Now it was my turn to lose my sense of humour. The smile faded from my lips and the laughter from my heart as I opened my mouth to reply, but the words were lost to me and I found myself stuttering a response that made him mock me then. It was true, I had never known a Flora-Jane Richardson, or any young girl like her: that was not where my life had led me to date. That was not something I had been allowed. My heart started to beat a little faster inside my chest and I closed my eyes for a moment; the images that I had tried to keep out of my head began to return. The nights in Mr Lewis's establishment. My brothers and I, lined up against a wall, ready to be of service, upon a determination. The gentlemen who came in and looked us up and down, putting a finger under our chins to lift our faces to them while they called us pretty things. I was naught but a lad when he took me in; I couldn't be blamed for it, could I?

'You know what they say about Otaheite?' asked Ellison then, and I looked up at him, barely hearing his words.

'What's that?' I asked, blinking a little in the bright sunlight.

'About the women there? You know what they say?'

I shook my head. I knew nothing about Otaheite at all and hadn't thought to ask much about it either. For me it was just a land at the end of our voyage, where the breadfruits were to be collected, and from where I might escape this servitude if I hadn't found freedom before then.

'Every one of them goes around naked as the day she was born,' said Ellison, with a big happy head on him.

'Go along!' said I, amazed.

'It's true. The men all talk of it on board. That's one of the reasons they wanted to get there as soon as possible. To have at them. They don't live like us there, you see. Not like decent people. They've no civilization there like what we 'ave in England, which means we can do what we want to them and take them

182

whenever we want. They love it, you see, on account of the fact that we're a civilized people. They think there's no shame in their nakedness either; that's why they don't cover themselves.'

'If they're handsome ladies, there ain't, as far as I can tell.'

'And not only that, but they are willing,' said he, giggling again, and I swear I wanted to palm his cheek to make him act like a fellow with a whistle between his legs and not like a lass.

'They're willing?' I asked him, confused.

'More than willing,' he said.

I waited for a moment or two, to see whether he would offer anything more, but words came there none.

'Willing to what?' I asked.

'They're *willing*,' he repeated then, as if saying the words again and again would explain things better. 'With anyone at all. With all of us if we want. It's their way. They don't care.'

I nodded. I knew what he meant now, for I had been described in just such terms myself on many an occasion in my life and I knew just how 'willing' I had been.

'Oh,' said I. 'Right you are.'

'And all I know is that I'm willing if they are,' said he then, clapping his hands together in delight.

'And what of Miss Flora-Jane Richardson?' asked I, growling at him. 'Has she been forgotten already?'

'That's different,' said he, turning away. 'A man must have a wife, of course, a decent woman to bear his children and keep his house.'

'You're marrying her now?' I asked with a snort. 'You're naught but a lad.'

'I'm older than you are,' he snapped, for we had established already that although we were of an age, his month was three before mine. 'And, yes, I intend to marry Miss Richardson, but in the meantime, if the ladies of Otaheite are willing, then so am—'

A rough slap on the shoulder made me spin round. Another of

our age, the scut Mr Heywood, was standing over me, squeezing his spots.

'There you are, Turnip,' said he. 'You deserve a flogging for your indolence. Didn't you heard your name being roared?'

'No,' I snapped, standing up and almost falling over again as my legs had gone unnatural under me, for I had been sitting cross-legged and the blood had gone astray in them. 'Who wants me, then?'

'The captain does,' he said with a sigh, as if the weight of the world was on his shoulders and it was all he could do to keep us afloat. 'Wants his tea, don't he?'

I nodded and walked away from them, heading downstairs to the cabin, all the time thinking of the willing women of Otaheite. And I'll say it as it was: I hoped it weren't true. I hoped that they were decent, Christian women who would keep their stays on and their hands to themselves, because I didn't want any part of that nastiness. I'd never known a woman in my life and didn't want to. My experience of matters of a physical nature had been dark and painful and all of it was behind me, I was determined on that. For several years I had thought little of it, though. In a way, I was grateful to Mr Lewis. Why, he fed me after all. And he clothed me. And he gave me a bed with a clean sheet on the first of every month. And had he never picked me from the streets when I was a boy, what might have become of me?

I had a brother once, a lad a year or two older than I, by the name of Olly Muster, and he was one of the most popular fellows at Mr Lewis's establishment on account of his little snub nose and rosy lips that made grown women turn and wink at him in the street. Now Olly and I, we were more than just brothers at Mr Lewis's establishment, we were more like *brothers*, if you follow my meaning. Olly was already living there when I arrived and, as it was Mr Lewis's particular way to place a new lad in the company of an older one while he settled in, I ended up having great fortune on my side as it was Olly who was given the job of looking after me. Most of the older lads bullied the new boys – it was expected of them – but Olly wasn't like that. A more decent soul never lived on this earth. A gentler, kinder lad never breathed air, and I'll fight the man who says otherwise of him.

In those early days, Olly and I would lie in our bunk together as the sun went down and he'd ask me whether there wasn't some family somewhere who could take me in.

'Why would I want that?' I asked him. 'Don't I have a home here?'

'If a home you can call it,' he said, shaking his head. 'There's nothing here for you, Johnny. You should leave while you can. I wish I had.'

I didn't like to hear him talk that way, as I feared the morning I would wake up and not find him snoring in the bed beside me, but I couldn't say anything in contradiction. He'd been there years longer than I and knew it better. At that time, I was still an innocent. Mr Lewis hadn't yet revealed my true job to me. I had yet to partake in Evening Selection. In the meantime, as I was too young for anything else, I was trained in the art of pickpocketing by Olly, which was the day job of my brothers and me and a better teacher I could not have found, for he could have picked the crown off the king's head at the coronation and been out of the Abbey and on his way back to Portsmouth with it perched atop his bonce before anyone was any the wiser.

But things were not right between him and Mr Lewis, I knew that, and as the months passed they grew worse and worse. They argued regularly and sometimes Mr Lewis would threaten to expel him from his establishment, and for all his bravado, Olly was afraid to leave and would always back down when this happened. There was one particular gentleman, a gentleman whose name you would know, so I dare not mention it here; I will call him Sir Charles ——. (And if you think you know him from the *newspapers*, particularly when matters of *politics* are raised, you would not be barking up the wrong tree.) Sir Charles was a regular

185

visitor and when he would arrive he was almost always in his cups and then he would cry out for Olly, who was his particular favourite, and Mr Lewis would instruct him to follow Sir Charles into the gentleman's room.

One evening, there was a great commotion from in there and the door was flung open to reveal Sir Charles running towards us all with blood pouring down his head, a hand to the side of his face, his trousers tripping him up as he ran. 'He bit me!' he was screaming. 'The lad clean bit my ear off! I am maimed! Help me, Mr Lewis, sir, I am maimed!'

Mr Lewis jumped out of his seat in fright and ran towards him; he tried to pull the hand away to inspect the damage and, when he did, all of us boys gathered there let out a terrific scream, for where his ear should have been there was naught but a bloody great mess of blood. And then we looked down the corridor and there was Olly Muster standing in the altogether, blood on his face too, spitting the ear from his mouth, and it bounced off the floor and landed in a corner. 'No more,' he was shouting in a voice that wasn't his own. 'Not once more, do you hear me? Not one more time!'

And, oh, the trouble there was then! A doctor had to be called to treat the wounded man and Sir Charles picked up a poker to beat the life from Olly and he would have succeeded too if Mr Lewis hadn't been determined that there would be no murders on his premises, for that would have been the ruination of us all. Of course, Sir Charles didn't go to the police, for to have done so would have caused trouble for him too. But Olly was taken away by Mr Lewis and I never saw him after that. I would wander the streets hoping to find him, hoping he would find me too, for if he was to leave then maybe I could go with him and we would be brothers somewhere else, but my eyes never rested on him again and no one I asked could offer any help as to his whereabouts. The last words he said to me before he left were words of warning; he took me into a corner and told me that I should get away, that I was better than all of this, that I should go before it became a part of me. But I was too young to understand and saw only my dinner at the end of the day and the mattress I slept on. Once he was gone, however, it was my turn to take his place. It shames me to say that I got to know Sir Charles —— better then. He was a man of unusual tastes.

Mr Lewis told him that I was willing. And now there were to be equally willing women on Otaheite? I wanted no part of it.

'It's extraordinary, isn't it?' I heard a voice saying as I stepped towards the cabin below. 'Mr Fryer has thirty-five years on him and yet holds the same position on board the *Bounty* as you did on the *Resolution* at a mere twenty-one.'

'But you hold that position now, Fletcher,' came the reply. 'Although I have a year on you yet, do I not?'

'You do, sir. I am twenty-two. I grow ancient.'

I knocked on the door and the two men spun round. 'There you are, Turnstile, at last,' roared the captain in a hearty voice. 'I began to fear we had a man overboard.'

'My apologies, sir,' said I. 'I was eating my lunch with Mr Ellison and we got into a conversation about—'

'Yes, yes,' he said quickly, interrupting me, for he didn't give a flying fig about the events of my day. 'It matters not. Tea for Mr Christian and me if you please. The thirst is too much.'

'Yes, sir,' said I, stepping over to fetch his teapot and cups.

'Twenty-two,' he continued then to Mr Christian. 'A fine age. And who knows, perhaps when you are my age, thirty-three, would you believe, you will captain a ship yourself. A ship like the *Bounty*.'

Mr Christian smiled and I left the room, shuddering. A ship with him as its captain? Why, we'd spend the day picking lint from our uniforms and combing our hair before mirrors and never get more than a mile away from land. The idea was a farce but, still, it gave me something amusing to consider while I made the tea, dismissing the memories of Mr Lewis's establishment from my head, not to mention the prospect of the willing ladies of Otaheite. A double bonus.

16

No one can go through life without getting a little luck on their side from time to time and I'll be damned if my little bit of luck didn't come around when we reached False Bay, an inlet where the *Bounty* docked after rounding the Cape of Good Hope at the southern tip of Africa. For weeks I had been hoping that the chance would come for me to get off the ship and make my escape and, finally, without warning, it was upon me and I saw my opportunity.

I had been following our progress daily on the charts in Captain Bligh's cabin and could tell that we had made good time through the waters that brought us from stormy South America to sunny South Africa and there was great relief and cheer among the men when land finally appeared in our sightlines. We anchored the ship while Mr Christian and Mr Fryer – together – went ashore to see whether this was a friendly environment, and when they returned we were informed that we might stay there for a week to replenish the ship and make repairs for the remainder of our outward journey towards Australia and Otaheite. They also brought with them an invitation from Commander Gordon, who was in charge of the Dutch settlement at False Bay, for Captain Bligh to dine with him. On the chosen evening I laid out his finest uniform for him in his cabin and was busy examining the local terrain on the wall charts when he came in to change.

'Turnstile, what's the matter with you, lad?' he asked me, blustering into the room, full of good cheer. 'Have you nothing better to do than stand around idly? Look lively, there's a good fellow. There's plenty of work to be done on deck if you can't find something to occupy your time down here.'

'Yes, sir, sorry, sir,' said I, wishing to study the map for a little longer as I was examining the area around the Bay for potential escape routes.

'What were you looking at there anyway?'

'Where, sir?' I asked nervously.

'You were looking at my maps,' said the captain, coming over now and looking at them suspiciously. 'Why would you be doing that? Finally taking an interest in the nautical life, are you?'

I felt my face take on the reddenings and a moment, an hour, a lifetime, seemed to pass as I sought an answer before, finally, a memory of how my story had begun came to me and I blurted it out, not caring how ridiculous I sounded.

'China, sir,' said I. 'I was looking for China.'

'China?' asked Captain Bligh, frowning and staring at me as if I was lying there in my cups and making no sense at all. 'Why on earth would you be looking for China on a map of Africa?'

'It's only that I wasn't sure where it was,' I replied. 'I happen to have read two books on China, as it goes, and they caused me a great deal of interest.'

'Did they indeed?' he asked, more willing to believe me now before turning round and examining the freshly laid-out suit for creases. 'And what were they about, these books of yours?'

'The first dealt with an adventure,' I told him, 'And a series of tasks, followed by a marriage. The second . . .' I hesitated now, remembering that the second was a saucy book, with pictures of an immoral nature contained within. 'The second was much the same,' I said then. 'Another adventure. Of a sort.'

'I see,' said he. 'And where did you get these books, might I ask? I don't recall there being much in the way of leisure reading on board the *Bounty*.'

'Mr Lewis gave them to me,' I explained. 'Him as looked after me when I was a lad.'

'Mr Lewis?' he asked. 'I don't recall you mentioning his name before.'

'I haven't,' I said. 'You've never asked me where I came from before I ended up here.'

He turned round slowly then and stared at me, narrowing his eyes, wondering whether I was cheeking him, I dare say, although I wasn't. It was merely a statement of fact. A silence hung in the air between us for a few moments, but finally he just sighed and turned back to his vestments.

'You may leave now while I change,' he said. 'I have what has the makings of a very pleasant evening ahead of me and I'll be damned if I haven't earned it.'

As things turned out it must have been an even more pleasant evening than he had imagined, for the next I saw of him was at the crack of dawn the following morning when, with the tip of his boot, he knocked me out of my bunk to the floor, returning me to consciousness without so much as a by-your-leave, a fate I was growing more and more accustomed to.

'Come along, lad,' he roared cheerfully. How he managed to keep his wits about him and retain an air of jollity at such an ungodly hour is anyone's guess. 'The two of us are going ashore this morning.'

'Ashore?' said I, opening my eyes wide now, for here was my chance to get off the blasted ship at last. 'Both of us?'

'Aye, both of us,' he snapped, suddenly irritated (he really was a one for a change of mood). 'I'm always having to repeat myself around you, Turnstile – why is that? Sir Robert is taking me to the hills to show me some of the excellent flora that graces the land here and is allowing me to take some cuttings back to Sir Joseph in London.'

I nodded and pulled myself together. He was already walking past me and marching down the corridor, so I suspected I was not to be given the benefit of breakfast; instead it was all I could do to keep pace with him in his excitement. (From that day to this, I'm not sure I've ever known a man who could survive on such little sleep as the captain and still manage to keep his wits about him.) On deck, he gave some instructions to Mr Christian, who looked at me a little uncertainly.

'Perhaps I should come with you, Captain,' he said, the smarm. 'Mr Fryer or Mr Elphinstone can take charge of the boat. Why take Turnip with you anyway? He's just a servant-lad.'

'And a very fine servant-lad he is too,' replied the captain, slapping me on the back as if I was his own son. 'Master Turnstile will be responsible for gathering the cuttings in a basket for me. But I need you here, Fletcher. Keeping the men busy with the repairs. I don't want us having to stay in Africa any longer than necessary even though it is, as you can see, a very pleasant diversion for a couple of days. We've lost enough time as it is.'

'Very good, sir,' said Mr Christian with a sigh.

I didn't dare offer him the smug look that I was harbouring inside lest it came back to haunt me at a later date. I knew that he would have preferred to stay a little longer, as the gossip had already spread around the ship about a dalliance he was enjoying with a local molly. I had the mark of him already, that was for sure.

A carriage awaited us at the end of the gangway and a few minutes later the captain and I were on our way through the dusty streets, leaving the shadow of the boat behind us.

'You mentioned Sir Joseph earlier, Captain,' said I after a few minutes, turning from looking out at the unfamiliar surroundings and back towards him in curiosity.

'I did indeed.'

'You've mentioned him many times on our voyage, in fact. Might I ask who he is?'

He stared at me and smiled. 'My dear boy, haven't you ever heard the name of Sir Joseph Banks?'

I shook my head. 'No, sir,' I replied. 'I haven't. Except from your own lips, of course.'

The captain looked startled by my innocence. 'Why, I thought every lad of your age knew the name of Sir Joseph and idolized him for it. He's a great man. A very great man indeed. Without him, none of us would be here.'

For a moment, I thought he was comparing him to the Saviour himself, but this was just a fancy; I said nothing, just continued to look at him and await an answer.

'Sir Joseph is the finest botanist in England,' he said finally. 'Ha! Said I England? I should say the world. A brilliant collector of rare and exotic plants. A man of great taste and sensibility. He sits on numerous boards and committees and advises Mr Pitt on many matters of social and ecological interest, as he did for Portland, Shelburne and Rockingham before him. He owns a great many conservatories and is the recipient of so much correspondence from keen botanists around the world that they say he keeps a dozen secretaries on hand to answer them all. And above all that, it was his idea for us to undertake our mission.'

I nodded, unembarrassed by my ignorance. 'I see,' I said, leaning forward. 'A famous chap, then, I imagine. And, Captain, may I ask one further question?'

'You may.'

'This mission of ours . . . what is it exactly?'

The captain stared at me before letting a roar of laughter escape his lips and shaking his head. 'My dear boy, how long have we been on the *Bounty* together now? Five months, is it? And every day you have stood around my cabin, or in it, and listened to the conversation of the officers and the men and you mean to tell me that you don't know what our mission is? Can you be quite so ignorant or are you performing a turn for me?'

'I apologize, sir,' said I, sitting back, my face scarlet with embarrassment. 'I didn't mean to make you ashamed of me.'

'No, it is I who should apologize,' he replied quickly. 'Truly,

Turnstile, I was not mocking you. I merely meant that this is a matter that must have crossed your mind on any number of occasions since we set sail and yet you have never raised it until now.'

'I didn't like to ask, sir,' I said.

'If you don't ask, you shall never discover. Our mission, my dear young boy, is one of the utmost importance. You are aware no doubt of England's slave colonies on the West Indies?'

I knew nothing of these so did the only thing that seemed sensible in the circumstances. I nodded my head and said that I was.

'Well,' continued he, 'the slaves there . . . regardless of their savage nature, they are still men and they want feeding. But as to the cost to the Crown of keeping them, well, I don't have the exact figures but they are considerable. Now some years ago, when Captain Cook and I were on board the *Resolution*, we brought home to England various samples of plant and food life which we discovered on the islands of the South Pacific and among them was a particular item known as the breadfruit. It's an extraordinary thing. Shaped rather like . . . like a coconut, if you can believe it, but growing in the soil. An excellent source of nourishment and protein, and cheap to produce too. We go to collect as many thousand of these breadfruit as we can procure and transport them on our way home to the West Indies, where they will be replanted and more grown, thus saving the Crown considerable expense.'

'And keeping the men in chains,' said I.

'What's that?' he asked.

'Our mission is to make it cheaper to keep men enslaved.'

He stared at me and hesitated before answering. 'You say that . . . Turnstile, I don't follow you. Do you feel that we shouldn't feed the men?'

'No, sir,' I said, shaking my head. He was not the type to follow my line of thinking; he was too well educated and of too high a social class to have respect for the rights of man. 'I'm glad I finally know, that's all. Our great cabin will be filled with these bread-fruit soon enough, then, I expect.'

'As soon as we can get there and collect them, yes. It's an adventure of great merit that we are engaged in, Turnstile,' he told me then, wagging his finger at me as if I was a babe in arms. 'Some day, when you are an old man, you will look back and tell your grandchildren of it. Perhaps their own slaves will be fed on breadfruit then too, and you will feel enormous pride at our achievements.'

I nodded but wasn't sure that I would. We travelled on in silence then for some time and I looked out of the window of the carriage, pleased to be able to lay my eyes on something other than the vast blue water of the ocean for a change. All the same, I felt disappointed that the terrain was mostly green and mountainous and seemed to offer little in the way of roads or villages to which I might escape.

We came to a stop in the centre of a small village and the pres-ence of our carriage, along with another of equal splendour, seemed out of place there, but as we pulled in, a man emerged from a saloon and strolled towards us with his arms outstretched, smiling pleasantly.

'William,' he cried in a hearty voice. 'So pleased you could make it.'

'Sir Robert,' replied the captain, stepping down and shaking his hand. 'I wouldn't have missed it for anything. I brought my lad with me to carry the cuttings. I hope that's all right.'

Sir Robert's face grimaced for a moment as he sized me up and down and finally he shook his head, as if he disapproved of me entirely. 'If you don't mind, William,' he said, leaning forward, 'my own man will accompany us for that. There are state matters of an urgent nature I wish to discuss with you and it would be inappropriate for me to do so in front of strangers. I dare say he is trustworthy, but—'

'Of course, of course,' said Captain Bligh quickly, taking the baskets off me and placing them back in the carriage; another fellow, older than I and far more serious-looking, emerged with baskets from the saloon and stood near by. 'Turnstile, you may go back to the boat.'

I looked around, disappointed, for I had been looking forward to a long walk and an opportunity to see the land and plan my route. It must have been obvious, for Sir Robert caught the expression on my face and clapped me on the back.

'The poor boy's been on that boat for so many months,' he said. 'Perhaps, William, you wouldn't object to him waiting for you in the saloon here where he can be given lunch and you can return together later?'

The captain thought about it for only a moment and then, to my delight, nodded his head. 'Certainly,' he said. 'A fair response. But let us begin, Sir Robert. I am anxious to see as much of your plant life as I can. As you know, Sir Joseph expects . . .'

His voice grew more distant as the two men strolled away from me and I turned to look at several of Sir Robert's servants, who nodded in my direction and motioned me indoors and out of the sun.

'No need to look so despondent,' one of them said as I walked. 'Believe you me, you're better off sitting here for the day than walking up and down mountainsides all afternoon.'

'You might not say that had you been stuck on board a ship for the last five months,' I countered, but the quick appearance of food changed my mind, as my plate contained meat and potatoes and vegetables, freshly cooked, a feast I had not expected or seen since before Christmas.

I ate quickly and hungrily as various members of Sir Robert's entourage talked to me, trying to learn as much about our ship as they could. The Dutch settlement had existed at False Bay for many decades and, as it turned out, most of the people working on it were as anxious to return to Holland as I was to escape the

Bounty. But would they leave me alone? They would not. Finally I got them engaged on the subject of geography and learned that the nearest city was Cape Town, and resolved that I would make my way there. It was only late in the evening, when alcohol was served, that I finally managed to make my way out of the saloon and find myself alone.

The sun had gone down and in truth I was surprised that the captain and Sir Robert had not returned yet, but it made it more difficult for me to find my way to the path. There were no signs anywhere and I knew nothing of Cape Town other than its general direction, north-west, and resolved that I would find somewhere to hide over night and then judge the compass by the rising of the sun the following morning. I had not gone ten minutes down the road when I started to hear sounds.

On board ship, all is either quiet or noise. Either we are in calm waters, when the men are silent and stare ahead and keep the ship at peace, or in noisy waters, when they shout and create a great clamour. At Mr Lewis's establishment, there was never anything but noise – from my brothers, from the streets below, from the gentlemen in their cups. But here, in this strange place with nothing but mountains and hills around me, I fancied that I could hear animal life ready to attack me and claim me as a worthy dinner. And then footsteps. And voices. I knew there were often criminals hiding out in places like this, but I convinced myself that these sounds were no more than my imagination playing tricks, until they grew louder and louder and I realized that from the direction in which I was walking there were men walking towards me. I hesitated, looked to my left and right in the darkness, and was about to break into a run in the opposite direction, when a hand landed heavily on my shoulder and I jumped and shouted out in fright.

'Turnstile,' roared the voice. 'What the devil are you doing here?'

My eyes grew accustomed to the darkness and my ears recognized the familiar voice.

'Captain,' said I. 'I got lost.'

'Lost?' asked Sir Robert. 'You're a good fifteen minutes away from the saloon. What has brought you out here at this time of night?'

I could tell that the captain was staring at me in surprise and I thought on my feet. 'I came outside to relieve myself, sir,' said I. 'And I went a little too far away from the saloon to do so. When I was finished I couldn't find my way back. I ended up here.'

'A good job we found you, then,' said Sir Robert, laughing. 'You might have wandered all night. You might have ended up in Cape Town, you're headed exactly in that direction.'

'Aren't there conveniences at the saloon?' asked the captain suspiciously.

'Oh, yes, sir,' said I. 'Only, I didn't think to use them on account of my being naught but a servant. I thought they were reserved for the quality.'

He nodded then and indicated that I should follow them, and so I did, angry with myself for getting caught, my first chance of escape destroyed. Sir Robert's man was laden down with baskets of cuttings, roots and smaller plants and when we arrived back at the carriage they were placed carefully on the floor between us.

'I hope I've not overdone it,' muttered Captain Bligh as we took the carriage back. 'But I swear that I could have taken a tenfold amount, there was so much of interest. I must give these to Mr Nelson when we're aboard and see that he keeps them well. Sir Joseph will be delighted.'

'Yes, sir,' said I, watching ahead for the ship. The water appeared suddenly, as if out of nowhere, and upon it I saw our tall sails blowing back and forth in the breeze.

'Turnstile,' said the captain as we drew closer to it. 'Earlier, when we found you, you *were* lost, weren't you?'

'Of course I was,' said I, unable to look him in the eye. 'I said as much, didn't I? I couldn't find my way back.'

'Only, there are serious penalties in His Majesty's navy for

197

deserters. Just so you remember that.'

I said nothing, just looked outside at the *Bounty*, the place I had lived for the past five months and which, to my surprise, I was not unhappy to see again. It was a home, of sorts.

17

THERE WAS ONE MORE incident that took place before our ship left South Africa and continued on her merry way and it left something of a dark cloud behind us after we departed.

The *Bounty* had suffered more than her share of hardship and rough weather since leaving England before Christmas and the so-called rest that the men were supposed to have enjoyed at False Bay was overtaken by almost as much hard work as we had endured during any of the stormy days that we had met at sea. The captain and the officers, on the other hand, were enjoying the hospitality of Sir Robert and the officers of the Dutch settlement, and as this usually involved an evening meal my own nights were not quite so busy as they had once been. In fact the only day that I was engaged upon my regular duties was on our last evening before setting sail again, when Sir Robert invited all the officers to a ball at his home and I was press-ganged into making sure that all their uniforms were clean and starched for the evening's entertainment. And you should have seen the bunch of fine fellows who went off that night, clean and shiny, ready to meet the ladies, their hair pomaded and their skin washed in cologne. Only poor Mr Elphinstone was left behind to watch the ship, and he wasn't happy about it one little bit, but good enough for him, for if we regular boys couldn't enjoy the festivity, then why should he, and he earned no sympathy from any of them.

Late the following afternoon I was on deck assisting in the polishing of the woodwork with Edward Young, a midshipman who had been allowed ashore every morning to worship at the local church on account of his religious fervour. I didn't let the fact of it put me off him; other than that, he was a perfectly rational and pleasant man.

'You'll be sorry to leave the church behind,' I said to him, for once we were under way again he'd have no recourse but to whisper his words to the Saviour from the vantage point of his bunk. 'You were a lucky dog to get off the boat every morning for it, though, weren't you?'

'The captain was generous in allowing it, aye,' he told me. 'And I thank him for it. You should have come with me, Turnip. You strike me as a lad who could do with a little more Bible in his life.'

I was about to answer this in a manner that he might not have liked, when what did I see, only Sir Robert's carriage charging down the path towards the ship.

'Here's another one who could use the Saviour,' said Young, nodding his head in the direction of the carriage. 'Come to invite them all to enjoy more frivolity at his lair, I imagine. Dancing, drinking and carnal behaviour that will damn their souls.'

'I didn't know he was expected,' said I, putting my brush down and looking up at the sky to judge the time, a talent I had grown more skilled at as the months had gone on. 'The captain never mentioned anything about it.'

I watched as Sir Robert stepped out of his carriage and stood there for a moment, staring at the *Bounty* with a thunderous look on his face, before marching towards the gangway and making his way to the top, where Mr Elphinstone stepped over to meet him. I noticed Mr Heywood, the scut, walking quickly away to a place where he would not be seen, but thought little of it at the time other than that he was an unsociable brute who would partake of a man's hospitality on one evening and then snub him the next day.

'Good afternoon, Sir Robert,' said Mr Elphinstone, acting as if he was master of the boat and not one of the more junior officers on board. 'I'm delighted to see you actually. It gives me an opportunity to thank you for the—'

'Out of my way, sir,' said Sir Robert, swatting him aside with the flat of his hand as he marched past while all the time looking back and forth along the deck, his eyes darting like ferrets, until he spied me hovering in the background and, remembering my face from our introduction earlier in the week, stepped towards me at such a pace that I retreated a few steps, thinking he was going to strike me down. My mind raced with the possibilities of what I might have done to offend him but, try as I might, I could think of naught. 'You,' he said, pointing his great fat finger at me. 'I know you, boy, don't I?'

'John Jacob Turnstile, sir,' said I. 'The captain's servant-lad.'

'Your name matters not a jot to me. Where is your master?'

His face was scarlet with barely suppressed rage and for a moment I was wary of telling him, lest their interview should end violently. I had seen him almost every day that we had been in False Bay and had never known him to have the tremors like this.

'I'll . . . I'll inform Captain Bligh that you seek an audience,' I said, making my way to the stairs. 'If you'd like to wait on deck and take the air for a moment.'

'Thank you, I'll follow if it's all the same to you,' he said, stepping into pace so close behind me that, had I stopped short for a moment, the two of us would have collided into each other and I would have come off the worse for it, for he was a large man – a fat one, if I want to be uncharitable. I would have landed on the deck. A mashed Turnip.

'This here's the great cabin,' said I as we trundled along, for even though the man was in a state close to collapse it gave me the giggles to pretend that none of it seemed in any way important to me, since he hadn't even been interested in having the polite acquaintance of my name. 'As you see, we have hundreds of pots here for the breadfruit when we reach Otaheite but they just sit here at the moment, getting in my way. Except of course for the plants the captain brought back from his botanizing with you. Now, they've been put in the care of Mr Nelson, him as—'

'Lad, I'll tell you this once and I'll not say it again,' said he then in a dark and troubled voice behind me. 'Close your mouth and keep it closed. I'll not hear any more of your garble.'

I did what he said, I closed my mouth, for it occurred to me then that maybe there wasn't a farce to be had here at all and that Sir Robert was on a more serious mission than I realized; what it could have been, I didn't dare imagine. I said nothing further for the rest of our short journey, save to tell him that the captain's cabin was just a little further along.

When we reached the door, it was – most unusually – shut. Captain Bligh almost never closed his cabin door, preferring the men to feel that they could approach him on any matter of import at any hour of the night or day. Even during the dark hours he left it partially open, which was a great grievance to me, as he was a fierce snorer and from my bunk outside his cabin I could hear every ingress and egress of his breathing as I tried to sleep and oftentimes it made me want to take a pillow and suffocate one or the pair of us with it.

'If you could just wait here a moment, sir,' I pleaded, turning round. 'I'll let him know that you're outside.'

Sir Robert nodded and I gave a quick two-tap knock on the door. There was no answer for a moment, so I knocked again and this time, the captain barked out an 'Enter!' from inside, so I turned the handle and stepped in. The captain was sitting with Mr Fryer and the two men were deep in conversation, but they looked across at me irritably when I entered.

'Yes, Turnstile, what is it?' asked the captain with a great deal of impatience in his voice.

I noted that he looked quite red-faced and angry and that Mr Fryer was a little paler and yet had a determined air to him.

'Very sorry to disturb you, Your Magnificence,' said I, all politeness now, 'only, you have a visitor as desires a moment of your time.'

'Tell the men I can't spare a moment right now,' he said quickly, dismissing me. 'Mr Christian and Mr Elphinstone are on deck. They can take care of whatever nonsense—'

'It's not one of the men, sir,' said I immediately. 'It's Sir Robert. From the settlement.'

The captain opened his mouth for a moment and then closed it again, turning to look at Mr Fryer, who raised an eyebrow at him, as if he wasn't in the least surprised by the identity of our visitor. 'Sir Robert is here?' asked the captain in something approaching a whisper.

'Standing outside your door,' I replied. 'Shall I ask him to wait?'

'Yes,' he said quickly, stroking his whiskers, before looking at Mr Fryer and changing his mind. 'No, I can't do that, can I? I can't ask a man like that to wait. Height of rudeness and discourtesy! You had better send him in. Mr Fryer, you'll remain here for this?'

'I don't know as I should, Captain,' came the reply. 'Wouldn't you prefer to—'

'For pity's sake, sir, you'll wait and show a little solidarity for once,' he hissed quietly. 'Show him in, Turnstile. No, stay that order! Tell me this. What kind of mood is he in?'

I stared at him, surprised by the question. 'I beg your pardon, sir?'

'His mood, lad, his mood,' he repeated irritably. 'Does he seem cheerful or—'

'Vexed, sir,' said I, considering it. 'All told, I would say he seems a trifle on the vexed side.'

'Right,' he said, standing up and sighing heavily. 'Well, we had better not keep him waiting any longer, then. Show him in.'

I nodded and opened the door and there was Sir Robert, pacing up and down the corridor, his hands clasped together behind his back, his face appearing like a cloud of thunder preparing to break over us all.

'Sir Robert,' said I, 'the captain will see you now.'

He barely acknowledged me then, the rude bollix, just marched right past me and straight into the captain's cabin. But any adventure is a break from the boredom of the day, and this being too great a lark to pass up I followed him inside too.

'Sir Robert,' said the captain, stepping forward with his hand outstretched, acting as if this was a great honour and not seeming as nervous as he had a moment before. 'How delightful to see you again. I . . .' He stopped for a moment then, saw me standing in the corner and glared at me. 'That will be all, Turnstile,' he said.

'I thought you might like some tea, sir,' said I. 'Or Sir Robert might care for a brandy,' I added, for the fellow did seem awful contraire.

The captain hesitated and narrowed his eyes at me before looking at his guest. 'A brandy, Sir Robert?'

'I know not what sailing men are like, but for my part I care not for brandy when I have yet to have my luncheon, sir,' he barked angrily. 'I do, however, require your full attention for what I have to tell you.'

'Thank you, Turnstile, you may leave us,' said the captain then and I had no choice but to go, but on this occasion I didn't pull the door fully behind me, though, and, after checking that no one was about at this end of the boat, I put my ear to it, and it was as good as being inside, especially with the volume Sir Robert was speaking at.

'I dare say you know why I am here, sir,' said Sir Robert.

'I do not,' replied the captain. 'Although I am of course delighted to see you. And may I take this opportunity to thank you and your lady wife for the delightful ball last night. I enjoyed it very much, as did my officers, who—'

'Aye, your officers, sir,' he snapped then, as aggressively as before. 'Your officers indeed, sir! It is those same officers whom I come to speak to you about, the same ones as enjoyed the hospitality of my home and ate my food and drank my wine. 'Tis one officer in particular I wish to discuss with you.'

'Really?' said the captain, not sounding as confident as he had before. 'I trust they all comported themselves as gentlemen?'

'Most of them, aye. But I stand here to tell you that one comported himself in the manner of a rabid dog in heat and I am here to demand satisfaction of you, because I swear to you that if I had a dog like that in my household I'd take out my pistol and shoot him dead and no one would think the worse of me for it.'

There was a long silence then and I could hear some muttering within, words I could not make out, but then the voices were louder again and it was Sir Robert speaking.

'. . . Into my house and meet my family and all the ladies and gentlemen of a settlement where, I promise you, sir, we have worked long and hard to establish homes and security and a decent, Christian way of life. And this so-called officer dares to insult a lady. Now, I don't know whether it is the habit of English officers—'

'I assure you, sir, it is not,' replied the captain, his voice raised now too, for as unwilling as he was to be abused on his own ship he would never have taken a slight on His Majesty's naval officers as anything to be endured without reply. 'It behoves me to declare there's not a man on board this ship who does not have the greatest respect for you, sir, and for the settlement you have established here in South Africa. They hold you in the highest esteem, sir,' he added fiercely.

'Behove me no behoves, sir!' shouted Sir Robert. 'Respect, is it? And if they have so much respect, perhaps you will let me know how such a low dog could suggest such a vile proposition to a young lady? It may be that he speaks to his harlots in England like that, his whores and his slatterns, his tarts and his fallen women, but Miss Wilton is a decent and upstanding Christian lady, a fine and respectable girl, and ever since her father died I have taken a particular interest in her well-being, so an insult against her is a glove across the cheek to me and a sting for which I will demand satisfaction. Had I known for one moment that an officer attached to this ship would have behaved in such a base fashion, I would never have invited any of you to take entertainment with us, nor would I have offered such assistance to you this last week as you have required. I would have had you all run off, I tell you!'

'And for that very hospitality, sir, I am deeply grateful,' replied Captain Bligh. 'Deeply grateful.' He hesitated for a few moments before saying anything else and I just knew that both Sir Robert and Mr Fryer were staring at him, waiting for him to make his judgement. 'The charge is a serious one,' he said finally. 'And as much as I will defend any man of mine to the bitter end until I have reason to do otherwise, I stand before you ashamed that you feel that you had to come on board and lay such a charge against one of my own. I am grateful for all that you have done for us and, if you will accept it, I offer you my word as a gentleman and as an officer of King George that I will take this charge up with the officer in question and deal with him accordingly. There will be no whitewash of this, I assure you. I happen to take courtesy and decent manners very seriously, and I take the proper respect shown to ladies even more seriously. My own dear wife, Betsey, would attest to that. I apologize on his behalf, sir, and promise that justice will be served.'

Another long silence followed as Sir Robert weighed this up. It was a fair response on the captain's behalf and there was little he could add to it. I stood at the door, desperate to know what the charge was and, even more importantly, against whom it was laid, but the sound of movement in the nearby galley from Mr Hall forced me to step away in case I was caught in the act of eavesdropping and received a box to my ears that would leave me hearing bells for the rest of the day. I hovered around the corridor, however, hoping for the cook to go back to wherever he had been

205

before so I might put my ear to the door again, but a few moments later it opened and Captain Bligh and Sir Robert emerged, the former looking at me for a moment and narrowing his eyes irritably.

'And you are leaving within the hour?' asked Sir Robert, who was not as red-faced now as he had been when he stormed on board; he was apparently placated by whatever had been agreed within.

'Indeed we are, sir,' said the captain. 'We have a long voyage ahead of us still. Around Australia and up to Otaheite. Another couple of months, I dare say.'

'Then, I wish you well with it and Godspeed,' said Sir Robert, offering his hand. 'I only regret that our acquaintance had to end in such a disappointing fashion.'

'As do I, Sir Robert, but please be assured that I will take whatever steps are necessary to redeem our standing in your eyes and I will write to you when I am satisfied with the result of my enquiries.' Sir Robert nodded his head and the captain turned to look at me. 'Turnstile,' said he, with a note of sarcasm in his voice, 'since you are so fortuitously and unexpectedly close at hand, perhaps you will see our guest back to the deck?'

'Of course, sir,' said I, unable to look him in the eye.

'And Mr Fryer, fetch Mr Heywood and Mr Christian, if you will.'

'Yes, sir,' said Mr Fryer.

A few minutes later I was back downstairs, having escorted Sir Robert back to the deck silently, and this time the captain had forgotten to close his cabin door fully, which allowed me to hear better the inquisition taking place inside. Happily for me I had not missed very much, for whatever Mr Christian was saying, the captain was having none of it.

'That is not what I have asked you here to discuss,' said the captain in a sharp voice. 'And I have only asked you to join Mr Heywood since you were present at the ball with him and know his character better than any other on board, perhaps.'

'Sir,' said the scut, 'I don't know what you've been informed, but—'

'And you, sir,' roared the captain in such a scream as I'd never heard emerge from him before, not even during one of his arguments with Mr Fryer, nor even in the aftermath of Matthew Quintal's lashing. 'You will keep that mouth of yours closed, shut firmly, until such times as I address you and ask you a question and demand of you an answer. You have brought shame on me, sir, and on this ship and on His Majesty's navy to wit, do you understand that? Are you aware what is being said about all of us back at Sir Robert's settlement? So keep your mouth closed until I invite you to do otherwise or I swear, by God, I'll take a lash to you myself, do you understand?'

A silence. And then a 'yes, sir' mumbled in a tiny voice that already sounded broken.

No one said anything more for a few moments and I could hear the captain pacing the floor within. 'Mr Christian,' he said finally in a calmer voice but one filled with anxiety nonetheless, 'tell me this. You were in Mr Heywood's company for much of the evening?'

'Much of it,' he replied. 'But not all of it.'

'And are you familiar with this Miss Wilton? I confess I can't recall meeting her myself.'

'I am, sir,' said Mr Christian. 'I made her acquaintance during the evening.'

'And you, young fellow-my-lad,' said Mr Bligh. 'You are aware of the charge?' No answer. 'You may speak,' barked the captain.

'I'm not, sir, honest I'm not, sir. I was just on deck, minding my business, working with the men, when Mr Fryer comes up and says you required my presence and I don't know what it is I'm meant to have done, I swears it.'

'Ha!' laughed the captain. 'You mean to tell me that you are completely in ignorance of what Sir Robert has accused you of?'

'Yes, sir.'

'Then, you're either an innocent and have been badly slandered or are guilty of barefaced lying to your commanding officer in addition to everything else. Which is it to be, sir?'

'I am innocent, sir.'

'Innocent of what?'

'Of whatever it is I am accused of, sir.'

'Well, there's a catch-all reply,' said the captain angrily after a moment. 'And you, Mr Christian, are you equally ignorant of the charge?'

'I confess, sir,' said Mr Christian, all quiet and calm, 'I have no knowledge of what it is that Sir Robert accuses Mr Heywood. I was under the impression that a pleasant evening was had by all.'

'As was I, sir, as was I!' snapped the captain. 'But now I am informed that Mr Heywood here, having been granted the honour of several dances by this Miss Wilton, a ward of Sir Robert's I might add—'

'I did dance with her,' said Mr Heywood quickly. 'I confess to that. I danced two waltzes and a polka, but I thought it an acceptable thing to do.'

'Two waltzes and a polka, is it?' asked the captain. 'And why, might I add, did you see fit to lavish so much attention on the lass?'

'Well, sir,' he replied after a slight hesitation, 'I can't pretend other than that she was bonny. And a fair dancer too. I thought she might enjoy the favour of it.'

'Did you indeed? And when these dances were over, what did you do then?'

'Sir, I thanked her most humbly for the kindness she had shown me and returned to Mr Christian's company.'

'Is that true, Mr Christian?'

'Sir, the night was a long one,' said Mr Christian. 'And we were, all of us, dancing and engaging in conversation with the other guests. I can't recall the moment precisely – I would have no reason for marking it – but as I spoke with Mr Heywood on many occasions, and as I know him to be a gentleman, I'm sure it must be true.'

'Well, then, we have a divergence of opinion, sir,' said the captain angrily. 'A most serious divergence of opinion. For Ms Wilton claims that you invited her to take a turn in the gardens with you for some refreshment and that while walking you made a most lewd and improper suggestion.'

'Not in this world, sir!' shouted Mr Heywood, and I confess that he sounded so wounded by the allegation that I half-believed him myself.

'Not in this world, is it? So it is your contention that you did not invite Miss Wilton for a constitutional?'

'I did not, sir!'

'And while doing so, you did not take her hand and push her against a tree where you attempted to make kiss with her?'

'Sir, I . . . I must protest,' he replied. 'In the strongest terms possible, I must protest. I did nothing of the sort. It is a lie.'

'A lie, is it? She says differently. She says you manhandled her and tried to press an advantage, and were she not taller and stronger and thus able to push you away she fears you might have compromised her for eternity and ruined her. And added to that, before Sir Robert arrived on deck, I had it from a reputable source that you were in your cups, sir, and disgracing yourself with a lascivious jest relating to the adventures of a late Russian empress and her charging-horse.'

Mr Heywood said nothing for a moment, but when he did speak his voice was as low as I had ever heard. 'Captain Bligh,' he says, 'you have my word as a gentleman, you have my word as an officer of King George, God bless his holy name, and you have my word as a Christian man, and an *English* Christian man at that, that the events you speak of did not take place. At least not with me as the leading player in the folly. If Miss Wilton found herself in an unhappy position with some gentleman at the ball and now regrets it, then she may take her fancies out on another, but she may think again about involving me in her naughty escapade, for it was not I, sir. Not I, sir, I swear it.'

A long silence ensued and when the captain finally spoke he sounded less angry than before and more perplexed and irritated by the whole mess of it. 'Fletcher, what say you to this, for I confess I find myself in a turmoil of opinion.'

'Sir, we are men here, yes? The words I speak will not leave this cabin?'

'Of course, Fletcher,' said the captain, sounding intrigued. 'You may speak freely.'

'Then, sir, I will say this, and I say it from the point of view of one who did not see any of the events that Sir Robert speaks of and so can only offer a character for the two players involved. I have known Mr Heywood since he was a lad and a fellow of better judgement I have yet to encounter. His family are gentle-people of the most proper type, and I could no more believe that he would force himself on a lady than I could imagine young Turnip bounding overboard and dancing a foxtrot atop the waves.'

Young Turnip indeed! He could leave me out of this game.

'And as for Miss Wilton,' continued Mr Christian, 'I confess that our paths crossed on several occasions yester-evening and she spoke to me of some of her fancies and I am not convinced she was as pure as Sir Robert might have thought. I believe she is a reader of novels, sir, which is hardly appropriate. She had a way about her, that is all that I will say. An experienced way, if you follow me, sir, that made me think she was a person of compromised character.'

Well, this put a different complexion on things, that was for sure. I was all in favour of Mr Heywood, the scut, getting keel-hauled for taking liberties, but, dislike the man as I did, even I would not have seen him punished on the basis of a malicious lie from a whore.

'This is all very distressing,' said Captain Bligh finally. 'Very distressing indeed. It leaves me in a position where I have no choice but to take you on your word as a gentleman, Mr

Heywood, and plan no further retribution.'

'I am relieved to hear it,' said Mr Heywood.

'But the incident will not be forgotten,' he added. 'For there is something in the dish that doesn't taste right to me, but that's where I'll leave it for now. However, my eyes are on you, Mr Heywood, do you hear me? My eyes are firmly fixed upon you.'

'Yes, sir, and might I say—'

I failed to hear what came next, for Mr Nelson, the gardener, and Mr Brown, his assistant, came round a corner on their way to the great cabin and gave me such a start that I jumped into the officers' cabin, intending to wait until I could be sure they were out of the way, but, to my despair, as I was standing there I heard the door of Captain Bligh's cabin open and the three men emerge together.

'Turnstile!' shouted the captain and what could I do but ignore him, for I had no excuse for standing where I was and to be discovered there was to be disgraced myself. 'Where is that lad now?' he added, marching off in the direction of the deck himself in search of me, no doubt. It was my intention to wait until Mr Christian and Mr Heywood left too before emerging from my hiding place, but to my horror Mr Christian grabbed the scut and pulled him towards their own cabin and I had no choice but to squat in a dark corner out of sight of them.

'In here,' Mr Christian said, closing the door behind him, and I did what I could to control my breathing so as not to alert them to my presence. 'You stupid fool,' he said, and then what did he go and do, only deliver Mr Heywood a fierce slap across the cheek, leading the scut to let out a shout of hurt and then burst into tears! 'I'll not lie for you again, do you hear me?'

'She was a whore,' said Mr Heywood, spitting out the words through his bawling tears like a child who has been disciplined. 'Why did she want to dance with me all those times if she didn't want to know me better?'

'No lady would want to know you,' said Mr Christian. 'Now I

211

have lied to protect you, but I swear that I won't do it again. Should you get yourself into further trouble, you will answer the charges alone, is that understood?' Mr Heywood went silent, merely sat on a bunk, wiping his eyes. 'And one day, I might call on you for help and I will expect it, is that understood?'

'A tease, that's what she was,' came the reply, which wasn't to Mr Christian's satisfaction.

'Is that understood?' he repeated.

'Yes,' sobbed Mr Heywood.

Mr Christian said nothing further, just stormed out of the cabin, and there was me, left in a corner, desperate for the privy, and unable to move until the scut finally pulled himself together, dried his eyes and left the room.

Well, now, I thought, this was a pretty state of affairs. The scut was bad, through and through. I had my proof of it now.

18

AND THEN, TO MY SURPRISE, all was at peace for a few weeks. Our cheerful boat brought us across the Indian Sea towards Australia and throughout that journey we had good fortune with the weather, which was clement. The sails remained aloft, dimpled outwards by the steady winds. The men were in good spirits, knowing that the most severe part of our journey was behind us.

The only incident of note during this time involved a personal conversation that took place two evenings before we were due to arrive at Van Diemen's land, an island off the southernmost tip of Australia, when I was alone with Captain Bligh in his cabin, organizing his undercrackers and uniforms in crates for when we arrived at our destination. The captain had been in mostly good form during this part of our voyage and his anger at the behaviour of the scut during our South African sojourn had dissipated a little, although I think it was not forgotten.

'So, Turnstile,' said the captain to me as I was getting along with my work, 'it won't be long now until we reach Otaheite. I dare say you'll enjoy your escape from the *Bounty* for a while?'

I looked across at him, surprised by his choice of words. Little did he know the escape that I had in mind. 'Well, sir,' said I, 'I must admit it'll be a good thing to set foot on dry ground again for a few weeks and not to feel the world moving beneath myself.'

'Does it move?' he asked in an absent-minded way. 'I have spent so many years at sea now that I fail to notice it any more. If anything, I find dry land difficult to negotiate.'

I nodded and got on with my work. It was the custom of the captain from time to time to engage me in conversation, usually when there was nothing urgent to attend to on board and (I had noticed) often when he had finished writing another letter to the missus and his boy.

'I must commend you,' he continued then after a few moments. 'You've done a fine job as servant. This was your first voyage, was it not?'

'It was sir,' said I.

'You'd never been to sea before?'

'No, sir.'

'Then, tell me,' he asked, sounding curious, 'what was it that brought you here?'

I put down one of his uniforms and heaved an old sigh as I looked at him. 'If you want the truth, sir, I had little choice in the matter. There was a misunderstanding of a sort back in Portsmouth and it led me to the ship.'

'A misunderstanding?' he asked, smiling at me a little. 'Might I enquire as to the manner of it?'

'You might,' said I then. 'Only, if I'm to be honest with you, I

213

suppose it wasn't really a misunderstanding at all, but a fair reading of what was before them.'

'But you just said—'

'I lied, sir,' said I, deciding that there was no benefit to be had in my not telling him the truth. 'I've built a character for myself as something of a petty thief,' I explained. 'Handkerchiefs, pocketwatches, the occasional purse or wallet if I was lucky. And I happened to get caught one too many times when I took a pocketwatch from a French gentleman on the morning the *Bounty* was due to set sail and, to put it bluntly, I had the choice of going to the gaol for a twelvemonth or coming to sea.'

The captain nodded and smiled. 'I put it to you that you made a wise choice,' he said quietly. 'Would you agree?'

'Aye,' said I with a shrug. 'For all the choice it was.'

We said nothing to each other for a few moments after that. I had the idea that the captain had formed a good opinion of me during our voyage and I surely had a good one of him, for he was a fair and decent man who treated all the men and officers alike and was as focused on keeping us all healthy and well-fed as he was in completing our mission as quickly as possible. But I was aware that he was watching me as I moved around and finally he spoke again.

'This . . . habit of yours,' he said finally.

'Habit, sir?'

'Pickpocketing. Stealing. Call it what you will. How long had you been engaged in it?'

I felt my face take on the reddenings a little when he asked me, but I wasn't about to lie now. I was not so ashamed of my past not to tell him about it when he asked, but I didn't want him to form a low opinion of me and put all the good that I might have earned so far to the bad. That would happen soon enough when I fled the ship for ever and he had nothing but his disappointment in me to use as my condemnation.

'As long as I can recall, sir,' said I, 'Mr Lewis – him as looked after me – he taught me the trade.'

'Now, let's not call it a trade, lad; that suggests it is honest work. This Mr Lewis, what class of a man is he?'

I thought about it. 'A bad 'un, sir. A bad 'un through and through.'

'I see,' he replied, nodding. 'He's a relative of some sort? An uncle perhaps?'

'No, sir,' said I. 'None of that. I don't have any family. None that I can recall anyway. Mr Lewis, he runs an establishment for boys and he took me in when I was a nipper.'

'An establishment?' he asked then, frowning. 'A school of some sort, do you mean?'

'Of a sort,' I said. 'You learn things there, that's for sure. Not the type of things you might want to know, but lessons all the same.'

He hesitated before speaking again, and when he did he took me by surprise with his words. 'You speak very angrily about him,' he said. 'Your voice, it trembles with rage, as if you hate the man.'

I opened my mouth to reply but found I had not the words. He was right, I did feel anger when I thought about Mr Lewis, but I was not aware that it came across in my speech.

'Well, sir,' said I, considering the matter, 'it was not a happy place.'

'But there were other boys there, of course? Lads your own age?'

'Lads of all ages up to about sixteen or seventeen, sir. Mr Lewis would take boys in at five or six and hold on to them until they were of age. The only ones he ever threw away were them as had no skill for the thieving or them as weren't pretty enough—'

'*Pretty* enough?' he asked, seizing on that which was out of my mouth before I could steal it back. 'What the devil can you mean by that?'

'I don't know, sir,' said I quickly. 'I only meant—'

'What would it matter if a lad were pretty enough? Does a boy have to be fair to be a thief?' He stared at me and I felt my face take on the reddenings even worse than before, until I thought my cheeks would singe if they were touched by water, and to my surprise I thought that I might burst into tears and shame myself entirely. This was not a conversation I had ever imagined having with the captain and I despised myself for getting dragged into it. 'Unless . . .' said he then, thinking about it and stroking his chin. He stood up from behind his desk and came towards me. 'Turnstile, what sort of a place was it, this establishment where you were reared?'

'I told you, didn't I?' I snapped, something I had never done in his presence before, something no one on board ever did. 'A bad place. A place I won't go back to, I swear on it now. I'd rather die than go back to it and you'll not make me, none of you will.'

We stood there, looking at each other, for what felt like a long time and I swear the captain's face reflected the misery I felt within myself for the things that had occurred in my life. He opened his mouth and I think he was about to offer words of con-solation, but Mr Christian appeared in the doorway at that moment and disturbed us.

'Captain, you might want to . . . Oh, I do apologize,' he said, taking in the scene before him. 'Am I interrupting something?'

'Nothing at all, Fletcher,' said the captain, stepping away from me and coughing deeply. 'What is it?'

'A most unusual school of dolphins, sir, running the ship at port and starboard. I thought they might interest you.'

'Indeed, indeed,' he said gruffly, not looking up at his master's mate. 'I will be on deck presently, Fletcher. Thank you for alerting me.'

Mr Christian nodded and gave me a curious look before leaving and I returned to my duties. I wished for nothing more than the captain to step up to the deck for a look at the dolphins and leave me alone with my thoughts and, to my pleasure, he walked towards the door, but not before turning round and speaking one last time.

'I think I have an idea what you may have been through, John Jacob,' he said, addressing me by my Christian names for the first time. 'I have heard of such dens of vice. Suffice to say that I won't allow you to return there. I take an interest in you, Master Turnstile, I confess it. You put me in mind of someone, someone I care for a great deal.'

His eyes flitted over to the portraits on his desk and I followed them there and thought it could hardly be that boy of his, who was half the age I was and had the look of a milksop about him. But I said nothing and a moment later he was gone. I looked up and, finding myself alone, put the uniforms down and half collapsed into a chair in the cabin, where I placed my head in my hands and wept like a baby with the memory of those things I tried never to think about.

19

THREE HUNDRED AND EIGHT DAYS.

That's how long I spent on board that rusty old tub, the *Bounty*, before we reached our final destination. To my surprise, though, about half of that time consisted of days when I didn't feel so bad about myself or my place in the world. I spent a long time resenting the crew for what they'd put me through when we were crossing the Equator, but after a while that, like so many other things, was forgotten. And then I spent a long time planning my escape from the clutches of the king's navy, but there was such little time spent ashore that I finally put that out of my mind too. And soon the weather changed and the waters changed and the smell in the air grew a little sweeter and the word went round that it would be any week now, any day, any hour, perhaps only a few minutes, before one of us would espy land and cry the word and be hailed a hero by all.

In preparation for this long anticipated moment, one fine morning as we drifted along the captain gathered together on deck the whole complement, officers and men alike, on a matter of what he called 'the highest urgency'. Usually I had some idea what this would be about, as I would hear him muttering to himself in his cabin with his thoughts on what he might say to the assembled throng, but on this particular morning I had no idea whatsoever and thought he had an uncomfortable look on his face as to address us he climbed on a box, the better to see every man.

'Well, men,' he shouted, and I swore I could hear a little nervousness in his tone, 'it looks as if it will be only a matter of hours before our ship reaches her destination and what a merry voyage it has been, wouldn't you agree?'

Among the men surfaced a polite murmur, which finally turned into a general nodding of heads. No one could deny that we hadn't done too badly. I knew from the conversations of sailing men I had listened to back in Portsmouth that they went through trickier times than we had and that there were captains in the navy with a greater affection for the lash than our own.

'We have suffered through some harsh weather, that's true enough,' continued Mr Bligh. 'But you have each shown great fortitude. And we saw our journey extended in a way that none of us had anticipated or hoped for. But nevertheless we saw it through and here we are, safe and well. And I think it's true to say that there has been no better disciplinary record of any ship in the history of the British navy. We officers have had to keep order at times, of course, but I appreciate the fact that there has been only a single flogging in all these thousands of miles. You should be commended for that, every one of you.'

'I'll take mine in gold,' cried the voice of Isaac Martin, an able seaman, to a cheer from all.

'Shut your trap, you,' shouted Mr Heywood, the scut, advancing on him despite the good humour of the remark. 'You'll keep a silence when the captain addresses you.'

'No, no, Mr Heywood,' said the captain loudly, waving his hands in the air to call the hound off his prey. 'No need for that. Mr Martin is right and his point is well made. Sadly, I'm not in a position to offer financial rewards to any of you men, but rest assured that if the coffers of Sir Joseph Banks belonged to me then I would see each of you fairly rewarded for your travails.'

A round of applause greeted this remark and I noticed how everyone on board felt like true members of a happy company now that the prospect of release from our prison was upon us.

'I am, however, in the position of being able to offer you some leisure time,' said the captain then in a cheerful tone. 'None of us know how long we will remain on Otaheite while we gather the breadfruit. There will be work to be done, of course. There are many plants to be gathered and stored. There are repairs to be made to the ship. But I expect that each of you will have more than your share of time to enjoy a rest from your labours; I intend to see to it that all the island work is shared out equitably between officers and men.'

Another murmur of appreciation came from the men and I thought that maybe that was the end of it; only, the captain looked at us then and frowned, staring down at the deck for a moment before looking up again, and this time I swear I could see the rouge in his cheeks.

'There is a matter . . . a matter of some importance, however, that I wish to address,' he stated finally, with more nervousness in his voice than I had ever heard before. 'As many of you know, I have visited these islands before, when I was a younger man, of course, in the company of the late Captain Cook.'

'God bless his sainted name!' cried a voice from the back to general cheers.

'God bless it,' echoed Mr Bligh. 'God bless it indeed. And well said, that man. But I mention this because the rest of you . . . well, you are novices here and may not understand the customs. I should warn you that . . . that the people who reside here may not know our Christian ways.'

He looked out at us as if that would explain things, but on this occasion the men simply stared back blankly, unsure what he was referring to.

'When I say our Christian ways, I of course mean the way that we comport ourselves as men, both here and at home, and the way that the . . . how shall I put it? . . . native ladies comport themselves. Differently from our good wives, I mean.'

'I should hope so,' roared William Muspratt. 'I have to give my wife a farthing every time I want her to kiss my whistle!'

The men exploded in laughter when he said this, but the captain looked merely embarrassed. 'Mr Muspratt, please,' he said, shaking his head. 'There's no call for such vulgarity. Let us not abase ourselves to the level of the savages. But look here . . .' He hesitated now and coughed and appeared to grow more confident for a moment. 'We are all men here, are we not? I shall put it bluntly. The women on these islands . . . they have known the favours of many of their menfolk. They are indiscriminate, do you see? This does not cheapen them, you understand, it is merely their way. They are not like us, cleaving to a wife and holding her dear for ever.'

Another few shouts were heard, more jokes, but the captain shouted over them.

'Many of them are in possession of cruel diseases,' he said. 'Venereal diseases, if I may call it by its proper name. And it is my advice to each and every one of you that you do not place your-self in a position where you may become susceptible to them. Of course, men will be men and you have been a long time at sea in one another's company, but I beseech you to think of your health when you associate with the natives . . . and if you cannot do that,

220

then I ask you to consider your morals. We may be among the savages but we are Englishmen, do you see?'

There was absolute silence among the men and I anticipated a great burst of laughter at any moment, but before it came a small voice piped up from my left; the voice of George Stewart, a midshipman.

'I'm a Scot,' he said in his thick brogue. 'So can I fuck whoever I want, Captain?'

The crew exploded in laughter and Mr Bligh stepped down from his box, shaking his head in a mixture of embarrassment and dis-illusionment; on any other occasion a remark such as this, directed at the captain, would have caused uproar, but with our being so close to the end of our journey, discipline had become more relaxed. 'Here, Turnstile,' said Mr Bligh, grabbing me by the collar as I passed him. 'I hope that you will heed my words anyway.'

'Of course, sir,' said I, although I confess that I had a cobbler's understanding of what a venereal disease was, only that it didn't sound pleasant.

'I doubt if any of the native ladies will take a shine to Turnip anyway,' said Mr Heywood, the scut, approaching us. 'He's a pasty fellow, don't you agree?'

'Still your tongue, sir,' said the captain, walking away, leaving the officer open-mouthed and humiliated. I gave him a wink and ran off myself.

It was very early the following morning; the sun was still on the horizon, but offering sufficient light to see anything that might appear before us in the distance, and I was at the tip of the ship, alone with my thoughts. Few of the men were around me, but Mr Linkletter, the quartermaster, was steering the ship and singing 'Sweet Jenny of Galway Bay' in a low and melodious voice not far from where I stood.

Somewhere out there lay our island, I thought, and on it lay

221

new adventures. My mind was filled with thoughts of the native women who had so dominated the conversations of the men for months. They said they ran naked as the day they were born, a concept that filled me with both excitement and terror. The truth was I had yet to know a woman and the thought of it was something that kept me awake at night with anxiety; for a moment I couldn't help but wonder whether it would not be a better thing entirely for me to stay on board this ship for ever more and never have to face the realities of what lay ahead.

'Turnip,' said Mr Linkletter quietly, ending his song, but I didn't turn round. I had sworn never to respond to that name again.

'Turnstile,' he said then, a little more urgently, but still under his breath.

Again, I held my position. I wasn't ready to surrender my thoughts just yet; I wasn't ready for the world.

'John,' he said finally, and this time I turned round to find him smiling at me. He nodded in the direction that I had been looking towards and I turned back again, narrowing my eyes to focus them better. 'Take a look,' he said, and despite my anxieties I felt my face breaking into a broad grin and the excitement of the moment overtaking me so much that I could have jumped overboard in my enthusiasm and started swimming.

Land.

We had arrived.

Part III

The Island

26 October 1788 – 28 April 1789

1

WHEN I WAS LITTLE MORE THAN A LAD, Mr Lewis used to complain that I was a feckless creature, one who could never be relied upon to finish a job that I started. It was one of the many accusations he flung at me whenever he was in one of his tantrums, if one of my brothers had come home with less of a pot than he had expected, say, or if a lad had got into a fight and bruised his face, making him a less pretty object and unlikely to be chosen during Evening Selection. If you weren't cleaning up the house, then you were out on the street snapping from pockets, and if you weren't doing that you were engaged in those other activities of which I prefer not to speak. But I think I would have him confounded if he saw all the work that I have put into this recollection so far.

All told, we were on board that blessed boat for just shy of a full calendar year. Our stay on the island lasted a mere half of that time, but the Saviour knows that it was no less of an eventful period. For if the crossing had been difficult at times, and wearying, and if there had been the occasional altercation between AB and boatswain, midshipman and officer, captain and master, then for all that we were still for the most part a happy crew, and a contented one, and a gang of men who saw Mr Bligh as our anointed leader, in much the same way that the Saviour himself had anointed King George to rule over us all. This was a sacred trust and one that we would not have questioned, and, as such, we were a community of little dissent. But it was on the island, where we were not all thrown together in such a small space as we had been while at sea, that things started to change. The men changed;

the officers changed; the captain changed. And I changed too, I do believe. Every one of us discovered something there that came upon us most unexpectedly. For better or worse, the events that took place there, and the pleasure that we all took in them, were set to make new men of the *Bounty* crew and the result of that would brand every one of us, from captain to servant-lad, in different ways for the rest of our lives.

2

THE FIRST THING TO CHANGE was the nature of authority and it fell face first into an unexpected place. The separation between the officers and the men was not so pronounced as it had once been, which gave each of us a sense of individuality that we had lacked when we were little more than sea-slaves, dragging a hulk of wood and iron through the great waters day after day. And when the uniforms were dispensed with, which they had to be on account of the scorching heat that burned down on us every day, why, we might have held the same status, every man jack of us.

There wasn't a single one of us who measured our days in the same way on Otaheite that we had when we were serving on board the ship. There, we had measured out our lives through the changing of the shifts, those two, and latterly three, separate periods of time during the day when we were either at work, at leisure or at rest; the changing of the hours dictated how we should employ ourselves, but now we had a sudden freedom and unexpected control over our own fate. On the island, we didn't notice time passing in the same way. The sun rose and set at regular hours, I'm sure, but we paid it little heed. We were on dry land and, although there was still work to do, it was a different class of labour entirely and we weren't left in fear of our lives at every shoddy hour of the day, as we had been during that bleak period when we were attempting to round the Horn. Some days I would cast my mind back to those traumatic weeks and it seemed to me to represent a different existence entirely. And if I thought of my days on the streets of Portsmouth? Well, that was just like something I'd dreamed up after eating a bad mango. That most of the men had left wives and sweethearts, parents and children, behind them in England was a fact that no one could deny, but during those months on Otaheite they may have never existed at all, so little did they enter our consciousness.

And as for the notion of fidelity? Well, you could throw a fig at that.

Truth to tell, it wasn't that we had been unhappy at sea. Our captain was a fair-minded and thoughtful man after all, but it was one thing to be engaged on a contented labour that some days felt passable and other days felt rotten and another to be without one and spending one's days resting under the shade of an overhanging tree with a ripened piece of fruit preparing to detach itself from its stalk and drop into your welcoming hands. The latter is better, I don't mind admitting to it.

But here's a strange fact for you. I have related already how it had taken me several days to grow accustomed to the tossing and turning of the ship when we first left Spithead and began our travels; even now I can recall the misery of the time I spent emptying the contents of my belly overboard back in those dark and miserable days and my stomach churns at the recollection. But it took almost as long for me to grow accustomed to standing on solid land once again after so much time away from it. When I first set foot on the beaches of our new home I expected the sand to rock back and forth at a steady pace, not sit still beneath my feet as was its nature. Indeed, when first I stood on the island I found it difficult to remain in the vertical and had to steady my hams at distances from each other in order to save myself the embarrassment of taking a tumble. Others did too, I saw it. And when I tried to sleep those first few nights, rather than allowing me to rest easier, the stillness and the peace that surrounded me filled my head with curious and unexpected thoughts that kept me awake, and I confess that by the third night I was so tired and in need of a fresh burst of energy that I considered taking a launch back to the *Bounty* and adopting my old place again in the bunk outside Captain Bligh's cabin; only, I knew that it would be a foolish and headstrong thing to do and I would be mocked mercilessly for it when the sun came up.

For most of us, the island was called Otaheite. Some of the men used the word 'Tahiti' from time to time, as that was the name the maps employed and the one by which the government back home had called it in the christening of our mission, but Otaheite was what the people there named it, the natives, the men and women who had spent their lives on its hills and beaches. It was their language and it was their name that the captain used out of respect for their culture and because it had also been how Captain Cook had referred to it, so naturally it became what I called it too. The men argued about what the word meant in English – there were varying and exotic suggestions, some poetic, others vulgar – but it seemed quite obvious and simple to me: Paradise.

I confess that I entertained a mixed set of feelings on that noisy afternoon when we dropped anchor just off the island and set the first launches off in its direction. It had taken the best part of a day to negotiate our approach and in the meantime many of the natives had gathered on the shore and were engaged in a cheering and riotous dance that both delighted and terrified me. There were hundreds of them and I knew them not for friend or foe, so I stood a little away from my whistling fellows on the deck as the launches were lowered. And as they advanced, I held back, unsure of going forward into this unknown territory, nervous of what might be out there.

'Last on, last off, is it, lad?' asked Mr Hall, taking a place beside me and looking towards the shore. I looked at him and frowned, unsure what he meant by this remark. 'You,' he explained. 'You were the final member of the ship's crew to set foot on the *Bounty* back when we were setting sail, were you not? Are you to be the last to leave it too?'

'I thought the captain might need me,' I said, dismissing the idea quickly, for I didn't want him to see the apprehension painted upon my features and call me a milksop. 'I'll leave when he leaves.'

'Well, you're too late for that, lad,' he said, clapping me on the back. 'The captain was in the second launch that set out, did you not see him go? Mr Christian went ahead in the first, to settle matters with their leaders, and when the signal came the captain was away. You can see him yonder, heading towards the shore.'

This came as a surprise to me, for, although I had not crossed paths that morning with Mr Bligh anywhere about the ship or near his cabin, I had expected that he would bring me with him when he left and his departure must have come when I was below-decks, packing some of his uniforms in crates. In truth I was sorry and even a little hurt that he had deserted me, for my confidence was at its lowest point and his protection would have meant something to me. I had heard many stories about how wonderful this island would be from my fellow sailors over the course of our voyage, but back in Portsmouth I had also heard many tales of how quickly these idylls could turn to the bad. Wasn't it true, after all, that Captain Cook had died in the most brutal and cruel fashion on an island just like this one? Hadn't his skin and bones been separated, parts of his body lost for ever, while the rest decomposed at the bottom of the ocean? What if such a fate lay in store for all of us? For me? I cared little for the notion of being boiled or flayed or dissected; the idea didn't sit with me at all.

'My oh my,' continued Mr Hall, whistling a little through his lips as he looked off into the distance at the natives dancing on the shore. 'I tell you now, Turnip, I have the greatest affection and regard for Mrs Hall – she's borne me six bonny lasses and another four lads, although one's a half-wit, I should say – but she would think me less of a man if I didn't look forward to enjoying some of the delights this island has to offer. Can you see them? Can you take your eyes off them, I should say!'

He was referring, of course, to the native women in particular who were parading themselves on the beaches and sailing towards the *Bounty* in launches of their own, throwing garlands into the water, unashamed of their half-naked state. I found myself wanting to stare but not wanting the men to catch me ogling the ladies and mock me for a nance; I look back now and wonder how foolish I must have been to think that, after a twelve-month at sea, there was a single one of my fellow sailors who cared a fig for what I was doing or where I was looking. They had other sights to observe.

'Look!' I cried suddenly, my eyes taken by a flurry of activity on the beach. 'What's this now?'

A large throne had appeared, carried on the shoulders of eight enormous men from the thickets behind, and was being placed carefully on the beach; a few moments later another eight men arrived by the shore, carrying what looked like a second throne, and this one was occupied by a robed creature whose features I could not make out from this distance. The natives bowed low to him and he stepped from one throne to the other and only when he was safely seated did more natives set forth in canoes, hollering and slapping their cheeks in a most distressing fashion, and approach the captain's own launch, which I observed now floating near the shore line, and accompany it in to the island.

The sounds ring in my ears still. Perhaps you have attended celebrations in Trafalgar Square to mark a great victory in this war or that. Perhaps you have gathered outside Westminster Abbey and seen a newly crowned king emerge to greet his subjects. But unless you have experienced the roar of shouting and cheering that ricocheted back and forth between the islanders coming out to meet us and the sailors desperate to make their acquaintance in return, you cannot understand how delirious we suddenly became. Some of the sailors jumped overboard in response and swam towards our new hosts. Others leaned over and pulled the native women up on to the *Bounty* itself and made kiss with them without so much as a by-your-leave. Either way, before I knew it I was surrounded by islanders, who placed flowers around my neck and stroked my cheeks in delight, as if my pale skin was enough by itself to excite them. One placed her hand within my shirt and stroked my belly, uttering sighs of delight as if I was a fine fellow entirely, and I was ashamed of it but I could neither stop her nor run away.

Every girl and woman who came our way was naked from the waist up and had a beauty that you couldn't see if you travelled round the world a dozen times but never came to visit Otaheite. And every boy and man could only stare and cheer and think of the happy times ahead, because we'd all heard the stories from the salts of long standing and we knew that these were treats worthy of men who'd been at sea for a year and who had enjoyed no female companionship during that time.

I confess, the whole thing gave me the motions.

3

DISTURBED BY THE ATTENTIONS OF THE ISLANDERS, I stepped quickly into the next launch that was setting out for the beaches and arrived in time to witness the captain's first exchange with the island leaders. There was noise a-plenty to be heard as we approached the shore – bloody great cheers from the Englishmen who had preceded or were accompanying us and a kind of terrified but exciting caterwauling from the natives dancing up and down the sand – but to my surprise the latter stopped the very moment Captain Bligh set foot on land. It was as if a great orchestra had suddenly been knocked out of their rhythm by their conductor dropping his baton. I took it as one of their customs, for even though it gave me the chills the captain seemed to have expected such a commotion and the sudden desisting of it, for it didn't make him turn on his heel and order that we all sail back to England immediately before every man jack of us was eaten alive. Instead he walked confidently towards the throne, stopped a little in front of it, and offered a short but efficient bow, the like of which I had never seen him give to any man before.

'Your Majesty,' said he, his voice taking on the affectations of a gentleman on an even higher social plane than the one on which he resided. 'Might I be so honoured that you remember me, William Bligh, lieutenant, from my last visit to your fine island, when, if you recall, I was led by Captain James Cook of the *Endurance*.'

There was a long silence from the man seated on the throne and he narrowed his eyes and smiled before looking suddenly angry and then smiling again. He stroked his chin where his beard might have been, but there were no whiskers there and his appearance was as clean-shaven as my own. 'Bligh,' he said finally, sounding out the name as if it were a longer one than its five letters implied. 'William Bligh,' he repeated then after a moment, watching as the launches filled with sailors headed towards his shore. I had an idea that he was not perhaps as excited by this invasion as the rest of his kinsmen. 'I am in the remembrance of you. The Captain Cook was joining you?'

The captain looked around for a moment and caught my eye; I dare say he could tell from my expression that I was at a loss what to think by this phrasing and the very question in itself. He glanced down at the sand for a moment then, as if he was ensuring for himself that the decision he had made was the right one, before looking back up at his inquisitor and smiling. 'The captain is very well,' said he and not a blush on his face despite the eloquence of the lie. 'I'm happy to say that he is enjoying a well-earned retirement in London, from where he sends his warmest regards to Your Majesty.'

I don't mind admitting that my mouth fell open at that last remark. I had never heard the captain utter a lie in all the time I had known him – at least I didn't think I had, and if he had it must have been on a subject of which I knew nothing – but this was the sauciest remark to be uttered so far since any of us had left Portsmouth and yet none of the men around us seemed surprised by it. By now several of the other launches had arrived on shore and the rest of the officers and most of the crew had taken up a position flanking the captain.

'Please to return my compliments to your brave captain when you see him next,' said the island king in response and Captain Bligh nodded graciously.

'I will, Your Majesty, and might I add my congratulations to you that your English has improved exceedingly since my last visit. You are speaking like a true gentleman who would not be out of place in King George's court.'

The king nodded and seemed pleased by the compliment. 'You are thanked,' he said with a deep nod of his head.

The two men watched each other for a moment and I wondered who would be next to speak, but as I waited a second throne was brought out and placed on the sand beside him and then who should appear out of the trees but a monster of a man, half-naked, with hair down to his waist and a look on his face that suggested he had recently eaten a weevil and was not the better for the experience.

'Captain Bligh,' said the king, 'may I have presented my wife Ideeah.'

Well, I don't mind admitting that you could have stepped up

beside me and given me a wink and I would have fallen over in surprise that the creature I was staring at was a woman, but blow me if he wasn't telling the truth, for when she sat down and looked around at all of us her hair moved out of the way slightly and what did I see but a pair of bloody great titties that would have kept a bairn in milk for a twelvemonth. I looked at the captain but he seemed less disturbed than I did by what he saw and even looked away out of shame.

'Delighted to make your acquaintance, ma'am,' he said, bowing again, although not as lowly as he had for the king. 'His Majesty, King Tynah, has been kind enough to accept the compliments of Captain Cook and King George; may I in turn extend them and the gracious felicitations of the lady Queen Caroline to you?'

Queen Ideeah, for that was the behemoth's name, seemed unhappy with the remark and turned to her husband, barking something rapidly and dramatically in a language I could not understand, but he dismissed her remarks quickly with a wave of his hand and she fell silent and looked down. I couldn't help but notice the marks that covered his hands and arm, and even portions of his face. Lines and drawings, deep etchings of black and blue and other colours, that lent him the phizzy of a painting and not of a man. The other islanders were similarly illustrated but not perhaps in so extraordinary a fashion. It was true that many of the sailors on board the *Bounty* had tattoos of their own, but they were small things, words and fancies, the smallest drawings stretching from wrist to elbow, which might breathe into life when the bicep was inflated, but none could compete for colour or artistry as the pictures that adorned the body of Tynah.

'My wife will not have learned the English tongue in as wonderful a way as I himself will have,' remarked the king, which led me to a moment's thought as I attempted to decipher it. 'But please to fall to your sleep tonight with the joy of knowing that she is enraptured by you.'

Well, I believed that was as warm a welcome as any of us could have expected to receive, and the captain appeared to think the same thing, for he smiled and looked towards Mr Heywood – whose face had grown so red in the sun that I imagined I could see a trail of smoke emerging from behind his ears – before clicking his fingers in his direction. It was at this point that I realized the scut was carrying a medium-sized wooden inlaid box in his hands, one I had observed on many occasions in the captain's cabin but had never had any cause to open or examine, as I had considered it merely one of the trifles that gentlemen carry with them to transport their snuff or their prayer-books in, whichever they rely on for sustenance more.

'Mr Heywood,' he said after a moment, when that foolish lad did not instantly march in his direction, and then we all looked at him and I saw that he was not paying attention to the scene playing itself out before him but was instead staring at a group of young females – more attractive, I will grant him, than the devilish woolly mammoth that occupied the throne beside King Tynah – and his eyes were out on stalks as he leered at their nakedness and I swear that his pustules were exploding with excitement.

'Mr Heywood, sir,' snapped the captain then and the scut sprang back to life just as Mr Christian pushed him forward, almost unsettling him and sending him arse over tea-kettle into the sand before us, which would have given me the rollickings for a fortnight had he not recovered and stood his ground. The captain glared at him as he came forward and I could see his face grow even worse red, on account of the fact that staring at the ladies had given him the motions, a development that was only too obvious through his loosened trousers. However, without an ounce of shame such as his sort never have, he handed the box across to Captain Bligh, who in turn stepped towards the king – a little cautiously, I thought, as if he was afraid that any sudden movements might lead to a spear between his shoulder-blades –

and opened it wide. A scene of a comic nature ensued, with the entire party behind the throne leaning forward and opening their mouths as one in delight before stepping back and nodding approvingly.

'Might I be permitted to offer Your Majesty this token of our undying friendship?' said Captain Bligh as the king reached forward and took the looking-glass from its place within. A fine piece it was too, silver with a gold edge circling the mirror. The king glanced at his face inside it and seemed unimpressed by what he saw, but then this was a man who had taken a creature from the depths for his wife and bed-mate so I knew not where his tastes lay. However, he accepted it graciously before placing it back in the box and handing it over to one of his attendants.

'I am enraptured by your kindness,' he said, sounding a little bored if I am honest, but then, as I was to realize, the king's English tended to live in the realm of the superlative. 'Might I dare hope that your visit will be an eternal one?'

'We would very much like to stay for a few months, if we may,' replied the captain. 'King George and Captain Cook have sent many more gifts for Your Majesty's pleasure; they are currently on board our vessel, but we will transport them to you presently.'

'I was delighted beyond words,' remarked the king, doing nothing to stifle a yawn. 'And while you were here, there are many things we have offered you in return?'

'Your generosity knows no equal,' said the captain, and I confess that at this point I thought they might strike up a dance and perform a waltz together, so delighted were they by each other's company. 'And, since you ask, there is something that Your Majesty, in his kindness and beneficence, could provide us with.'

'Which will be?'

And that was when the subject of the breadfruit came up.

4

TWO DAYS AFTER OUR ARRIVAL on Otaheite, the captain woke me early that morning with undue ceremony, by placing the toe of his boot quickly into my ribcage and dislodging me from my hammock. I woke with a start and was so close to letting loose an oath that half the phrase was out of my mouth before I could pull it back in. I swallowed nervously, looking up at him with a mixture of embarrassment and dismay, but he merely smiled and shook it off.

'Keep a civil tongue in your head, young Turnstile,' he said, throwing a handful of documents at me. 'There may be ladies near by. What do you mean by still being asleep at this time of the day anyway?'

I raised an eyebrow and looked at him, wondering whether he was making a farce of me. It was true that the morning was bright but I knew for a fact that I had not slept for more than two or three hours and was desirous of many more yet.

'Begging your pardon, Captain,' I replied, trying to stifle a yawn. 'Was there something you needed of me?'

'Your company, sir,' he said then. 'And the use of your arms for carrying these small items. I am visiting Point Venus this morning and thought you could do with the exercise. You will grow flabby on this island, all of you men will. I've seen it before. A decent walk will do you the world of good.'

I frowned and exhaled the most enormous yawn before him, the kind I would never have released had we been back at our rightful places below decks, and as I did so he stared at me with distaste and shook his head. For myself, I thought there was little chance that the captain was interested in my health or physical well-being but, rather, he needed a dogsbody and I was it, but it mattered not, because before I could say a further word on the topic he was away from me, marching eastward, and what choice did I have only to follow him and hold my tongue. It was a warm morning, I recall that much, and having taken more than my rightful share of grog the night before I had been suffering the hallucinations in my sleep and did not feel the better for it yet. I looked ahead at the vast surroundings of the island as I caught up with Mr Bligh and asked him an indecorous question.

'Is it far, sir?' said I.

'Is what far?' he asked, turning round and staring at me as if my presence was a complete surprise to him and not something he had demanded.

'Point Venus,' I replied. 'Where you're taking me.'

He looked at me with a quizzical expression on his face and for a moment I thought he was going to burst out laughing, something I had never seen him do before. 'I'm not *taking* you anywhere, Turnstile. You are accompanying me, as is my desire. We may be on land but I am still captain and you are still servant-lad, are we not?'

'Yes, sir,' I muttered.

'This is what happens when ships dock on these islands,' he continued, looking ahead now. 'I have observed it on many occasions. We each forget our place. Discipline slackens. The natural order of things is subverted. Had we not enjoyed such a peaceful voyage to Otaheite, I confess that I would be more concerned about these matters.' I liked that he thought it had been a peaceful voyage. It had held more than its share of dramas for me. 'But in reply to your question, Turnstile, if it is of such importance to you,' he conceded finally, 'no, it is not far.'

'Well, I'm glad to hear it, sir,' said I, 'as I believe my health is compromised this morning.'

'I'm not surprised. Don't think word of your escapades did not

238

reach me. You may rest assured that I have eyes and ears everywhere on this island.'

I wasn't sure whether that was true or not, for as far as I could see during our short residency so far, the men had already grown accustomed to island life and were settling in quite nicely. I thought it unlikely that any of them had set themselves up as informers or tattle-tales. If anything, I suspected the captain was feeling a little isolated now that the close confines of *Bounty* life were behind us for a time. When you can see all the men in your charge at any time you choose, it is vastly different from when you cannot.

'My escapades, sir?' asked I. 'I don't know what you mean.'

'Do you know that I was eighteen years of age before I tasted my first drop of alcohol?' he replied, keeping up such a pace as he walked that I feared I would fall over in my eagerness to keep astep with him. 'And I swear that I didn't care for it neither. Of course I know that all of you need some leisure time after your long voyage, and I promised you as much, but that can't continue for too long. We have a job to do here, you're aware of that. Duty must come first. You're not much older than my own boy, William. If I found him in the condition that I found you this morning, I would kick his rump for him and he would thank me for it too.'

I suspected that he would not but said nothing about it for now and simply continued to follow him as we climbed higher.

'It's a curious thing, but I was around the same age as you were when I first came to Otaheite,' he mentioned after some more time had passed. 'A little older, perhaps, but not by much.'

I nodded and considered it. The captain was a decidedly elderly gentleman, thirty-three or -four if he was a day, which meant that it had been between one and two decades since he had last set foot on these shores.

'With Captain Cook, sir?' I asked.

'Aye, with the captain,' he replied sadly.

I hesitated before speaking again; there had been something

239

that had been on my mind since arriving on the island but I was unsure how to phrase it. 'Sir,' said I finally, 'might I ask you a question?'

'Of course you can, Turnstile,' he said with a laugh. 'Why, you sound quite terrified in the asking of it too. Are you that afeared of me?'

'No, sir,' said I. 'Only, you might think me a scamp to ask it and I don't relish the thought of a flogging.' I meant the words in jest, but no sooner had they escaped my mouth than I could tell that I had spoken ill. Perhaps it wasn't the words at all, perhaps it was the tone of them, but either way the captain spun round and suddenly his previously cheerful countenance had grown dark, as I had seen it do on a few other occasions to date.

'A flogging?' he asked. 'Is that what you think of me after nearly a year toiling alongside me? That I would flog a boy for an ill-advised question?'

'No, sir,' I said quickly, attempting desperately to salvage the situation, for even though I was tired and would have welcomed a longer stay in my pit, it was a fact that I enjoyed spending time with the captain and appreciated how it made me feel when he thought well of me. I had never enjoyed the benefit of a father, Mr Lewis being the closest I had got to such a thing and he had precious little to recommend himself, and the captain had increasingly played that role in my life. 'You misunderstand me—'

'You're a fine fellow to make such an accusation,' he snapped. 'How many floggings have you seen me administer in our time since we left Portsmouth?'

'Only one, sir,' I admitted.

'Only one, sir,' he repeated, nodding ferociously. 'And are you aware that that in itself will constitute something of a record for the British navy? I believe the least number of floggings on board a ship travelling our distance heretofore was seventeen. Seventeen, Turnstile! And I administered one, and even that I would have preferred to have ignored. Ours is a disciplinary record second to none and I have proved a friend to you boys and men, I thought.'

A silence hung in the air between us for quite some time after that. I could tell that he was torn between anger and injured feelings and knew that to say anything too soon would only precipitate more drama from him, and so I waited a spell before offering my apology.

'I misspoke earlier, sir,' said I finally, conjuring up as regretful a tone as I could find within myself. 'I meant no harm.'

'Perhaps you should think before you speak in future, then,' said he, refusing to turn his head to look at me.

I swear that I felt we were an old, married couple, lost between the twin passions of love and resentment. 'Aye, I should,' said I. 'I knew little of ship life before stepping on board the *Bounty*, but I do know from the salts I met back in Portsmouth that whippings and beatings are the norms on other boats, not the exceptions, as they have been on ours.'

'Hmm,' he said, mollified a little at last. 'I wonder, do the other men realize that? I feel no gratitude coming my way from them on that score. Not that I expect it. A captain can never expect to be loved by the men who work beneath him, but I have tried hard to create a harmonious atmosphere on board. I have worked at it day and night. But you had a question, Turnstile, before this whole sorry business began.'

'Aye,' said I, recalling it now. 'I only wondered why you told the island king that Captain Cook sent his greetings to him and that he was alive and well and living the fine life back in London, when you of all people must know that he is—'

'Dead?' he said, interrupting me. 'Of course I know it, lad, for was I not with him at the terrible moment?' He sighed and shook his head. 'You consider me a liar, perhaps, but there's more to this than you realize. Tynah and Captain Cook had established a successful friendship on the last occasion that Englishmen visited these islands, a cordiality that brought us all the things we needed from that voyage and allowed our mission to end successfully. It seemed to me that if he knew that Captain Cook had been killed on another island, our friendship might suffer, as he might consider me suspicious of him. He might think that we were here to avenge the loss. He might consider striking first. And in turn we would very likely fail to acquire the breadfruit, which is, of course, our only reason to be here among these savages in the first place. These are delicate negotiations, lad, and I must play our hosts carefully if I am to be successful.'

I confess I was surprised by his use of the word savages; I thought he had more respect for the islanders than that. But then he spoke it with little regard for insult but rather with the natural disdain for other forms of life that only an English gentleman can have.

'Ah,' he said, stopping for a moment and looking at a clearing before us that in turn led to a crag overlooking a valley. 'Step this way, Turnstile. I have something to show you here if I am where I think I am. I think you will find it rather interesting.'

I followed him carefully, for the ground was becoming uncertain beneath our feet and a false step could have meant an unhappy slide into the valley below, but in a moment we were standing beside a set of tall, green trees, trees that to my eye looked as if they might have stood there since the dawn of time. I wondered why the captain had brought me there and watched as he examined the bark of each tree in turn. He went from one to another, touching them, narrowing his eyes and staring at them, but then finally he appeared to find what he had been searching for, for a wide smile crossed his face and he beckoned me over excitedly.

'Here,' he said, pointing out a carving in the wood before me. 'Read it.'

I narrowed my eyes and peered closer. The writing was difficult to make out, but a close examination revealed the words: *Wm Bligh, w/Cook, April 1769.*

'It's you, sir,' said I, astonished, and turning to face him.

'It is,' he replied, delighted. 'I came up here with the captain one morning to look out at the valley below and he allowed me to carve my name in the tree. As I did so, he said that I would be a captain myself one day, perhaps a great captain, and that when I was I should return here some day on the king's business.'

Feeling astonished that I was standing in the very spot where Captain Cook had stood before me, I reached a hand out to touch the bark of the tree. I thought that if my brothers at Mr Lewis's establishment could see me now, why, they would turn green with envy at the shock of it.

'We must keep moving, lad, anyway,' he said a moment later. 'There is much to see at Point Venus. But I thought this might interest you.'

'It does, sir,' I said. 'I wonder . . .' I hesitated, unsure whether I should say such a thing or not.

'Wonder what, Turnstile?'

'Whether I should be a great captain someday,' I said in an almost embarrassed tone, as if the very idea was outrageous even to me.

His reply, however, both shocked and disappointed me, for he burst into a laugh, the like of which I had never observed on him before. 'You, Turnstile?' he asked. 'Why, you're just a servant-lad!'

'I shall grow older,' I protested.

'The captaincy of His Majesty's naval ships is for . . . how shall I put this?' he mused. 'Well, there are those of good stock, do you see, and who have a fine education. Whose characters are of a higher calibre than the men off the street. If England is to remain the great power that it is, then these traditions must be maintained.'

I raised an eyebrow but tried not to display my contempt for his words; he seemed ignorant of how insulting they were. But then I suspected that a man of his class did not realize that it was even possible to insult a member of mine.

'So I could never improve myself?' I asked.

'Why, you are improving yourself,' he replied. 'You have improved yourself every day on board the *Bounty*. Surely you recognize that you have a better understanding of the ship than you had when you boarded?'

I conceded that this was true, that despite myself I knew almost as much about the day-to-day duties of an AB as any of them ABs themselves.

'Then, let that be enough for you,' he said. 'Now, come along,' he added, turning away from me and stepping over some rocks that were in his way and that refused to move for him, despite his exalted status. 'I wanted to see the valley again and I have done so. Let us keep on.'

'One moment, sir, if you will,' said I, removing my own knife from my belt and setting about the tree carefully but still with a lesser hand than his had been. I cursed at the fact that my name was such a long one and reduced it to a mere *Turnstile, w/Bligh, 1789*.

'Ready, sir,' said I then, turning and following him up the mountain, all the time wondering whether he was right, that a lad of my station must stay with what he knows for ever or whether there was a way out of drudgery and obedience.

5

THE FIRST TIME I LAID EYES ON KAIKALA I was wearing naught but my britches and was lying on the beach, roasting in the noonday sun, tracing a journey up and down my chest with the tip of my finger. It had been more than a week since the crew of the *Bounty* had arrived on Otaheite and the days were rolling by in what I considered to be a very pleasant fashion indeed. It was at moments like this that I realized how fortunate I was to be the captain's servant-lad, rather than a regular sailor, as they had all manner of tasks to do both day and night, whereas I had a little more independence and nothing more was expected of me other than that I would be available as and when the captain had need of me.

On this particular afternoon, however, the captain was away with Mr Christian and Mr Elphinstone, making a chart of a part of the island that he hadn't seen before where even more generous supplies of breadfruit were supposedly located and I was taking advantage of his absence to enjoy a little well-earned rest in the sun. Lying on my back, looking up at the sky, I felt that I would be more than happy to spend the rest of my life on this island paradise; despite the fact that we had only been here a short time, there was already a palpable sense among the men, and one that I shared too, that none of us was relishing the moment that we would be summoned back to the *Bounty* and the long return voyage to England. Of course I had already decided that that was a country I would never lay eyes on again – the thought of what Mr Lewis would do to me when he caught up with me was enough to secure that fact in my head; I had little doubt by now that a few discrete enquiries on his part would have led him to hear of my arrest, my brief trial, incarceration and then the offer that had been made to me – and if I hadn't been forced to pay for my crimes back in Spithead there was little doubt that I would have to make up for my absence upon my return. But that did leave me with the devil of a dilemma: how to escape? Otaheite was a relatively large-sized island compared with some that we had passed, but it was an island nonetheless. There was precious little chance that I could disappear some day and not be discovered. And what would happen if I did? A flogging? A hanging? There was only one legal punishment for desertion and I couldn't risk that. There had to be another way. I just had to wait for my chance.

However, lying there as I was, thoughts of escape were far from my mind and I was engaged instead in a pleasant fantasy in which I was a boy of monkey-like tendencies, able to swing from tree to tree with ne'er a care for my safety. This was a happy enough day-dream to allow me to enjoy the peace and serenity and I would have gladly stayed flat on my back until the captain reappeared later in the day were it not for a footful of sand being kicked crudely into my face, landing in my eyes and mouth, which was open at the time, engaged in the act of a yawn. I spluttered and tried to open my eyes to name and massacre the miscreant who had disturbed me, but before I could scrape the grains from the sockets I heard the scut's voice barking above me.

'Turnip, you lazy jackanapes, what in blazes do you think you're doing?'

I looked up at Mr Heywood and frowned. 'I am engaged in a contemplation,' I told him, maintaining my horizontal position on the ground, which was as flagrant an act of disrespect that I could manage, for we were supposed to leap to our feet in deference to their sanctified state whenever an officer approached us. Nevertheless, I shifted slightly in the sands so that I was not so obviously beneath him; the memory of him standing above me and taking his shrivelled cock from his pants to piss on me during my outbound trial lingered unpleasantly in my memory.

'Engaged in what?' he asked, for his schooling was such as a nine-year-old girl might have vied with him in a competition of wits and not disgraced herself. 'Contem-what?'

'Contemplation, Mr Heywood,' said I. 'It refers to the moment when a chap is lost in thought and considering his past, present and future and their relative worths. The concept might be a new one to you.'

'Past, present and future?' he asked with a sarcastic laugh. 'Your past was as an urchin on the slimy streets of Portsmouth; your present is as the lowest of the low on board His Majesty's frigates; and your future will be determined by one singular fact: that you will end your days as a drunkard under the king's pleasures at one of his gaols.'

'Not a bad life, all told,' I remarked. 'Now, Mr Heywood, if you please, sir,' I added, shifting further left again, 'you're blocking the sun.'

'Less of your sauce,' he replied, not so sure in tone now. He let out a sigh, as if the heat and the conditions were enough to distract him from any further attempts to assert his authority. 'Stand up, will you at least, and let the king look at the cat.'

I rose to my feet slowly and brushed myself down, for a direct order was a direct order and I knew well that I could get away with a certain amount of banter but that he'd see me swing if I disobeyed him. I considered for a moment which was the more unusual, the fact that he considered me to be a feline creature or his own regal pretensions, but it was neither here nor there for the moment, so I held my tongue on it. He was looking at me with that mixture of contempt and revulsion that he always pierced me with. For my part I could only consider why the heat of the Otaheite sun had burned his skin so bad. It made his pimples look like dormant volcanoes.

'You're a lazy good-for-nothing, do you know that, Turnip?' asked he, and for once my composure around him dropped.

'Turnstile,' said I. 'My name is Turnstile, Mr Heywood. John Jacob Turnstile. Is it so difficult for a fellow like you to remember that? And you supposedly of intellect.'

'Your name could be Margaret Delacroix for all I care, Turnip,' he replied with a shrug. 'You're just a servant-lad and I'm an officer, which means—'

'You're above me, I know,' I replied with a sigh. 'I'm familiar with the ladder by now.'

'What were you doing anyway?' he asked then.

'I should have thought it was plain to see,' said I. 'The captain is away for the afternoon with the senior officers' – I threw that in for a farce even though it was beneath me – 'which meant that I had a little time to myself.'

Mr Heywood laughed and shook his head. 'My God, Turnip . . . *Turnstile*,' he said then dramatically, 'you really don't have a whisper of a clue, do you? There is no free time for His Majesty's men. Just because the captain has decided that you're of little use to him today does not give you cause for idleness. You seek out work! You come and find me and ask what needs doing!'

'Ah,' said I, considering it. 'I was unfamiliar with the rules. I'll bear it in mind for future occasions although, I must confess, the captain gives me very little free time indeed. He can't bear to be parted from those he considers most worthy of his attentions.' Even as I spoke, I concluded that this exchange, which was spoiling my afternoon, was entirely my own fault anyway. I should have been hiding out of sight, not lying around where any old scut could find me. I would not make such an error of judgement again.

'I need you over by the gardens,' said Mr Heywood then, dismissing our badinage suddenly. 'Pull yourself together and follow me, if you please.'

Over the course of the weeks since our arrival many of the crew members had been engaged in the occupation of digging a garden at a nearby part of the island. The task involved cutting the soil, then turning it, then laying out neat rows side by side that stretched on for quite some distance. I had gone to visit it a day or two earlier, having little else to do, and been impressed by the level of activity taking place, but had made sure to keep myself out of sight lest I be offered the chance to take part in it. The captain had sat down with King Tynah and explained the reason for his mission – the collection of the breadfruit – and after a little appropriate flattery the king had happily agreed that we might take all we liked. The island was littered with them after all and there was no risk of our making the item extinct. However, the plan was not, as I had imagined, to take the breadfruit themselves and transport them back to the ship; on the contrary, we were going to grow as many fresh samples as we could from original shoots, then plant those saplings in the earthenware pots near the captain's cabin, before transporting them onwards to our next destination, the West Indies, before returning home.

'I had better not, if it's all the same to you, sir,' said I, resolving to be polite if it would mean that he would leave me in peace. 'The captain might return at any minute and if he wants me for something I have to be available.'

'The captain,' stated Mr Heywood in a firm voice, 'will be away until sunset. He will have no need of you in the meantime. He didn't take you with him, did he?'

'No, sir,' I admitted. 'He left us both behind.'

'In which case you are free to help with the gardens.'

I opened my mouth, attempting to locate a further piece of sauce that might serve the twin pleasures of excusing me from the work while also irritating him to the point that his head might explode, but I could discover none and before I knew what day of the week it was I was being led back in the direction of that area of the island where hard work was undertaken.

An hour later and there I was, tilling soil with nine or ten other crew members, my arms protesting the strange weight of the hoes, so uncomfortable in the heat that I had stripped down as far as decency would allow, but the sweat off my body could have greased up a cog-wheel nonetheless. If I was to grow flabby, as Captain Bligh had suggested, I could scarcely imagine when it might happen. I had been a skinny lad to begin with but a twelve-month on board had taken all the fat from my body and I swear that I could run a finger along my rib-cage and feel the bumpity-bumpity-bump as I passed each one along the way. I had muscle though, newly acquired since my Portsmouth days, and a level of energy that sometimes surprised me. Near to me was midship-man George Stewart, whose pale skin was burning up and would,

I knew, present him with a pretty pain later in the day, and he looked as if he might pass out at any moment. Fortunately, the native girls had a strange concoction of medicines, which they trampled together in bowls into a fine paste and which they then massaged into the bare skin of the burnt men at the end of each day. I suspected that the men were happy for the scorching if it meant they got the familiar attentions as a result of it.

'Here, George Stewart,' said I, and perhaps the heat had given me the head-hysterics to make the following suggestion, even in jest. 'What say you we take our hoes and bash Mr Heywood's brains in so that we might make our escape?'

I meant the whole thing as a terrific farce, but the look on Stewart's face instantly told me that I had erred badly. He stared at me with the contempt that only the most junior of the crewmen ever displayed towards me – as the captain's servant I had no official ranking on the boat and so that meant that the lowest of the low had someone to look down their noses at – and shook his head before returning to his work.

'I didn't mean it,' I said quickly. 'It was just a joke.'

Something inside me made me regret my casual comments and I was about to go over and explain that I meant nothing by them, when all the men stood up and dropped their hoes and I followed their gaze westward to where a chain of four young girls were walking in our directions, carrying large urns on their heads. They walked with ease and seemed not to notice the great weight they were transporting; I suspected that they could have broken into a running chase and still they would not have spilled a drop. They wore naught but a strip of fabric around their waists to cover their shame, but after a week here the tendency of the men to whistle and leer at their titties had waned somewhat. We still looked, of course, and they gave me the motions so much that I was at tug more times during the day than I considered healthy, but for the moment the thing that interested us the most was the jars on their heads, for they contained something far more special to us now than the feminine form; they were filled with icy water from a nearby cold stream.

The men rushed towards the girls and they lowered the jars to fill the tall cups that sat near the gardens and each man swallowed his rapidly in order to have it refilled as many times as was possible before the supply was drained. I was slow in joining the group and the last to be served and, when I was, it was the final member of the group who poured for me, a girl I had not seen before, a girl around my own age, perhaps a little older. I stared at her as she filled my cup and astonished myself to discover that my dry palate could grow dryer still. I held the cup but didn't taste the water.

'Drink,' she said, smiling at me now, and her white teeth set against that brown skin dazzled me momentarily and I obeyed her instructions, as I would have done had she commanded me to lift the knife from Mr Heywood's belt and slit my own throat with it, ear to ear. I swallowed the water in one rush, feeling it make its sudden descent through my gut and chilling me delight-fully, and begged her to serve me some more, which she did with a laugh. Only, this time as she poured, her head was bowed but her eyes were lifted and she held my own while she smiled.

I'll make it clear to you now and save you the flowery language. This girl was Kaikala, a word that meant 'all the coldness of the sea and all the heat of the sun', and from that moment on I was smitten. She held me in her hands. The sound of the men fell to nothing beside me and only when Mr Heywood, the scut, came over and led her away by the arm did I snap back to life.

'Here, take a look at Turnip,' cried John Hallett, the lad nearest my age on board. 'He's lost his reason.'

I looked around then and all the men were looking at me, some amused, some bored. I shook my head and went back to my digging, and little more can I remember from that afternoon's labours, for my mind was elsewhere entirely, in a land I had never visited, a place that I wished to call home.

6

ALTHOUGH RELATIONS BETWEEN THEM appeared to have improved considerably towards the end of our voyage to Otaheite and across the span of our earliest weeks on the island, a further dispute eventually broke out between Captain Bligh and Mr Fryer. On this occasion, I confess my sympathies were with the ship's master, for he was hard done by in the argument by both the captain himself and the crew members who blamed him for the fault of it.

The matter started, as these matters often do, with a trifle so insignificant that it might not have been of any consequence at all had it not led to something else, which in turn led to something else, which in turn led to the dispute. But initially the entire conflict turned on a pin: the captain was suffering the squits.

There wasn't a man or boy from the *Bounty's* crew who had not been indulging in more food and drink since arriving at the island than we had on board the ship, and although our skin and hair were the better for it, and all cases of scurvy had quickly cleared up with the sudden influx of vitamins afforded by the limitless supply of fresh fruit and vegetables that the island afforded us, there were some who overdid things too quickly and felt the worse for it. One of those was the captain, who had developed a great taste for the papaya fruit and ate so many of them one day that they affected his digestive system something terrible and he was back and forth to his privy like nobody's business.

When I brought him his breakfast on that particular morning I could tell that there was something amiss on account of the paleness of his face, the dark sacs that hung beneath his eyes and the drops of perspiration about his forehead, but my mind being fully distracted by my new love, Kaikala, I thought little of it at the time.

'Good morning, Captain, your holiness, sir,' said I, all joy and cheer. 'And a fine morning it is, to be sure.'

'Good Lord, Turnstile, if I didn't know better I'd have taken you for an Irishman,' said the captain, looking across at me irritably. I didn't care for the accusation. The suggestion that I had impersonated an Irishman had been one of the charges that King Neptune, the donkey, had made to me when I was a slimy polly-wog and which had resulted in my terrible trial as we had crossed the Equator. 'Your turn of phrase becomes more perverse by the day.'

'Oh, no, Captain,' said I quickly, shaking my head. 'You have me mistaken. I knew many an Irishman when I lived in Portsmouth, I don't mind admitting it, but they were a rum lot and given to expressing themselves in an overly affectionate manner after they had taken a drink, which was often, so I snubbed them for the most part.'

'Yes, yes,' he replied, as if I was a terrible nuisance altogether, sitting up and poking around at the plate I'd brought with a growing look of distaste about his chops. I could tell that he was in no humour for my particular brand of prattle, even if I was in the form for it myself. 'Heavens above, Turnstile, didn't you think to bring me any fresh water?'

I thought he must have gone mad, because there was a jug of fresh cold water, which I'd drawn myself from a stream not ten minutes before, sitting at the side of the tray beside his bread and fruit.

'It's right there, Captain,' I said, pushing it forward a little. 'Will you have me pour you a cup?'

'I'm not an infant,' he snapped, staring at it in surprise, for it did seem a little curious that he had failed to notice it before. 'I think I can manage to feed myself without your assistance.'

'As you please, sir,' said I, picking up a few items that he'd casually dropped to the ground the night before, in the manner that gentlemen do when they know there's another who'll come along after them to collect their mess. It's something their mamas teach them. I held my tongue as I did this, sensible enough to know that the captain was neither in the form nor the mood for chatter. His mood had darkened over the weeks that we had been here, despite the fact that the work upon which we were engaged was continuing at a strong pace. I suspected that he was finding the change of circumstances unhappy, however. By the nature of things, there were days when he did not see some of his officers at all, and the entire crew had not been gathered together as one since the evening before we had first spotted land. He was as aware as anyone that the men were enjoying the physical side of being on Otaheite and making themselves free and easy with their new friends.

A special hut had been erected for him in the shade of some trees near the shoreline but far enough removed from it that he did not need to worry about getting his groundsheets damp. Most of the men were sleeping in hammocks and on the beaches. Of course, many of the men had already found a girl to spend those nights with and not be left alone. Or two girls. Or, in Mr Hall's case, four girls and a lad, but that is another story and one he would have to take up with Mrs Hall on his return to England and not for these pages. As I had yet to know a feminine touch myself, I tried desperately not to focus too much of my time on my longings for it. But the captain's hut was particularly fine. He had a desk set up with some maps upon it, and his log-book and daily information sheets about the breadfruits were there too, and he spent much of his time filling it in and writing letters about their progress to Sir Joseph, although how he imagined these would be transported to their recipient I knew not.

'The fruit isn't very good this morning,' said the captain after a moment and I was surprised to hear it, for I'd stolen a little myself and thought it exceptionally fine. Sweet and juicy, as I liked it.

'Isn't it, sir?' asked I and was about to say more and possibly contradict him, when he took me by surprise by suddenly leaping from his bunk with an oath and charging towards me at a speed I had never seen him manage before. For a moment I thought the inferiority of the fruit had turned his head so badly that he was going to knock me to the ground and pull my head from my shoulders but before I knew it he had rushed past me to his privy, wherein he relieved himself quickly and at length in a loud and deeply unpleasant fashion. I thought about leaving, but the mornings were typically set aside for him to set me some tasks that he needed doing during the day and I knew that in his present mood I would be in for trouble if I departed without being dismissed.

When he finally emerged again, he was walking unsteadily and there was a great deal of perspiration on his face; the heavy bags under his eyes had grown even darker still.

'Are you all right, sir?' I asked.

'Yes, yes,' he snapped, pushing me out of the way as he returned to his bunk. 'I've eaten enough, though. I don't want any more of that. Feed me something edible in the future, will you, boy? I haven't the stomach to be poisoned.' I glanced at the tray. He had barely touched any of his food, but I said nothing of that for now; I would set it aside and enjoy it for my own lunch later. 'Have you seen Mr Christian today, Turnstile?' he asked me then. 'The increase of daily collection numbers seems to be levelling out at the moment and I want to know the reason why.'

'I saw him not twenty feet from where we are speaking now,' I replied. 'He was outside when I was coming in, organizing the shifts for today.'

'Only now?' he asked irritably. 'Hang it, boy, look at the time.'

He crawled out of the bunk again and set a robe about his person before marching out on to the sand; he hesitated for a moment when the sun hit him and shielded his eyes before pressing his hand to his forehead, and then continued on, picking up his pace even as his face grew more and more irritated. Mr Christian and Mr Fryer were standing at no distance from us, engaged in a rare moment of light-heartedness, when he stormed in their direction and demanded to know what the devil was going on.

'Going on with what, sir?' asked Mr Christian, and I confess that no man's hair had ever looked as dark as his did in the sunlight that morning. He was standing there without a shirt on and it was not difficult to see why the ladies of the island had taken such a fancy to him; he had a structure to him that seemed as if the Saviour himself had been present at his formation and presented a design of his own construct. Gossip around the camp was that he had already had his way with more than a dozen of the native girls and was determined to work his way through the whole shoddy lot of them by the close of business on Friday.

'With the breadfruit, Mr Christian,' snapped the captain. 'So far we have transported fewer than two hundred to the nursery, when the schedule clearly states that we were to have broken the three-hundred mark by yesterday. How are they to mature and be ready for transportation to the ship's cargo hold at this rate?'

Mr Christian gave an almost imperceptible shrug of his shoulder and looked at Mr Fryer for a moment, before stalling for time. 'Is there really that much of a shortfall?' he asked.

'I wouldn't have said it if there wasn't,' insisted the captain. 'And what time of the day is this to be organizing the rotas anyway? The men should have been at their work an hour ago.'

'We were just waiting for Martin and Skinner to return, sir,' said Mr Fryer, speaking for the first time now, and from my vantage point several feet away I wondered why he didn't hold his tongue entirely, for there was precious little that was guaranteed to stir the captain's temper more when he was already in a commotion than discourse with the ship's master.

256

'Waiting for Martin and Skinner?' asked the captain in astonishment. He hesitated before continuing and seemed to utter a slight groan; I could tell it was the squits playing with him. He took the weight off his right leg and transferred it to his left, but his body seemed to sink a little in the sand even as he did so. 'What do you mean "waiting for them"?'

'To return from last night's . . . escapades,' replied Mr Fryer, choosing his words carefully.

'Escapades?' asked the captain, staring at him as if the man had suffered an embolism. 'What sort of escapades? Is it a circus we are running here now?'

'Well, sir . . !' replied Mr Fryer, hesitating, and laughing for a moment before turning that laugh into a cough and recalling his serious countenance, 'you are a man of the world. I dare say you understand.'

'I understand nothing, sir, that you do not explain to me,' snapped the captain, and I wondered whether that was entirely what he wanted to say and suspected not. 'What escapades are they about? Answer me, sir!'

'I believe they took some of the native girls inland a little for the evening's sport,' replied Mr Fryer cheerfully. 'They'll be back here at any moment, I guarantee it.'

Captain Bligh stared at him in amazement and his mouth lay open for a moment; I dreaded to think what was to come. But to my surprise he turned away from Mr Fryer and chose his companion to address instead. 'Mr Christian,' he began, 'are you seriously telling me that—' He halted again and offered a small grunt of agony, his face contorting something rotten. 'Stay here a moment, the both of you. Neither of you are to leave.'

And with that he vanished back inside his hut and from there to his privy and when he returned a few moments later he appeared both embarrassed by his absence and more annoyed than he had been before.

'There's too much indolence around here for my liking,' he

roared immediately, not allowing either of them a chance to speak first. 'And you're at the heart of it, the pair of you. Standing around like a couple of ladies' maids while the men have deserted—'

'Sir, they have hardly deserted—' began Mr Fryer, but the captain was not to be interrupted.

'They have deserted their posts even if they have not deserted their king,' he shouted. 'They should be here and ready for work at the scheduled time. It's all this sleeping on shore that's doing it to them. The whole thing needs to be brought to a swift end and now. You, Mr Christian, you're in charge of the nursery. How many men do you need there on a shift every day?'

'Well, sir,' said Mr Christian, smoothing down his eyebrows and examining the condition of his fingernails as he considered the question, 'I suppose a dozen and a half would do us at any one time to tend the gardens, half working, half on rest.'

'Then, Mr Fryer, the men who are not part of the nursery duties, those men who are engaged in transportation during the day, they will return to the ship every evening when their duties are completed and sleep on board. Is that understood?'

The three of us who were not of the captain's rank stood silently for a moment and I was pleased to note the look of disbelief that passed between the two officers. For my part, I wished that the captain's squits would come on again and he'd be taken unawares and forget about this suggestion, for even I knew what trouble this would lead to.

'Captain,' said Mr Fryer, 'are you sure that's wise?'

'Wise?' asked Mr Bligh with a laugh. 'Are you questioning my decision?'

'I only ask, sir,' he replied patiently, 'because you yourself informed the men when we arrived at Otaheite that their sacrifices along the way were received in gratitude and that things would be a little less . . . regimental on the island. As long as the work is done I see no reason why the men shouldn't be allowed to enjoy a little leisure time in the evening. It's good for morale and so on.'

This was a pretty speech to have delivered without suffering the sensation of having his head ripped from his shoulders, and even as he spoke it Mr Christian caught my eye and we shared an unexpected moment of silent agreement, the accord being that neither of us would like to be on the receiving end of what was to come next.

'Mr Fryer,' said the captain finally, and I was even more nervous to note that he held his tone steady as he spoke. 'You are truly a disgrace to your uniform, sir.'

The recipient of this insult stood there, open-mouthed, and Mr Christian swallowed nervously as the tirade continued.

'You stand there in front of me and tell me that the men made sacrifices on our journey. The men made no sacrifices, Mr Fryer. The men are part of His Majesty's navy, God bless his name, and what they do they do in his name and it is their duty, sir, aye their sworn duty. As it is your duty, sir, to listen to my every word and obey my every order and question me not. Why must we have this continual back-and-forth between us, Mr Fryer? Why can you not simply fulfil the role for which you were put on board the Bounty?'

'Sir,' replied Mr Fryer after a moment, and he held himself to his full height as he spoke and his voice didn't quiver, for which I admired him, 'if those are your orders I will of course see them through. I wish it to be stated for the record, however, that I consider it ill-advised to punish the men at this time, and that is what it will be seen as, sir, punishment, on the trifling matter of two men being late for work detail. There are better ways to tackle the problem than breaking a promise that was made to all at once.'

'Ways you are familiar with, no doubt?'

'Allow Fletcher and me to speak to the men, sir. We can make it clear to them that a little fun is one thing, but we are here with a mission to achieve and—'

'We'll not speak to the men,' said the captain quietly, his voice filled with exhaustion, his face growing pale again, and I could tell that he was about to have another turn and would need to go to relieve himself. 'I have spoken to you and you will tell them and what I have said will happen and that is an end to the matter, is that understood?'

'Yes, sir,' said Mr Fryer, an obvious tone of dissatisfaction in his voice. 'As you say.'

'As I say, indeed, sir,' snapped Mr Bligh. 'And you, Mr Christian, you will keep your men at the nursery on a tight leash from now on and see that every man pulls his weight, but there will be no more nocturnal fraternizing with . . . with . . .'

'With whom, sir?' asked Mr Christian.

'With the *savages*,' he replied.

At this his body bent over halfway with the pain of it and he was forced to run back to the hut again, leaving Mr Christian, Mr Fryer and me standing in his wake, filled with a mixture of amazement, dismay and wonder.

'What say you to that?' asked Mr Fryer.

Mr Christian sucked in his breath and shook his head. 'Not easy to tell them,' he replied. 'There'll be a lot of unhappy sailors, I can promise you that.'

'Perhaps if we speak to him later? Or if you do, Fletcher. He listens to you.'

I knew that Mr Fryer was right, but knew even better that the chances of Mr Christian attempting to change the captain's mind in order to improve the lot of the common sailing man was about as likely as wings appearing out of my shoulder-blades and my flying off to a land where there was plenty to eat and drink and Kaikala was by my side, hoping to pleasure me every hour on the hour from now until the Saviour called us home.

'I don't know, John,' said Mr Christian. 'Have you ever considered that—' At this he turned and saw me standing there and hesitated. 'Turnip, what the devil do you think you're doing?'

'I thought the captain was coming back, sir,' said I, all innocence.

'I think he's gone for now,' he replied. 'Go after him. He might need your help.'

The last place I wanted to be was back in that hut, but I followed reluctantly and the captain was not in sight; he was locked in the privy again.

And that is the story of how a case of the squits let to an ill-considered decision, which in turn laid the first seeds of discontent for the mountain of trouble that was to follow. Had I known then what lay ahead, I would have mixed into the captain's tea a little nutmeg and olive extract the night before, as everyone knows the good that does for the stomach and the manner in which it keeps the squits at bay.

7

THAT WAS THE START OF IT. The captain's personality began to alter something terrible during the weeks that followed and I started to suspect that the heat on the island was playing games with his mind, for the good-humoured and kindly man I had known on board the *Bounty* became irritable and prone to out-bursts against all.

Mr Fryer, observing me having the head practically lifted from my shoulders over a small trifle one evening, took me aside and earned my eternal gratitude by asking after my well-being, a question that had barely been put to me once in my life, let alone since joining that shoddy crew.

'I'm extremely well,' said I, lying through my teeth. 'Here I am, a lad on a tropical island with the sun on my face and my belly full. What should I have to complain about?'

Mr Fryer smiled and for a moment I was afraid that he was going to embrace me. 'You're a good lad, Master Turnstile,' he replied. 'You care a lot for the captain, do you not?'

I thought about it and considered my reply carefully. 'He's been good to me,' I admitted. 'You don't know the kind of men I had to deal with before him.'

'Then, let me encourage you not to take it to heart when he scolds you,' he said. Scolding was a good word for it! A few minutes earlier I had brought him his tea and forgot the lemon and I swear that he was ready to reach for his cutlass. 'The thing about men like Mr Bligh,' continued Mr Fryer, 'is that they are primarily sea-faring men. When the land beneath their feet is solid, when the tides do not surround them, when the smell of salt water is not in their nostrils, they become irritable and likely to abuse. It is both a rational and irrational fancy and I would encourage you to think nothing of it. What I'm saying, Turnip, is you would be wise not to take it personally.'

There was another possibility to it. There were only two men, as far as I could tell, from the crew of the *Bounty* who had yet to taste the offerings of the native women. One of them was Captain Bligh, who kept his portrait of Betsey close by at all times and who, unlike the other married men of the crew, even the quality ones as were officers, appeared to take as sanctity the vows he had made on his wedding day. I began to wonder whether a juicy dalliance or two would not improve his mood somewhat; I know it would have done wonders for mine. For I, of course, was the other person who remained untouched.

I heeded Mr Fryer's advice, nevertheless, and appreciated his offering of it. A year before, when we had first met, I had often thought him a difficult fellow to get to know. He had a way about him, mostly in the mutton of his chops and that long horse-like face of his, that made a fellow want to avoid him. But he was a kindly soul. Thoughtful to the men and attentive to his duties.

And I liked him for it. Unlike that prancing popinjay Mr Christian, who spent more time addressing his own features in a glass than considering the men who toiled around him.

When I returned to the captain's hut from Mr Fryer's talk, he invited me to inform all the crew, officers and men alike, that they were to gather on board the *Bounty* that evening as he wished to address them as a group and in private. I had half a notion to ask him to take me into his confidence in advance to ascertain what it was he wished to discuss with us, but I feared that to do so would have seen me scalped and skinned before I even reached the end of my sentence.

And so I did as he asked and at seven bells that evening the entire complement of the *Bounty* were gathered on deck once more. Seeing the men together as one for the first time since we had reached the island gave me time to consider how they had changed in the weeks since we had got here. They looked a healthier lot, that was for sure. Their complexions were ruddy, the bags that had drooped from under their eyes had vanished, and they had a fairly cheerful air to them, although I could tell that the unexpected proximity of all being on the boat again gave them a certain air of nervousness. They were already in dread of the day that the captain gave the order to up anchor.

The officers stood at the front, Mr Fryer and Mr Elphinstone dressed appropriately, while Mr Christian and Mr Heywood appeared in a pair of slip-trousers and a chemise open at the collar. I add this for the clarity of the record: I believe that Mr Heywood was inebriated.

I had had the good fortune not to see much of either of these two while on Otaheite, as Mr Christian was in charge of the nursery and, with Mr Heywood as his second-in-command, they lived and spent most of their time there. The captain visited every day, of course, and seemed pleased upon his return by what he had seen, but it was while he was gone that I took my opportunity to clean his lodgings and wash his dirty vestments. But I had heard gossip, of course, that following the work that prospered during the day there was a level of bacchanal enduring through the night that would have put the Greeks and Romans to shame. I saw none of it – yet – but that was because I was not of their number and was too closely associated with the captain to be invited to join their sport. But what I did know was that almost every other man from the crew was finding his way there at the dead of night and making friendly with the island women, and as ne'er a one of them was a Christian lady they had no qualms about allowing them congress.

The captain appeared on deck in full uniform and breathed in deeply through his nose as he observed each and every one of his charges. I recalled what Mr Fryer had said about the captain needing the smell of sea water in his nostrils and wondered whether he wasn't stocking up for later and filling his lungs with enough that he might ration it out for himself as the night wore on. He glanced at his officers and frowned when he saw the outfits that Mr Christian and Mr Heywood had appeared in but looked away for the time being, shaking his head slowly.

'Men,' he declared, silencing the low murmurs with a word, 'I brought you here tonight as it has been some time since we gathered together as a crew. I wanted to . . .' He hesitated here, searching for the appropriate word and seemed loathe to offer it, '*thank* you for all the hard work you are undertaking on the island. Having consulted with Mr Christian at the nursery earlier today and the botanist, Mr Nelson, I can confirm that our work is going according to plan and the success of our mission, should we continue at our current pace, is guaranteed.

'However, there are one or two things I should mention to you as we still have at least a month left on this island and I want to ensure that things continue to go as smoothly as they have so far. The following are a list of . . . not rules, exactly; I think our company is a cheerful enough one without that. Consider them more a list of recommendations that I would like you all to keep in mind as the weeks follow.'

There was a murmuring among the men again at this, but as there was no suggestion that we were preparing to stay on the ship and sail away to England, it was not a nervous one.

'Firstly,' continued the captain, 'as you are no doubt aware, the natives on the island believe that Captain Cook is alive and well and residing in Belgravia. In reality, of course, this heroic man was murdered by savages on nearby islands some years ago. I wish the lie, if you can call it such, to be continued. It is in our interests to maintain the deceit that a friendship continues between the late captain and our host, Tynah, who naturally looks up to him with the respect and adulation that such an Englishman deserves. I will take most seriously the actions of any man who violates this lie.

'Secondly, I am aware that there is a certain amount of . . . friendliness between you men and the island women. This is not an uncommon thing and of course the ladies here, and I use the term liberally, have none of the decencies that our wives and sweethearts have at home, so do with them as you will but I urge you to treat them kindly and take a care for your own health as you do so.'

There was raucous laughter that greeted this remark and a series of bawdy shouts from the men that I won't repeat here, for they're beneath me. After a few moments had passed, the captain raised his hand, the men calmed, and he spoke again.

'As you know, we have taken many items from the ship to the shore to assist us in our endeavours, and King Tynah has been kind enough to offer us the use of knives and cutting implements to assist us too. Every man should take care of them and see that nothing is lost or stolen. The value of any lost items shall be charged against their protector's wages at a later date.'

I can assure you that the men didn't care for that last remark and made it clear, but it seemed only decent to me. If a chap can't be trusted to take care of items, then he's not worth his salt.

'I am sure,' continued the captain, 'that no man is engaged in the act of what I suggest next, but it has happened on previous voyages, on other ships, so I merely bring it to your attention. All ship items, everything we collect on the island, any part of our stores, is not yours, nor mine, but the king's, and any man who embezzles any of it for the purposes of trading or bartering will be guilty of the most serious breach of standing orders and be dealt with accordingly.'

I looked round and saw some guilty-looking faces. It happened regularly, we all knew that – even the captain knew that – but this was his way of attempting to put a stop to it.

'I shall appoint one of the officers to be placed in charge of regular trade between the island and the ship as part of an act of commerce and if any man here wishes to purchase something from the island he shall apply directly to this officer for permission. Mr Christian,' he said, turning to the first officer, 'I had intended offering this position to you.'

'Thank you, sir,' he replied, practically rubbing his hands together in glee, for it was obvious that such a position held the right to earn more money than any other job on board. 'I shall be glad to—'

'Only, I note, sir, that you think it appropriate to stand on deck, facing the men, with your collar exposed.'

Mr Christian's mouth opened a little in surprise and his face reddened; he was not accustomed to being chastised in front of any of us. 'Sir?' he asked nervously.

'You think your garb appropriate, do you, sir?' asked the captain. 'And you, Mr Heywood, if Mr Christian was to drink his own bath water would you follow suit, sir?'

Mr Heywood glared at him but answer had he none.

'Discipline is falling apart here, gentlemen,' stated the captain in a serious tone, but not as serious as it was to become in the following weeks. 'I would ask you not to present yourself during your official duties in such a naked fashion. Mr Fryer, perhaps you would be good enough to take over the trade duties.'

'Thank you, sir,' said Mr Fryer, displaying no emotion on his face, and I must admit I thought it a fair thing indeed to see him rewarded for once, rather than damned.

'Then, that's an end to the lecture, men,' said the captain with a tone of forced jollity. 'I believe I will sleep on board tonight. Mr Christian, you will lead your nursery men back to the island. The rest shall stay on the *Bounty*.'

And that was how we left things that night, a set of rules before us, a warranted officer chastised in front of us, and a feeling among us all that the good times we had been enjoying might shortly be due to end.

Quicker than any of us expected.

8

HERE'S HOW WE DID THINGS. Every afternoon, around four bells, the captain went to his tent for his afternoon nap. He was always an early riser, was Captain Bligh, and if he didn't get to sleep for a few hours before his evening meal he could be a real tartar. Before he drifted off, I made sure to leave a bowl of fresh water by his bedside so that he could splash himself back to life when he woke up if I hadn't yet returned. And then I left.

I ran southwards from the camp into an overgrown area of trees and bushes, the type of flora I had never encountered in my life before, but I saw little of it as I hurried along, eager for my destination. I was not there for a sightseeing exercise, nor was I interested in pretty garlands; I had a finer prize awaiting me. I continued running and took a left here, a right there, a leap over some rocks that would appear before me by surprise, a circle round a mound of trees that gathered together in a circle as if protecting some creature in its home within. And then I came out into a clearing where the island fauna scurried around with a sense of great importance; I paid them as little heed as they did me.

By now I would be able to hear the gentle lapping of the water in the streams and the fall of the water slipping into the lake below and I would know that I was close, and when that happened I'd get the motions, knowing what lay ahead for me. There were more trees then, and a sudden burst of sunlight, and before very many more minutes had passed I was greeted with the sight I had been longing since our last parting: Kaikala.

She was the same age as me, I think, maybe a year older. Perhaps two at a stretch. Probably three, if I'm to be entirely honest. And when she smiled at me she made me feel that no one in my life had ever thought as highly of me as she did, or considered me quite such a dashing chap, an assessment that was probably a fair one. She couldn't get her mouth around the name John, and had no ability whatsoever for Turnstile. Fortunately, having never seen a turnip in her life, she had no intention of calling me by that blasted name either and I believe it would have brought tears from my eyes had some miscreant told her of it and she had found it amusing. And so she settled on my middle name, Jacob, which she pronounced to sound like Yay-Ko, and in this way the two of us, Kaikala and Yay-Ko, formed our alliance.

It was common knowledge that every man on the island had sought companionship with the womenfolk – every man with the exception of Captain Bligh, that is, whose heart belonged to Betsey back home in London. These were not affairs of the heart, for the most part, but some of the younger fellows, such as myself, less accustomed to the affections and intimacies of women than our elder colleagues, perhaps mistook these signs of warmth for something more than they truly were. Kaikala had made it clear from the day that we had first met that I belonged to her and that

I was to be her willing slave, ready to go where she wanted, when she wanted, and to do whatever she bade me. This was a role I accepted with willingness and delight. The more she asked of me, the happier I was to fulfil her desires; I was no longer Mr Bligh's servant-lad, I was hers. As we lay by the lake together, touching each other gently, my fingers able to explore her titties now as freely as I might have shaken the captain's hand, she asked me about my life back home in England.

'My home is in London,' I told her, playing the toff even though I had never been north of Portsmouth in my life. 'I have a charming house just off Piccadilly Circus. The floors are marble and the banisters are made of gold, although the sheen has come off them a little so I left instructions with my servants to have them buffed and shined for my eventual return. I summer at the country house, however, in Dorset. London is a frightful bore in the summer, don't you think?'

'You are a rich man?' she asked me, eyes opening wide.

'Well, the thing you have to remember is that it's vulgar to say that you are,' I explained, stroking my chin sagely. 'So let us just say that I am comfortable. Very, very comfortable.'

'I wish to be comfortable,' she said. 'You have many friends in England?'

'Oh, but of course,' said I. 'We are heady members of society, my family and I. Why, only last year my sister Elizabeth had her coming-out ball and within ten days she had received four proposals of marriage and a rabbit of unusual colour from an admirer. A maiden aunt has taken her for a companion in the meantime as she completes a walking tour of Europe, where I dare say she will engage herself in any number of romantic misunderstandings and alliances, and she can recite her numbers in French, German and Spanish.'

She smiled and looked away and I could see that she liked the idea of this. She had an air about her of someone who knew nothing of the world outside her own, but who was aware

269

nonetheless that there was one out there, a better one, and she wanted some of it.

'But why then is Yay-Ko here on this ship?' she asked me. 'Do you not want to stay in England and count your money?'

'It's my old papa,' I told her with a terrible sigh. 'He made his money in shipping, you see, and before handing the business over to me he insisted that I learn something about the sea. Terribly old-fashioned, but what can you do? One must humour the old pater. And so he arranged for me to have this posting. He's a game old thing, but he might not have long left in him and he wanted to be sure that he was handing over to someone who knew the ropes. I am Captain Bligh's closest adviser, though,' I assured her. 'The *Bounty* would practically sink if I wasn't on board.'

'The captain, he scares me,' she said with a shudder. 'I see him look at me and I think he wants to kill me.'

'His bark is worse than his bite,' I reassured her. 'I will tell him what a wonderful girl you are and then he will treat you differently. He listens to me more than anyone else.'

'And those two at the gardens,' she added, shaking her head and curling her lip. 'I do not like them at all.'

'That's Mr Christian and Mr Heywood,' said I. 'One's a popinjay and the other's a scut, but you don't need to worry about them. I'm above them and they must do as they are bid. If they attempt anything unpleasant with you, then you must tell me at once.' This is what I lived in fear of the most, hearing that Mr Christian had pursued an advantage with Kaikala. Or – worse still – that Mr Heywood had.

'They are bad men,' she hissed under her breath. 'The men from your ship are kind, mostly, but not them. They treat us badly. They treat all the girls badly. We are afraid of them.'

There was something in her tone that made me want to know more and yet at the same time made me not want to listen. I had never got along with the scut or the dandy but, still, they were

270

Englishmen and I didn't like to hear that they were behaving in an upsetting fashion towards the natives.

'And the king,' she asked afterwards. 'King George. You are acquainted with him?'

'Acquainted?' said I with a laugh and sitting up on my elbows. 'Acquainted, you ask? Why, me oh my, I have been good friends with His Majesty since I was a bairn. Many's the time he's had me up to the palace and we sit around and play cheroot together or maybe a hand of Ruff and Trump and stay up late into the night, talking affairs of state while drinking the finest wine.'

Kaikala looked thrilled by this idea. 'And ladies?' she asked. 'There are ladies at his court?'

'Many ladies,' said I. 'The most beautiful ladies in England.'

She looked away from me then and turned her lip. 'Yay-Ko has a lady he loves at the court,' she said sadly.

I jumped to my own defence. 'Never!' I cried. 'Not in this world! I held out against them, waiting for the right one. The most beautiful woman, not in England, but in the whole world. That is what I came to Otaheite for. And that is what I discovered here.'

I took her hand at that, acting like such a nance that I'm ashamed to recall the moment now, and moved closer towards her, wishing that we could be left alone in that place together for ever.

'I make you happy,' she said, moving around so that I was lying on my back and she was seated atop me. 'You want Kaikala to give you pleasure?'

'Yes,' I squeaked, but even as she undid my britches I could feel the motions, which had hitherto been full of purpose, leaving me until I was naught but a shrivelled wreck beneath her. She looked down at me in disappointment, for it happened every day, and then looked directly into my eyes.

'What is the matter?' she asked. 'Yay-Ko doesn't like me?'

'I do,' I replied defensively, willing myself into action. I reached up and cupped her titties in my hands and, much pleasure as I got from the touch, I could not transfer that into action. My head became filled with pictures of the past, the time before, Mr Lewis's establishment and all that he had made me do there. If I closed my eyes I could hear the sound of gentlemen's boots on the step and the clod-clod-clod as they ascended the stairs towards us boys. And so our afternoons together always ended the same way; with me running back through the jungle, pulling my pants up as I went, returning close to the camp, only to find that what had failed me before was full of life now, and hiding in the hedges to find a little pained relief before returning to the captain's side and my duties.

I hated Mr Lewis and all he had done to me. And I sought a cure.

9

CAPTAIN BLIGH'S DECISION TO LEAVE Mr Fryer in charge of all the trade between the islanders and the crewmen had seemed to be a sensible one at first and for a time there were no serious incidents of theft or illegal bartering taking place, at least none that were brought to the captain's attention. However, I was attending on Mr Bligh one morning at the home of King Tynah, when a report was made to him that set about another turn in our fortunes.

The king and the captain got along very well; in fact there were even days when I believed that the captain appeared to have more respect for Tynah than he did for the majority of his own officers any more. Almost every morning, he would visit His Majesty at his home and inform him how well their mission was coming along and how grateful both Captain Cook and King George would be when they learned how accommodating their Pacific brother had been to their plans. It was patronizing, certainly, and I would have been keen to slap any man who'd spoken down to me with as much condescension as the captain did towards our host, but the native king was susceptible to such flattery, that was for sure, and everyone was happy, and so it continued and in this way the mission moved towards its conclusion.

'The men,' the king asked one morning as they sat over cups of the mucous liquid that the king's servants prepared for him on a regular basis and which contained some mixture of banana, mango, water and a flavour with which I was unfamiliar, 'they eat well on the island, yes?'

'Very well, Your Majesty, thank you,' said Captain Bligh, sampling some of the lighter refreshments that the servants had left out on the trays before him. 'Let me see now . . . our stores have been well stocked at all our stops along the way and the fruit and vegetables of Otaheite make a most pleasant variation from our standard fare.'

The king nodded his head very slowly, as if the matter of movement was a great inconvenience to such a man as he, but his mouth was pursed, as if he had just discovered a taste in his mouth that he did not care for. 'You know that I think of you with friendship, William,' he said, and he is the only man in these pages who I ever heard address the captain with that level of familiarity.

'Of course, Your Majesty,' replied Mr Bligh, looking up cautiously, for he knew as I did that only bad sentences began with phrases such as that. 'As I do of you.'

'And you and your men are welcome to the fruit and vegetables of the island, as you say. They are God's gift to all who are here. But the pigs . . .' He shook his head and wagged his thick old brute of a finger in the captain's face. 'No more of the pigs.'

Captain Bligh stared at him and then across at me for a

moment as if he had not fully understood the statement. 'I beg your pardon,' he said, smiling quizzically. 'I don't understand, Your Majesty. What of the pigs?'

'You must not eat our pigs,' replied the king forcefully, looking ahead as if his pronouncement was enough and there need be no further conversation on the matter.

'But, Your Majesty,' continued the captain, 'we do not eat your livestock. You made that clear when we arrived and we have honoured that commitment.'

The king looked at him and raised an eyebrow. '*You* do not, perhaps, William, but your men? They are a different tale. You must tell them to stop. You must tell them now. There will be unhappiness between us if this continues.'

Captain Bligh said nothing for a moment, merely looked at his host as he considered this before bowing his head and breathing heavily through his nose. I could see that he was angered by what had been said. His orders – I remembered his issuing them myself – had been quite explicit on this subject. The conversation between the two men dried up considerably after this and we left the tent in a state of some humiliation.

An hour later, Mr Fryer was summoned to the captain's tent, where he was quizzed on the matter in such a way that you would have thought the master was going around the island all day chewing on a side of bacon.

'Did I not make it clear to all when we got here that the men were disbarred from eating the livestock of the island unless it was served to us by the islanders themselves?'

'Of course, sir,' replied Mr Fryer. 'And to the best of my knowledge, we have all adhered to that rule.'

'To the best of your knowledge,' replied the captain with a sneer that was beneath him. 'Well, let us see how far that gets us, shall we? Are you telling me that you have heard no rumours of pigs being illegally slaughtered and roasted?'

'None, sir.'

'Then, I must take you at your word. But the king believes it to be the case and I imagine he has cause for it. He is not the type to create a fancy. And it will not do, Mr Fryer. I won't stand to be disobeyed. Let me put a notion to you.' He sat down behind his desk and invited Mr Fryer to sit opposite him; it was another of those rare occasions when the two men seemed to have more in common than their differences. 'Your duties take you around a large portion of this island, do they not?'

'They do, sir,' he replied.

'If a man were to steal a pig and bring it somewhere to kill and gut it, roast it and eat it, a place where the smell of burning bacon would not be detected by his fellows or by the officers, where do you suppose he might go?'

Mr Fryer considered it for a moment and I could see his eyes darting back and forth a little nervously as he mentally scanned the terrain with which he had become so familiar. 'It's difficult to say, sir,' he said finally, a half-hearted answer and not worthy of him.

'Then, think, man,' replied the captain, keeping his temper at bay. 'You're a resourceful fellow, Mr Fryer. If it was you, where would you go?'

'Captain, I hope you're not suggesting—'

'Oh, I'm not suggesting anything of the sort, man,' snapped the captain. 'Keep your wig atop your head, for pity's sake. I'm asking that *if* you were to do such a thing, and let us all be assured that you never would,' he added in a sarcastic tone, 'but if you *were* to, then where would you go?'

'It's a conundrum, Captain,' he replied finally. 'The breadfruit are scattered widely, so Mr Christian and Mr Heywood's men are about various parts of the island collecting the specimens throughout the day. They would be distracted by the scent of the meat if it were as you suggest. However . . .' He tapped his nose for a moment and considered it.

'What is it, Mr Fryer?'

'Sir, there's an area of thicket-land, tall trees and undergrowth too heavy for the breadfruit to grow in on the north-east shore. Not a great distance from here actually, no more than a twenty-minute walk in all. The exposure traps the winds that are sweeping in towards it and holds them there, so, in theory, a man who wanted to cover the smell of meat could do worse than commit his crime in such a place.'

The captain nodded. 'You think it's likely?' he asked.

'I hope it is not,' replied Mr Fryer. 'But, to my mind, it is the only possible place where such a thing could take place.'

'Then, let us go there together,' said the captain. 'You and I, sir.'

'Now?'

'Of course now,' he said, standing up with a cheerful look on his face, no doubt pleased to have something constructive to do at last, an opportunity to exert his authority once again. 'Tynah has expressed his displeasure with our crew. Should the matter continue he may decide that we are no longer friends and become indisposed towards us. In which case all our work here would have come to naught. Would you have that, Mr Fryer?'

'No, of course not.'

'Then, let us go. Turnstile, fetch my cane.'

And with that they were out of the cabin for their walk together. I knew not what they would find, whether they would discover anything at all indeed, but I felt pity for the miscreant there should Mr Fryer be proved to be right.

The captain, after all, was just waiting for an opportunity such as this.

Evening times on the island were generally quiet affairs. The men had finished their work, they were ready to enjoy their victuals and then to take their pleasures with the ladies. The natives were happy to stay on the beach, lighting fires, performing dances, making us all feel like gods among men. When the beach was filled with crewmen and natives it was typically a night of laughter and debauchery. And that same night, the night of the day when the captain and Mr Fryer went a-walking, the beach was as full as it ever was, but there was no laughter in the air and no potential for licentiousness or dissipation of any kind.

The crew were gathered together in their lines, the officers standing by their sides, and every man jack of them had the startled look of a fellow who has forgotten what his role in life is and has just descended back down to the earth with a bang. Running around the beach, becoming increasingly distraught, were many dozens of natives, mostly women, screaming and crying in despair.

And at the centre of this throng stood Captain Bligh, alongside Mr Fryer and James Morrison, the boatswain's mate; facing them, tied to a stump, stripped to the waist, his bare back on display, was the cooper, Henry Hilbrant.

'Men,' announced the captain, taking a step forward and addressing us, 'I have spoken to you before regarding discipline and its breakdown while we are on this island. It goes too far when we discover a thief among our number. I made clear to all of you the rules regarding trade, barter and theft; this morning, our island host, His Majesty King Tynah, had cause to reprimand me over the continual loss of his piglets by one of our number. Later in the day I discovered Mr Hilbrant alone with one of his ill-gotten gains, enjoying the bacon. Shamelessly enjoying the bacon, I say! And I tell you now, it will not stand. Mr Morrison, step forward, sir, and comb the cat.'

The bo'sun took a few steps away from Mr Fryer and revealed the cat-o'-nine-tails which he had been holding behind his back and lifted it into the air, giving it a shake to loosen the tendrils. At its appearance the native women let up an almighty cry of pain that put the heart half-crossways in me.

'Go ahead,' said the captain.

Mr Morrison stepped forward and began the flogging and we counted the numbers off in our heads. As they increased past the first dozen I found myself unable to remove my eyes from the face of Hilbrant, who let out a great scream of agony every time the tool made contact with his ripped skin. The only thing more disturbing than the sound of this was the screams of the women who encircled us, some of whom had lifted stones from the beach shore and were dragging them across their foreheads, ripping their own skin and allowing the blood to pour dramatically down their faces. The men watched them and I could see the pain they felt, for they had all formed terrible close bonds with these women and hated to see them hurting themselves so. I searched in vain for Kaikala, but was pleased to see that she had not joined in the self-mutilation and had, I supposed, remained behind in her own tent.

Finally, the lashing stopped, at three dozen, which seemed an awful high price to pay for the theft of such an ignorant animal as a pig, and Hilbrant was cut down.

'There will be no more thievery,' shouted the captain, marching around before us, his face filled with fury, and I swear that I scarcely recognized him at a moment like that. He caught my eye at one point and it seemed to me that he didn't know me at all. This was not the man who had taken care of me when I had been ill at the start of my *Bounty* voyage; nor the man who had come close to being moved when he had discovered the truth of my past exploits at Mr Lewis's establishment. Nor was it the kind and affectionate father who had brought me to the mountain trees to show me his name carved there many years before and allowed me to add my own name to his. This was someone else entirely. Someone who was breaking down before our eyes.

He stopped shouting then for a moment and looked out to where the *Bounty* sat in the water, bathed in the glow of a full moon. I watched his face and saw it crumble when his eyes lit on it; by heaven, he might as well have been entering his bedchamber in London for the first time in two years to discover his beloved Betsey sitting by her dressing table in her shift, as she turned to lay eyes on him again and smile at his return, so tender was the glance. He swallowed, he gasped and his eyes filled with tears, before he reluctantly dragged them away and looked at all of us again.

'We are here to work, men,' he roared. 'Not steal, not dally, not satisfy our carnal pleasures. But to work. For the glory of King George! Let tonight's proceedings be a lesson to you all and a warning of what will happen to the next man who dares to disobey me. This will seem light in comparison, I promise you that.'

And then, exhausted by his own anger, he turned and walked hesitantly back towards his quarters, his head slightly bowed in grief. The men watched him in despair as the women continued to cry and rend at their features.

It occurred to me that it would be a good thing if we finished our work here and returned to the *Bounty*, to the sea, to our voyage, as soon as possible. There was a demon in the air between us, set there not by the men or by the captain, but by those twin creatures that glared at each other constantly – the boat and the island, the one calling its captain home, the other dragging its new captives ever deeper in.

10

WHEN KAIKALA AND I first made love, I'm not ashamed to admit that I let a scream of delight out of me that echoed any of the cries that I had ever heard on the island before. We were in our usual place, by the stream near the waterfall, and she had helped and guided me until my nerves were finally overtaken by my desires and I was able to be one with her. Afterwards, lying side by side as naked as a couple of new-born babes, she quizzed me once again on life in England.

'I have four horses,' I told her. 'Two for my carriages and two for riding. I treat them well, of course. Feed them the finest oats, keep them clean and brushed. Or I have a man who does that for me anyway. He lives in the stables with the horses. And I'm above him.'

'You employ a man to live with horses?' she asked me, sitting up a little on one elbow and staring at me in surprise. I thought about it. I'd never known anyone who kept horses, so wasn't sure who looked after them usually or where they typically resided. However, I still knew more about them than she did, so I believed myself to be fairly safe in the lie.

'Well . . . he lives near by,' I told her. 'Not in the actual . . . not in the actual stable itself.'

'Will you let me ride your horses when I come to England?' she asked me.

I nodded quickly, anxious to please her. 'Of course,' I said. 'You can do whatever you want. You will be the wife of a famous, wealthy man. No one will be able to tell you what you can and cannot do. Except me, of course, as I'll be your husband and there are laws about things like that.'

She smiled at me and leaned back again. The issue of marriage had come up on our previous encounter, when she had done as much to excite me as had ever been done in my life and we had only stopped short of consummating our relationship then by an unfortunate accident that had come over me while she was playing with my bits and pieces. I had told her that I would bring her back to England and make her a fine woman and she had seemed thrilled by the idea of it.

Whenever I was with Kaikala, these lies came easily to me and, in truth, they seemed to be little more than harmless fibs. I didn't imagine she really saw herself sailing across the seas to a new life with me, and I wasn't entirely sure that she believed all the things I said about my supposedly wealthy existence back home either. I thought it was just a game, something that two young lovers might pretend to each other in order to imagine a different life from the one that they actually had.

'But what about you?' I asked her. 'Won't you miss your family, your home on Otaheite? It's unlikely we'll ever come back here again, you know.'

'Oh, no,' she said, shaking her head quickly. 'I won't miss it. My mother and father, they don't care much for me anyway. And they care even less for each other. And anyway, Yay-Ko, I am different from them.'

'Different?' I asked. 'Different how?'

She shrugged her shoulders and I watched as she ran a finger down to her titty and encircled the dark bud at its centre in a distracted fashion. I wanted to kiss it, but even after all that we had done I still did not feel the courage to do so without a proper invitation.

'When I was a child, my mother told me about the men who came before,' she explained. 'She was my age, you see, when they were here.'

'The men who came before?' I asked. 'You mean Captain Cook and the *Endeavour*?'

'Yes, them,' she said. 'She told me about those men: how kind they were, the gifts they brought, and how they stayed and made love to the women time and again.' I gasped a little in surprise; she had no shame in her story-telling and I admired her for it. 'It was my favourite story. I asked her about it frequently. But I always had to imagine it in my mind. What it was like. What they were like. And I thought that if they ever came back here, then they would take me with them when they left. This is a paradise to you, Yay-Ko. To me, it is a prison. I've been a captive here all my life, knowing there's more out there, knowing there's a world that I have not seen. And I want to see it. My parents will never leave. No one here ever leaves. They would never show me the world. Tanemahuta would never show me the world. So I waited. And then you came.'

I nodded, and it struck me that the fantasies of people the world over held a lot more in common than might generally be recognized, and while I was considering her words again one jumped out at me as being something that I did not understand.

'What did you say?' I asked her. 'Who would not show you the world?'

'My parents,' she replied with a smile.

'After them.'

She thought about it, recalling. 'Tanemahuta,' she said. 'He would not.'

I raised my eyebrows and sat up, staring down at her in surprise. 'Who's that?' I asked. 'I haven't heard you mention that name before.'

'He is nobody,' she said with a shrug. 'No one special. He is my husband, that is all.'

My eyes opened wide when she said this and my mouth fell open. 'Your husband?' I asked. 'You're married?' This was fresh news to me and I immediately felt the excitement that was upon me from lying here naked with her drifting away again.

'I *was* married,' she said, as if it was the most natural thing in the world. 'He died.'

'Oh,' I said, a little relieved, but still not entirely happy. 'When did you marry?'

'I don't know,' she said, staring at me as if she couldn't fully understand why I was so interested. 'I was twelve, I think.'

'Twelve? And how old was he?'

'A little older. We married on his fourteenth birthday.'

I gave a low whistle and tried to imagine that happening back home in Portsmouth. You'd be locked up for less, I knew that from personal experience.

'What happened to him?' I asked her then. 'How did he die?'

'It was a year ago,' she told me. 'He fell from a tree one morn-ing. He was always doing foolish things. He was not a clever boy. Not like you, Yay-Ko.'

'He fell from a tree?'

'And broke his neck.'

I thought about this and lay back down, surprised that this was the first I had heard of him. 'Did you love him?' I asked.

'Of course,' she said. 'He was my husband. I loved him every morning and every night and sometimes in the afternoon too.' I frowned, suspecting that we were talking to each other about something different. 'Why do you ask me about him?' she said then. 'He doesn't matter. He's dead. We are alive. And you are going to take me with you to England.'

I nodded. I was under no illusion that Kaikala had been untouched when she had met me; after all, she was the one who had taught me how to make love, an art I was sadly unskilled at and still wanted teaching in. And why should she have told me about her past anyway? I had told her naught of mine except a bunch of fanciful lies. She could tell that my mood had altered a little and rolled over on top of me, exciting me once again.

'Yay-Ko still happy?' she asked me.

'Oh, yes,' I replied quickly. 'Very happy, thanks very much.'

'Yay-Ko will not leave me behind when he leaves?'

'Never,' I promised. 'If it came to a choice, I would stay on the island with you.'

She seemed displeased with this answer. 'But I don't want to stay on the island,' she insisted. 'I want to leave.'

'And you will,' I said. 'When I go.'

'When is that?'

'Soon,' I promised. 'Our work comes to an end shortly and we will depart. Then I will take you with me.'

This appeared to satisfy her and she leaned down to kiss me. I rolled around the grass with her and in a moment I was above her again, making love, lost to all thoughts of the world except the act that we were committing and the pleasure that she was giving me. Almost lost, anyway. For at a particularly unfortunate moment I found myself distracted a little by the sound of snapping near by.

I paused in my movements and looked around.

'What was that?' I asked.

'What?' she asked, looking around. 'Don't stop, Yay-Ko, please.'

I hesitated, convinced for a moment that there was someone there, someone in the thickets observing us at our play, but the forest had returned to its natural sounds now and I shook my head, sure that I was being foolish.

'It doesn't matter,' I said, kissing her. 'I must have been imagining things.'

An hour later I emerged from beneath the waterfall, where I had gone to wash my body clean before saying goodbye to Kaikala. As I stepped towards her, soaking wet and pulling the hair from my eyes, I felt self-conscious and awkward allowing her to observe my nakedness, despite all that we had done.

'Don't look,' I said, covering myself.

'Why not?'

'I'm shy.'

'What is this?' she asked, frowning; it was a word that none of the natives there were familiar with.

'It doesn't matter,' I said, pulling my britches on and dragging my shirt over my head. 'I must go back now, Kaikala. The captain will miss me soon and it's best not to keep him waiting.'

She stood and kissed me one last time and my hands ran down her spine to her rump, which I squeezed joyfully. Of course, I had the motions again, but there was no time to satisfy them; it would be more than my life was worth if I was found missing when the captain needed me, so we said a final goodbye, arranged to meet again the following afternoon, and I made my way back whence I had come, through the trees, letting them close behind me as I saw her beautiful form disappear.

As I left her alone in this secret place of ours, my face filled with a smile of satisfaction, I looked down and noticed my boot-prints, which were crushed into the grass beneath me, pointing back in the direction from which I had come, the place where Kaikala and I made love every day. I frowned, realizing that anyone who came near this spot might see them and follow them and find us. I resolved to be more careful in future.

I am not always a clever person.

Another few minutes passed before I stopped suddenly, my face growing scarlet with embarrassment, rage and suspicion. I looked down once again. I never wore boots when I came to visit Kaikala. I was barefoot.

The tracks were not mine.

11

A CHAP WILL DO SOME STRANGE THINGS for love and in recognition of that I come to a part of my story that is both painful to recount and humiliating to recall.

There were many customs prevalent on the island which we, as Englishmen, were not familiar with, but there was one in particular which had become something of a fad among sailing folk and that was the art of the tattoo. It was Captain Cook, when he first visited the Pacific Islands on the *Endeavour*, which numbered a young William Bligh among its crew members, who first permitted his crew to copy the traditions of the Pacific people by adorning their bodies with colourful imprints that remained indelible for ever after. On returning to England and displaying these badges of experience, it was said that a fair number of ladies swooned into a fainting fit, but it had become more and more common over the previous ten or fifteen years for a salt to consider a tattoo a mark of honour. I had seen many of them on the arms and torsos of the sailors in Portsmouth. Some were small and careful designs; others, bright and bold and lively, as if their images might come to life and dance a jig towards me.

It was Kaikala who first suggested to me that I might join this group myself, on another afternoon when we were swimming in our private lagoon. Ever since the incident when I believed we had been espied in our love-making, I had grown more cautious. It wasn't that it was against the ship rules to form alliances with the native girls; on the contrary, it was the norm. But I was not one of those who grew excited by the idea of being watched by another while I was about this saucy business, and had I discovered who had observed us that day I would have boxed his ears.

I had emerged from my plunge and was running at speed around the lake, the better to burn off my excess of energy as well as dry my body, when I noticed Kaikala staring at me and laughing. I slowed down to a halt, instantly discouraged that she was mocking me in my nakedness, but when I demanded an explanation for her outburst she simply shrugged her shoulders and told me that I was impossibly white.

'Well, I am a white man,' I told her. 'What else would you expect?'

'But you are *so* white,' she insisted. 'Yay-Ko is like ghost.'

I frowned. It was true that when I had left Portsmouth more than a year before, I might have been a pasty class of individual, but there was little doubt, as far as I was concerned, that I had changed for the better over the course of my experiences. I had aged a year and three months, after all, and that showed in the improved size of my body, my stance, my complexion, the ruddiness of my cheeks, the length of my whistle and my strengths as a man. And as for my colour, well, the sun of Otaheite had transformed me, to my eyes at least, to a rather attractive shade of bronzed brown.

'How can you say that?' I asked. 'I have never been so tanned before.'

'Are all Englishmen as white as you?' she asked.

'I'm delightfully brown,' I protested. 'But, yes, they are.'

'You can never marry me with such pale skin,' she said then and looked down at her own body in the water with sadness in her eyes. I followed the direction she was looking in and stepped over to her, leaning down to touch her shoulder.

'And why is that?' I asked. 'I thought we had an understanding.'

'Haven't you seen the men here?' she asked. 'You know what you must do.'

I sighed. For some time I thought this had been coming and I had not been looking forward to it. Many of the crew members had already undergone the tattooing process. The scut Mr Heywood, to my immense surprise, had been among the first to do so, installing the three-legged insignia of his native Isle of Man on his right leg. (It was no shock to me that his screams were heard halfway across the island, and probably all the way to England too, when the adornment was being applied.) Others had followed his lead and improved upon it. James Morrison had the date of our arrival in Otaheite emblazoned upon his forearm. Even Mr Christian had submitted to the process and had a curious design drawn on his back, a creature that was unfamiliar to me, with arms outstretched, peering at his observer as if he wished to eat him alive. He had recently added to his collection with native designs on his arms, his shoulders and across his torso, so that he appeared to be becoming more like a native than an Englishman.

'Before a man can marry,' Kaikala informed me, 'he must be tattooed.'

'Well, perhaps a small one,' I suggested, for I have never been a one for pain. 'A small flag on my shoulder.'

'No, no,' she said, laughing. 'A man cannot marry without having the proper adornment. The tattoo protects the wearer from the evil spirits by sealing your sacredness inside you.'

I frowned and thought about it and immediately shook my head. 'Oh, no,' I said. 'Not in this world.' I knew exactly what she was referring to, for I had seen the process take place on a local lad who was preparing for marriage only a few weeks before. Here's the fact of it: his buttocks were entirely tattooed a dark shade of black. The young fool lay on a block for half a day and allowed two artists to complete the job, one working on the left, the other working on the right, and despite how painful it appeared to be he never uttered a cry throughout the whole procedure. I admired him for that but thought he looked a damn fool when he stood up for all the world to see, men and women alike, with his freshly darkened skin. I also heard it told that he could not sit for the best part of two weeks afterwards; indeed, I had seen him only the previous day and he still seemed to be walking with some difficulty.

'I'm sorry, Kaikala,' I told her, 'but that's not something I can do. Even if I could submit to the pain, which I can't on account of the fact that I'm fierce cowardly, I don't want to spend the rest of my life with a colourful rump. I couldn't stand it. I'd be ashamed.'

She looked downcast, but something in my tone or phrasing told her that I was serious, for she nodded her head and seemed to accept this as the case.

'Perhaps just a small one, then,' she said, reverting to my earlier offer.

Reluctantly, I nodded; if it had to be done, it had to be done. I wanted to please her, after all.

And so it was that two days later I was taken to Kaikala's uncle, who was a master tattoo artist, and I explained to him what I wanted, what it should be, and where it should be placed. I had brought a thick stick with me to lock between my gnashers in order to have something to bite down on while the artwork was being created. I had told no one, not even Kaikala, the design that I had chosen and refused to allow her to be present while it was being created, and in my foolishness, oh, sweet mother of God, in the innocent foolishness of my fifteenth year, I had come up with something that I thought would secure her heart for me for ever.

I explained my plan to her uncle and he stared at me as if I was a bedlamite, but I insisted and he simply shrugged his shoulders, told me to disrobe, and then he fetched the ink-pots and sharpened the animal bones that were the tools of his trade and then at last he set about creating his latest masterpiece.

It was late evening when I returned to camp and even from some distance I could hear Captain Bligh calling my name loudly. By the sound of it, he had been calling me for some time and I tried to pick my legs up and move faster but, suffering such tremendous pain as I was, I found it difficult to move. The perspiration was teeming from my forehead and my shirt was fairly stuck to my back. I was glad that evening had fallen at least as the cool breezes floating in my direction made my agony a little easier to endure.

'Turnstile,' said the captain when I stepped inside his tent. 'Where the devil have you been, lad? Didn't you hear me calling you?'

'Begging your apologies, sir,' said I, edging inside and looking around at the faces of the full complement of officers – Mr Christian, Mr Fryer, Mr Elphinstone and Mr Heywood, the scut – who were gathered around the table, wearing serious expressions on their phizzys. 'I was elsewhere and lost track of time.'

'With his molly, I bet,' said Mr Christian. 'Haven't you heard, Captain, that young Turnip is an innocent no more?'

I glared at the master's mate and then looked at the captain, my face taking on the reddenings, as I did not want these private matters to be discussed in his presence. To his credit, he looked embarrassed too and shook his head.

'I care not for this line of discussion, Fletcher,' he said dis-missively. 'Turnstile, tea, if you please, fast as you can. We are all in need.'

I nodded and made my way towards the fire to boil the water, catching the eye of Mr Heywood as I went; his lip was twisted in distaste and I could tell that he had not enjoyed Mr Christian's attempt to make a farce of me. Perhaps, I thought, he knew who my beloved was and, knowing her to be the fairest creature on the island, wanted her for himself. I set the kettle over the flames and made for the cups, careful not to upset my wounds as I went.

'Turnstile,' said the captain, interrupting his conversation and looking at me. 'Are you all right, lad?'

'Fair to middling, Captain, sir,' said I. 'Fair to middling.'

'You appear to be moving with some difficulty.'

'Do I? I must have been sitting wrong and my legs have taken a seizure.'

He frowned for a moment, shook his head as if to dismiss the nonsense from the table and looked back at the officers. 'So, tomorrow morning it is, then,' he said. 'Around eleven bells?'

'Eleven bells,' muttered a few of the officers, and I couldn't help but notice the air of sorrow that pervaded them.

Mr Fryer noticed my staring and turned towards me. 'You'll not have heard the news, Turnstile, I imagine. If you were absent on . . . other business.'

'News, sir?' said I. 'What news?'

'Surgeon Huggan,' he replied. 'He was saved this afternoon.'

I stared at him and tried to comprehend his meaning. 'Saved?' asked I. 'Was he in some trouble?'

'Mr Fryer means that he was called home,' said Mr Elphinstone, which produced even less understanding in my face, for I could scarcely conceive of another ship's arriving at Otaheite for no other reason than to transport our drunken surgeon back to Portsmouth.

'Dead, Turnip, dead,' snapped Mr Christian. 'Dr Huggan has gone and died on us. We will be burying him in the morning.'

'Oh,' said I, 'I'm sorry to hear it, sir.' In truth, it mattered little to me, as I had exchanged no more than a few dozen words with the man in all the time I had known him. He was permanently in his cups and of such obese weight and proclivities that to sit near him was to suffer the imminent possibility of a gassing.

'Yes, well, it looks like you could have done with a surgeon, Turnstile,' said Captain Bligh, his voice rising as he stood up and came towards me. 'What's wrong with you, boy? You're walking in a most curious fashion and perspiring like a laboured horse.'

'There's nothing, sir, I . . . oh!' In trying to step away from him I moved too fast and the pain in my lower regions was so extreme that both hands went to my rump to soothe it.

'Have you been tattooed, Turnip?' asked Mr Elphinstone, a note of humour coming into his voice.

'No,' I said. 'Well, yes. But it's not a matter of importance. It's—'

'Good God, I know what he's done,' said Mr Christian, standing up and breaking into a smile. 'He believes he's going to marry his tart and so he has blackened his arse for her.'

If I had been willing to go along with the farce of it before, the mention of Kaikala's name as a tart was too much for me now and I felt a strong desire to challenge him on it and demand satisfaction, but I kept my counsel for the moment.

'Let us see, then, Turnstile. You won't be sitting for weeks if I'm right.'

'No, sir,' I snapped. 'Leave me be. Captain, tell him!' I appealed to Mr Bligh, but he was standing by my side with a half-smile on his face, bemused by the whole business.

'You haven't, lad, have you? You've not gone native on me?'

'Hold him there, William,' said Mr Christian, referring to Mr Elphinstone, I might add, and not the captain. 'Hold him straight.'

'No, please,' I cried as he took me by the arms and spun me round. 'Leave me be! Captain, stop them . . .'

It was too late for begging: a gust of wind at my bare behind told me that they had pulled my britches down and I was exposed before them. I silenced myself and closed my eyes. The air, thankfully, was a balm to the burning sensation and I was grateful for that at least.

'But there's nothing there,' said the captain. 'Aren't they usually fully covered?'

'Look!' said Mr Christian, pointing a finger towards the left edge of my left buttock. 'It's here. But it's so small as to be almost insignificant!'

I might explain that it was not at all small. In fact the tattoo that adorns my person is a good two inches in width and height and can be clearly observed by anyone with ready access to that part of my anatomy.

'But what is it?' asked Mr Christian in wonder. 'Is it a turnip? How appropriate!'

'I believe it's a potato of some sort,' said Mr Heywood, the scut, who had come over for a closer look.

'No, it's a pineapple,' said Mr Fryer, who was observing too.

Now all the officers and the captain were gathered before my bare rump, studying it carefully.

'It's clearly a coconut,' said Mr Elphinstone. 'Why, you just have to look at the shape and detail.'

'It's none of those things, is it, my lad?' asked Captain Bligh, and I swear that for the first time in our acquaintance I saw the man laugh. The whole thing was almost worth it in order to see that too, for his moods had been so contraire of late that I thought a moment like this could do him the world of good. 'The thing is neither a turnip nor a potato nor a pineapple nor a coconut, but it does represent the island and it does bear testament to young Turnstile's time here. Can't you guess, gentlemen?'

The officers stood up and looked at the captain expectantly and he smiled broadly, extending his arms as if to point out that it was entirely obvious, and he told them what it was, leading to all five of them almost falling out of their stance with hilarity. I pulled up my britches, tried to recover my dignity and returned to the kettle to make their tea, ignoring the hoots of derision and the tears of laughter that were pouring down their cheeks.

The captain was by far the most perceptive of every man there, because he had guessed it at once.

It was a breadfruit.

12

IT SEEMS TO ME THAT A MAN can live among other men, thinking he is part of their community, believing himself to be privy to their thoughts and plans, and never really know the truth of what is taking place around him. Even when I look back on those days from the distance of time, it seems to me that the crew of the *Bounty* were working harmoniously together on Otaheite, gathering breadfruit, planting the seeds, watching as the shoots appeared after a few weeks, then transporting them to the ship and the care of Mr Nelson. The days were filled with work and the nights with play. Our bellies were full, our mattresses soft, and our desires as men were being satisfied many times over. There were incidents, of course – men who were angry about this or that, complaints about some trivial matter or another – and from time to time the captain lost his senses entirely on account of being stuck on dry land, but all in all I considered us to be a happy lot.

Which made it all the more surprising when, during the afternoon of 5th January 1789, Mr Fryer and Mr Elphinstone appeared together in the captain's tent, with a look of great distress upon their faces, while he was engaged in the act of writing a letter to his missus and I was starching a uniform for a dinner that was taking place later that evening with King Tynah.

'Captain,' said Mr Fryer, stepping inside, 'might I disturb you?'

The captain looked up from his writing paper with a slight air of distraction and glanced from one man to the other. 'Of course you can, John, William,' he said, an odd characteristic that I had noticed in him whereby he held each man on more friendly terms whenever he was engaged on the heart-warming task of writing to his wife. 'What can I do for you?'

I glanced across, without paying particular attention at first, but the moment the words were out of Mr Fryer's mouth I stopped what I was doing and looked in his direction.

'Sir, there's no way to put this other than to state it plainly. Three of the men have deserted.'

Mr Bligh put his quill down and stared down at his desk for a moment; I watched his face. He was shocked, I could see it, but did not want to react too quickly. He paused for the best part of half a minute before looking up again. 'Who?' he asked.

'William Muspratt,' began Mr Fryer.

'Mr Hall's assistant?' asked the captain.

'The very same. And John Millward with him. Also Charles Churchill, the master-at-arms.'

'I can't believe it,' said Mr Bligh.

'I'm afraid it's true, sir.'

'My own jaunty is one of those who has deserted? The man trusted with policing the ship has contravened its laws?'

Mr Fryer hesitated, but finally nodded; the irony did not need to be pointed out to anyone.

'But how?' asked the captain. 'How do you know this for sure?'

'Sir, we should have informed you earlier and I take responsibility for that. The men did not return from work duties yesterday and I believed they had simply taken themselves off somewhere with their womenfolk. It had been my intention to give them the scalding of their lives when they returned. Unfortunately there has been no sight of them this morning, they have not reported for work, and the afternoon is nearly behind us and they have still failed to appear. Sir, I recognize that I should have brought this information to you sooner . . .'

'It's all right, Mr Fryer,' said the captain, surprising all of us in the room, perhaps, by the manner in which he was absolving the master of responsibility. 'I have no doubt you did what you considered to be right.'

'Indeed, sir. And, in truth, I believed they would return.'

'And how do we know for sure that they will not?'

'Captain,' said Mr Elphinstone, speaking up for the first time, 'a member of the crew has spoken to me in confidentiality, telling me that he heard rumours that the three men planned to desert. He spoke to me on condition that the other men would not find out his name.'

'Which is what, Mr Elphinstone?'

'Ellison, sir. Thomas Ellison.'

I gave a laugh within myself. Thomas Ellison – he of the Flora-Jane Richardson waiting for him back in England, she who had allowed him to kiss her and take a liberty before the journey had begun, he who was above me and happy to point it out – was little more than a snitch. It took some beating, it surely did.

The captain took the news badly and I could see his face grow dark. He paced the tent for a few minutes, considering the matter, before stepping over and facing the two officers again. 'But why?' he asked. 'That is what I fail to understand. Why would they do this? Aren't the conditions good here? Haven't I created a harmonious camp? Don't they appreciate at the very least the fact that there are so few disciplinary issues in our group? Why would they go? And *where*, for that matter, *where* would they go? We are on an island, gentlemen, for pity's sake!'

'Sir, there is the possibility that they might get off the island, by stealing a launch or canoe, and perhaps make their way to one of the neighbouring atolls. There are so many, sir, that if they do that, I fail to see how we can recapture them.'

295

'I am aware of the local geography, Mr Fryer,' said the captain, reverting to irritation. 'But you haven't offered an explanation as to the why.'

'Sir, there could be many reasons.'

'And your theory?'

'Shall I state it plainly, sir?'

Mr Bligh narrowed his eyes. 'Please do.'

'Our work here is nearly completed. Mr Nelson walks the beach daily, informing us how well the shoots are doing on board. Soon all the pots will be filled and there will be no further need for us to gather plants or nurture their seeds.'

'But of course,' said Mr Bligh, his face betraying his confusion. 'That is obvious: our work is finite. What of it? Are you suggesting that the men are so beloved of labour that they fear the end of their chores?'

'No, sir; what I'm saying is that one day soon Mr Nelson will come to this tent, he will come to you, sir, and he will tell you that the part of our mission centred on the island of Otaheite has come to an end. And at that moment, sir, you are very likely to give the command to pack up our tents, gather our belongings and return to the ship.'

'It'll be anchors aweigh and goodbye Otaheite,' chipped in Mr Elphinstone unhelpfully.

Mr Bligh nodded and a smile crossed his face. He glanced across at me, as I tried desperately to stay busy with the uniform. 'Are you hearing this, Master Turnstile? The men will be happy that their work is over and they can return home to their loved ones with money in their pockets. I beg your pardon, Mr Fryer,' he added, turning back to him. 'I dare say you are making a most sensible point here but I am at a loss as to what it is.'

'It's as simple as this, sir. The men don't want to leave.'

The captain stepped back a little and raised his eyebrows. 'Don't want to leave, is it?' he asked. 'When their wives and sweethearts are standing by the docks in Spithead expecting their safe return?'

'Sir, their wives and sweethearts may be there, but their lovers are here.'

'Their lovers?'

'The women of the island. The ones for whom they have had their bodies marked.' He shot me a look at this point, having had the good fortune to get an eyeful of my rump tattoo a week or so earlier. 'The men have had a great deal of freedom while here. Their lives here are, for want of a better phrase, extremely pleasant. You have . . .' He paused and corrected himself. 'What we have done here—'

He may have tripped over his words but the captain wasn't so stupid that he hadn't noticed. 'What I've done, sir, is what you're getting at.'

'No, sir, I merely—'

'You're saying that I've given the men an easy time of it. That I've made their lives a lot less disciplined than they might have been. You're saying that if I had been a little more forceful, then they wouldn't want to stay in this place, they would want to return to where they belong. They would be desperate for England, for Portsmouth, for dear old London town.' His voice was rising to a crescendo as he spoke. 'You're saying this entire catastrophe is my fault.'

'I don't think he is, to be fair,' said Mr Elphinstone. 'I believe Mr Fryer is simply saying—'

'Hold your tongue, if you please, Mr Elphinstone,' said the captain, silencing him by raising a hand in the air. 'When I want an opinion from you, I will ask for it. As it happens, for once I find myself entirely in agreement with Mr Fryer. It is my fault. I have made the men's lives too happy and they have repaid my kindness by choosing to abandon their duties and stay on a savage land for no other reason than that they might satisfy their lusts at any hour of the day or night. I believe Mr Fryer might have a very sensible point. And if I am at fault, I stand guilty of it and must mend my ways. Mr Fryer, all men, save those currently under the watch of Mr Christian at the nursery, are to return to the ship immediately. And when I say immediately I mean that when you leave this tent you gather the launches and the men go to the *Bounty*. From this moment on, there will be no fraternizing with the natives, no leisure time on the island, and no opportunities for their blasted games and perversions. This will happen now, Mr Fryer,' he continued, his voice becoming a shout. 'This very minute, do you understand me?'

'Yes, sir,' he replied quietly but urgently. 'But if I might suggest a grace period whereby they may say farewell to their ladies . . .'

'I said *now*, Mr Fryer.'

'But the morale, sir—'

'I care not for it!' roared the captain. 'Three men have deserted their posts. The penalty for this, when they are caught, and they will be caught, Mr Fryer, mark me on that, the penalty for this is death. Hanging by the neck until dead, sir. And the gift that they have left their fellows is an end to luxury and a cessation of my generosity. Gather the men, Mr Fryer. The *Bounty* awaits them.'

They left immediately and the captain paced the floor, lost in thought. I was lost too. My mind was with Kaikala. I needed to find a way to speak to her.

That was a bleak evening. One of the bleakest. By nightfall, every man jack of the *Bounty* crew, save the three deserters Muspratt, Millward and Churchill, were back on the boat. Mr Byrn attempted to cheer us all up by playing his fiddle, but a suggestion was made that it be cracked over his head and the pair of them tossed overboard, and he took notice of the intelligence and silenced himself. The captain spoke to the gathered crew and told them of the new rules for our last weeks on Otaheite, and they went down badly, very badly indeed. The men spoke out in ways I'd never heard before and it was all that the captain could do to control them. Every time he had peace to make his statement, a noise would erupt from the island shore, where the fires had been lit and the women were dancing around them, screaming in misery and tearing what little clothes they wore; I had no doubt they were injuring themselves too and prayed that Kaikala had the sense to leave her beauty intact. I confess that at one point I feared for the captain's safety when he informed the crew that there would be only two states of being from that moment until we set sail: either at work under an officer's eye or on board the ship. I believe that had the officers not been there the scene might have grown nastier and, indeed, when we were all below decks again, I could see that Mr Bligh was visibly shaken by his ordeal.

A few hours later, I was lying in my bunk, so filled with the motions and the knowledge that I might never touch Kaikala's skin again or taste her kiss that I thought I might explode. I reached down to relieve myself and was nearly discovered in the act by Mr Fryer, striding in my direction, knocking on the captain's cabin door and marching inside without so much as a by-your-leave. Naturally I sprang from where I lay and put an ear to the door, but on this occasion the two men were speaking too low and I could hear ne'er a word.

Within a half-hour of the clock, Mr Fryer emerged again and strode off purposefully and I looked up to see the captain standing by his door, a look of utter defeat and perplexion on his face.

'Are you all right, sir?' I asked. 'Can I get you something?'

'No,' he muttered. 'Thank you, lad. Get you some sleep.'

He stepped back inside then and I would have heeded him and drifted off, only, the sound of boots re-emerged and this time it was Mr Fryer accompanied by Mr Christian and Mr Heywood. I jumped up and knocked on the captain's cabin door to let them in. They marched past me without an acknowledgement and I followed them inside.

'Out,' said the captain immediately, pointing a finger in my direction.

'Sir, perhaps the officers might like some—'

'Get out,' he repeated. 'Now.'

I did as I was told, closing the door carefully behind me, but doing everything in my power to leave an inch of air space whereby I might hear what was going on inside. I could not make it all out, but what words I did hear were shocking.

'. . . In Mr Churchill's belongings, you say?' the captain asked.

'Yes, sir,' said Mr Fryer. 'Discovered by my own hand not an hour ago.'

'And this list of names,' he said. 'What do you suppose it means?'

'That is for you to decide, Captain. But, as you can see, the names of the three deserters are on it. At the top.'

'Aye, I see that. And the names of several other seamen. What do you make of this, Mr Christian?'

I know not where he was standing but I could hear only a muffled sound as he replied and made out none of his words.

'But nine of them, sir?' asked the captain. 'Nine men who planned to desert and stay on the island? It seems preposterous!' Mr Christian spoke again, followed by Mr Heywood, but neither were distinguishable; then the captain's words came through once more. 'No, the list stays with me, Fletcher. As few people as possible should know the identities of these men. I realize that is frustrating for you but I prefer to handle this my way.'

The voices were getting closer now, so I jumped into my bunk, pulled the sheet atop me and feigned sleep. A minute or two later, all four men emerged and the three officers dispersed silently. I could sense the captain standing above me, watching me, but I dared not move. After a few moments, he went back inside and shut his door behind him. Shortly after that, I did fall asleep.

I woke in the darkness to the sound of voices. I could tell by the noises around me that it was the middle of the night and that most of the men and the officers were in their bunks, but something had woken me up: the sound of footsteps passing me quietly and a gentle tapping on the captain's door. By the time I was fully conscious I had missed most of their conversation, but I remained totally still, my breathing consistent, my eyes closed to hear how it ended.

'Should you not have challenged them, sir?' came a question and I knew the voice to be that of Mr Fryer.

'Perhaps,' replied Captain Bligh. 'But what good would it have done? We have no real idea why Mr Churchill included their names on his list.'

'They weren't just *on* the list, captain,' he replied. 'They were at the head of the list.'

'It's simply impossible,' said Captain Bligh. 'Two warranted officers? It's simply impossible,' he repeated. 'Go to your bed, Mr Fryer. Do not speak of this matter again.'

There was silence for a few further moments and then the master crossed past me again and returned to his cabin, while the captain stepped back into his and closed the door.

This time I did not fall asleep.

13

THE DAYS PASSED AND, to my dismay, I was left on board the *Bounty* with little opportunity to return to shore. I had been afforded no opportunity to say goodbye to Kaikala, so suddenly had the captain's decision for the crew to return to the *Bounty* come about. Night after night I lay in my bunk dreaming about her and what she must think of me, but when I asked the captain whether I could join him on his daily trips to the island to inspect the gardens he would shake his head and tell me that he needed no one to attend on him and my time would be better spent helping to prepare the ship for its imminent departure.

But if I was lying, broken-hearted, in the corner of a dusty corridor, it was as nothing compared with the rumblings of the men on board the *Bounty*, who were increasingly angry about their confinement. Of course there was a part of them that blamed Muspratt, Millward and Churchill, the three deserters, for being the catalysts for this unhappy turn in our fortunes, but more than that their contempt was saved for the captain, who to my mind had merely reacted to the insubordination of a group of malcontents rather than instigating a campaign of senseless authority for himself.

'Why, I should have gone with them and I wish to blazes I had now,' said Isaac Martin one evening as we sat on the deck of the *Bounty*, staring across at the beach fires and the women who surrounded them, so tantalizingly close but too far away to do us any good.

'Had you planned on it, then, Isaac?' asked the quartermaster's mate, George Simpson, a tricky old cove trusted by no one on account of an incident during Ruff and Trump shortly after we had crossed the 55th parallel; there was a matter of some deuces being held down the seat of his britches and reappearing at opportune moments. The incident had come to blows and he had been con-sidered a villain by all for some time afterwards and even now was not fully trusted. Honesty at the cards was a tenet of naval life.

'I had not,' replied Martin, careful not to utter mutinous words when such a man as Simpson was listening. 'I would never desert my post, not in this world. I merely say that I envy them their free-dom and the luxuries that freedom brings.'

'Lucky devils,' said James Morrison, the man who, by privilege of being the boatswain's mate, would be the unfortunate creature who would have to tie the rope around the men's necks should they ever be discovered. 'They won't have gone far, if you ask

302

me. They'll be in and out of that camp at night whenever the officers are on the ship and their whistles need tending to.'

Here was the truth of it already. The malcontent was based on little more than the fact that the men had been among women who had allowed them to take liberties as many times during the day as they liked. We were soaked in the physical, every man jack of us. I was no better than any of them, although to the surprise of many of my fellow sailors I had saved my attentions for only one.

'Bloody Bligh,' came a deep murmur from behind me and I turned round to see the face of the cooper, Henry Hilbrant, now fully recovered from his flogging some weeks before. 'He does it because he's jealous, that's all. That's his only reason.'

'Jealous?' I asked, uncertain why he should say such a thing. 'And what does the captain have to be jealous of, if you please?'

'Of us, you wee pup,' he replied, not looking me in the face but looking towards the shore instead. 'Every man here knows that the captain hasn't laid a finger on a woman since the day we left Spithead. All these treats here before us and is he interested in them? Not a bit of it. Perhaps he can't manage it, that's what I say. Perhaps he hasn't a manhood at all.'

I stared at him in disgust, for it was a vile thing to say, a calumny of the worst nature. In my heart I wanted to defend the captain, for he had been good to me, but I couldn't help but wonder whether there was some truth in the charge. Of course the captain loved his wife, but I knew from my conversations with the men that there were many who loved their wives and would have died rather than cause them pain. This, however, this life we were living on Otaheite, this was not betrayal. Or it was not seen as such anyway. It was seen as reward for the length of time we had spent at sea and the indignities we had suffered during our difficult crossing. It was a physical matter, not an emotional one. A need satisfied.

'He's gone mad, if you ask me,' said Hilbrant. 'A man goes mad if he does not take his pleasures. Wouldn't you agree, Turnip? Sure, you're half crazed already and it's only been a few days since you last dipped your wick. There's a madness in your eyes, can't you see it? Should the moon come out I dread to think what might become of you!'

I ignored the comment for fear that it might be true. There was a long voyage home ahead of us. And now that I had partaken regularly in the act of love I could not imagine my mornings, afternoons and evenings without those particular pleasures. The very idea sent a pain southwards in me.

'We should say a prayer that the *Bounty* will be destroyed,' said Isaac Martin. 'And then we would be forced to stay.' There was a silence for a long moment and then he started to laugh. 'I jest, of course,' he said.

'Still, it'd be quite the thing, wouldn't it?' asked Hilbrant. 'To be able to stay for ever?'

'And if we were stuck here, then no man would be in charge. Not the captain, not the officers, no one. We would rule over ourselves as the Saviour intended.'

'Pipe-dreams, lads, pipe-dreams,' said James Morrison, standing up and blocking my sight of the other men for a moment. He stood there quite still and I saw his head turn from man to man and settle on them for a few moments. I thought nothing of it at the time, only marvelled at how quickly the conversation changed from talk of the island to a tale that Hilbrant had about the time his brother Hugo had engaged in a wrestling match with an alligator of some renown. Indeed, the conversation, which had seemed a trivial thing to me at the time, vanished from my mind quite quickly and I was left to contemplate more important matters, such as how I would ever manage to see Kaikala again.

Every day more and more seedlings were being planted in the earthenware pots in the lower hold and I watched as the rows and rows, many hundreds of them, lined up. When they reached the far door I knew that our time was nearly up; and when, one particular afternoon, I saw that at the rate we were going that day was fast approaching, I determined to put a plan of some risk into action.

When I was a lad, living off my wits and the especial generosity of Mr Lewis in Portsmouth, I was not what you would call a particular specimen of manliness. I was small and slight, my arms were reedy and my chest a little sunken. I could walk around the town all day and not feel the exhaustions, but break into a run – as I did whenever a blue saw me pocketing an item that was not mine or a trick felt my nimble fingers pulling their pocket-watch from its home – and you could be assured that when I found my hiding place I would be stuck there, gasping for breath, for an hour hence. All that had changed, however, over the previous eighteen months. I had grown strong. I had grown able. I was what you might call a healthy fellow.

The *Bounty* was anchored a mile from the beaches of Otaheite; this was as close as we could get without the ship running aground and, although it was not something I had ever had cause to do in the past, it occurred to me that a nimble lad such as myself, with all his capacities intact and a determined rudder pointing him towards his destination, could swim that distance without finding himself in jeopardy. And if I was to be denied any further visits to shore until we left our paradise home, then I was determined to see Kaikala one more time and decided that I would wait until nightfall and swim the distance myself.

The officers were, of course, able to move freely between the island and the ship – Captain Bligh drew the line at limiting their freedoms – and this was another thing that was causing malcontent among the men. The idea of Mr Christian, Mr Elphinstone, Mr Heywood and even Mr Fryer suddenly having the pick of all the ladies of the island, ladies who had previously been under certain attachment to particular coves, dismayed all the

305

men and caused a great deal of anger about the issue of how one fell into the role of being an officer in the first place, whether it was by just deserts or by a father's deep pockets.

But each of them went back and forth, taking the launches with them, and those officers who were on board at night took a count of those tubs to make sure that none had been stolen – not that any man would have been able to sail one of them back to the island without being seen; they were too big for that. Each launch was twenty-three feet in length, not big enough to hold very many occupants, but too small to make such a journey unseen either. And so this was not a possibility for me. I had a simple choice: swim or stay. And I chose the former.

I waited until what I felt sure could only be our third or fourth last night there and was fortunate that the moon was half covered by clouds, so the possibility of being spotted and apprehended was more slight. The captain had gone to his cabin late but had fallen asleep almost immediately – I could tell by the sound of snoring emerging from his bunk – and the ship had fallen to silence. I was aware that the two officers on board were Mr Elphinstone and Mr Fryer, but the latter had already taken to his cabin too, so the footsteps I heard pacing the deck when I ascended were those of Mr Elphinstone.

I emerged from beneath and looked around cautiously. He was nowhere to be seen, so I assumed he had made his way to the foredeck, and I in turn made my way to the rear and quickly slipped over the side of the boat, descended by the ladder and allowed my body to glide gently into the water beneath.

Glory to God, it was shoddy freezing as I recall. I had dressed light, naught more than a pair of britches and a chemise, in order to make the swim easier, but it did little more than cause me immediate concern that I would freeze to death before I could complete my journey. I clung close to the boat still and waited until I heard Mr Elphinstone's feet make their way to a spot above me, whereupon I waited for him to turn back, the point at which

I planned to begin my swim. He took his sweet time about it too, standing there for what felt like an eternity, whistling a tune to himself, then singing a ditty in a low voice. I could feel the sensations in my feet starting to disappear and began to worry whether I would even make it to the island, but finally he turned and began his walk to the foredeck again and I was away.

I was forced to swim quite slowly, with long stretches under water, for this would limit the sound of my journey through the waves being carried back to the ship. I believed it unlikely that anyone could hear me, but I was resolved to play this game carefully. And what looked to be a short and surmountable distance from the deck of the *Bounty* seemed another thing altogether from the vantage point of the waves: the island suddenly appeared fierce far away. Determined, however, I set my mind to it, swam as if my very life depended on it and not just my passions.

When I eventually swept up on shore I believed my lungs were going to give way inside me, so exhausted was I by the swim. I lay there gasping, then reached down to massage my frozen feet, but my hands were so cold that I could barely get the circulation into them either. A part of me wanted to lie there, to simply lie there and sleep, but I knew that if I did there was a chance that either Mr Christian or Mr Heywood would discover me and I would be hanged for a traitor. So instead I stood up and made my way carefully through the forest towards Kaikala's home.

It took some time to reach it and when I peered through the gaps between the reeds I failed to see her. I walked round all sides and could make out her sister and parents asleep, but she was missing. This was a curious thing. I sat on the sand and considered it. After a few moments' thought, I wondered whether she might be waiting at our special place by the lagoon. There was always the possibility that she knew I would come back for her – I had yet to decide how I would smuggle her on board the *Bounty* and hide her during the journey home – and was lying in wait for me every night, expecting me to find her.

The thought of it sent me to my feet once again and I left the small village of houses and headed towards the waterfall. At night, with a darkened moon overhead, it was not so easy to find my way and I took several wrong turnings as I walked. Finally I was forced to stop every few yards and reassess where I stood. Time was not on my side. I had to find it, then find her, enjoy some time together, plan our escape and make it back to the ship before anyone discovered my absence; even now the captain could be calling my name and demanding his tea. I was no longer worried about the cold but about capture.

After what I felt was too long a time I finally crossed by a familiar series of small copses and knew that I was close. My heart jumped at the idea that she would be there waiting for me and I tried not to imagine where I would go next if she was not. I began to hear the gentle sound of the lagoon water and before very much longer I was close to the spot. I hesitated, peering through the trees, desiring to observe my beauty for a few moments without her seeing me, and I was not disappointed, for through the split of the trees between I could make her out, lying by the lake, waiting for me.

I smiled. My heart leaped. And I am not ashamed to admit that I got a sudden rush of the motions. But I held my ground for now. I wanted to just watch her for a little longer. And then she spoke.

'You have promised to take me with you to England,' she said, and my face broke into a smile. She was too good for me. She could sense my presence. 'You will not betray me? You will take me there and make me a fine lady?'

I opened my mouth to respond, to tell her that, yes, yes of course I would, that I would never desert her and I would never betray her. My right foot lifted from the ground so that I might emerge through the trees and take her as my own. But before I could move, her question was answered by another.

'Of course I will,' said the voice. 'I will take you wherever you want to go. I promised you that and I'm a man of my word.'

'Peet-a,' said Kaikala, her voice purring like a kitten now, 'how I long to be your wife. I will keep your palace for you and be kind to your servants, if they behave themselves. And I will make love to you four, five, times a day. As often as you want.'

Peet-a? My breathing seemed to have slowed down to a halt, and then what did I see but the figure of a naked man, no more than a boy really, emerge from a spot to the right and go over and lie beside her. My eyes opened wide, and I swear it, I swear that I had never felt such a pain so deep within myself.

It was Mr Heywood. The scut himself.

My fingers grasped on to branches and I knew immediately that it had been he who had followed me that time before, he who had sat and watched our love-making and had a tug to it, no doubt. But he had cuckolded me into the bargain, stolen that which had been pure, with a lie to take her to England. I would have seen it through, I told myself, I would have found a way. I looked around and, seeing a branch that had fallen, I reached down to pick it up. With that in my hands, I knew that all I would have to do was swing it once and his brains, such as they were, would be spattered over Kaikala's body. Swing it twice and hers would be floating in the lagoon alongside his. I held it, I clutched it tight and I began my charge.

Whether Mr Heywood or Kaikala ever heard my feet running through the forest away from them, I know not. I no longer cared about being caught or considered a deserter. But there were many things I had done and many things I had been in my life, not all of which caused me shame, nor all of which afforded me pride either. But there was one thing that I was not.

I was not a murderer.

I made my way back to the beach quickly, my heart broken inside my chest, my eyes streaming with tears, an agony playing out its game in my brain like no suffering I had ever known before, the pain of love. The awful pain of it. I knew not who I was, where I was, how I would survive this betrayal. But somehow

I found my way back to the shore, into the water – whose frozen temperatures caused me little pain now – and back to the ladder. I gave no thought to danger and simply ascended to the deck, caring not whether I was discovered in my return, but no one saw and I returned numbly to the lower deck, to the corridor outside the captain's cabin, and to my bunk.

14

THE WORD SPREAD LIKE WILDFIRE around the ship the evening that the three deserters were caught and brought back to the *Bounty*.

The captain was in his cabin, plotting a course for the West Indies, where we were shortly to head with the breadfruit plans, when Mr Elphinstone marched down the corridor at a tremendous pace and ran inside without so much as a knock. Naturally, I was presently engaged in clearing away Mr Bligh's dinner.

'Sir,' he said, taking both of us by surprise, and the captain spun round, a hand to his chest in fright.

'Good God, man, take a care when you enter my cabin, will you?' he said testily. 'You nearly frightened me to death.'

'I apologize, Captain,' he said. 'But I thought you'd want to know immediately, sir. Mr Fryer and Mr Linkletter are approaching the ship in a launch; they have returned from the island.'

The captain stared at him for a moment, and then across at me, before shaking his head. 'And you're only telling me now, Mr Elphinstone?' He sighed and shook his head. 'Why the blazes would it be of interest to me that Mr Fryer is returning to the ship?'

'Because he has Muspratt, Churchill and Millward with him, sir. He's captured them.'

This put a different spin on things entirely and the captain set aside his charts immediately and made for the upper deck. I followed at just such a pace, for this would be an event worth seeing and a pleasant interlude to a dull evening.

It had been two days since I had discovered how Kaikala had betrayed me, and with Mr Heywood too, which only made matters worse. How she could have allowed that scrawny, pimpled body anywhere near her own was a mystery to me, but it was clear that she had been using us both. She wanted away from Otaheite almost as much as the sailing men wanted to stay there and it was anyone's guess how many other salts had made equal promises to her in return for her favours. I felt like a fool for having believed her. But I found it hard to hate her, for she had been my first love and even to think on her was to feel a great ache inside my body that sent my spirits low and my eyes a-weeping. As for the scut, I picked no fight with him for now. He had been as big a fool as I had been.

The deck of the *Bounty* was swarming with men when we three arrived there and they each fell silent as Captain Bligh took his place at the side of the boat, watching as the launch drifted towards us and was elevated so that the men might step aboard. Neither Mr Fryer nor Mr Linkletter, who had been engaged for some time in tracking the three men, had a look of triumph on his face; indeed if I was to tell it as I recall it, I would say they looked almost sorrowful, for the penalty for desertion was death and the captain had proved in recent times that he was in no mood to be lenient.

The men for their part watched as their former fellows appeared before them with a mixture of emotions; it had been their fault that we were all confined to the ship again; the blame was entirely theirs that no man had placed so much as a finger on his sweetheart in a week. But, still, they were part of one crew. And there was admiration for their courage in escaping in the first place. So they said nothing. Just stood and watched. As I did.

'Captain,' said Mr Fryer, stepping on to the deck first and removing his hat. 'The three men who deserted, William Muspratt, John Millward and Charles Churchill.'

Mr Bligh breathed heavily through his nose and nodded slowly. 'Where did you find them, Mr Fryer?'

'Tettahah,' he replied, indicating a part of the island about five miles away. 'Gathered round a campfire.'

'Were they eating a stolen piglet by any chance?'

'No, sir.'

The captain raised an eyebrow, a little surprised. 'Well, that much at least is to their credit. Gentlemen,' he added, stepping forward, 'lift your heads, then. Let me take a look at you.'

The three men looked up slowly and for the first time I was able to see their faces. They were blackened with dirt; John Millward, the youngest of the three, looked as if he had been weeping, for there were streaks and channels laying waste to his smooth cheeks. Charles Churchill had a bruised eye, which had turned a mixture of the purple and green shade.

'Mr Churchill,' said the captain. 'What happened to your eye?'

'A dispute, sir,' he replied, his voice filled with contrition. 'A small matter of my own fault.'

'Indeed,' he said. 'Well, gentlemen, you are discovered. What have you to say to that?'

They said nothing for a moment and we all held our breaths, waiting for their excuses to pour from their mouths. They were pathetically weak, though, and no sound came from the men other than a muffled series of apologies.

'It's a little late to be sorry,' said the captain. 'You know the penalty for desertion, I assume?' The men looked up, Millward particularly quickly with a panicked look in his eye, and the captain frowned. 'I can see that you do. Yes, by the looks on your faces I can see that you very well do. And you knew it when you left your posts as you know it now.'

'Captain, if I may, please, sir,' began Muspratt suddenly, but the captain shook his head.

'No, Mr Muspratt, you may not. I'll not hear it now. Mr Morrison,' he said, shouting at the boatswain's mate, who was standing not three feet from him. 'You and Mr Linkletter, take these . . . men downstairs and place them in irons. Their punishment will be meted out on the morrow.'

'Yes, sir,' said the two men together and they took their prisoners down to the lower deck, leaving each one of us above with a mixture of excitement at what might lie ahead and dread at the sheer awfulness of it.

The captain looked round at the assembled crew and seemed about to say something, but changed his mind, shook his head, and stepped back down to the lower deck to make his way back to his corridor. He was followed quickly by Mr Christian and then by me.

'What will you do, sir?' asked Mr Christian when they were away from the men.

'What will I do, you ask?' replied Mr Bligh, spinning round in surprise. 'Is it your place to ask me that, Mr Christian?'

'No, sir,' he said quickly. 'I merely wondered—'

'There are rules, sir,' said the captain in a tremulous voice. 'There are terms of employment, sir. There are articles of war, sir. And they must be adhered to. I suppose you have followed me down here to suggest leniency? For your friends,' he added cautiously.

Mr Christian seemed momentarily thrown by those last three words and considered them carefully before speaking. It seemed to me, and I could have been wrong, that at that phrase he made a decision to change tack. 'Not at all, Captain,' he stated firmly. 'Indeed, I followed you to let you know that you will have my utmost support in whatever decision you make.'

'But of course I will, Fletcher,' replied the captain, smiling. 'I am captain. You are not. You'll support me or I'll know the reason why.'

Mr Christian swallowed nervously and I could tell that, some-how over the course of our stay on the island, the direction of the wind between these two men had shifted a little. Mr Christian no longer had the confidence of the captain; indeed, Mr Bligh seemed to consider him in much the same way he had considered Mr Fryer during the first part of our voyage. I traced this back to two events: first, the fact that Mr Christian above all others had made himself free with the ladies of Otaheite, a perversion that was not lost on the captain, and, second, the piece of paper dis-covered in Churchill's belonging listing the names of the deserters alongside Mr Christian's own. It was too much of a thing to challenge a warranted officer on a charge such as this, but the suspicion was there and Mr Bligh could not afford to ignore it.

'I'll see you on deck in the morning, Mr Christian,' he said. 'Muster the crew for eight bells.'

He nodded and left us and the captain glanced at me for a few moments. 'See that I'm not disturbed, will you?' he said quietly. 'I must think deeply tonight. I must consult my conscience and our Saviour.'

I said nothing, understanding the gravity of the affair, but he took my silence as consent and closed his door behind him.

Mr Christian did not have to try too hard to muster the ship, for we were all awake early and gathered on deck before the captain emerged. He was wearing one of his formal uniforms and hats, which I took as a bad sign. The crew, most of whom were wearing blackened rags encircling their arms as a sign of solidarity for their disgraced comrades, went silent when they saw him. He looked tired to me, as if he had not slept, and was still unsure as to his decision.

Once he was in position he nodded at Mr Fryer, who led the prisoners in chains to the deck. The two elder men, Churchill and Muspratt, looked scared but brave, ready to accept their fate, but poor John Millward, all eighteen years of him, was already

314

half-dead on his feet, his legs slipping beneath him. As he stepped into the daylight I saw his eyes shoot upwards, left and right, and imagined that he was looking to see whether a noose had already been fitted from the mast. The fact that it hadn't seemed of no comfort to him, for he was visibly a-trembling and could barely look in the captain's direction out of fear.

'Men,' said Captain Bligh in a deep voice and the crew stayed silent to hear him out. 'We have dark business before us this morning. Our lives have swung dramatically through good times and bad these past eighteen months. We have weathered storms, turned our ship around adding thousands of miles to our journey, but we reached our island, we completed our mission, and within days we will be ready to depart for the West Indies, and then onward to home. And we did this together, as a crew, every man a part of it. And, if I may say, with a disciplinary record second to none. And so it grieves me, men, it grieves me that we have among us three cowards. Three men unworthy to be named part of the king's navy. William Muspratt, Charles Churchill and John Millward, you have been tracked down in your disgrace. You are guilty of desertion, are you not?'

'Yes, sir,' they mumbled one by one.

'Yes, sir,' repeated the captain. 'You have brought shame on the ship and dishonour upon your families. It is clearly stated in the navy constitution that there is only one fitting punishment for your crime and that is death.'

They each looked up sharply at him now and there was fear in all their eyes. My own stomach lurched, wondering what horrors I was about to witness. The entire crew stayed silent, officers and men alike, waiting to hear what the captain might say next, whether it would begin with that one simple word that would mean a reprieve. They did not have to wait long, for that word was soon upon his lips.

'However,' he said, looking down for a moment and considering things, then nodding his head as if he had only now

315

convinced himself of the justice of it, 'I am minded that men do strange and unusual things when they have been away from home for too long, suffering under the heat of the sun, and corrupted by the natural pleasures of a place like Otaheite. I feel that in this instance the death penalty might be reprieved.'

The defendants all relaxed instantly and I swear that Millward's legs went from under him again in relief, but he was quickly righted. The men all let up a ferocious cheer and I found myself beaming from ear to ear in relief. Only Mr Christian seemed unmoved by the spectacle.

'Mr Morrison,' said the captain. 'Each man will receive two dozen lashes for their behaviour. A week from now, when their wounds are healed, they will receive two dozen more. Upon their return to England they will each receive a court martial. But they will live. And that will be an end to the matter. Strap them up, sir.'

The officers took the three men to the masts, tied them there, stripped their shirts down and the punishments began. And although this was the most serious discipline that had been meted out to date, there was a sense of relief around the deck that only skin was to be broken and necks were not to be snapped.

'Will they thank me for it, Turnstile?' asked the captain of me later that evening when I was settling matters in his cabin. He had looked up from his letter-writing and caught my eye and, for my part, I was a little surprised by the question.

'I beg your pardon, sir?' I said.

'I asked whether they would thank me for it,' he repeated. 'Will they even remember my leniency?'

'Of course, sir,' I said. 'They will hold you in great esteem. You would have been within your rights as captain to end their three lives and you did not. Every man on deck will consider you a fine fellow for it and you will have their undivided loyalty.'

He smiled and nodded. 'You are a naïve lad, aren't you, Turnstile?' he said. 'Has the island taught you nothing?'

I didn't know how to answer this question, and felt uncomfortable in thinking about it, so said nothing in response, gathered what items I needed to take and went on my way, wondering what he could possibly have meant by such a thing.

I would find out before the week was over.

15

THE MORNING THAT WE WERE DUE to leave Otaheite was one of the strangest of all the days I spent at sea. The captain was up before five bells and insisted on my being up to join him.

'What a beautiful morning, Turnstile,' he said cheerfully as I prepared his breakfast. 'A good day to up-anchor.'

'Yes, sir,' said I, betraying the fact that I did not feel quite as good about this prospect as he did.

'What's the matter, boy? Aren't you glad to be starting the home stretch?'

I thought about it for a moment. 'Begging your pardon, sir, but it's not as if we'll be back in time for our dinner, now, is it? It will be many months before we are home. We have the West Indies to get to first before we start for England.'

'True, but the return journey will be nothing like as difficult as the crossing was. Trust me on this, Turnstile. We shall make it wonderfully well.'

I had scarcely seen the captain in better humour than he was now that we were about to leave the island and return to the seas. It was true that his temper had improved considerably since he had bound the men back to the boat, but this was in a directly inverse proportion to the tempers of the men, who did not want to leave. This was a clear fact. Given the chance, the majority of them would have stayed on Otaheite for ever, but that chance was not afforded them. We had a mission to complete and no man had the freedom to make his own choices, not I, not the sailors, not even the captain himself.

'You will accompany me to bid farewell to King Tynah?' he asked me. 'One last visit to the shores for you? It's been some time since you've been there, I imagine.'

'As you wish, sir,' I replied, for I was unsure whether or not I wanted to cross paths with Kaikala. My mind was still obsessing over what I had seen that night and the manner in which she had played me for a fool – aye, and Mr Heywood too. Although the last laugh, I suspected, would be on her, for while I might have found some clever way to smuggle her on board and home with me had I still been well disposed towards her, I did not think that Mr Heywood, the scut, had any similar intention.

'I do so wish, Turnstile. What's the matter with you, boy? Why are you so downhearted? The men are the same. Every one of them looking glum, as if they didn't want to see their homes again.'

There was no talking to him when he was in a mood like this; it was as if he simply did not want to acknowledge that the way he felt about things was not necessarily the way the rest of us felt. For my part, I was starting to think about how I would avoid returning to England. We had only one stop to make en route and that was at the West Indies, and it was quite a simple equation: I had to make my escape there or find my way back into the clutches of Mr Lewis. The penalties I would face at home would be too terrible to ignore.

'How long will we be docked?' I asked him. 'At the West Indies, I mean.'

'Not long, I shouldn't think,' replied the captain. 'A couple of weeks. We have more than a thousand breadfruit plants to trans-plant and I dare say by the time we get there we shall need to make some repairs to the ship and take on fresh supplies. Three weeks at most. Then it's homeward bound.'

Three weeks. More than enough time to make my move. And at least when I did so it would not be from an island, so I would not be caught as easily as Muspratt, Millward and Churchill. They wouldn't see me for dust.

The king was seated on his throne with Queen Ideeah by his side, just as he had been on the day, some three and a half months earlier, when we had first arrived to pay our respects. A servant was standing behind him, feeding him chunks of mango, for it was against protocol for the regal hand to feed the regal mouth itself. Our party consisted of the captain, all the officers with the exception of Mr Elphinstone, who remained on board the *Bounty*, and myself.

Although the captain had presented Tynah with many gifts over the course of our stay, there were some final tokens to be presented and he did this with a flourish. Tynah accepted them gratefully and it seemed as if most of the islanders had come out to say goodbye to us. There was a terrible crying and wailing emerging from them as usual – I wondered whether it might not be in their interest for us to leave so that they might finally be cheered – and the women ran to the seashore, waving their arms hysterically at the sailors in the boat beyond.

After the formalities were over, Tynah stood and took Captain Bligh aside to speak to him privately and the officers and natives milled around, speaking to one another. Stepping out of the forest at this time, who should I see but Kaikala, waving at me to come forward. I stood my ground for a moment or two but was finally led by another part of my anatomy and went towards her and was quickly dragged into the thickets out of sight of the rest of our party.

'Yay-Ko,' she said, kissing me again and again about the lips and cheeks as if her very life depended on it. 'Where have you been? I have not seen you.'

'The captain insisted we all stay on board,' I explained. 'I'm sure you know this.'

'Yes, but couldn't you find a way to escape? To come see your Kaikala?'

'I suppose I could have,' I said, stepping away from her and removing her arms from my body, despite the fact that every part of me wanted to throw her to the ground and take her there and then. 'I suppose I could have swum ashore one night at great risk to my person and come to see you, but, had I done so, who knows what I might have discovered? I might have come to our special place and found you there, playing with Mr Heywood's whistle in my place!'

She looked at me as I said this and frowned. 'Peet-a, you mean,' she asked.

'Yes, Peter,' I said. 'Peter Heywood, who is the lowest scut that the Saviour has ever put on hind legs. I find it astonishing that any Christian woman could lay a finger on him, so deformed is he.'

'But Yay-Ko,' she said with a smile, 'I am not a Christian woman.'

I opened my mouth to respond, but answer had I none to that. 'How could you do it, Kaikala?' I asked her, pleading with her now. 'How could you betray me like that?'

She shook her head and appeared genuinely mystified by what I was saying. 'I have not betrayed you, Yay-Ko,' she said.

'I saw you with him,' I insisted. 'You took him as a lover.'

'And that is a betrayal? Why?'

I stared at her. At first I believed this was little more than further proof that we were from different cultures, but then I recalled my own idea that the men of the *Bounty* did not see relations with the women of the island as an infidelity, but merely as a need satisfied. Could it be that the women of the island felt the same way?

'You asked him to take you back to England with him,' I said.

'He has denied me,' she replied. 'He came to see me last night. He told me there would be no more between us and that I could not come with him.'

'Then, you are as badly deceived as I.'

'So I told him that you would take me instead. I said that Yay-Ko would never leave Otaheite without me, that you would bring me to England and make me your wife and I would live in your palace and ride your horses and meet the king with you.'

'Ah,' I said, shrinking back a little. 'That.'

'And you know what Peet-a did? He laughed at me. He said that you were talking lies to me. That you have no palace, no horses. That you are not a rich man at all. And you talk to me of betrayal?'

'Kaikala,' I said, feeling suitably ashamed of myself, 'I'm sorry. It seemed harmless at the time. I just thought that—'

'Oh, Yay-Ko, it doesn't matter,' she said quickly. 'I don't care. I just want to leave. Will you take me with you?'

'Turnstile!' I heard a voice calling me from the beach; Captain Bligh's.

'It's the captain,' I said, turning away from her. 'I must leave.'

'No, wait,' she shrieked, grabbing me by the arm. 'Take me with you.'

'I cannot,' I said. 'I have other plans. And as much as I care for you, after Mr Heywood . . . ? Never! Not in this world!'

I made my way through the clearing and back to the beach, where the officers were standing by the launch, looking in all directions for me.

'There you are, Turnstile,' shouted the captain. 'For a moment there I worried you had deserted us yourself. Get a move on, boy. We return to the ship.'

'Sorry, Captain,' said I. 'I didn't hear—'

No further did I get in my sentence, for I heard the sound of running and screaming behind me and saw the eyes of the officers open wide. I thought for a moment I had been murdered, for something landed on my back and knocked me off my feet to the sand below. It was Kaikala.

'Take me with you, Yay-Ko,' she cried. 'Please. I will be good wife to you.'

I sat up and scrambled back, shocked by the look of madness in her eyes, and looked towards the officers and captain, each of whom was laughing wildly at my situation, except for Mr Heywood, who looked furious that Kaikala was beseeching me to marry her, and not begging him instead.

'I can't,' I said, rushing for the launch. 'Captain, tell her!'

'Oh, Turnstile, I think you have made a pretty bed here!'

'Captain, *please*!'

'I'm sorry, miss,' he replied then, wiping a tear of laughter from his eye. 'It's quite impossible. A ship is no place for a lady.'

We jumped in and the launch sailed out into the water, but it did not stop her yet, for she came swimming after us and almost received a bang on her head from the oars for her trouble.

'Good God, Turnip,' said Mr Christian. 'You must have hidden talents of which we were unaware.'

I frowned and didn't dare look at Mr Heywood. Within minutes she was tiring and we were getting closer to the *Bounty*. I watched as the men still laughed and saw her turn for the shore, her head bobbing up and down in the surf as she disappeared out of my life for ever.

She had hurt me, it was true.

She had betrayed me, although she did not see it as a betrayal.

And she had certainly behaved in a fashion at the end that made me glad that I had chosen to leave her behind.

But still, I had loved her for a time. My first love. And she had taught me things about myself. I was sorry to see her go. There, that's the truth of it. And if it makes me sound a nance, then so be it.

16

AND SO WE LEFT.
The island disappeared behind us, the men resumed their duties, the breadfruit plants were safely stored in the hold, the captain was happy to be back at sea, the officers appeared satisfied to walk the decks and issue orders, and I returned to my place outside the captain's cabin, ready to give service, plotting my escape, and wondering where my life might take me after the West Indies.

If you had asked me, I would have said that the men – *all* the men – were sorry to have left Otaheite behind them but understood that all good things must cease. That is what I would have said and it was what I believed.

But then, as you know very well, I would have been quite wrong.

17

WHEN I LOOK BACK at the few short weeks that passed between leaving Otaheite and the night of which I write now, it astonishes me to recall that there was an entire universe of disappointment, despondency and conspiracy taking place on board the *Bounty* of which I was entirely ignorant. It seems to me now that there were four separate groups on board the ship: the first was a party of one, the captain himself; the second, his officers; the third, the sailors; and the fourth, another party consisting of only one soul – myself – a boy trapped between his responsibilities to the ship's commander and the separation that existed between the crew and me. Many was the night that I went on deck in search of conversation and company, only to be snubbed by my fellows, who thought that anything they might say to me would be transported directly back to the captain. An unfair charge, certainly, considering that I had never once betrayed a trust in more than eighteen months on board, and if my dishonesty was to be asserted simply by regard to the proximity of my bunk to the captain's, well, then there was naught I could do to change minds.

There was, at times, a certain level of jealousy attached to my position too. I had the ear of the captain, that was plain to all. He looked at me with a certain fondness, although had he known of my continuing desire to escape the ship that fondness might have altered into something more sinister. But the men also liked to make kiss with him; whenever he was on deck, in tolerant form, and willing to exchange pleasantries with a sailor, then that sailor would be up on his hind legs telling the captain every piece of information he required and plenty more besides, offering intelligence about his own life back home and the people he missed. It came down to this: the captain was in charge, he was the power, and every man likes to be under the rays of the sun.

But still, it meant that I was privy to nothing.

On the evening of 28th April, I was restless of spirit. We had been away from Otaheite for almost three weeks but we were a long distance yet from the West Indies. The weather was unremarkable and a spirit of ennui had settled over all. From those conversations that I did hear, I knew that the men, rather than putting their experiences on the island behind them, appeared to be missing them more and more. They talked of the women they had left behind, of the peaceful days they had enjoyed there and that had ended all too soon. They spoke of a paradise lost to them for ever. And then they got back down on their hands and knees and scrubbed the deck.

At nights, when Mr Byrn would take out his fiddle so that we might dance, as were the captain's orders, to keep our bodies exercised, there was scarcely a man who did not look around at these sweating, tired sailors kicking their skinny limbs around them and imagine the fires, and the natives, and the music of the islands; the dancing that would lead to them being dragged into the sands and given as much pleasure as they could take on any night. The *Bounty*, it was clear to all, was no substitute for the island.

The captain was suffering a sick headache and had gone to bed early, which was a blessing in itself, for he had been in a foul mood all day, damn-and-blasting his way around the decks, throwing insults at the officers more than the men, and I had made sure to stay close enough to him that I was near by if needed, but far enough away that I wouldn't catch his eye and suffer a roasting of my own. What was inspiring this fit of pique, I knew not, only that when he entered his bed that evening there was a spirit of antipathy present around all the decks and scarcely a man on board who would not have wished that he might sleep for several days hence.

It was too early for me to sleep, however, and so I wandered on to the main deck in search of a little fresh air. I saw most of the crew gathered together towards the foresail, Mr Byrn playing his fiddle quietly, as the low hum of conversation came my way. Before stepping towards them, however, I took a fit of irritation and thought that I did not seek company after all, not that evening. They would only end their conversation when they saw me anyway and I did not desire the snub. I turned on my heel instead and walked towards the mizzen-sail, where, as far as my eye could see, there was peace and solitude to be had. I had left my shoes below deck, so my approach made no sound as I walked along.

I stood by the rail and looked out into the dark night, staring in the direction from which we had come, and quickly I realized that near by, but not at a point where I could see who was there, a conversation was taking place. One of the voices quite obviously belonged to Mr Christian; the other, I was unsure about. I barely took any notice of it at all until something in the tone and the wordplay made me cock up my ears. I recount that conversation now as I heard it.

'I am in *hell*,' said Mr Christian, stressing the final word, and I swear by the sound of his voice he sounded like a man who was suffering an extreme of the anxieties. 'I cannot take it any longer.'

'We are all in hell, sir,' said the second voice. 'But the days are passing by. We get further away with every hour of the clock. It must be tonight.'

'I can't . . . I am unsure,' he replied. 'But his insults are too much, his madness. Why should he be in charge anyway? Do you know who his people are? Does anyone? And I, sired by a great family, am reduced to this?'

'Sir, it's not a question of charge, it's a question of where we choose to live. And how.'

A great silence ensued and I frowned, wondering what they could be talking of. Perhaps now it seems ignorant of me not to have realized it, but it is only with the knowledge of how that night ended that such an accusation could be made of me. I would never have thought that matters had come to such a head.

'Will it be tonight, sir?' said the second voice.

'Do not push me!' cried Mr Christian.

'Will it be tonight?' insisted the man, and I wondered who it could be that would speak to the master's mate in such a tone; only a fellow officer? But no, the officers, even the scut, had voices of the gentry. This man did not.

'It will,' replied Mr Christian finally. 'You believe that we will have all the men?'

'I would swear on it. Their memories are short. Their hearts are on the island.'

There was further conversation for a few more moments before the two men separated; I looked over to my left and saw a figure walking back towards the sailors, but in the darkness of the late night I could not make out his form. Instead I turned back to the sea and frowned, considering the words I had heard. And here's the farce of it: I was all set to put the matter out of my head and think no more of it, considering it to have been a conversation about some trifling matter of little concern to me, only at that moment Mr Christian himself appeared from my other side, walking quickly and purposefully towards me, before stopping suddenly when we met, his mouth falling open in surprise as if he had never laid eyes on so glorious a form as mine before.

'Turnip,' he said. 'You are here.'

'Aye, sir,' I replied, turning to look at him. 'The captain is asleep. I thought I would take the air.'

'You have been standing there long?'

I stared at him and frowned, suddenly aware that to suggest I had overheard their words could be to my detriment. 'No, sir,' I replied. 'I just got here.'

He narrowed his eyes and looked at me. 'You wouldn't be lying to me, Turnip, now, would you?'

'I, sir?' I asked, all innocence. 'Not in this world! The last time I told a lie was to a shopkeeper in Portsmouth, when I said that his apples had worms in them and I wanted a sixpence or I would tell the street.'

He shook his head quickly and turned to look in the same direction as I. 'You are looking towards the island,' he said, in a more friendly tone now than before. 'You are faced towards Otaheite.'

'So I am,' I replied. 'I hadn't thought of it.'

'Hadn't you? You don't think there's a part of you that brought you here to look longingly in that direction?'

I laughed a little, but his stony face urged me to stop. 'What good are longings, sir?' I asked. 'I shall never look on that beach again.'

'No, perhaps not. There was a girl there for you, was there not?'

'You know there was, sir.'

'Did you love her?'

I stared at him; this manner of conversation between two men on board was most unusual. For it to be taking place between Mr Christian and me was downright surprising. 'Yes, sir,' I replied. 'Sometimes three times a day.'

He laughed and shook his head. 'I believe I had something of a reputation on that island myself,' he observed.

'Did you, sir?' I replied, unwilling to flatter him by feigning the knowledge. 'I hadn't heard of it.'

'It was all false anyway,' he said. 'Yes, I took my pleasures where I could find them, what natural man would not, but there was one woman . . . one in particular. Different from the rest.'

'Did you love *her*, sir?'

'Sometimes four times a day,' he replied with a smile and I confess that I laughed at the comment. He was not my type of fellow, that was for sure, we had never got along. I despised him for the pomade in his hair and the mirror by his bunk and the cleanliness of his nails and the fact that he and Mr Heywood had proved little more than scourges to me during my time on board the *Bounty*, but there are moments between all men, friends and enemies alike, when defences are dropped and something approaching candour can be the result. I looked away and, foolish me, I allowed my natural guard to drop.

What happened next came about so suddenly that I barely knew it was happening until it was already over. Without warning he had me by the throat and was leaning over the railings.

'You heard it all, didn't you, bastard?' he hissed at me. 'You were eavesdropping.'

'No, sir,' I whispered, my voice all but lost as he clenched my voice box. I turned my eyes to see the waves crashing along beside us. 'I don't know what you mean.'

'I say you are the captain's spy,' he insisted. 'Sent here to listen in to things that are not your concern and report them back to your master. Tell me I am wrong!'

'You are wrong, sir,' I said. 'Terrible wrong. I was standing here, that was all. I was thinking on other things.'

'You swear it?'

'On my mother's life,' I promised, although who that naughty lady was, and whether she yet lived or not, was a mystery to me.

He loosened his grip only a little and seemed to relent. 'You know that I could just throw you overboard,' he told me. 'I could send you to your death and no one would be the wiser for it. It would be seen as a tragedy. And life here would go on as before.'

'Please, sir . . .' I whispered, a fierce longing to survive surging through me, a desire for continued existence that only appears when that very lifeblood is threatened.

'But I'm no killer,' he said, releasing me.

I fell to the deck instantly, coughing in a most unpleasant fashion, and rubbed at my throat, looking up at him with hatred in my eyes. I swear that if I had been in possession of a cutlass or a musket I would have ended him right there and said damn and blast you to the consequences. But I had neither of them, and nor did I have the courage to wrestle him overboard. So I simply sat there, and felt tears behind my eyes, which I forced myself to stay.

'Go down below,' he said now in a distracted tone. 'Go to your bunk. Men are on deck.'

He walked past me, the toe of his boot grazing against my leg, and when he was out of sight I did exactly as he said. I ran back to the comfort of my hammock and pulled the sheet over my head, allowing the tears to flow freely then, tears that lasted for so long and caused me so much pain that they finally blended into sleep. Before I knew it, the rest was silence until a few hours later, when I sat bolt upright. The conversation between the two men, Mr Christian and his fellow conspirator, I knew what it meant. I had it now. It was obvious. I reached up a hand to lever myself out of the hammock and was immediately pushed back by the force of a blow.

Four men. Marching past me. Breaking into the captain's cabin. It had begun.

'What the—?'

I heard the captain's words from outside and could tell the shock of surprise and the immediacy of the lack of understanding. He had never woken to something like this before. In the astonishment of the awakening, he knew not what was happening.

'Mr Christian,' he roared. 'What's the meaning of this?'

'Meaning?' cried Mr Christian. 'Let us not seek meanings. And ask no questions, Mr Bligh. The time for your questions has come to an end.'

'What?' roared the captain. 'What in God's name—?'

I jumped from my hammock and ran inside in time to see two men – the midshipman George Stewart and the AB Thomas Burkett, he who had once tumbled from the fore topgallant sail and narrowly avoided opening his brains on the deck below – pulling the captain from his bunk and dragging him in his night-shirt into a stance. They were rough with their handling and shouting phrases at him. *Get up! On your feet, dog! Do as we tell or you'll be damned.* Phrases such as those. They turned to look at me as I appeared in the doorway, but dismissed me immediately and went back to their dirty business.

'Mr Christian!' shouted the captain, trying to unhand himself from his captors. 'What do you think you're doing? I am a captain in His Majesty's—'

'A captain must have a ship,' stated Mr Christian flatly. 'Yours is forfeit.'

'Forfeit, you say? Damn you if she is! To whom is she forfeit?'

'To me, sir,' he replied, equalling the roar. 'I am taking the ship.'

A silence seemed to descend on the room at that phrase. The captain ceased his struggle and looked at his master's mate with a mixture of disbelief and abject terror in his eyes. The three men who held him stood still too, as if the utterance of the words was enough to give them pause for thought.

'You never are,' said the captain in a level voice.

'You have put us through *hell*, sir,' shouted Mr Christian. 'If you could only have seen . . . if you could have thought what it was like for us. To be there. To experience that. And then you take it away from us? You show us a paradise, and then expel us from it, as if you are the very Saviour himself. What had we done to deserve your unkindness?'

The captain stared at him and appeared to be genuinely amazed by what he was hearing. 'A paradise?' he asked. 'What paradise? Fletcher, I don't—'

'Otaheite!' he replied, pacing the floor now. 'You gave it to us, don't you see? You brought us there! And for what? For a few plants?'

'But that's our mission,' cried the captain. 'You knew this when you . . . Oh, unhand me, you men, or I will see you hanged in the morning!'

He wrestled himself free of his two captors and they stood by him for a moment, looking to Mr Christian for guidance in what to do next.

'Fletcher, you have taken the sun, that is what it is,' said the captain, taking a step towards him and holding his hands out in a conciliatory gesture. 'It has gone to your head, that is what it is. You have debased yourself with illustration and alcohol and the depravity of whores and your mind is diseased by it. Stop this now, stop it *now*, Fletcher, and allow me to help you and the matter may end here.'

He was standing directly in front of Mr Christian then and I saw the master's mate's head dip slightly and a hand reach up to his own eyes, as if to wipe the tears from them. I thought for a moment that this was over, that he would concede his madness and equilibrium would be restored. Instead, he betrayed his code and his own honour by performing an unspeakable act; he lifted his hand to Captain Bligh and brought it across his face.

The captain was knocked sideways by the blow but he neither retaliated, nor allowed himself to look back at Mr Christian immediately. We watched him, all four of us, and it was perhaps half a minute before the two men were eye to eye again and I could tell by looking at Mr Bligh that his generosity had come to an end.

'What do you mean to do?' he asked.

'It's quite simple,' said Mr Christian. 'We do not wish to return to England.'

'We? Who is this "we"?'

'We, the men of the *Bounty*.'

'You three?' asked the captain with an embittered laugh. 'You believe that three men can take a ship like this? I have near forty alongside me.'

'They are with me, sir,' replied Mr Christian.

'Never.'

'Oh, but they are.'

The captain swallowed and I shook my head in amazement; how could this conspiracy be gathered among the whole crew? How had it happened without some warning being obvious? The closest I had come to it was the overheard conversation earlier, but I had not the sense to translate the words at that time. My movement caught the captain's eye and he looked in my direction, his eyebrows raised.

'And you, Turnstile?' he asked. 'Even you?'

'No, sir, not I,' I replied quickly and defiantly. 'You think I would stand by a diseased cur like Mr Christian?'

The words were not out of my mouth when Mr Christian turned and hit me a slap with such force that I fell directly backwards, over the captain's desk, taking two of the portraits with me; I landed, dazed, upon the ground, with Betsey Blair so close to my lips that I might have kissed her.

'Infamous,' said the captain, appalled by the blow. 'You'll hang for this, Fletcher.'

'For the beating of a servant-lad? I rather think not.'

'For assaulting a senior officer, for taking a ship—'

'We will not be found, captain, don't you understand it yet? It will be as if we never existed. You cannot hang a spectre. Take him, lads.'

Stewart and Burkett took the captain by the arms again and this time he did not struggle, but allowed himself to be led by them towards the door. I was still on the ground, putting a hand to my lip and attempting to stay the flow of blood that was coming from it.

'Wait,' said Mr Christian, before looking down at me. 'Fetch Mr Bligh's overcoat,' he instructed me.

'I'll do naught on your say-so,' I replied.

'Fetch his overcoat, Turnip, or as God is my witness I will carry you to the deck and throw you overboard before this minute is out. Now fetch it!'

I scrambled to my feet and took the heavy, dark blue coat from its place and handed it to the captain, who took it without a word and put it on, for he was wearing naught but an undershirt and it was a fierce unsightly way to present oneself to another man.

'Take him up, lads,' said Mr Christian before turning to me. 'You can come with us or I can lead you there myself. Which is it to be?'

I nodded and agreed to follow them and he stepped out first, leading the way through the great rooms beyond. Mr Bligh proceeded to curse the men who were holding him, informing them in no uncertain terms of the great damage they were doing to their own lives, the shame they were bringing on their families, the disrepute they were bringing on their names, but they were having none of it. They seemed caught up in a sort of blood thirst that allowed them to damn their captain with the names they would have been afeared to employ when he had control of the ship, lest he set them to the gunner's daughter and had them flogged for their cheek.

They took us at great speed through the lane ways where the breadfruit were stored, and as we came to the stairs to the upper deck the sound of a great commotion up ahead finally reached my ears and my stomach turned in fright as I wondered what ordeal would face us when we hit the night air.

Mr Christian went first and a great cheer broke out when he appeared on deck.

The two men and the captain came next and there was a sudden silence, followed by more cheering and stamping of feet.

In the great din of it, I dare say no one saw me appear as well, but I was shocked by the sight that was presented to me.

The mood on deck was not quite so in Mr Christian's favour as he would have had us believe. On the contrary, from the moment the captain set foot among the men his natural authority was enough to cause most of them to become a little less vocal in their support for the new regime. I could see that not everyone was behind the mutiny either; Mr Fryer, loyal and trustworthy regardless of his personal relationship with the captain, was being restrained by several of the men, and some of the sailors were arguing among themselves about what was the right course of action.

'Quieten down, lads,' cried Mr Christian, raising an arm, and the crew fell silent as they waited for him to speak; he appeared to have regained some of the composure that he was lacking when making his initial arrest in the captain's cabin. 'Mr Bligh has been informed of the new structure on board the *Bounty* and has agreed that he has behaved for the bad.'

'I have agreed nothing of the sort, you damned blasted cur!' cried the captain, practically foaming at the mouth in anger. 'You'll all hang for this, every one of you that follows Mr Christian. If you want to stand a chance, I suggest that you arrest him and bind him in chains this minute.'

'I'm with you, Captain,' cried William Cole, the boatswain, and he was immediately surrounded by angry sailors.

'And I,' shouted the quartermaster's mate, George Simpson.

'So, Mr Christian?' said the captain with a smile. 'You have the whole crew, is it? Who else is with me? You, Surgeon Ledward?'

Thomas Ledward had been assistant to Surgeon Huggan and had taken over his responsibilities after his death. The young doctor looked around nervously and finally nodded his head.

'Aye, Captain,' he said. 'I'm with you.'

'You see, Christian?' he asked triumphantly. 'And you, Mr Sumner?' he said, sure that he could rely on the young AB. 'You'll take my side, won't you?'

'Not I,' he replied, stepping forward. 'I mean you no harm, sir, but if you think I want to live out my days sailing the seas to line another's pockets, when I could return to paradise and be with the woman I fell in love with, then you're a Bedlamite.'

'And you're a mutineer, sir!' cried the captain. 'You're a damned mutineer, you're a damned disgrace, and you'll be damned to hell for your actions.'

'Aye, maybe so,' he replied. 'But I'll have a happier time of it between now and then all the same.'

The captain looked away and scanned the ranks. 'You,' he called, pointing over at one of his midshipmen, George Stewart. 'You, Mr Stewart, where do you stand on the matter?'

'Four-square behind Mr Christian, sir,' he replied.

'And you, William Muspratt?'

'With Mr Christian, sir.'

'I might have known it too. A deserter and a mutineer. And not an ounce of remorse on your face despite the fact that I spared you from the hangman's noose.'

Muspratt shrugged his shoulders. 'I couldn't give a flying fuck,' he said, laughing in the captain's face.

'Matthew Quintal, what say you?'

'Mr Christian, sir.'

'And you, Matthew Thompson?

'Mr Christian.'

'William Brown?'

'Mr Christian.'

'Enough of this!' cried the same Mr Christian. 'The men are with me, sir, that's all you need to know. Your time here is over.'

The captain nodded and breathed heavily through his nose; I could see that he was desperately trying to think what he might do next to regain his command. 'So what happens now, then?' he asked. 'What are your intentions, Fletcher? Do you mean to cut my throat?'

'I told you I am no murderer.'

'You're as good as one, so let us not play with niceties.'

'Skinner, Sumner, Ellison,' he replied, looking in the direction of three of the men. 'Lower one of the launches.'

'Aye, sir.'

They ran to the side of the boat and lowered a launch into the water, keeping it on its ropes yet.

'This ship,' shouted Mr Christian loudly so that every man jack of us could hear, 'will not be returning to England. Nor will it be going to the West Indies. It has another destination in mind. Any of you who wish to stay with it, your presence will be welcomed, although do not fool yourselves that there will be no work to do. Any who wish to go with Mr Bligh, you may step into the launch now.'

Silence fell and the men looked at one another in surprise. It was finally broken by the captain himself.

'Not a murderer, are you?' he asked. 'Not a murderer? You will set me adrift, thousands of miles from home, with naught to guide my way. If that is not murder, then I'd like to know the name of it.'

'You will have a compass, sir,' said Mr Christian. 'And any man who chooses to accompany you. That is all I can spare. After that, the rest is down to your skill.'

'You may dress it in as many fancy ways as you like. It is murder.'

At that, John Norton, a young seaman who had been of little

use or interest to anyone since the beginning of the voyage, broke through from the ranks of the sailors. So surprised were his fellows – for Norton was a timid thing, given to silences and poetic thoughts – that they let him through and he stepped all the way towards the captain. I feared for a moment that he had lost his reason in the excitement and was about to do Mr Bligh an injury, but instead he merely nodded his head at him for a moment and then did the most unusual thing. He walked to the side of the boat, climbed over the side and lowered himself into the launch. The men watched him, astonished, and then as one broke into a cacophonous melody of jeers and whistles, taunting the loyal sailor for his fidelity. Norton seemed not to care. He took a seat and awaited companions.

He had little need to worry. Before long, others stepped forward and made the journey into the launch. The gardener, Mr Nelson, joined him, although I noted he was trembling as he did so. The clerk, Mr Samuel. The quartermaster's mate, George Simpson, stepped down. The midshipman, John Hallett. The boatswain, Mr Cole. The gunner, Mr Peckover. The carpenter, Mr Purcell. They went down one by one until there were sixteen men below and thirty above.

'Mr Heywood,' said the captain, his voice breaking now, intimations of doom ahead of him. 'I feel I need hardly ask, but what of you? You are an officer in His Majesty's navy.'

'And His Majesty may suck on my whistle for all I care of him,' he replied, and the captain merely nodded, refusing to be shocked by the scandalous remark.

'I am with you, Captain,' said a voice from my left. 'Right to the end.' I looked over and watched as Mr Fryer made his way towards the side of the boat.

'You, sir?' asked the captain, a note of tenderness edging into his voice.

'To the end,' he repeated and climbed over the side. The captain nodded and swallowed slightly, his eyes looking down on the deck sorrowfully. I thought he might have been considering his own behaviour towards that fine fellow over the course of their time together and regretting it.

'Anyone else?' cried Mr Christian, looking around, and the rest of the men shook their heads. 'Then, get you down, Mr Bligh.'

Without hesitation the captain stepped towards the side of the boat and turned back once to make a final remark. 'You will lay eyes on me again,' he said without any rancour in his voice. 'Every man jack of you will. You will see me standing before you as the hood is placed over your heads before you swing. Mine will be the last face you will see, you may mark that.'

The men hooted and jeered and he turned to step over the side, but as he did so I caught his eye.

I confess, and I confess it to my shame, that I had been hiding a little out of the sightlines of the others, keeping my head down, hoping that a resolution might be reached and we would not come to this. It was clear that the men in the launch and the captain himself would not survive; they could not. It was a nautical impossibility. They knew not where they were, in which direction they should aim; nor did they have food or drink. And the launch itself was already overfilled, for it was a mere twenty-three feet in length and not designed for the seventeen men already inside it, and the captain too.

'Turnstile,' said the captain. 'You must decide.'

I looked at him and at Mr Christian, who I despised with all my heart now. But the truth of it was in my soul. I did not wish to return to England and to my fate at the hands of Mr Lewis. And I did not wish to die at sea in the launch, my body eaten by fish, my bones scattered about the foot of the sea. Should I stay with the *Bounty*, then I might return to the island, to paradise, perhaps to a reconciliation with Kaikala. Mr Lewis would never find me. I would have a happy life. It was not a difficult choice.

I stepped over to Mr Bligh, shook his hand and smiled at him.

'You've been very kind to me, sir,' I said. 'And I will be eternally grateful for it.'

I thought I could see his whole body collapse slightly in sorrow as he nodded his head, but nevertheless he did not take his hand away instantly. When he did, he patted my shoulder, turned away and walked to the launch. I watched him descend, and then turned round to face Mr Christian.

'This has been a most unexpected experience,' I said with a smile on my face, before turning to Mr Heywood, pulling back my right arm into a fist, and hitting the scut so hard on the jaw that he fell backwards, arse over tea-kettle, and lay sprawled on the deck in a daze. The men, and Mr Christian, stared at him and then back at me.

'I'm with the captain,' I said then in a steady voice, before turning round, climbing over the side of the *Bounty*, and stepping down into the launch and into an uncertain future.

Part IV

The Tub

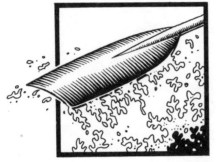

28 APRIL – 14 JUNE 1789

Day 1: 28 April

JOHN JACOB TURNSTILE, prize fool. I'll be damned if I know what came over me.

Although I'd had precious little time to consider my options, it had been my intention during the whole sorry mess to stay on board the *Bounty* and return to the island with the mutineers. It's true I could barely stand any of them, and considered them a fine set of cowards and scoundrels to have behaved in such a fashion towards a man as decent as the captain, but I did not believe that I harboured sufficient loyalties to any man or cause to look after the well-being of a single creature other than John Jacob Turnstile himself. Throughout the prosecution of the whole palaver, I thought that once we were back on Otaheite I could fashion a craft of my own and set out, travelling island by island, in search of a better life and a happier world. And instead I cheeked Mr Christian, thumped Mr Heywood and ended up as a passenger of one of the *Bounty*'s launches on a cold, dark night, certain of nothing other than the surety of my approaching demise.

There were nineteen of us, all told. Of the officers, only Mr Fryer, Mr Elphinstone and the captain himself were present. Surgeon Ledward was with us, and the botanist Mr Nelson. The quartermasters, John Norton and Peter Linkletter, had both seen fit to remain loyal to Mr Bligh, but as we had no lines to stow or cables to reel, their regular employments would be of little use. I noticed the cook, Mr Hall, sitting at the side with a panicked expression upon his face and wondered which of us he would fillet first. The butcher, Mr Lamb, was no great navigator. Nor was the carpenter, Mr Purcell. And nor, for that matter, was I. We did not have a single AB among our unhappy number; every one of those rough fellows was already on his way back to make merry with the women of Otaheite.

As we were cut free from the ship, the men who had once been afeared of the captain whistled at him and called him base names, and I felt my gorge rise with anger at the dirt of it. It was a low thing, a very low thing indeed, to set other Christian men off to their certain deaths in a boat in the middle of the night, but it was a worse thing to take a pleasure in it. The captain, for his part, seemed unperturbed and rose not to their taunts, for such was his dignified way. I watched him and he seemed oblivious to the whole thing, as if this was simply another part of the voyage home. His narrowed eyes were darting back and forth, staring into the black night as if he could espy a white line appearing through it that would lead us safely back to England, and I swear it was as if he was reading a map in the darkness of the night.

As our launch drifted away from the *Bounty* I heard a loud sound of splashing behind us and when I turned I could see by the fire-torches that the pirates were engaged in a commotion at the rear of the ship, pouring a discharge through the very port-holes I had walked past a thousand times as I made my way towards the captain's cabin. The discharge was accompanied by a heavy thudding sound and great cheers from the men on deck.

'What are they doing?' I asked Mr Nelson, the botanist, who rose to his feet a little and narrowed his eyes for a better observance. 'It's as if they're throwing away the ship's fine things.'

'It's more precious than that, Turnip,' said he, shaking his head and locking his jaw in anger. 'Can't you see? It's the breadfruit. Those dogs are drowning them in the sea.'

My mouth dropped open in surprise and I turned to face the captain, but the light had grown so low now that I could only make out the bulk of his person as he shifted in his seat and stared; his demeanour was hidden from me.

'That's a crime,' I shouted, appalled by it. 'A terrible crime after all we have been through. Why did we come here, after all, if it wasn't for them? Why did we risk our lives, again and again? Why are we left out here in the middle of this blessed ocean if it wasn't on account of them damnable breadfruit?'

A low, thunderous snorting sound emerged from Mr Nelson's mouth and I swear that I had never seem him look so angered. He had always been a most mild-mannered fellow, happy to have his nose in a set of leaves. For him to see the plants that he had nurtured so carefully be thrown to their demise in such a careless fashion was enough to make him want to dive overboard, swim back to the ship, and have at every man there in hand-to-hand combat.

'They'll be hanged!' I heard one man say from the other side of the launch; I knew not who.

'Every one of them will face justice,' said another.

'We won't see it if they do,' came a low voice that I knew to be that of Mr Hall. 'We'll be at the bottom of the sea, a fine supper for the fish.'

'That's enough of that,' said Mr Fryer, his voice uncertain now as he considered what lay ahead, but his very words were echoed by the captain who snapped them out, not so much in anger but in a desire to have our attention.

'Hold your tongue, Mr Hall,' said he. 'Their punishment, and they will receive one, you can mark that, is not our concern for now. We have a calm night at the moment. We may not have many more ahead of us. Keep the launch steady while I think. I am still your captain. I will bring us to safety. You must have faith.'

The men said nothing, but in truth there was nothing for us to say; the waves were as placid as they had ever been and in that moment I began to think that perhaps we did not have as much to worry about as I had previously thought; and, believing that the next day would bring a solution to our problem and a quick return to civilization, I did the only thing that I could think of that would be of any use under the circumstances.

I lay back, closed my eyes and promptly fell asleep.

Day 2: 29 April

WHEN DAYLIGHT CAME on the second day I was able to take full account of the predicament that we found ourselves in. The launch being no more than twenty-three feet in length and with nineteen loyalists on board, we were put together in a most intimate and unpleasant fashion. The captain was seated at the fore, engaged in consultations with the quartermaster John Norton and Mr Fryer, while two of the men sailed the vessel without a great deal of enthusiasm and the rest tried to sleep. We were pointed in the direction of the island of Tofoa, which the captain said was not a great distance for us to travel, and where we might land our small craft and send a party ashore in search of provisions for the journey ahead. I confess that I was not filled with the trepidations at this time; indeed, I felt almost cheerful that we were all gathered together in such confinement with little work to do, save the task of keeping ourselves alive. For I had been sailing alongside Mr Bligh for long enough – aye, and alongside Mr Fryer too – that I felt a confidence in their abilities to see us to safety.

'This was a foolish thing,' I heard the second quartermaster, Mr Linkletter, whisper to his mate, Mr Simpson. 'What possibility is there of survival, I ask you that? We know not where we are and we have few provisions. We shall be dead before the day is out.'

'You shouldn't say such a thing,' came the braver reply. 'The captain knows what he's about, don't he? How quickly you give up!'

This was confidence all right, but it was only the second day. None of us knew what the weeks ahead held in store for us.

We arrived in sight of Tofoa by midday and it gave each of us a terrific boost to see the craggy rocks and stone aspect of that god-forsaken island, as if it was the smooth-walled harbour of Portsmouth herself that was coming into sight. I was at the rear of the launch, but the captain sat at the foremost part, watching directly ahead, occasionally staring bleakly into the waters below before shouting orders to the sailing men behind him in such a tone that we might have all been back on board the *Bounty* and not stuck on that miserable craft.

'Ho there, men,' he cried, raising an arm. 'Keep her steady a moment.'

The launch came to rest and the men looked overboard. Through the blue waters we could see a long range of stone beneath us, ready to break our small craft into pieces should we venture across it. The land was still too far away for us to anchor and it was fierce miserable to be stuck at such a distance when a landing would have brought great hope to us all.

'Turn her around,' roared the captain. 'Nor' by nor'west.'

The launch turned and we sailed slowly and carefully, rounding the pointed tip of Tofoa until we came to a darker stretch of water, which indicated that an easier passage to shore might be available to us. Mr Fryer gave the order to make for the land and we did so, stopping only when the waters changed again and it became clear that to risk further ingress was to risk our own transport and, by extension, our lives.

'Mr Samuel,' said the captain, selecting the ship's clerk at random. 'You and Mr Purcell and Mr Elphinstone. Into the waters with you and over to shore. See what provisions you might find there and report back as soon as you can.'

'Aye, sir,' said the three men, plunging out and swimming for the island, not a great distance away, if truth be told. They were walking with the water lapping their waists in only a minute or two. As they did so, I moved my position near to the fore of the launch to be closer to the captain; it was the position I preferred for most of the voyage to come.

'What say you, Mr Fryer?' asked the captain quietly of his first officer. 'Not the most helpful of islands, I suspect.'

'Perhaps not, sir,' acknowledged the master. 'We may be forced to sail on and take a care with what provisions we have in the meantime.'

'Oh, we shall take care of them, sir,' said the captain with a half-laugh. 'I can promise you that.' I glanced to his left where a small crate lay, filled with bread and a few pieces of fruit, the only nourishment that our erstwhile shipmates had deemed necessary to provide us with. 'It might surprise you how little a man needs in his belly to survive.'

'Yes, it might,' said Mr Fryer flatly before turning away and I thought it a curious reply.

We sat there for several hours, bobbing up and down in the water, each man considering how he had found himself in this unhappy position. Very few words were spoken, but if spirits dipped, then the man in question would look to port, espy the rocky island of Tofoa and take solace. The reason why is hard to know. Perhaps any sort of solid ground seemed comforting.

Our three fellows swam back to us as the sun started to fall and their reply was an unhappy one. There was nothing there, they stated. Nothing to eat. No fruit trees. No natural vegetables. One tame spring that had provided only two flagons of water, which they brought with them and which the captain took quickly out of their hands. We were each of us possessed by a terrible thirst at that point and there was little question in my mind that Mr Elphinstone, Mr Samuel and Mr Purcell had drunk several quantities of these flagons themselves before rejoining us, but there was naught that could be done about that. They settled back into their seats and we all looked to the captain to know what might come next.

'We sail on, then,' he said after a few moments, answering our unspoken question. 'And if there is a man aboard who doubts that we can do it, then he may keep his infamous thoughts to himself, for we have difficult days ahead and only a positive outlook will be permitted or, I swear, I shall feed you all to the fish myself. Mr Fryer, hand me that loaf.'

The master reached into the crate and removed one of the larger loaves and I stared at it in horror, for although it was bigger than its fellows, there was scarcely enough in the captain's hands to satisfy three men, let alone more than six times that number. And then, to my surprise, Mr Bligh tore the loaf in two, and then in two again, replaced three of those worthy quarters in their crated home and held the fourth aloft for all of us to see. The men stared at it wordlessly, appalled that this morsel was to be divided between nineteen of us – it seemed impossible that such a feat could be achieved – but before too long each of us held a few crumbs in our hands and were swallowing them quickly, teasing our appetites so cruelly that they cried out in complaint.

'Where to now, sir?' asked Mr Fryer, settling the sailors on either side of the launch, awaiting directions.

'Isn't it obvious, Mr Fryer?' asked the captain, half-smiling. 'Homeward, sir. Point us homeward.'

Day 3: 30 April

TOWARDS HOME we may have been aiming, but towards home we did not yet advance, for a series of islands were lying to the north-east of Tofoa and Mr Bligh determined that it would be a sensible thing for us to rest at another of these on this day and discover whether there might be something edible to be discovered on their terrain. The island that he selected was chosen on account of the fact that there was an easy inlet through which we could land close to the rock-face of the atoll itself and also because there was a row of thick, long-lying vines strung from the top of that same rock to the ground below, left there no doubt by natives of these islands who had used them to find their way to the top.

'I shall venture up myself, I believe,' said the captain, surprising each one of us by the decision, for it would be no mean feat to scale that sheer face; it would require monkey-powers.

'You, Captain?' asked Mr Fryer in surprise. 'Would it not be more sensible to send one of the men?'

'I am a man, Mr Fryer,' came the saucy reply. 'In case you haven't noticed, His Majesty places his best men in command of his ships, so why should I not ascend? Mr Nelson, sir, you will join me?'

All heads turned at once to stare at the botanist, Mr Nelson, who appeared at that moment to be engaged in the fine art of scratching his bollix, for his hand was tucked within his breeches and was finding quick purchase there. He had not perhaps been listening to the conversation between the two officers but, becoming aware of our sudden interest in him, he removed his hand from his nether regions without an ounce of shame, sniffed at it for a moment, pulled an appreciative face as if he was mightily pleased with what it offered him, and then looked towards the assembled audience, raising an eyebrow in surprise.

'What?' he asked. 'Can a man not scratch himself without charging a penny for viewing-rights?'

'Mr Nelson, you have not heard me, sir,' shouted the captain from the fore, straining to keep a note of jollity in his tone. 'I plan to scale the rock-face we see before us by means of the vines that lie along them to determine whether there is aught to be found at the top. Will you join me?'

Mr Nelson frowned for a moment and looked at the sight ahead of him and shook his head as if he was actually considering it. 'My legs are a little weak this morning, sir,' he said. 'And my arms too. I don't know if I have the strength for it.'

'Nonsense,' said the captain cheerfully, standing to his feet and beckoning the botanist to do the same. 'On your feet, man. The exercise will do you good. Between the two of us, I say that the second man to reach the top is a dandy.'

Mr Nelson gave a deep sigh but stood up, aware that the captain's request was no request at all, but an order, and one that must be obeyed, even if the boatswain did not have the tools of his trade alongside him to punish the mischievous. The rest of us, I recall, shrank back in our places, eager that the captain and his chosen companion would be on their way and that none of us would be enjoined to accompany them.

'Captain,' said Mr Elphinstone, helping Mr Bligh out of the boat, whereupon he was immediately submerged waist high in water but had no more than twenty feet to walk to where the vines hung. 'Do you think this is sensible?'

'I think it is a mighty sensible thing to discover whether there might be food atop those cliffs,' said the captain. 'I don't know about the condition of your belly, Mr Elphinstone, but mine wants filling.'

'I only ask, sir,' he replied, 'because it is a dangerous climb, and a difficult one, and if there is naught at the top of interest, then it will have been a wasted one as well.'

The captain nodded for a moment and looked over at the vines and then upwards to the top of the cliff, whose bounty was hidden to us from this vantage point. 'I would ask you this, Mr Elphinstone,' said the captain eventually, as if he was explaining an obvious matter to a simpleton child: 'why would the natives of these islands put so much effort into creating these floral ladders were there not something of interest to be discovered at the top of them? Can you think of a reason for it, sir?'

Mr Elphinstone considered the sense of this for a moment before shrugging his shoulders, nodding his head and retaking his place in the tub. Mr Nelson, in the meantime, had stood erect but failed to place one foot before the other and the captain summoned him with a click of his fingers. 'Quick, quick, now, Mr Nelson,' he said. 'Join me, if you please.'

Within a few minutes our small crew, depleted now to seventeen, were in our places, turning our heads to watch the climbing-race of the two men up the side of the cliff. It was not difficult to guess who would be the winner; the captain was a fine healthy specimen of a man and, despite a few initial difficulties finding purchase between hand, feet and mossy stone, he ascended with no more difficulty than a spider along a wall-face. Mr Nelson, on the other hand, struggled a little more and we could not help but show concern that he might fall backwards, crash on to the rocks below, and provide a more permanent depletion to our crew.

Among much cheering from the men, however, our two fellows were soon at the top and struggled their way over, disappearing from our sight for a time. We sat and talked among ourselves, at first happy that they had made it, and then slowly beginning to worry why it was taking so long for them to reappear. I looked across at the two remaining officers, Mr Fryer and Mr Elphinstone, and watched their faces for similar signs of concern, but if they had any they kept them carefully concealed.

The sun was high in the sky and I looked down at my feet in order to ease the light in my eyes and the crick in my neck, and then a strange thing happened. The men let out a roar at once and looked upwards. I turned to look too and, as I did so, their faces turned to surprise and I thought they were pulling away from me. Knowing not what was the matter I tried to look up again, but the sun was too bright and I could see naught but a blinding sensation, and then what appeared to be a missile heading towards me, and then before I could scramble out of the way my own lights went out and a blackness took its place.

It was, I was told, some fifteen minutes before I returned to full consciousness. In the meantime, the men had been throwing sea water in my face, taking care that I would swallow none of it, and slapping my cheeks to revive me, but it took a time for my sensibilities to return and, when they did, it was with a great sickness of the head. I reached a hand up and felt a tender mark above my eyes and what appeared to be the beginnings of a great bruise. I hissed when my fingers touched it and attempted to sit up and when I did so, who was seated before me only the captain himself, looking both amused and embarrassed.

'Sorry about that, Master Turnstile,' he said. 'You don't seem to have an awful lot of luck, do you?'

'I was attacked, sir,' I cried. 'A missile of some sort.'

'A coconut,' he replied, indicating a dozen or so of these hairy items that were now placed at the fore of the boat. 'Very few to be found, I will grant you, but they will be of great assistance to us in the days ahead. Mr Nelson and I threw them from the top. I think you got in the way.'

I nodded and felt insulted by the whole experience, but a few minutes later, when the captain deigned to crack open one of the coconuts and distribute its flesh among the men, he handed me a slightly larger portion than was my due – and for that, if nothing else, I was grateful.

I forgot my injury quickly, but I began to worry that these stomach pangs were of a more serious nature than any of us was conceding. We could only hover among these islands for so long; at some point we would have to put to sea, and when we did, what would become of us then?

Day 4: 1 May

BETTER NEWS TODAY in that we set out for yet another of the small islands dotted around those regions that the late Captain Cook had christened the Friendly Islands – which gave me a warm and satisfying feeling – and on this occasion we discovered a small cove where our boat could rest and we could, every one of us, emerge from our confinement and stretch our legs, walk on the sand, or lie on our backs without fear of kicking another three fellows in the face, just as we fancied. After seventy-two hours trapped on the launch I could scarcely believe how liberating it was to feel the freedom of my pins once again, and I leapt and danced and twirled around the beach like a Bedlamite until the captain himself marched over to me and boxed my ears, as if the injury of the coconut on my forehead was not disfigurement enough.

'Have a care with yourself, Master Turnstile,' he said, shaking his head irritably. 'Just because there is no one to observe your behaviour does not mean that you should carry on in such a ridiculous fashion. Think you to be a dancer at the Covent Garden?'

'No, sir, not I,' said I, pirouetting on my toes for a moment with my hands stretched wide above my head, a sensation that felt so good I could have held the ludicrous pose for a weekend and a day. 'I merely meant to return some of the blood to my extremities as it's been fierce cramped in the *Bounty*-tub.'

The captain snorted and stared at my continued prancing, wondering whether he should put an end to my nonsense once and for all with either a command or a swipe of his hand, but when he turned he was presented with a further tableau to test him: seven or eight of my fellows, engaged in similarly buffoon-ish behaviour, stretching and a-posing and a-dancing with abandon.

'A bunch of fools is what I have in my company,' said the captain finally, shaking his head but allowing himself a hint of a smile, hidden as it was in the growth of his moustache and beard, which were beginning to take precedence on his face. 'A bunch of frolicking fools.' But, still, for all that he let us be, perhaps aware that it was exercise at least, not indifferent to the dancing he had commanded on board the ship. Or perhaps he knew that the nature of authority had undergone a change over those past four days and it would be wise of him to relax his rules a little.

A scouting group of four men were assembled and sent to investigate the island, which appeared at first glance to be of a far more hospitable nature than any we had seen in recent days. Already the men were dining off fruit-trees and berries, filling their stomachs as they would, although the lack of water con-tinued to prove a difficulty as our hydration levels were low. Indeed, one of the things that the men were sent to look out for carefully was a spring, that we might drink and fill our flagons before setting off again.

To our surprise, they went as four but returned as six, the crew on the beach turning in surprise as a young woman – not pretty, but worth a glance nonetheless – and a boy of three or four years of age appeared in their company, the men wearing broad smiles at what they had discovered, as well as carrying a bushel of plantains, some breadfruit and some more coconuts. The woman did not speak English but wore a smile that suggested she was simple in the head and cracked coconuts open on her noggin with scarce a thought for the brain within. Indeed, she seemed to take pleasure in it.

To the men, this was great sport, for she was a new person to take an interest in, but perhaps the interest grew too strong, for as we all surrounded her she took fright and then took a hold of her boy and the two of them turned and ran away, with no more than one or two men following in half-hearted pursuit, among them Lawrence LeBogue, who was singing a bawdy song and threatening her virtue, the filthy fellow.

'We shall rest here the night, men,' the captain announced. 'Sleep will come easier to us all, I think, if we are flat on our backs on the sand for an evening rather than locked together on the launch. What say you?'

The men gave a hearty cheer, for at that moment I swear that we would have happily stayed there for ever. There were things that we could have done, of course. We could have searched for more food and water. We could have checked the launch for any repairs that needed doing and set about them with wood from the island. But at that moment no one wanted to do much other than exercise their limbs and then rest them, which is what we did.

It was two hours later when the midshipman Robert Tinkler let out a shout and we all turned to look in the direction he was pointing. Coming around a hill were a group of men, women and children, carrying gifts in their arms but spears on their backs, walking at such a pace that they would be upon us in minutes.

'Stay close, every man,' said the captain, moving to our front, as was only right and proper. 'No one is to make a sudden movement or antagonize the savages. They may be friendly.'

'They outnumber us, sir,' said I, slipping to his side. 'There must be thirty of them, if not more.'

'And what of it, Turnstile?' he said. 'Half are women. Another quarter children. And we are all men, are we not?'

The group arrived in front of us and stopped, not gathered together quite as close as we were, and although their apparent leader stood face to face with the captain the others began to spread out and surround us, looking at each one of us as if we were the savages and not them. They pointed at our faces and white skin and appeared to find us highly amusing, which was both an insult and a bore. A girl of indeterminate age came over to me and I stood my ground like the fierce soldier I believed myself to be and she leaned forward and what did she do, only take a dirty great sniff at me! I didn't know whether to run away or sniff back.

The leader of the group handed a slab of pork to the captain, thrusting it at him as if there was any chance Mr Bligh would not accept it, and in return the captain took a scarf from his neck and wrapped it around the chief's own neck, providing much hilarity for his fellows. Words were spoken on both sides, but they were inconsistent with each other and so a conversation ensued where neither man knew what the other was saying, or whether it was friendly or threatening.

After an hour or so of this lunacy had passed, the chief let out a cry and his group gathered behind him again, and without any ceremony whatsoever they turned on their heels and departed, leaving us alone on the beach, Englishmen together again.

'Well, Captain,' said Mr Fryer, 'they seemed friendly enough. And there are healthy provisions to be had here. Should we stay a spell?'

The captain considered it; his face gave away little of his thoughts. 'For tonight, yes,' he said. 'We shall let the men sleep. And fill their bellies. But organize a watch, Mr Fryer, would you? Three men alert at all times. This place may not be all it seems.'

And so it was that we had our first good night's sleep since leaving the *Bounty* and woke refreshed and alert, ready for our next adventure. The captain had appeared to distrust the people of the island, but me, I thought him a sorry fellow for it, for they seemed happy and generous and determined on doing us no harm. And it was with such cheerful and optimistic sentiments that I closed my own eyes and found a much-needed slumber.

Day 5: 2 May

THE FOLLOWING MORNING I awoke to a face peering down into mine and I gave a start, uttered the Saviour's oath, and scrambled to my feet before backing away into some of the bush that stood behind me. The fellow who had been observing me was about my age, I supposed, perhaps a little older, although it was difficult to tell with some of the savages, as they had a raw look to them that suggested they might be of any age from fifteen, perhaps, to about forty.

'What's to look at?' I enquired of him, trying to keep the note of trepidation out of my voice, although it was most decidedly lodged within my bonce. 'Can't a fellow sleep no more without observation?'

The fellow started a low laugh and wagged his finger at me before turning around and displaying his rump, which was tattoo-blackened like the married men of Otaheite, although this of itself offered no clue to his age, as the fellows there were at it like rabbits or Frenchmen from the time their hair grew in below.

'The name's Turnstile,' said I then, attempting to establish a conversation. 'John Jacob Turnstile. And I'm pleased to meet you, I'm sure.' Taking my life in my hands I extended a hand to his, but he seemed to interpret this as an offensive gesture, for he stopped laughing immediately and offered me a dirty frown before walking away, disappearing into the undergrowth as quick as you like. He was back out no more than a minute later, just at the point when I was pacing up and down and feeling perturbed at the encounter, but this time he was accompanied by three men, taller and broader than he, and every man jack of them was speaking loudly and pointing angrily in my direction. They stared at me for a few moments, pinning me with a look of such incivility that I had a mind to start a fight with them, but then as before they simply turned round and vanished into the trees, leaving me unsettled by the whole encounter.

While thirty natives had surrounded us the previous afternoon, that day they brought even more of their number with them, perhaps half as many again, and three canoes appeared from around the island, each carrying two rowers and a proud silent man seated between them. They were friendly to the captain, happy to allow him to skin some plantains and coconuts and carry their meat to our crate, but the tension in the air was there for all to feel and made us nervous for our souls.

Mr Purcell, the carpenter, and a few of the men were engaged in repairing some of the wood of the launch, which had held for us so far but was not as tough as might be needed for a longer voyage, and the captain enquired of them how much longer it would take.

'Tomorrow afternoon and we should be ready,' said Mr Purcell, who had brewed up some glue from the sap of the trees and a log fire to hold the planks and nails together. 'Are we to set forth, then?'

'I think so,' said the captain, looking around carefully. 'I feel that our welcome here may be a short-lived one.'

I couldn't help but feel that our lack of ability to communicate with the natives contributed to the unhappy atmosphere. We Englishmen and they, the savages, spoke constantly, as if our very lives depended on it, but as neither side had any understanding of what was being said to them, the whole thing seemed a terrific farce.

As the evening drew in there was another drama when a young savage – who had gone to every man one by one, pointed at his own heart before saying the word 'Eefor', which we interpreted as being his name – appeared with two others on a canoe, full of smiles and laughter, as if we were all engaged in a matter of some hilarity, before stepping out to where our feeble *Bounty*-tub was steadied in the water and did his damndest to drag it in to shore.

'Stop there, that man!' cried Mr Fryer, marching towards him, followed by the captain and Mr Elphinstone and some of the braver men. 'Unhand that launch!'

Eefor made a long and unintelligible argument for why he should be permitted to continue with his dragging, and before long he was surrounded by ten of his own fellows, who did not assist him but watched, grinning and laughing like madmen.

'Young Eefor,' said the captain, bursting into laughter too, as if to prove his friendly nature, and showing his face to the savages, 'I must ask you to take your hands from our craft. It is ours; we do not wish to trade.'

Eefor smiled and shrugged and continued trying to drag it ashore, although it was far too heavy for him to manage on his own, so he looked to his fellows who had been observing the scene and shouted something towards them. At this, conscious that a further development could mean the end of our travels, the captain placed a hand on the cutlass that hung by his side and unsheathed it only a fraction, allowing the blade to glisten in the sun; he turned it slightly so that for a moment the light caught the steel and the eyes of Eefor were momentarily blinded. Immediately he dropped the craft and stepped away, his face fallen, looking for all the world as if we had just insulted him terribly and he might begin to cry like a baby.

'Mr Fryer, take six men and sit in the launch; take it out to sea a little, would you, please,' said the captain in a low voice and the master's mate replied with an 'Aye, Captain' and before any more time had passed the tub was safely back in the hands of those who owned it.

The captain approached the savages and bowed to them briefly before turning his back again and this time the crowd began to disperse until, before long, there was only the loyal crew of the *Bounty* left ashore.

'Tomorrow, you say, Mr Purcell?' called the captain to the carpenter, who was seated on the launch itself at sea.

'Aye, sir,' he shouted back. 'Early, do you think?'

'I think early would be wise,' was his dark reply.

Day 6: 3 May

THE LAST TIME I HAD BEEN so afeared was the morning I had been taken from my bunk by dirty hands and dragged to the court of King Neptune. On the sixth day of our voyage away from the *Bounty*, I spent the morning aware that if my heart was still beating by the end of it, then I would be a lucky lad, a very lucky lad indeed.

There was no question that the time to leave this particular Friendly Island was at hand. The captain and the officers had consulted with Mr Purcell that morning and it was agreed that our tub was ready to set out again. We had placed as much provisions within it as we deemed safe while still maintaining our own weights, which were diminishing by the day.

'No one is to board the launch until my signal,' said the captain. 'When I say it is time for us to leave, I want every man to make his way there very slowly, gathering up whatever belongings he may have. No one is to seem in the least afraid or aggressive. We act as if everything is perfectly normal.'

It was easy for him to say that. When I turned away from him the sights and sounds that were before me suggested that everything was far from normal. It seemed as if all the savages had come to the shore that morning. There was at least one hundred of them, six for every one of us, and they surrounded us, observing our every move, those damnable cheerful smiles still pasted across their chops. In itself that was nerve-racking enough, but added to this was the fact that every one of them, men, women and children alike, held a large stone in their hands, a stone that was as big as a man's head and could cave one in without fear of disappointment. They banged the stones together at regular intervals, a great cacophonous sound echoing around us that suggested there was trouble to come. The louder the noise, the more I started to get the trepidations.

'The stones mean they are preparing to attack,' the captain told the officers quietly. 'I saw it before when I sailed with the captain—'

'Captain Cook, sir?' asked I, piping up with one of my questions at an inappropriate time.

'Yes, of course Captain Cook,' he replied testily. 'Look, Turnstile, will you prepare yourself for the journey, please? Have you collected as much water as you can?'

'Yes, sir,' said I.

'Then, stand with the midshipmen until it is time for us to leave.'

As I walked away, I noticed one of the savages approaching the captain's group and he took Mr Bligh gently by the arm, attempting to pull him back towards their line with a wide smile plastered across his chops; the suggestion was that he should stay on the island and, I presumed, that we should all stay too.

'No, no,' said the captain, laughing gently and releasing himself from the man's grip. 'We cannot stay, I'm afraid. There is nothing any of us would like more, of course; you have been uncommonly kind to us, but it is time we pressed on. Farewell to you all and the king's blessings upon you.'

I shook my head, wondering why he continued to speak English to a group of people who couldn't understand him, but speak it he did. As he turned, the clanging of the stones began to grow louder and I observed some of the savages beginning to move towards us.

'Quickly now, but carefully,' said the captain in a clear voice that we all might hear. 'Make your way towards the launch.'

We did as he said, stepping into the water even as the savages tried to pull us back. It was all that we could do to release ourselves from them and I felt that at any moment now the scene could turn murderous. There was a chance that they would let us go, aggrieved no doubt, but without menaces. Or they might charge at us. I was in the launch by now and watching as the captain and a few others made their way slowly towards us. In my mind I urged them on, wishing that they might step more lively, but the captain did not want to give off the appearance that any of us, himself included, was the least bit afeared.

By the time we were all in the launch, the natives of the island were half in the water too, shouting at us, laughing no longer, but they seemed as if they did not intend to attack after all. I took my place in the rear of the boat, unhappily the closest man to them, and from the side of my eyes I noted John Norton, the quartermaster, leaping overboard and heading back to the shore, or to the pole that we had planted there to rope the launch sturdily; it was obvious that he was setting to in order to release us and allow us on our way.

'Get back here,' cried Mr Fryer, but his voice was overtaken by the captain, standing and calling loudly.

'Mr Norton, return immediately. We will cut the launch free.'

Norton turned at the sound of his captain's voice, and I watched as a great roar went up from the savages the moment his back was turned. At that sound he turned back again as perhaps thirty of them descended on him. He tripped backwards into the water and then the great sound of splashing and murder as they fell on him and raised their stones, crashing them down into his skull with laughter and delight.

'Cut us free, Turnstile!' cried the captain and I looked around just in time to grab hold of the knife he had flung in my direction by the handle; I momentarily wondered whether it might have hit my head or sliced my hand off. I stared at it, unsure what to do, and looked out again at the terrible scene playing out before me. The water was already scarlet with Mr Norton's blood and the savages seemed keen for more. They turned in our direction and I quickly cut the rope and the launch gave a great heave, allowing us to sail further out. There was no question that the savages could have caught us or sailed after us and killed us all, but once we were free of their beach they appeared inclined to let us go.

My last sight of that place was a picture of the body of John Norton, his head smashed clear from his body revealing a contorted and bloody stump below, being taken back to the island for who-knew-what terrible reason. The tub was quiet now as we sat silent and still, terrified as one, grief-stricken for our fallen comrade. I turned away from the grizzly scene and looked ahead.

There was nothing to see there. Nothing to take my mind off it.

Day 7: 4 May

IT WAS SOME RELIEF to be away from that blasted place and those damnable murderers, but being back in the tub reminded me how poor our chances of surviving this adventure truly were. We had lost a man after less than a week – and a good man too, for John Norton had always been kind to me and was one of the few men on board the *Bounty* who resisted the urge to call me by the blasted nickname Turnip – and each of us felt the worse for it, although one dark voice was heard to mutter an obscene remark regarding how much more space there would have been for each of us on the launch had the savages managed to take a few more alongside Mr Norton.

The sea was rough that day, as I recall, and although the tub felt more sturdy and secure than it had when we arrived at the Friendly Islands, the roar of the waves crashing around us meant that we were spending much of our time scooping the water from the floor of the launch and returning it whence it had come. It was thankless work and continued for so long that I swore my arms would fall off with the strain of it; by the time the winds died down a little and we were allowed to sit back and take rest, my muscles felt like jelly and they appeared to be trembling within my skin at the horror of what they had been asked to do.

'Mr Fryer,' said Robert Lamb, the butcher, late that afternoon, turning his head a little to look in all four points of the compass and seeing nothing but open sea, 'where are we headed, sir, does the captain know?'

'Of course he knows, Lamb,' replied the master's mate. 'The captain has a fine nose for these things and you should trust in him. We're keeping west by nor'west, in the direction of the Feejees.'

'The Feejees, you say?' asked the butcher, his voice betraying the fact that he was less than happy with this as an answer.

'Yes, Mr Lamb. Is there a problem with that?'

'Oh, no, sir,' he said quickly, shaking his head. 'I hear they are very beautiful islands indeed.'

It struck me that there was something he was not saying, for I could hear a trembling in his tone and spy a look of concern about his phizzy, but I waited until Mr Fryer had returned to the fore of the launch before inching closer to my sailing mate and poking him in the ribs.

'What was that for, young Turnip?' he asked, turning towards me with a look of irritation on his face, although his earlier predilection towards violence, which had been much on display in the sailors' quarters of the *Bounty*, had diminished in these trim surroundings.

'The Feejees,' I said. 'You know of them?'

'I know a little of them,' he said. 'But take an honest man's word for it, Turnip: you don't want to know what I have heard.'

I swallowed a little nervously and furrowed my brow. 'Tell me, Mr Lamb,' said I. 'I have an interest in it.'

He looked around for a moment to check that we were not being overheard, but most of the men were taking their rest at that time, the decent wind carrying us in the correct direction.

'Is it more women?' I asked. 'Are they like the women of Otaheite? Free with their virtue, I mean?' I may have been stuck on this launch for a week and I may have been exhausted beyond all that was natural or holy, but I was still a fifteen-year-old lad and the motions were playing up with me something terrible and as I had had no opportunity to play at tug since being evicted from the *Bounty*, there was a fierce longing inside me. Even mentioning the freedom of women's virtue was enough to send the blood rushing southwards.

'It's not that, lad,' he confided in me. 'I had a friend once, a right suitable fellow, name of Charles Conway. He sailed with Captain Clerk and they stopped at the Feejees on one visit and what happened, only the natives captured three of their fellows, strung them up, dropped them in a pot of water, boiled them alive and ate them.'

'Bones and all?' I asked, wide-eyed.

'They used the bones to pick their teeth,' he said. 'Like the trolls in the fairytales you read as a lad.'

'I don't think we should go to these Feejees,' I said, not bothering to disillusion him of the fact that I had been a childhood reader. 'I have no desire to be eaten alive.'

'You're boiled first, in fairness,' he stated then with a shrug, as if this made the whole practice a far more agreeable matter. 'I imagine the life has gone out of you after that.'

'Still, it's not a happy way to go.'

'No,' he conceded. 'No, it's not. But listen here, you have the ear of the captain. Perhaps you should be the one to tell him that we ought to seek an alternative island, preferably one of a hospitable nature?'

I looked towards the fore of the boat where Captain Bligh had just begun the process of dividing out the evening feast. One by one we were called before him and he handed us a morsel of coconut, a scrap of plantain, and a teaspoon full of rum. It was scarcely enough to fill the belly of a babe at wean, but we were grateful for it, especially now that our stomachs had grown accustomed to sustenance again after our short stay on the Friendlies.

'Captain,' I whispered as he handed me my allotted amount.

'Move along, Turnstile,' he said, waving me away. 'There are other men awaiting their repast.'

'But, Captain, the Feejees,' I said. 'There's fierce terrible stories about—'

'Move *along*, Turnstile,' he repeated, more forcibly now, and before he could say anything more I had been cruelly manhandled by Mr Elphinstone and sent back to my seat

But I was determined that no savage would make a meal of John Jacob Turnstile. Not in this life.

Day 8: 5 May

A DISPUTE OF A SORT broke out today between Mr Hall, who had been cook of the *Bounty*, and Surgeon Ledward. It began over a trifle, the surgeon suggesting that a cook with half a wit about him would be able to take our meagre provision and turn it into something more delicious for us all.

'And what would you have me do, Surgeon?' asked Mr Hall, who had a sweet nature about him for most of the time but could turn cantankerous if his culinary skills were called into question. 'What have we after all only a few coconuts and plantains, a little rum and some bread that grows harder to the touch by the hour?

Am I to be like the Saviour?' he continued, ignorant of the blasphemy. 'Turning water into wine for every man on board?'

'I know not what you might do with it,' replied the surgeon, leaning against the side of the tub and scratching his beard irritably. 'I have not been trained in the art of the kitchen. But I know that a skilled man might find a way to—'

'And a skilled *surgeon* might have leapt into the surf and taken the dead body of John Norton from the arms of the savages and brought him back to life,' rejoined Mr Hall, sitting forward and wagging his finger like an old washerwoman. 'Speak not to me of skilled men, Surgeon Ledward, when you yourself have shown no such abilities.'

The surgeon breathed heavily through his nose for a moment before shaking his head and narrowing his eyes. I could sense that such an argument might lead to fisticuffs had we been on either Otaheite or the deck of the *Bounty*, but here in the tub there was no such freedom to move around; men could cause friction and then find no way to resolve matters. I began to consider that this might ultimately be our undoing.

'John Norton was dead, Mr Hall,' he said finally. 'It does not take a talented surgeon to revive those who have gone to their reward, it takes the will of God.'

'Aye, and it would take the will of God to turn the few scraps the captain keeps under lock and key into anything fit to eat. We're in this together, Surgeon Ledward. I suggest you maintain your dignity and allow your unhappy state not to cast aspersions on your fellow drifters.'

The surgeon nodded and was happy to let it go at that. Tempers had been stirred, voices raised, an argument distributed, but had they continued it would only have forced one of the officers to attend to them and such a thing was already being seen as unfair. We were a small society, the nineteen of us. The eighteen of us, as we were now. We could not fight among ourselves.

A fierce wind came upon us that evening, but it blew east by nor'east, pushing us along in the direction that the captain insisted would bring us home. I found myself drifting in and out of sleep and on one occasion awoke with a start, convinced that I was back in Mr Lewis's establishment in Portsmouth. The lapping of the water around me did not stir my senses yet to inform me that I was nowhere near England and had precious little hope of seeing it again, and when I finally returned to full consciousness and an awareness of who and where I was, I found that to my surprise I missed my sometime home. Not Mr Lewis, of course. I could not have given a fig for him. But I missed England. And Portsmouth. And some of my brothers. The good ones. The ones I cared for.

I sat up, rubbing my eyes, and looked around at our desperate crew with a sensation of hope in my heart. We were a raggle-taggle lot and no mistake. Dirty, smelly, bearded – even my own chin was beginning to be tickled by soft whiskers – but we were a crew. And we had been cast out to sea without a care for our survival. And we would survive. The captain would see to that. Aye, and every last one of us.

I narrowed my eyes and peered into the distance. Somewhere out there, perhaps half a world away, lay England. Lay Portsmouth. Lay Mr Lewis. It was a place I had been running away from for sixteen months, a place I had sworn never to revisit. But that night, sitting in the tub with the farting, stinking evicted crew of the *Bounty* around me, I swore that I would do the opposite of all of that. I would return there. I would go back and seek my own vengeance. And then I would begin again. Life might hold a lot of treasures for John Jacob Turnstile yet and I would allow no man to play liberties with me again.

'You have a look of fire in your eyes, Turnstile,' said the captain, opening his own eyes to look at me; he was seated only a few feet from me, his body twisted in its sleep as he tried to find a comfortable position. I smiled at him and nodded but offered no reply. And when he closed his eyes again and his snoring began, I watched him and thought to myself that here was a great man. Here was a heroic sort. Here was a fellow that another fellow might follow into battle. And at that moment I found my own life's ambition.

I would be a great man like Captain Bligh too, one day. I would survive, I would thrive and I would succeed.

And we would all, every man jack of us, return to England safely.

Day 9: 6 May

WE FINALLY SPOTTED a new island and a great cheer went up among our hungry, thirsty and exhausted crew as the possibility of rest and sustenance became more likely.

'Turn us there, men,' cried the captain to the rowers, pointing in the direction of the green, mountainous region before us; a great stretch of sandy beach at its fore was a delight to behold. I couldn't help but note how the captain's voice had changed during the nine days since we had been away from the *Bounty*; like all of us, he was dehydrated, but there was a croak in it that had not been there previously. I suspected he was growing increasingly depressed by the turn of events. Still, there was a general feeling among us that if we could survive from island to island, and then make that great stretch of sea between the two last, then we might yet live to tell our tale, and the sight of the new island before us gave ever more hope for that.

We all watched the land hopefully as we got closer, but then, what did we see only a group of savages emerging from the thickets to spy on us. We were still some way from the shore, far enough that they would not be able to reach us, but the captain gave the order to maintain our position and the oarsmen lifted their oars and we all watched.

'Captain?' said Mr Fryer. 'What do you think?'

The men on the shore, who numbered about thirty or forty, appeared friendly enough. They were waving in our direction and some were dancing a most curious dance, but they were not carrying stones in their hands, as the savages on the Friendly Islands were.

'I think we are outnumbered to begin with,' said the captain. 'But they may mean to greet us.'

'It might be some days before we reach another island,' remarked Mr Elphinstone, who was taller than most of us and who was beginning to suffer badly from the cramped conditions, as he could never stretch his legs out and was barely able to sleep. 'Perhaps we could send a few men over to discover whether they mean us any harm and then decide? I'd be happy to volunteer.'

'And I thank you for it, Mr Elphinstone,' replied the captain. 'But I do not desire to send any man towards his demise. We have the example of Mr Norton to remember, do we not?'

'Look!' cried a voice from my left, that of Peter Linkletter, the quartermaster. 'Look what they have!'

All our eyes turned in the direction of the shore, where some more savages, perhaps a dozen or so, were carrying great barrels of fruit and placing them before us. Some more appeared quickly after them with sides of meat. Even looking at this sight prompted my mouth to salivate with hunger. And then what, only caskets of water to wash the feast down. They beckoned us over and the men cheered in delight, rising up so quickly that they threatened to turn our tub over.

'Sit ye down, men!' roared the captain, the croak in his voice affecting his ability to shout. 'Maintain your places: we'll have none of it.'

'None of it, Mr Bligh?' cried William Purcell. 'You can't mean it! We could survive for weeks on the offerings they have for us.'

'We can survive on nothing if we are murdered into the bargain,' replied the captain. 'You think they are amicable, do you?'

'I think they would not bring such treats to the shore for us if they were not a hospitable people.'

'Then, the sun has gone to your head, sir,' said Mr Bligh. 'For if you cannot spot a trap when you see one, you are not in possession of half the wit for which I had you pegged. They are luring us, Mr Purcell, can you not see that? We sail over there, eat their food, partake of their vittles, and within an hour we will have our heads caved in and never see home.'

My mind turned at this to thoughts of what Robert Lamb had told me two days earlier, about the Feejee Islands, and I began to wonder whether filling my belly was a reasonable payment for the loss of my life. And such was my hunger and thirst that at that moment I half believed I would offer the trade.

'Turn us, Mr Fryer,' said the captain to a great cry of pain from the crew. 'Turn us, I say!' he repeated, louder, looking at none of us and sounding more like the man who had commanded the *Bounty* for more than a year without having his authority called into question.

'Rowers,' said Mr Fryer, with a note of disappointment in his voice too, although I dare say he could see the sense in what the captain had said, 'nor' by nor'east again.'

A low murmuring went up among the men and I sat back, defeated and disappointed, but there was a sense to it. The savages on the shoreline gave up a great cry when they saw that we had nobbled their ruse and some splashed into the water to follow us, revealing short spears which they aimed in our direction, but we were too far away from them either to be a potential target or for us to have any fear of their intentions.

'We will find a safe harbour, men,' said the captain after a suitable amount of time had gone by. 'I know you are all hungry and in need of water, but we cannot accept these things at risk to our lives. We have already survived this long. Let us make it home.'

'But how, Captain?' asked John Samuel, the clerk, a note of utter desperation creeping into his voice. 'How shall we with little food and less water? What's to become of us?'

The captain stared at him for a moment, shook his head and turned away, and at that moment his face changed slightly. I saw him stare into the water and what came next was a great triumph. We had all tried at different times to capture a fish on a spear but had been unsuccessful. It was thought that it would be a tremendous feather to whoever did so first. And right then, surprising us all, giving some a start it all happened so quickly, the captain lifted one of the spears from the floor of the keel, stabbed it quickly and smartly into the waves, and when it emerged it held a great fish, some twelve pounds worth, I would say, taken directly through the centre, and threw it on the deck, where it flapped around for a few moments before lying still, its glassy eye staring out at us with as much shock and surprise as we felt ourselves.

'We shall survive,' repeated the captain, looking out at all of us, who were, to a man, too amazed and hungry to do anything but wait for it to be divided among us all.

Day 10: 7 May

THE CAPTAIN ORGANIZED US into two shifts, whereby half of our crew would sit round the edges of the tub while the other half tried to find a place to lie as horizontal as possible along the floor. It was almost impossible to do so and, as it was a sodden mess down there, sleep was hindered by the constant pain of soaking. Our bones were already creaking with it. It was a miserable existence.

As the captain slept I found my way closer to Mr Fryer and

discovered him lost in thought as he stared out to sea. I was forced to say his name on three occasions before he turned to look at me and even then he stared at me for a moment as if he had not the slightest idea who I was.

'Ah, Turnstile,' he said finally, rubbing his eyes as if he had just woken up. 'You're here. Were you addressing me?'

'I was, sir. You seemed to be in a different world entirely.'

'Well, there's something captivating about it, don't you think?' he asked, looking out towards the vast expanse of blue that surrounded us. 'A man could get lost just looking.'

I nodded. It occurred to me how some of the lines between captain, officers, men and servant-boys were getting blurred as day followed day. We were speaking to one another with much more familiarity than we ever had on board the *Bounty* and the captain treated us all as near-equals, although perhaps this had something to do with the fact that we were a crew of loyalists and he was naturally well disposed towards us.

'Yes, sir,' I said. 'Mr Fryer, sir, might I ask you a question?'

'Of course,' he replied, turning to look at me.

'It's just . . .' I thought about it, hopeful that I might phrase it correctly. 'Our course, sir,' I said. 'You do know the course that we have set?'

'The captain sets the course, my boy, you know that. Don't you have faith in Mr Bligh?'

'Oh, yes, sir,' I replied quickly. 'Of course I do. He's a fine gentleman, as fine as ever lived. I only ask because, like the other men, sir, I'm getting fierce hungry and thirsty and weak in my legs and I wonder sometimes whether we will ever spy land again.'

Mr Fryer smiled a little and nodded. 'It's natural that you should be worried,' he said. 'My father was a sailor too, you know. He went to sea when he was around your age. Younger even.'

'Did he, sir?' asked I, wondering whether the combination of sea and sun had taken to his head, as I had not asked about his family circumstances.

'Yes, he did,' he confirmed. 'And when he was not much older than you are now he was involved in a shipwreck off the coast of Africa. He was nowhere near as far away from home as we are, of course, but he and his fellows – there were seven of them – managed to make it to the southernmost tip of Spain in a tub a quarter the size of this one. They had no captain and only one officer among their number. But they survived. And he became a great man, my father.'

My eyes widened. I had never known anything of Mr Fryer's family before and thought it terrible decent of him to tell me of them.

'Is he a wealthy man, sir?' I asked.

'Wealthy is as wealthy does, Turnstile,' he replied, a phrase that meant nothing to me. 'It is not for his riches that I remember him. Yes, I see you frown: he died several years ago. Of the typhoid.'

'I'm sorry to hear it, sir.'

'We all were. He lived a life filled with adventure. It was he who sent me to sea in the first place. And I've never regretted it. Not even though I leave my wife and young 'uns at home for months at a time and miss them growing up. But I don't regret it. I tell you this, Turnstile, if he could have seen the actions of Fletcher Christian on board the *Bounty* on that last night . . . why, he would have taken a cutlass to him without a second's thought.'

'Was he a violent man, sir?' I asked, recalling my younger days at Mr Lewis's establishment. 'Did he take a switch to you when you were a lad?'

'You're missing the point, Turnstile,' he said irritably. 'I mean that he would have never allowed the mutiny to take place. He would have found a way to stop it. And Christian would have swung for his misdeeds. I wonder whether he was watching us all that night and lamenting the fact that I did nothing to prevent it.'

'You, sir?' I asked. 'But what could you do? There were so many of them!'

'And I was the ship's master. They might have listened to me had I spoken up. But I didn't. Oh, I remained loyal, that's the truth. And do you know why?'

'No, sir.'

'Because of the captain, Turnstile. Because of my regard for him.'

I narrowed my eyes and considered this. It was a fine thing that a man of his stature was deigning to talk to me at all, but an even more curious thing that he was speaking so candidly. I half wondered whether he realized my station, as he would never have sounded so emotional had he been of his full senses.

'I know what you must think,' he continued with a smile. 'That the captain and I never got along. And it's true that he was unusually . . . severe with me. But he's a younger man than I, Turnstile, and a captain in His Majesty's navy. Or as good as, anyway. And the career he's had so far . . . I admire him so much, that's why I sought this position. His map-making skills are perhaps the finest since da Vinci's – did you know that, Turnstile?'

'I knew he held a pretty pen,' I said. 'But I didn't know that—'

'A pretty pen, you say?' he replied with a laugh. 'You don't know the half of it. The maps he drew when he was with Captain Cook, why, they have proved indispensable for the last decade to all of us. It is as if he can see the world from a great distance and reproduce it. Only a great man can have such talents. No, if I could go back to that night I would unsheath my sword and have at the mutineers myself.'

'And you would be cut down for it, sir,' said a deep voice from my right. I swung round to see the captain, maintaining the position in which he had been sleeping, but with his eyes open now.

'Captain,' said Mr Fryer, flushing slightly, embarrassed by his generous words.

'Turnstile, perhaps you shall leave us alone for a few minutes,' said the captain. 'Down the boat with you.'

'Aye, sir,' said I, fierce reluctant to go, as I was interested to know how the captain would take this vote of appreciation from the man he had put down on so many occasions, but an order is an order and so I stepped away and took my place beside Robert Tinkler, who was one of those on watch.

'What was that all about?' asked Tinkler. 'You and Mr Fryer?'

'I don't know,' I replied. 'I merely asked about the course we were taking and the conversation took an unexpected turn.'

'Officers,' he said with a snort. 'They can never give you a straight answer.'

I watched for only a few more moments as Mr Bligh and Mr Fryer engaged in a quiet conversation. I wondered what it was about; I wondered whether the captain was telling Mr Fryer how much he respected him too and thanked him for his loyalty, but they were out of earshot and there was no way to tell. I wonder about it still.

Day 11: 8 May

L AND APPEARED BEFORE US once again today and as usual we all felt a great start of joy at the possibility of leaving the tub and enjoying rest and sustenance. All four rowers automatically began to turn their oars in the direction of the island, but immediately sensing the turn the captain gave a great holler and told them in no uncertain terms to maintain their course.

'But, Captain,' said William Cole in exasperation, pointing eastwards in the direction of the land. 'Haven't you seen the island?'

'Of course I've seen it, Mr Cole,' snapped the captain. 'I have two eyes in my head and I haven't gone blind, you know. But we must be wary. Let us take a tour around the coastline first before venturing further in.'

Our spirits sank a little, but Mr Bligh had to be obeyed, so the rowers turned again and set about circling the island, which lay a good distance from us yet.

'Where are we, Mr Bligh?' asked George Simpson. 'Have you visited here before?'

'I believe these are the Feejee Islands,' he proclaimed. 'And, yes, I was here once before with the captain.' His reference was to Captain Cook, of course, as all such references were. 'But we must take care. There are friendly natives of Feejee and some not so friendly ones. Cannibals and the like.'

My heart gave a jump at the sound of that word and it put me in mind of what Mr Lamb had told me before about the ways of the people at this area of the world. I had travelled a long way from Portsmouth and been through many adventures in sixteen months and I was damned if I was going to end up as a luncheon feast for a group of savages. As much as I wanted to lie on the beach and exercise my limbs once again, I started to wonder whether we were not much safer staying in our little craft.

'Captain,' said Mr Elphinstone, 'look yonder.'

We each of us looked in the direction that he had indicated and what did we see, only a group of natives taking canoes to the shoreline, pushing them into the water and setting out in our direction.

'Ah,' said the captain, frowning. 'I was afraid of this.'

'What's happening, Mr Bligh?' I shouted. 'Are they a welcoming party?'

'None that we would like to meet, I would warrant,' he replied. 'Oarsmen, turn again, we continue on our travels.'

A great cry went up among those men who were willing to risk their lives for a chance to land the boat. I looked back at the shore and two canoes were rowing towards us, each filled with four men, a lesser number than our cargo.

'There's only nine of them, sir,' said I. 'We are eighteen.'

'There's eight of them, Turnip, you young fool,' said Mr Elphinstone. 'Don't you know your two times tables?'

'Eight, then,' I said, irritated by his pedantry, for after all it only made my point more valid. 'Less than a third of our number!'

'Less than a third!' snapped Mr Elphinstone again and was about to say more, only he was interrupted by the captain.

'Where there are eight there will be eighty more,' he said. 'Row fast, men. We continue on our voyage. They will stop giving chase soon enough.'

He was right on that, for within a very few minutes the two canoes slowed down until they were simply bobbing along in the water and four of the men, the central parties on either canoe, stood up and waved spears at us, spears that might have been intended to hold us on a skewer over an open fire.

'Don't look so downhearted, men,' said the captain. 'We shall find somewhere safe. We have done well so far, have we not?'

'But when, sir?' asked Surgeon Ledward, a great strain entering his voice now, as if he was a child who had been denied his rattle. 'Do we even know the direction we are heading? We have no maps, after all.'

'Our maps are up here, Surgeon,' replied the captain, tapping his bonce. 'My memory is all we need. You forget to whom you are speaking.'

'I forget nothing, sir, and I meant no disrespect. I only say that we cannot sail like this indefinitely.'

A low murmur went up among the crew and the captain peered round at all of us with a certain look of displeasure on his face. It wasn't that he was fearing another mutiny – after all there was no way to mutiny now, short of throwing him overboard, and that would hardly be helpful to our cause – but that he knew low spirits were the greatest enemy we could have. Savages, cannibals, murderers, they were one thing. A lack of belief that we would survive was something else entirely.

'We continue westward,' said the captain. 'And on to the New Hebrides islands. I can picture them in my mind, men. They are there before us. I know they are. And from there we aim for the

Endeavour Strait at the tip of Northern Australia. An isolated place, yes, but we can regroup there before making the final sailing to Timor. We will find friends in Timor and a safe passage home. I can picture the waters as clear as I can picture the face of my wife and children, men. And the thought of seeing them again is what spurs me on. But I need you with me, sailors. Are you with me?'

'Aye, Captain,' we all cried halfheartedly.

'I said are you with me, men?'

'Aye!' we roared, more happily, and to our delight the heavens opened at that moment and a great rain fell that allowed us to refill our flagons and open our mouths to the heavens until we were hydrated once again. It felt for a moment as if the Saviour himself was on our side.

Day 12: 9 May

IF WE HAD BEEN HAPPY about the rainfall the evening before, we woke in a state of chaos, as the men who had managed a few hours' sleep could barely move with stiffness. This, the captain assured us, would be a common complaint as the days passed. If we slept in damp clothes, then we would wake with the water having seeped through to our bones. I dreaded to think what difficulties this might present us with as our lives progressed. For my part I could barely move my head at all and any attempt to turn either left or right would result in such untold agony that I resolved to maintain my place for the entire day and attempt nothing more than slow movements of the arms and legs until all circulation was restored.

'Ledward, Peckover, Purcell and Turnip, assume the oars,' cried

Mr Fryer just after our so-called breakfast, a thimbleful of water and a husk of coconut. I shrank in my seat and attempted to appear inconspicuous, which is a difficult feat in a tub measuring no more than twenty-three feet in length. I watched as the previous four rowers lay their oars down and my three fellows shuffled over to their seats, but I remained still for now. 'Turnip!' yelled Mr Fryer. 'Did you hear me?'

'I am indisposed,' I called back. 'I send my apologies.'

'Indisposed?' he said, staring around with a look of amazement on his face. 'Did that lad say he was indisposed?' I knew not who he was addressing but answer came there none. 'Indisposed doing what?' he asked.

'It's a terrible thing, sir,' said I. 'But I awoke with a crick in my neck and an ache in my body that shows no signs of disappearing. I fear that if I was to attempt to sail the tub, then I would only succeed in steering us round and round in circles.'

'Not with me to watch over you, you won't,' he pronounced. 'Now, get your lazy arse over here and pick up your oar before I give you a thrashing you won't forget.'

I grumbled and groaned and grunted, but it was of no use, the die had been cast. Lowering myself into position beside William Purcell, I attempted a half-smile of resignation, but the carpenter took it as a sign of insolence and threw me back a filthy look.

'We all have to do it,' he said. 'You're not the captain's servant-boy any more, you know.'

'I certainly am,' I replied. 'If I hold any position in His Majesty's navy, then that's the one I hold.'

'You have no special privileges,' he said then with a sneer. 'It's not as it was. We're in this together, every man jack of us.'

I frowned. Was this how the men had seen me over these past sixteen months? As a fellow who held special conditions different from their own simply on account of my proximity to the captain's cabin and person? Little did they know how hard I had worked. Why, I was up in the morning to prepare the captain's breakfast and after that there would be his clothes to take care of, and then lunch, and then perhaps a little free time if I could hide away somewhere he wouldn't find me, and then it was dinner and, sure, after that it was time for bed. How on earth did they think that they had endured a more difficult time of it than I had?

'I know that, William Purcell,' said I, insulted. 'It's only the crick in my neck that—'

'Ah, you can kiss the crack in my arse if you say one more word about the crick in your neck,' he snapped, the filthy beggar. 'Now, start a-rowing and let's see if we can get where we are going a little quicker.'

Every man in the tub took a turn at the oars, even the captain himself, and the officers, and this at least offered us a sense of unity and equality. Two hours at a time, four men on a shift. Over the first few days of our escapade I had felt the muscles in my arms turn to jelly and I swore that if I was forced to pick up the oars one more time they would snap off at the shoulder, but now, having been at it for nearly two weeks, the muscles in my arms had developed and it no longer felt like such a trauma. I could cheerfully row for my two hours without feeling any the worse for wear. But that day, with such a waterlogged body and an unhappy skeleton, it was a terrible trial.

In the meantime the captain was creating a sort of weighing scales from two shelled halves of a coconut and a couple of pistol balls as weights, and he announced that from then until we reached our next destination – the New Hebrides – rations would be cut again and divided equally by weight determined by this contraption. A great cry went up, for our stomachs were already feeling as if they were never fed any more due to the meagre amounts he offered us three times a day, but there was nothing we could say or do to change things and the captain would listen to no argument.

It was a dark day, as I recall. A depressing day. A day when I felt my spirits very low, very low indeed.

Day 13: 10 May

HUNGER. HUNGER. HUNGER. HUNGER.
And thirst.

If the word hunger could have been spun on its head and turned into a living, breathing human being, then I swear he would have been a young English lad, no more than five feet and six inches in height, with tousled dark hair, a chipped front tooth, and answering to the name of John Jacob Turnstile. I woke this day with a pain in my belly the like of which I could never remember having endured before, the sort of pain you get that bends you over and makes you howl.

Rising from my place on the floor of the tub after a few hours of restless sleep, where my feet had been stuck in the face of Thomas Hall and I had suffered the indignity of having the feet of John Hallett in my own, I felt as if my whole body was protesting at the trauma that I was causing it. My arms and legs ached, my head pounded, but, sweet Saviour, it was the pain in my belly that hurt me the most. Dragging my sorry carcass over to the side of the launch, I picked up a spear and watched in the waters below for any sign of fish. If I could just spike one, I thought, then I could squirrel it away under my shirt – such as it was, a thin layer of fabric, torn and shredded in parts – and chew on it raw whenever I felt like it. It would be a mean thing not to offer it to the others, of course, and would surely cause a commotion should the intelligence be revealed, but it was every one of us for himself now and I swore in my head that if I found a fish it would soon find its way into my belly.

The waters in that area had a curious blueness to them, with something approaching a green shade dusting the base and a roll of blackness appearing from time to time to add an extra colour to the rainbow. Watching it I felt myself entranced, as Mr Fryer had been on the occasion that I had discovered him to be lost in his reveries and looking out to sea. Concentrating, I found I could see my own reflection in the water and, when I put a hand down to disturb it, in a moment my eyes, my mouth, my nose, my ears, had spread out into a kaleidoscope of Turnstile, spilling to all four points of the compass before the call of each other proved too much and the water settled and the parts of my phizzy re-assembled beneath my gaze. It caused me a smile and a sigh.

Another moment and then I jumped. I opened my eyes wide and wondered who it was that was looking back up at me. Was that John Jacob Turnstile, late of Mr Lewis's establishment? Late of Portsmouth? Englishman? I thought not. For was not his jaw too strong and fixed for a lad of fifteen? Were not his cheeks too sunken? Was that not a trim of mustachio and beard upon his chops? I put a hand to my face and touched the whiskers that were growing there and felt a momentary pride in my own masculinity. For a few vital seconds it was a wonderful thing to be alive. I wondered whether anyone would even recognize me back in Portsmouth, should the unlikeliest of things happen and we eighteen return to the king's land; and it crossed my mind that I might start again, aye, even in my own home town, and no one would know the employment I had endured before, either during the day or, darker, during the night. But such thoughts could only last a second, like my dissolved features in the water, before rejoining and the truth reappearing.

I blinked and heard activity behind me; others waking. Sailors rising unsteadily to their feet, anxious to stretch their arms heaven-ward, lift one foot from the deck and hold it out, shake it, while trying to maintain a balance, to allow the blood to flow again. Voices called to the captain and asked when our fasts would be broken and he replied with an answer that was not to everyone's taste.

But I didn't look around. I continued to stare at the water. And then I saw it: a long fish. Red in its colour, was it? Or a dark green? It mattered not. It was a fish. It contained meat. I picked up the short spear and held it over the side, and just at that moment the pain in my belly attacked me like a kick to the privates and it was all that I could do not to scream aloud in agony, and when my eyes opened again the spear was gone, one of only two that we had. I had dropped it. It had plunged to the depths of the ocean. I gasped in horror and waited for a hand to the seat of my pants that might throw me over in search of it, but none was forthcoming. No one had seen.

I looked round cautiously, anxious not to give away the terror in my face, but none of my companions was facing in my direction. The captain turned to look at me and noted my features.

'Turnstile,' he said, 'are you all right? You look quite anxious.'

'I'm fine, sir,' said I. I would keep my secret. The absence of the spear would be noticed soon enough, but I would say nothing. It would be more than my life was worth.

Day 14: 11 May

THEY WERE A RUM BUNCH of conversationalists on board the tub, that's for sure. While on rowing duty I tried to strike up a chatter with William Peckover, the gunner, and got a whole lot of nothing for my trouble. We were side by side in the craft and as he was a much bigger man than I – taller, broader and a great deal thicker, take that as you will – his shoulders kept banging on mine every time we swung the oars back towards us. It gave me a proper set of annoyances, but tempers had been swift on board the tub that morning so I thought a little idle chatter would be better.

'I hear tell that you sailed with Mr Bligh before,' I said, and at my words he turned and stared at me with such a look of offence on his face that you'd swear he was the king of England and I'd just left his presence while displaying my arse.

'You heard that, Turnip, did you?' he asked. 'And what of it if I did? What business it is of yours?'

'No business at all, friend,' said I. 'I only mention it for something to say.'

He stared a little longer and then went back to his rowing. 'Aye,' he said after a long while, by which time I'd already forgotten my question and was more engaged with a memory of a particularly unchristian but highly enjoyable afternoon that Kaikala and I had spent at our lagoon, a recollection that would have given me the motions at any other time but which, on this occasion, were rebutted due to the exhaustion of my body and the emptiness of my belly. 'Aye, it's true. I sailed with him on the *Endeavour* when he was master and Captain Cook led us.'

'Was he much different then?' I asked, for it was hard for me to imagine the captain being in Mr Fryer's position, not handing out the orders but receiving and obeying them.

'Somewhat,' he replied. 'He were younger, that much is true.' I sighed, unsure whether he was being deliberately evasive or thought that this was a reasonable answer to my question. 'I'll tell you this much,' he said after a few more minutes had passed. 'Captain Cook never would have allowed this to happen.'

'What's that?' I asked ignorantly.

'This, Turnip. This! Our crew out here in the middle of nowhere sailing to the Saviour knows where, little knowing whether we might live or die. He never would have allowed matters to come to this.'

'But the captain was surprised by it,' I protested, for even though circumstances had changed, I still thought it my duty to stand by him. 'He had no idea what Mr Christian was planning.'

'Hadn't he?' asked Peckover. 'Then, I suggest he should have kept his eyes and ears open when we were on Otaheite, for there was more than one man knew of the plot, and there were others not far from us here who were torn between their two ideas: fornication and duty.'

I looked around and wondered who among us was the lazy dog who had considered standing against the captain, but it occurred to me that I too had had moments of doubt as to where I would stand.

'Did you know of it?' I asked quietly. 'Did you know the mutiny was to take place?'

'I knew there was a chance of it,' he said with a shrug. 'I knew that Mr Christian never wanted to leave the island and I knew there were those who said they would follow him no matter what.'

'And you? You never thought to join him?'

'Not I,' he said, shaking his head quickly. 'I'm the king's man, always have been since the day I was born. No, there's nothing I would have liked more than a little more frolics with the ladies of Otaheite, but I never could have stayed there and added my name to the list of mutineers. My family would have been disgraced. I wonder that you joined us, though, Turnip. I wonder that you didn't decide to enjoy the freedoms on offer.'

'I've not much to go home to, I'll give you that,' I admitted. 'But the captain was good to me from the moment I joined the ship. He looked after me in those early days when I was ill. He took me into his confidence during the voyage. He taught me things.'

'Aye, there were some who were jealous of that,' he said with a laugh.

'There were?' I asked.

'Of course! You think the younger officers liked the way you came to and from his cabin at any hour of the night or day? You think they thought it right that you could be in there, cleaning or clearing, while they were engaged on the ship's business? Both Mr Christian and Mr Heywood spoke to the captain about it. They said they had concerns.'

'Concerns about me?' I asked, my blood boiling. 'The scuts! Why, I never gave them any cause to!'

'And then there was the list,' he said, smiling a little as if he was enjoying the knowledge that he held over me.

'The list?' I asked. 'And what list might that have been?'

'The list that was discovered. The one that named those men who might have been engaged in a conspiracy. Mr Christian's name was on it. Aye, and Mr Heywood's.'

'I remember it,' I said, recalling the night that I had lain in my bunk, pretending to be asleep, while Mr Fryer and Mr Bligh discussed this newly discovered list and whether or not the names should be exposed. 'The captain was unsure what to do about it.'

'I dare say,' said Peckover. 'Only, there was another name on that list too, young Turnip. Someone who you may have been surprised to see there. Or perhaps not.'

I frowned. I couldn't imagine who it might have been, save the mutineers themselves. 'Who?' I asked. 'Who was it?'

'Do you really claim not to know?' he asked, turning his head a little and giving me a quizzical look, the better to decide whether I was being honest or not.

'Of course I don't,' I said. 'I never saw it. Whose name was there? Another of the officers? Thomas Burkett? He was always a bad 'un. Edward Young? He never had a good word for the captain.'

'None of them,' said Peckover, shaking his head. 'Although their names may well have been on the list too. But none of them. No, the name I refer to is that of someone much closer to the captain than them.'

I considered it. There was only one name seemed possible, although it was unlikely. 'Not Mr Fryer?' I asked.

'No, not Mr Fryer,' he replied with a laugh. 'The name was Turnstile. John Jacob Turnstile.'

Day 15: 12 May

TWO DAYS PASSED before anyone discovered that a spear was missing. Mr Elphinstone, who had taken to murmuring in his sleep, calling out the name Bessie time and again – a disconcerting fact considering that was the name of the captain's own wife – was organizing that day's shift of rowers when Lawrence LeBogue noticed a shoal of fish passing by the tub.

'Look, sir,' he said, pointing into the water, and half the crew looked starboard, almost over tipping us. 'We could catch some if we try.'

'Spears,' said Mr Elphinstone, looking around to discover them, as it had been several days since we had seen any fish at all so there had been no call for the spears. George Simpson produced one from beneath his seat and every man looked around for the second. 'Well, come on, men,' he said. 'It must be here somewhere.'

'What's this?' asked the captain, who had been asleep, and now sat up at the disturbance we were making. 'What goes on here, Mr Elphinstone?'

'The spears, sir,' he replied. 'We can only find one.'

'But there are two.'

'Yes, sir.'

Mr Bligh sighed and shook his head as if the whole thing was beneath his consideration. 'Well, it's not as if we could have left it anywhere, is it?' he asked. 'Every man look around him; it must be here somewhere.'

Everyone looked, including me, who could feel the blood pumping faster within my chest as the search continued. It occurred to me that I should have admitted to my crime immediately it happened. I would have been in trouble, of course, but at least I would have been honest with it. My worry had been that the men would pick me up and throw me overboard in search of it and that would have been the end of my adventuring.

'Sir, it doesn't appear to be here,' said Mr Elphinstone finally, sitting down and shaking his head. For a moment I thought he might collapse in a heap of tears at the upset of it.

'Not here?' cried the captain. 'Then, someone must have lost it overboard, wouldn't you agree?'

'Yes, sir.'

'So who was it?' he asked, standing up and looking around the tub. 'You, William Purcell, did you lose the spear?'

'As God is my witness, I did not,' he said, sounding mortally offended at the very suggestion.

'And you, John Hallett, did you lose it?'

'Not I, sir. I've never even held it in my hands.'

A voice from the back of the ship piped up. 'It was me, sir.' Before I knew it I was on my feet in the realization that I had spoken and admitted the loss. The fact of it took even me by surprise, but I knew for certain that the captain would have interrogated every man on board one at a time and I could no sooner lie to him, or hide the lie, than I could kiss a monkey. 'I lost the spear.'

'You, Turnstile?' he asked, his voice betraying his disappointment in me.

'Aye, sir,' I said. 'I had it in my hands. I was trying to catch a fish. And it slipped. And it vanished.'

He breathed heavily and shook his head, narrowing his eyes to observe me all the better. 'When was this?' he asked.

'Two days ago,' I said. 'As the sun slipped.'

'Two days ago and you saw fit only to admit to this now?'

'I'm sorry for it, sir,' I said. 'Truly I am.'

'Aye, and so you should be,' yelled David Nelson, the botanist, scrambling to his feet and him usually as placid as a duck in a pond. 'We had only two spears and now we have one. How shall we survive? What if we should encounter more savages?'

'Sit down, that man,' roared the captain, and Mr Nelson turned to look at him, not obeying him immediately.

'But, captain,' he said, 'the lad lied about it and—'

'He lied about nothing; he simply omitted to tell the truth. It's a subtle distinction, I grant you, but a distinction nonetheless. Sit down, I tell you, Mr Nelson, and, Turnstile, come up here to me.'

The botanist took his seat again, still a-grumbling, and I made my way slowly to the fore of the tub, passing by the other men, who gave me evil looks and muttered low comments about my birth and my mother, as if I had ever known that honest woman. The captain was standing with his hands on his hips and I swallowed nervously as I reached him.

'I do apologize, sir,' I explained. 'It was an accident.'

'And accidents will happen to all of us,' he said. 'But how shall we survive if we are not honest with one another? Look at Mr Lamb and Mr Linkletter there.'

I turned and faced those two men, who were seated on either side of the boat with small buckets, bailing out water from the tub, a task that had become as much a constant part of our day as the rowing or the pains in our bellies.

'If either of them was to lose his bucket, don't you think it would be important for him to inform us all and admit to the loss?'

'Yes, sir, of course,' I said.

'Well, you must be punished for it,' he said. 'You will do a double shift all this day at the oars and let that be a lesson to you.' And he boxed my ears then to finish off. 'Mr Samuel, allow Turnstile here to take your place.'

The ship's clerk stood up and I sat down and began rowing, my face burning with shame, aware of the looks of condemnation I was receiving from the others, but it mattered not. It would be forgotten by the next day. We had more things to worry about than this.

Day 16: 13 May

NOTHING OF ANY INTEREST to any of us took place this day. It was just tedium. Tedium and hunger.

Day 17: 14 May

A BAD DAY WAS MADE WORSE when I was awakened in the middle of the night by a great wave tumbling into the tub and landing directly on my person. I spat water from my mouth and sat up straight, wondering why the other seven or eight men who were asleep beside and atop me did not waken too. No doubt it had something to do with the fact that we were all so tired and feeble by now that it would take more than a little splash of water to disturb them. I looked around and was surprised to see the captain sitting behind me at the rear of the launch – his usual position was at the fore – and, sensing my eyes on him, he turned round to look at me.

'Not asleep, Turnstile?' he asked quietly.

'I was,' I said. 'I was awakened.'

'You should try to sleep again,' he replied, turning away from me and looking out at the water; the moon was full in the sky that night and lent his face a spectral aspect. 'We must all rest when we can to maintain our strength.'

'Are you all right, sir?' I asked, stepping over the snoring body of Robert Lamb and making my way to the seat beside him. 'Is there anything I can do for you?'

'We're not on the *Bounty* now, lad,' he said sadly. 'There's little that you can do for me. I lost the ship, don't you remember?'

'I remember it being stolen from you, sir,' said I. 'I remember it being taken. By mutineers and pirates.'

'Aye, but I'll not see it again, I know that much.'

I nodded and considered what I might say to lift his spirits. By now we were simply two men drawn together at a difficult time rather than captain and servant. I wanted to tell him something that would make him feel more like his old cheerful self, but I have never been much of a one on occasions like this. Fortunately for me he chose to speak first.

'Do you know why they did it, John?' he asked me, employing my Christian name for once, a rare treat. 'Why they took my boat, I mean?'

'Because they're blackguards, sir,' I replied. 'There's no way around it. They're a rum lot, every one. I never trusted that Mr Christian, if you want to know the truth. There was always the air of a nance about him. I know he's an officer, sir, but I can say that now, can't I? I can say what I think?'

'He's not an officer any more,' he said with a shrug. 'He's a pirate. A traitor. Treasonous. He'll be a wanted man when we return home. And he'll hang for it sooner or later.'

I smiled, appreciative of how the captain always referred to *when* we returned to England, not *if*. 'I never saw a man with cleaner hair than he,' I continued then, warming to my theme. 'Or neater nails. Or one who smelled so good. I never knew whether I should obey him or whistle at him. And as for that scut Mr Heywood . . . He were a bad lot from the start.'

'Fletcher and I . . . Mr Christian, I mean . . . we had known each other a long time. I know his family. I promoted him, Turnstile. It vexes me. Why would they do it?'

I bit my lip and considered the matter. There was something that had been preying on my mind for days, but I had not yet had the opportunity to speak to the captain about it. 'There was a list, Captain,' I said finally.

'A list?'

'Mr Fryer found it. It had the names of the mutineers on it. Mr Christian's name was there. And Mr Heywood's. And the others too.'

'Aye, you know about that, do you?' he asked, narrowing his eyes to stare at me. 'Who told you about it?'

'Truthfully, I was awake that evening, sir,' said I. 'When the two officers were summoned to your cabin. When Mr Fryer spoke to you about it. I heard the conversation.'

'I suspect you have heard rather a lot over the course of our voyage, Turnstile,' he said. 'I have always thought that you are a young man who keeps his ears open and his mouth shut.'

'It's right enough,' I admitted.

'I'm glad of it, in truth,' he said. 'I might need your memory when we return to England.' There it was again. 'When the courts convene, and they will convene. When my name is blackened.' He hesitated and I thought I could hear a catch in his voice. 'And it will be blackened,' he added.

'Yours, sir?' said I, appalled. 'But why? What have you done to deserve that?'

'We live in strange times,' he said with a shrug. 'Stories have a way of altering. There will be those who will ask why a group of men, including officers from decent families, would turn on their captain in the way that they did. They will blame me, some of them. Only one story will be remembered in the end. Either my own or theirs.'

'But yours is the truth, sir,' said I, surprised that he could be so pessimistic. 'A fairer captain never lived. That is what they will remember.'

'Do you think so? Who is to say, after all? One of us – Mr Christian and me, I mean – will be remembered as a tyrant and a blackguard. And the other will be recalled as a hero. I may need your ears and your memory to assume my rightful place.'

'Sir, was my name on the list?' I asked, blurting this out quicker than I had expected.

'What's that?'

'The list of mutineers,' I said. 'Was my name there?'

He breathed heavily through his nose and looked me in the eye; the waves splashed towards the side of the tub as he hesitated. 'It was there,' he said.

'Then it's a slander,' I replied quickly. 'For I never would have joined them, sir. Not ever. I never heard of it and I never enjoined in any such conversation.'

'It was not a list of mutineers,' he replied, shaking his head. 'It was a list of men who Christian thought would join him. People he considered to be . . . unhappy with their lot. Were you unhappy, Turnstile? Did I give you cause to be unhappy?'

'Not I, sir,' I replied. 'I was unhappy at home. I was unhappy in England.'

'Ah, yes,' he said thoughtfully. 'That.'

'That, sir.'

'You will not be returning to the same life, lad,' he said. 'I promise you that.'

'I know it.'

He smiled and patted me on the shoulder. 'Do you know something?' he said. 'By my calculations today is the fourteenth of May. My own boy's birthday. I miss him.'

I nodded but said nothing. I could see that he was emotional at the memory of his son, and before a few more moments had passed I stepped back to my seat, lay down and tried to sleep. And it came, fitfully at first, and then deeper.

Day 18: 15 May

IWAS ON ROWING DUTY an hour or two after sun-up when the mid-shipman Robert Tinkler suffered the first of his hallucinations. Surgeon Ledward was rowing to my left and we were both engaged about our work without conversation, our arms pulling the oars forwards and backwards without thought any more. The weather had taken an unexpected turn and for once we were not spending our time bailing water from the boat; indeed, some of the men had taken their sodden shirts and britches off and were laying them out in the hope that they might dry over the course of a few hours.

'Charles,' said Mr Tinkler, appearing from behind us and turn-ing his attention to Surgeon Ledward, whose Christian name was not Charles at all, but Thomas. 'They say the mare in the high paddock is with foal again. You never told me she had been put out to the stud-horse.'

Ledward turned his head for a moment and stared at the other man, a look of surprise mingled with disinterest plastered about his features. As he did so, I noticed a long stretch of white flaky skin scabbing its way along his neck and into his shirt and wondered what the surgeon himself made of it.

'I told Father that we should purchase our own stud-horse,' con-tinued Tinkler, oblivious to his lunacy. 'The shillings it costs every time we—'

'What madness is this?' asked Ledward. 'Who do you think I am, Robert, some brother of yours? Some friend?'

Tinkler stared at him and I thought I caught a nasty look in his eye, as if he was more accustomed to arguing with

396

whoever he believed the surgeon to be than appeasing him.

'You're no longer my brother, is that it?' he snapped. 'I told you that those were nothing but lies that you had about me and Mary Martinfield. I would never lay a finger on someone who you had your heart set on. If we allow this to come between us—'

'Robert, take a rest,' said the surgeon in a soothing voice. 'Lay your head down over there where there's space and close your eyes a spell. When you awaken, things will seem much brighter.'

Mr Tinkler opened his mouth to say more, but appeared to soften then, nodding his head and turning away for the direction that the surgeon had indicated. I watched him stretch out and close his eyes and within a very few seconds his body was inching upwards and downwards in the act of sleep.

'Is he for the madhouse?' I asked the surgeon, nodding my own head in the direction of our departed friend.

'Perhaps,' he replied. 'It's hard to tell. The voyage is playing tricks with his head. As is the hunger. And the lack of water.'

'That's playing tricks with all of us,' I pointed out. 'But I don't believe myself to be the Duke of Portland on account of it.'

'It will affect each of us in different ways,' he said. 'What you must not do is aggravate the situation. Mr Tinkler may be in a state of dementia or it may be a passing folly. But our quarters are too small to have him stimulated. I would suggest that if he starts speaking like that again, then you simply humour him and play the part that he assigns you.'

'Merciful Saviour,' I said, astonished by this, wondering which of us the madness might strike next. 'You've seen this sort of thing before, then?' I asked.

'I've not been stuck in the middle of the Pacific Ocean on a launch barely designed for eight, let alone eighteen, with no opportunity for sustenance and a near certainty of death on my hands, Turnip, no.' I raised an eyebrow and glared at him and he gave a half-smile and shook his head. 'I apologize,' he said. 'That was unfair.'

397

'It was a simple enough question,' I stated. 'I merely wanted to know whether you had experience of Bedlamites and how to treat them.'

'Not I,' he admitted. 'My father and grandfather were physicians before me but we have each dealt with matters of the body, not of the mind. It's an area of little interest to most true surgeons as there are no cures for those whose brains are diseased. Incarceration is the fairest solution for society.'

'I've heard terrible stories about those places,' I said with a shudder. 'I wouldn't care for them myself.'

'Then you must remain healthy and not give in to vice. Lads of your own age give in to vice constantly and I swear it is one of the reasons for lunacy in later life.'

I said nothing; I had observed on occasion that Mr Ledward was a religious man and I wondered whether he was suggesting that spending too much time at tug, which it was true that I did, would send me demented. He had carried a Bible with him during the course of the outward voyage, and read from it frequently, although unlike many of his ilk he did not see fit to impose its tracts upon the rest of us.

'I have never given in to vice in my life,' I protested, sniffing slightly and turning away from him. 'And I consider the suggestion a slander on my character.'

'Yes, yes, Turnip,' he said irritably. 'I shall take your word on it, then.'

I turned away from him, intending to stare out to sea in silence again, but was disturbed by Mr Tinkler sitting up and commenting on the condition of the streets of Cardiff these days and their tendency to be over-polluted by the manure of the horses, and I shook my head and sighed, hoping that the surgeon was wrong, for if I was to survive this voyage at all I wanted it to be as a healthy lad and not as one who would be sent to the madhouse immediately upon my return.

Day 19: 16 May

I F THE SAVIOUR HAD SEEN FIT to give us a bit of sunshine on our backs the day before, he took a great delight in spinning us the other way round on this day, for the gales and storms blew up like nobody's business and threatened to send us all downwards to a watery grave for some six or seven hours. Our strongest and best rowers – John Hallett, Peter Linkletter, William Peckover and Lawrence LeBogue – took on the oars themselves and worked as if they were one man with four limbs to keep us afloat. Others bailed water from the deck, while the rest of us dared to utter a few terrified prayers in our heads that we might survive this escapade.

When the hurricanes finally died down and we had nothing left to contend with but wind and rain, the captain sensed our misery and offered us a little salt-pork, which was our finest remnant from our brief time on the Friendly Islands, as well as a morsel of bread and a thimbleful of water. I confess that the three items taken together felt like a great feast, and had my stomach not been screaming that this was not enough for it, not enough by far, I would have lain back a happy and sated Turnstile and thought myself a fine fellow altogether.

'Captain,' said Mr Tinkler, who had briefly returned to his senses, although perhaps they were still a little impaired considering the impudence that was to come. 'Captain, you can't mean to give us just this?' he asked.

'Just what, Mr Tinkler?' replied the captain, running the back of his hand across his eyes, wiping the rain from them, the dark bags beneath them betraying his exhaustion.

'These morsels,' said Mr Tinkler, a note of utter frustration creeping into his tone. 'Why, they wouldn't be enough to feed a budgerigar, let alone a crew of grown men and the lad Turnip.'

I took exception to this but said nothing for now, merely adding it in my mind to a list of perceived insults and slights.

'Mr Tinkler,' replied the captain with a sigh, 'that is all there is. Should I give you more and starve you tomorrow? And the next day? Is that what you would have me do?'

The former Bedlamite stood up at this, stretched his arms out before him slowly and curled his hands into fists, not in order to make assault on the captain but to pump them up and down in the air in anger. 'Tomorrow is tomorrow,' he said, stating the clear and obvious. 'May we not worry about that then?'

'No,' said the captain, shaking his head.

'But I am starving,' came the screaming reply. 'I shall die of my hunger. Look here,' he added, lifting his chemise to reveal a set of fine ribs, on which I might have run a spoon and produced a harmonious effect. 'I am skin and bone!'

'We are all skin and bone, sir,' cried the captain. 'And we will remain skin and bone until we have saved ourselves. It is the price we pay for the crimes of our erstwhile sailors.'

'The price we pay for our folly in joining you, you mean,' he shouted, incensed, turning round to look at the rest of us, his face both pale with illness and scarlet with fury, if such a description can be understood. He turned to an unlistening audience, however, for none of us was in a mood to listen to his disputes. 'What say you, men?' he cried. 'We are deprived. We are starved. There is . . .' He looked up towards the crate that sat locked beside the captain at all times, its key suspended from his neck. 'There is food in there,' he roared. 'Food that Mr Bligh decides when and if we should dine off. Who gave him this authority? Why do we allow it?'

At this the captain leapt from his seat at the fore of the launch and in a trice was about Mr Tinkler with the back of his hand; there was a madness in his eyes and for a moment I worried about where this might end. 'Sit you down, sir,' he roared in a voice so loud that even Mr Christian might have heard him. 'I'll not have talk like this, do you hear me? Have we not had enough of mutiny for one lifetime? Who gave me my authority? you ask. The king, sir! The king gave it and only the king might take it away.'

Mr Tinkler locked eyes with the captain for five, six, seven, seconds and it was anyone's guess whether he might come back at him again and attack him. I saw Mr Fryer and Mr Elphinstone ready to pounce should the situation become untenable, but holding their muster for the moment. I was half off the seat myself, ready to defend the captain should he need assistance, but it was all in vain, for the stare of power was enough for Tinkler and his face collapsed in a mixture of pain, upset, starvation and madness, before he sank to the deck and wept like a molly. The captain's hand lifted again for a moment, preparing to touch his shoulder, I believed, but he thought better of it and turned back for his seat.

'You shall eat when I say you shall eat,' he shouted for us all to hear. 'And you shall eat what I give you. I swallow no more than any man on board, you know that. We shall survive, do you hear me? We shall survive this! And you *will* obey me!'

There was a low murmuring of cheers, but, in truth, we were half the men we had been and even a scene like this could do little to break the monotony of our voyage and the terror of our new lives. A few minutes after it had begun we were back at our duties and it was all forgotten, except for that one fact which had so incensed Robert Tinkler to begin with.

We were, every man jack of us, the captain included, starving.

Day 20: 17 May

I DREAMT THAT OUR SMALL TUB had done the impossible and sailed all the way from our current place to the harbour at Spithead, and as we got closer who did I see waiting on the shore, hands on hips, with a look of fury on his phizzy, but Mr Lewis. I dreamt that when I set foot on shore I was not given a hero's welcome but was taken away by Mr Lewis and brought back to his establishment, where I was made an example of by him in front of my brothers.

And then I woke up with a start.

We had long since passed the point where someone shouting or screaming in their sleep was enough to wake any of the others on board; we cared little for another fellow's disturbances. But as I lay there, the splashes of the waves falling upon my face with the regular upswing and downturn of the launch, I wondered whether he would indeed be waiting for me or whether by now he had forgotten about my very existence.

I had but vague memories of our first meeting. I was no more than a child of four or five, living hand to mouth, eating scraps whenever I could find them, and he passed me on the street one afternoon as I held a hand out for whatever he might be able to offer me. He walked by without a word, but then appeared to stop a little further along in his tracks and remain still for a moment. I watched him, wondering whether he had changed his mind and would root in his pocket for a couple of loose farthings, but instead he turned and smiled at me, looked me up and down and came over again.

'Hello, lad,' said he, crouching down so that he was closer to my level, although he still maintained a height over me.

'Good afternoon, sir,' said I, as polite as I could.

'You look like a hungry fellow,' he said. 'Don't your mam feed you, then?'

'I have no mam, sir,' I replied, looking down for a moment at the unhappy words.

'No mam? No pater either, then?'

'No, sir,' I admitted.

'What a sad story,' he said, shaking his head and stroking his whiskers. 'A terrible sad story for one so young. Where do you make a bed for the night, then?'

'Where I can, sir,' I said. 'But if you could spare a farthing, then I might do better tonight than I did last night when I curled up with a stinking dog for the warmth of it.'

'Yes, I can tell you have a stench off you,' he said with a smile, and I noted that he did not take a step back in disgust. 'Let me see what I have here,' he muttered, rooting in his pockets. 'I've no farthings, but perhaps you could make use of two pennies?'

I opened my eyes wide. It took eight farthings to make two pennies; I was young and innocent but my knowledge of money was keen. 'Thank you, sir,' I said, taking them quickly before he changed his mind. 'I'm most grateful for it.'

'You're welcome, lad,' he said, laughing a little and running a finger along my arm in a way that caused me no concern then, for I was suddenly wealthy and was considering how to spend my fortune. 'You have a name, lad?'

'Aye, sir,' I replied.

'And what is it, then?'

'John,' I said.

'John what?'

'John Jacob Turnstile,' I told him.

He nodded and smiled. 'You're a pretty lad, ain't you?' he said, but in a way that seemed not to require an answer and so I offered none. 'Do you know who I am, John Jacob Turnstile?'

'No, sir,' I replied.

'My name is Lewis,' he said. 'Mr Lewis to you, lad. I run a . . . how shall I put this? . . . an establishment for boys such as yourself. A place where the homeless may be given shelter. The hungry may be given food. The tired may be offered a bed. There are plenty of lads your age there. It's a fine Christian establishment, of course.'

'It sounds very fine, sir,' said I, wondering what it would be like to be offered food and bedding every day without having to pick up the one off the streets or find the other at the back of a fetid alley.

'It is very fine, John Jacob Turnstile,' he said, standing up so that I had to stretch my neck back to look up at him; his phizzy was hidden then by the sun shining in my eyes. 'It is very fine indeed. Perhaps you would like to see it sometime?'

'I should like that very much, sir,' said I.

'And there's no one . . . there's no one who will miss you? No parents, you have said. But not a favoured aunt perhaps? A devoted uncle? An old crone of a granny?'

'No one, sir,' said I, feeling a little sad at the admittance of it. 'I am entirely alone in the world.'

He smiled and shook his head. 'No, you're not, lad,' he said. 'You're not alone. You'll never be alone now.'

And at that he extended his hand towards me. I hesitated for only a second or two.

And then I took it.

Day 21: 18 May

MORE MISERY THIS DAY after a morning of relentless gales and rain, the former tipping the tub up and down so violently that I was convinced we would die and also making it impossible for us to replenish our water supplies. When we settled again and were sailing forward – now in the direction of New Holland, which the captain assured us was perhaps sixty or seventy leagues hence – it became obvious that some of the men were in extreme distress. The clerk John Samuel was unfit for any duty and his countenance was such that I wondered whether he had long to live; he had given up complaining or asking for extra provisions and seemed resigned to his fate. The botanist Mr Nelson was in a similar condition but would frighten me every few hours by leaning forward and clutching his stomach, as if a spear was being slowly guided through his skin and piercing his intestines, before letting out a cry such as a fox might make after being caught in a snare. I dreaded to imagine how such an ache felt for the sufferer; the look of sheer agony on his face explained enough to me and I fel sure that given the choice between continued hope or certain death he would not have hesitated with an answer. The officers were not immune either. Mr Elphinstone was in a state of extreme distress; his phizzy was paler than anyone else's and his stomach appeared distended now with the hunger. He had not spoken in two days, even to the captain, who appeared grief-stricken by the fellow's fall. And as for Mr Tinkler, his descent into dementia had grown apace, although he had quietened somewhat as the lack of food and water diminished his energies.

I considered myself lucky in that – hungry and desperate for water as I was – I appeared still to have some strength in my body and was not suffering the grasping stomach pains that some of the others were. Of course this meant that I was spending more time at the oars than before, but it was a duty I was content to undertake. If anything, I found the constant stretching back and forth as I dragged us through the water provided a release within myself that I found comforting. It also gave me an idea that I was in control of our own destiny and, by default, my own. If I could just keep sailing, then perhaps I would be the one to see land again. After all, it had been my eyes that had first observed Otaheite ... when was it? It felt like a lifetime before.

Three times a day the captain divided a morsel of bread eighteen ways. How he managed to maintain an equality between the crumbs was a mystery to me, but he succeeded at it nonetheless, for no man got more than his due, not even those who were suffering the most, which I was grateful for as it would only lead to dishonesty among the rest of us.

I suffered one bad hour that evening, however, of which I have little to say other than reporting that I felt quite certain I would die on that tub.

It depressed my spirits entirely.

Day 22: 19 May

A DREADFUL OCCURRENCE TODAY when a flock of gannets appeared near by and buzzed over our heads, cackling away something terrible. We grew terribly excited, each one of us, for if we could manage to catch one, it would make fine eating. Mr Fryer picked up the spear slowly and told us all to sit still in the tub, no one was to move; we were to wait and see if one of the gannets would land on the edge of our launch.

'If we had two spears, then things would be a damn sight better,' came a voice from behind me – I was unsure whose, but I kept my eyes facing forward and did not turn round to give the scut any pleasure from the remark.

'Quiet, please, gentlemen,' said Mr Fryer in a low, peaceful voice. 'Mr Bligh, perhaps a morsel of bread on the rim?'

'If we lose it, it will be a terrible waste,' he said, unsure whether to agree to the request or not.

'And if it brings one of these birds down to rest I promise you that he shall not fly again.'

The captain hesitated for a few moments, but none of the gannets showed any sign of landing and, rather than risk their flying away, he grabbed a tasty chunk from the crate and placed it carefully on the side of the boat, close to the master himself.

'If you can kill him before he eats it, all the better,' he said quietly as he placed it down.

It was a fine piece, that was for sure, more than he ever offered any of us, but then again it was necessary to be that size in order for the birds to see it and think it worthy of a swoop. My stomach growled and lurched in famished pain as I stared at it and I dare say I was not the only one on board who had an urge to lunge forward, grab it and swallow it before anyone could stop me, although to do so may well have resulted in instantaneous murder.

'Come on now,' came Mr Fryer's voice, and I swear he locked eyes with one of the birds, because a few moments later one started to descend and hover above the bread, watching it carefully, watching us, waiting to see whether we meant it any harm. 'Quite still, everyone,' he said and not a man on the boat dared to breathe, let alone shift in his seat. The moments felt like hours but then, to our delight, the bird rested his legs on the side of the tub, pecked down on the bread and swallowed it before any of us could stop him, but he was rewarded a moment later by Mr Fryer's spear piercing through his skin quite cleanly and pinning him to the deck.

The sound of the bird's surprised screech coincided with our raucous cheer and the flapping of the gannets overhead, who flew away immediately, and I swear I could not remember when I had last felt so deliriously happy.

'Three cheers for Mr Fryer,' cried Mr Elphinstone and in our delight we went along with the farce, and the look of relieved joy on the master's face was a sight to behold. I could not remember ever seeing him so pleased with himself. He turned to the captain and offered him the dead bird and Mr Bligh clapped him on the back soundly.

'Well done, Mr Fryer,' he said, trying to keep his enthusiasm in check. 'I don't believe I've ever seen such a clean shot.'

We watched as the captain pulled the spear from the bird's body and set about plucking the feathers from the carcass. There was none of us who thought for a moment that he was about to divide the bird eighteen ways – on the contrary, we knew only too well that the meat would be finely separated and might last us four or five days if the captain took care with it – but, nevertheless, it was a welcome change from the morsels of bread we were accustomed to, a healthy chunk of which had just been digested by our victim.

Mr Bligh held the plucked bird at the side of the boat and took his knife to gut it and, as he did so, as the blade entered the flesh and pressed northwards to divide the body equally along the centre, those of us close enough to see let out a disgusted cry. Rather than the healthy white meat and red blood and organs we expected to see, a black, tar-like substance emerged instead. The captain hesitated, curling his lip, before resuming his slicing and then a moment later, to our surprise, let go of the body, flinging it back to the sea with a cry.

'Captain!' I cried, shocked by what he had done.

'He was diseased,' said the captain, and I swear that had he had food in his stomach he would have retched it overboard as well. 'There was nothing to eat. A taste would have killed us all.'

'It's an omen,' said William Peckover, standing up and looking thoroughly defeated by the experience. 'It's an omen, men,' he repeated. 'The black diseased bird says that we shall all die.'

'Sit down, Mr Peckover!' snapped the captain.

Peckover opened his mouth to repeat his assertion, but then thought better of it, resumed his place and shook his head. No one spoke, the rowers continued to row, the tub continued to go forward, the rain started to fall, and each one of us wondered whether Mr Fryer had just been unlucky in the gannet that had landed or whether Mr Peckover had reason in his comments.

Day 23: 20 May

SURGEON LEDWARD, who by a stroke of good fortune appeared to be among the healthiest of our crew, spent much of the afternoon visiting every man in turn under Mr Bligh's orders to assess the condition of each one. I was not close enough to hear the conversation that he and the captain had at the end of it, but there were many concerned faces and low whispers, and after they had spoken the captain ordered that we would no longer be at the oars for two hours apiece but for one hour instead. This had the effect of decreasing the amount of time we had to rest but at least we did not finish a shift half dead.

Looking around, it was clear to see that we were in a terrible condition. Most of the men, myself included, were weakened, smelt filthy and had skin peeling in flakes from our burnt heads. There were some – John Hallett and Peter Linkletter among them

– who had been excused rowing duties for twenty-four hours on account of their condition. I myself had been excused two shifts a couple of days earlier but I had mysteriously rallied in the days in between.

'Captain, what's to become of us?' I asked at one point, hoping for consolation.

'Survival and long lives, Master Turnstile,' he told me with a half-smile. 'Survival and long lives.'

Day 24: 21 May

THE WORST DAY SO FAR. The rain started early and continued without cessation throughout the day, bloody great sheets of it falling on us so heavily that we could scarcely see our hands when we held them out before us. There was no question of our steering the tub in the direction of New Holland, which the captain insisted we were pointed towards; instead, we simply did all we could to keep afloat. Even the men who had collapsed over the last few days in a delirium found their way to their feet and used their cupped hands to help bail water from the deck, as we were in imminent danger of sinking. Never had I felt the insanity of a project more than this. From all sides the gales blew the rain at us and still we reached our hands down, linked our fingers together to form something that might hold a cupful of water, and threw it overboard, where the wind caught it in mid-flight and sent it directly back into our eyes and mouths. It was a terrible game, no more than that. A fight between us men and nature, in which we were struggling to keep ourselves from annihilation. I fell backwards at one point, thrown there by the force of the hurricane, and came to rest against the side of the tub;

at that moment we were so unbalanced that I felt I would only have to tilt my head backwards a little to submerge it in the Pacific waters, and for a split-second that is what I did. Beneath the water all was silent and I opened my eyes, imagining how easy it would be simply to allow my body to fall backwards, not to struggle but to float for a moment instead, to sink, to drown, to die. There was utter quiet beneath the surf and I swear it was unholy relaxing.

A hand reached down and lifted me from my madness, pulled me to my feet and deposited me on the deck again, where I instantly began bailing once more. I could not tell who had collected me – there was simply no way to identify people or understand voices – but whoever it was no doubt thought that I had collapsed utterly and was about to drown. He had saved me, although I was not yet there. Another moment or two of peace, that was all I required, and then I would have been restored.

My hands moved as if independent of my body and I could tell by the rocking back and forth of the boat how others were doing the same thing. A man crashed into me suddenly, knocking me off balance, and I fell forwards, knocking into another as if we were a set of bowls on a gentleman's lawn. There was no time to remonstrate: we each had no choice but to resume our duties wherever we found ourselves stationed. Eighteen men in twenty feet of wood and glue and nails, fighting for their very lives. Was this what I had left Portsmouth for? Was this what I had abandoned the *Bounty* and the island of Otaheite for?

I pulled back once more and a wave hit my face so hard that I felt as if it had torn the very skin from my cheeks and eyes and I let out a scream, a cry of such self-pity and horror that it contained the elements of many screams I had hidden away in the corners of my soul for so many years. I screamed louder, my mouth as wide open as it could possibly be, and yet I heard not a note of the cry, so strong were the gales and tempests that tossed us from wave to wave, above the water, below the water, sea-swept. How could the Saviour have abandoned us in this way, I

411

wondered. I might have wept in frustration at this pitiful turn of events had there been anything left in my body for the exertion. But there was not. And so I did the only thing I could do in the circumstances.

I bailed water.

And I bailed more water.

And I bailed more water still.

And I prayed that somehow I would survive just one more night.

Day 25: 22 May

I DID SURVIVE IT. We all survived it. But at great further cost, for now there were only a few of us who remained in any condition to row.

'I feel we cannot be far now from New Guinea,' said the captain, who looked as unhealthy as all of us did and whose beard, I noticed, was of a much greyer shade than his hair. We were sitting together watching the horizon and he had just finished writing his daily notes in the small notebook that Mr Christian, the donkey, had allowed him to take with him.

'Do you know who I was thinking of this morning, sir?' I ventured.

'No, Turnstile,' he said with a sigh. 'Who was it? Some friend back home? One of the brothers you have spoken of?'

'No, not them,' I replied, shaking my head. 'I was thinking of the lad Smith. John Smith, I believe his name was.'

The captain frowned and turned to look at me, raising an eyebrow. 'John Smith,' he said slowly. 'The name means something to me, I am sure, but then it is a most common name. Was he—? '

'He was the lad who had my position before I did,' I said.

'Isn't it curious how everyone thinks they can interrupt me here,' said the captain. 'On the launch, I mean. Back on the *Bounty*, no one would have dared.'

'No, sir, they mutinied instead,' I replied. It was a saucy comment, not designed to insult, and one that would have seen me flogged six months previously, but the captain merely shook his head and looked away.

'I suppose you're right on that,' he said sadly.

'John Smith was your servant-lad,' I explained. 'He was due to sail on the *Bounty* before me. But he cracked his legs in an accident.'

'Oh, I remember him now,' he said, nodding. 'He sailed with me a year before. A terrible fellow, as it happened. Stank to the heavens and back. No matter how often I sent him to the wash-room he came back with a malodorous stench that would have brought a corpse back to life. But it was no accident, Turnstile. I think Mr Hallett had at him one day and he fell down the gang-way as a result of it.'

'Well, he had the last laugh, I expect,' I said, smiling at the irony of it. 'For here we are, you, me and Mr Hallett, all on board this blasted tub, and he's most likely back in Spithead with his legs rested, drinking a mug of rum and eating a fine meal in the warmth of a local hostelry.'

'You were unfortunate then,' he admitted. 'I hope you felt that the rest of your voyage, before the . . . unpleasantness, I mean, was of worth.'

'Aye, sir, I did,' I said, smiling at the use of the word 'un-pleasantness' to describe our misadventure. 'To my surprise I did.'

We sat in silence a while longer before the boredom caught up with us both and he turned to look at me again. 'So how did you come to join the crew, then, Turnstile? I don't think I ever heard.'

'The truth of it,' I began, feeling no shame for what were the facts of the case, 'is that I was apprehended by the blues for stealing a Frenchman's watch and that same Frenchman made a case to the magistrate for me to join you on your voyage rather than face the gaol for a twelvemonth.'

'A Frenchman?' asked Captain Bligh.

'A Mr Zéla,' I said.

'Ah, Matthieu,' he replied, nodding his head. 'Yes, I have not known him long but he's proved to be a fine fellow. He is much in favour with Sir Joseph Banks.'

'Him what bankrolled our mission?'

'Him what . . . he who bankrolled it, yes, Turnstile.'

'The funny thing is if Mr Zéla had left me alone, I would have been freed from the gaol by now. My sentence, as it turned out, was a shorter one than the one I have endured here.'

'He meant you no harm. I dare say both Mr Zéla and Sir Joseph will be distraught when they hear what has happened to us.'

'But how will they hear, sir?' I asked, confused. 'The mutineers will surely never be able to return to England.'

'*We* shall return to England, Turnstile,' he said confidently. 'And we shall tell them.'

'And what will happen then, sir?'

'Who knows?' he replied with a shrug. 'I dare say the admirals will send a ship to locate Mr Christian and his followers. I look forward to leading it.'

'You, sir?'

'Yes, me, sir,' he said quickly. 'Don't you think I would want to?'

'I think you would be right enough never to want to venture to this godforsaken part of the world again, Captain. I know I never will.'

'Of course you will, Turnstile.'

'I certainly will not, sir,' I replied. 'Not wishing to contradict you, Mr Bligh, but I do not intend even to look at water again after my return to Portsmouth, should I ever get there, let alone come here. I'll be loath to take so much as a bath.'

He shook his head. 'We shall see,' he said.

Day 26: 23 May

BY NOW IT FELT as if the days when the weather did not torment us were always followed by the days when it did, and yet again we found ourselves thrown around the ocean, clinging to the sides of the tub for safety, hoping that this would not be the day when we would finally perish. Later, exhausted and starving, I found a patch of comfort near the fore of the boat, lay my head down and closed my eyes, desperate for sleep and the peace it would offer. A quiet conversation was taking place between the captain and Mr Fryer and I heard some of it.

'A week,' said the captain. 'Maybe two at the most.'

'Two weeks?' came the whispered reply. 'Captain, some of the men have less than two days left in them, I would warrant. How can we survive two weeks?'

'We survive because we have no choice,' he replied with an air of resignation. 'There is nothing that either you or I can do to alter that fact. What would you have me do?'

Mr Fryer sighed and breathed heavily through his nose. The captain had a point. We were all in this together and it was not as if he was gaining something from this voyage that we were losing. 'Perhaps we should alter our course,' he said finally. 'We seem to be drifting aimlessly.'

'We are not drifting aimlessly,' replied the captain quickly and I could hear that note of irritation creeping into his voice that had for so long been a marker of his relationship with the ship's master. 'We shall make our way north of New Holland, through the Endeavour Strait and onwards to Timor. There is a Dutch settlement there. They will feed us and nurse us to health and send us home on one of their boats.'

'You know this for a certainty, sir?'

'It is what we would do if a launch of half-dead Dutchmen appeared at one of our settlements. We can do no more than rely on their Christianity. To alter course now, Mr Fryer, would be disastrous.'

'I know it,' he said sadly. 'I am, like all of us, simply exhausted of this constant trudging through water.'

'You want to go home,' replied the captain. 'It is what we all want.' He hesitated for a few moments before speaking again. 'You will sail again when we return?' he asked.

'Perhaps,' he said. 'My wife and I . . . we have spent little time together.'

'Yes, I heard you had remarried,' replied the captain. 'I was glad of it. I met the first Mrs Fryer on one occasion and thought her a hearty woman.' Mr Fryer said nothing and a long silence ensued before the captain broke it. 'You are happy with your new wife?'

'Very happy,' he said. 'After Annabel died, I thought I would never find such happiness again. But then I met Mary and within a week of our marriage I left her for this voyage. Am I a fool, Mr Bligh?'

'Not a fool, no,' he replied. 'Men like you and me . . . our duties are to the king and to the sea. Our wives must understand that. Mrs Bligh knew the kind of man she was marrying.'

'But if we have only so few years in front of us,' continued Mr Fryer, who was clearly given to contemplation, 'then why should we spend it among other men, thousands of miles from home? Why should we do it when there is the comfort of a hearth and a family to be had in England?'

'Because it is how we are made,' said the captain, his tone implying that this was simply the way the world was designed and he would hear no more on it. 'The men on this launch, how many of them do you think will sail again when we return home?'

'None, sir,' he replied.

'And I would say most. It's in their blood. You mark my words, by

416

this time next year they will be on another ship, seeking adventure and excitement, leaving their wives and sweethearts at home.'

From my vantage point I wondered whether this was true or not and thought that perhaps the captain had a point, but it would not be true of me. I tried to imagine what my own future would hold, but sleep caught up with me then and I allowed it to sweep over me and drag me under.

Day 27: 24 May

TERRIBLE TROUBLE THIS DAY and I swore that maybe we were headed for a fight the like of which we had not yet seen on the tub. Around midday I was sitting next to the sail-maker Lawrence LeBogue, reminiscing with him about the island of Otaheite and the sport we had had there before our troubles began. After some time had passed, however – perhaps more time than by rights it should have taken me to notice – I realized that Mr LeBogue had passed into a state of unconsciousness and was not hearing a word of my prattlings.

'Captain!' I cried, raising my voice so that it might carry from the rear of the boat, where I was seated, to the fore, where Mr Bligh was in his usual place. 'Captain! Ho there!'

'What is it, lad?' he asked, turning his head to me.

'It's Mr LeBogue, sir,' I replied. 'I think he's only gone and died on us.'

Every man's head turned in our direction now and I swear that I could see a look of greed in some of their eyes; if LeBogue was gone, then there was one-eighteenth of our tub space left for us to spread our arms and legs into, and one-eighteenth of our few provisions available for us to eat.

'Step aside, lad,' said Surgeon Ledward, making his way down towards us, and I did as he said as he knelt down and felt for a pulse at Mr LeBogue's wrist and neck. We waited silently for a response, but before offering one the doctor placed his ear against the patient's chest and sat up, turned towards the captain and nodded. 'He's not dead, sir,' he said. 'But he's in a bad way, that's for sure. Passed out. I'd say he's completely dehydrated and starved.'

'An excellent diagnosis, Surgeon,' said William Peckover with a snarl. 'Now, how many years did you spend at the 'varsity in order to learn so much about human anatomy?'

'Quiet there, that man,' said Mr Fryer, although in truth Mr Peckover had a fair point. We were all starved, after all. We were each of us dehydrated. It took no great genius to identify that.

The captain hesitated for only a few moments before reaching into his crate and producing some bread and water; the bread would scarcely have satisfied a field-mouse, it was so feeble, but to each of our eyes it was a feast, weighing as much in one sitting as our meals weighed in a day. The water was no more than half a minute's rain would fall into a cup but, again, to us it was an ocean of fresh supply.

'Pass this along, Mr Fryer,' said the captain, clever enough not to trust any of us with it; it might surely have disappeared in the time it took to travel the twenty-three feet of the launch.

'Captain, no!' cried Robert Lamb immediately, and at the sound of his protest at least half a dozen found themselves complaining too.

'It's too much!'

'What about us?'

'Must we each pass out if we are to survive?'

'Silence!' roared the captain, raising his voice now, although it was a shadow of the voice that had been raised before on either boat or island. 'One of our fellows is ill. He must be saved.'

'But at what cost?' asked Mr Samuel. 'At the cost of our own lives?'

'The cost will be counted as the days go on,' said the captain. 'But we won't start to sacrifice each other simply because our bodies let us down. Where would it end if that were the case? By noon of the morrow there would be just one man left on board, the strongest of us all.'

We all murmured and griped under our breaths, but it was obvious that he was right. If we started to get a notion that we could allow one another to die at the first sign of weakness, then there was no telling how soon we would each find ourselves thrown overboard to end our lives as fish-food. Still, it was a terrible harsh thing to see all that food disappearing down Mr LeBogue's throat and scant compensation when he opened his eyes and returned to our company a few hours later, licking his lips and looking around as if he could scarcely understand the looks of contempt being thrown in his direction by his fellow passengers.

'What?' he asked, looking for all the world like a member of the Angelic Boys' Choir. 'What am I supposed to have done now? I've been asleep, after all!'

Day 28: 25 May

A BETTER DAY IN THAT MANY BIRDS were seen in the skies and there was a chance that we might catch one. After the incident almost a week before with the gannet whose darkened entrails suggested a bad omen for us all, there was a tension among us that should we be successful in our catch we would receive further ill portents, but on this occasion that was not the case. To our great delight a bird landed directly on the deck of the tub before we could even conceive of a plan to trap one, and stood there with its head bobbing back and forth as it examined us all before we jumped almost an entire crew atop it; when the throng disassembled and equilibrium was restored, its neck was broken and it was handed to the captain directly by the hand of Lawrence LeBogue, who had much recovered from the previous afternoon's misadventure.

'Men, we are lucky today,' cried the captain cheerfully, for truly after a month at sea this was a great delight to us all. I can scarcely recall such a feeling of elation as when the captain slid his knife into the gut of the bird to produce a healthy stream of blood and flesh of the most delicious hue. 'A feast is before us today, my fellows,' said the captain. 'We shall divide the bird equitably and dine off it in lieu of bread today. We are agreed on this?'

'Aye, sir!' we all shouted in reply, for there was ne'er a man among us who was not happy to forfeit his share of the daily bread if it meant that we might eat some meat. The captain sliced the bird – flesh, organs, even the small bones – into eighteen parts, trying his best to cut evenly, although there were some pieces that were a little bigger than others. In truth, a man on shore looking at the meagre offerings that each of us was about to enjoy would scarcely have found the interest in opening his mouth to receive them, but we were not men on shore. We were eighteen parts of skin and bone, gathered in twenty-three feet of damp wood, trying to keep our blood pumping and our hearts beating. We looked at the portions when they were ready, waiting for the captain to hand them out, each of us with our eyes focused on pieces that looked particularly satisfying to us.

'Mr Fryer?' said the captain.

The master nodded as the captain turned away from us all with the plate of bird pieces, and his second-in-command assumed his place at the fore, looking from man to man. The captain could see none of us now and held up the first morsel for us all to lay eyes on. The only man who could not see it, in fact, was Mr Fryer himself.

420

'Who shall have this?' asked the captain loudly.

Mr Fryer glanced around the waiting faces, selected one, and announced in an equally formal tone, 'William Purcell.'

The captain handed the piece – a good-sized chunk – to Mr Fryer, who in turn passed it to Mr Purcell, who looked at it with astonishment, as if he could not believe his luck to be served first, before nibbling the side of it cautiously and then devouring it in one.

'Slowly, men,' chastised Mr Fryer in a cautious tone. 'Allow your mouths to savour the meat before sending it to your stomach.'

'Who shall have this?' asked the captain again, holding another piece in the air, and we held our breaths; it was larger than the first.

'Peter Linkletter,' said Mr Fryer, and the named man gave a whoop of delight before claiming his prize, which he nurtured carefully, eating small amounts at a time, trying all that he could to make the piece last longer. I stared at him, my mouth salivating with desire, hopeful that I too would receive a piece of such value.

'And who shall have this?' asked the captain, who appeared to be enjoying his new role as much as Mr Fryer was.

'Surgeon Ledward shall have it,' came the reply and the third piece was gone.

'And this?' asked the captain, lifting the next morsel, which, to our starving eyes, was clearly a lesser amount than the three pieces that had gone before. 'Who shall have this?'

We all held our breaths, not wanting to influence Mr Fryer in any way by the look of panic in our eyes.

'The master's mate,' said Mr Fryer. 'William Elphinstone.'

We were men enough not to give a cry of joy that the piece was not for any of us, and Mr Elphinstone, to his credit as an officer, claimed his food with a 'thanking you most kindly, sir' and did not betray any disappointment or seek a second vote. The men nodded; we approved of him whole-heartedly.

'Who shall have this?' asked the captain time and again, and on each occasion a man stepped forward, betraying neither delight not disappointment. I felt a warmth in the pit of my stomach at what a crew we were, what a decent crew, what unity we held. There was such feeling during those moments that day that I swore we could sail directly to England and each man would survive.

Finally there were only four pieces of the bird left, and Thomas Hall the cook and I were the only men yet to eat besides the captain and Mr Fryer.

'Who shall have this?' asked the captain, raising the largest of the four remaining pieces; it struck me that, whatever happened, our two leaders would see the harsh end of this game.

'John Jacob Turnstile,' said Mr Fryer, and I reached forward and accepted my dinner gratefully. It was no bigger than the length of my thumb, and no thicker either, but I gave thanks to the Saviour, for it was as grand a meal as ever I could have wished for, and when I chewed into it, it gave up both a meaty texture and a rich sauce. My mouth came to life in an instant: the taste-buds on my tongue woke up with a start and wondered why they had been ignored for so long; my stomach turned nervously, receiving early signals that it was soon to begin the act of digestion. Salivating, I ate it as slowly as I could, savouring every texture and moment of flavour; I didn't even see the piece that Mr Hall got in the end.

'Who shall have this?' asked the captain a few moments later, holding the second-to-final piece in his hand.

'You shall, Captain,' said Mr Fryer.

The captain nodded, turned back to face his crew and handed him the final piece, which was of almost identical shape and size to his own and both of which were clearly the two smallest portions of the bird that had been there from the start, a fact that was lost on none of our admiring eyes. 'Then you shall have this,' said the captain to Mr Fryer and the two men lowered their heads to eat.

'Three cheers for Captain Bligh,' cried John Hallett in a surge of emotion. 'Hip, hip . . .'

'Hooray!' we replied, and again and again, for we were in a

great state of excitement after the drama of the division and the joy of the eating.

'And three cheers for Mr Fryer,' I added, for he had been a part of it too and suffered the smaller share on account of it. 'Hip, hip . . .' I cried.

'Hooray!' the men shouted, even more forcibly, and both the captain and the master grinned, a little embarrassed, but delighted by the turn of events.

'Perhaps we'll catch another,' said the captain, looking up at the skies, which had cleared of birds now but darkened considerably as our happy moments were inevitably to be followed by hurricanes and rain.

The men nodded, hoping the same thing but not counting on it. In the meantime, however, before the heavens opened, I swear that we were happy. Every man jack of us.

Day 29: 26 May

THERE WAS HEAVY RAIN overnight, but we had suffered worse days, and it cleared a little in the brightness of the day. More birds were spotted overhead and we tried hard to catch one, but they were not as ignorant as the one the previous day and neither landed in our tub nor flew so close overhead that we could catch one by hand. We were not made despondent by this, however, for the general agreement was that the increase in the number of birds meant that we were reaching closer to land.

The only drama of note came when John Samuel passed out in a faint, like a molly would on a hot day on the streets of London. He was quickly revived when we threw sea water on his face, he taking care to keep his lips locked so that he would swallow none of it, and it was generally agreed that he was a nance for the trauma, particularly considering how well we had eaten the day before and how positive our spirits were. He sought sympathy for a matter of an hour or so, it was declined on all quarters, and he retired to a corner of the tub to nurse his pride.

I found myself a victim of self-pity, however, a little later in the afternoon when I ran a hand across my head to cure an itch and flowery flakes of I-knew-not-what appeared to descend from my hair and phizzy to the deck. I stared at them, wondering whether my skin was falling off me, touched my head once more and the powdery rain continued. I kept my own counsel on it for some time, afeared that I had caught some virulent pestilence that would see me thrown overboard before it could spread, but finally, so terrified that I might be about to die, I consulted Surgeon Ledward on the matter.

He took a look and shook his head contemptuously. 'You have the scurvy, that is all,' he said. 'Most every man on board has it. There's a lack of iron and protein in our diets, lad, that causes it.'

'It's the lack of a diet in our diet,' I suggested.

'Quiet, lad, you ate yesterday,' he replied sharply, and I considered taking him to task for it, for he was not my master; that was the captain.

'I'll live, then?' I asked.

'Of course you'll live,' he said. 'Assuming we all live. Now get back to your place, Turnip. You have a stench off you that would send a cat a-scampering.'

I went back to my seat with a sigh, taking a sniff at myself for good measure, and sure enough I was not a clean lad by any means, but I don't think any of us were. I took a look around me and all I could see was skin-and-bone men, their faces covered in rough beards, their eyes hollow and dark, some searching the horizon for signs of life, some watching the skies for birds, some rowing, some sleeping, some lost in thought, some with blank faces.

Day 30: 27 May

L ATE IN THE AFTERNOON more birds appeared overhead; one was caught and killed and the captain played 'Who Shall Have This?' again and we were happy to dine on our catch. We were even happier, however, to catch sight of the occasional piece of driftwood passing by our small tub, for we took this as a sign that it should be only a matter of hours before we arrived at the Great Reefs of the Endeavour Strait, still a sizeable distance from our destination but nevertheless a place where we might be able to reach a shore and rest after so much time at sea.

I noted that I was becoming a little more light-headed in the bright sunlight than I had been previously and that it was becoming more and more difficult for me to stay awake. I did not regret sleeping so much, for it passed the time when I was not rowing, but it was not a solid sleep and never resulted in recuperation as much as more exhaustion, but I said nothing on it for now and kept my counsel.

The captain mentioned that he had visited here with Captain Cook when they were on the *Resolution*. 'We hoped to replenish our stocks there,' he explained to a few of us who were seated near by, 'but there was precious little to be found. The captain named the inlet through which we sailed Thirsty Bay on account of it,' he added with a smile. 'Aye, it were rightly christened, as I recall.'

'Something to look forward to, then,' said William Peckover in a saucy tone, and Mr Fryer shot him a dirty look in reply to it.

'It may have changed,' suggested the captain. 'But if we can rest, then that at least will be something, don't you agree?'

Mr Peckover nodded his head and looked away, and I hope he was ashamed on account of his insolence.

'There was a story you were to tell me, sir, if you recall,' I suggested after a little more time had passed.

'A story?' said the captain, turning to look at me with a raised eyebrow.

'About Captain Cook,' I reminded him. 'Of how you were with him at the end. When he died.'

'When he was murdered, you mean,' he said quickly, correcting me.

'Aye, sir. When he was murdered.'

Captain Bligh sighed a little and shook his head. 'I shall tell you it, Turnstile,' he said. 'Do not convince yourself that we are close to the end of our travels yet. We have many more nights to while away before the end. I shall tell you, worry not.'

'But, sir—'

'Not today, lad,' he said, silencing me by placing a hand on my thin shoulder. 'Today we seek the Reefs. That is what is important.'

I sat back and frowned. I would have that story yet before I was done.

Day 31: 28 May

THE DAY WAS SPENT IN A FLUX between anticipation and disappointment, for we had hoped to make our way through the reefs and onwards to the tip of New Holland for rest and sustenance, but, damn and blast those waters, for they would offer us no entry. After several hours of attempts we began to notice breaker waves stirring around us and, afeared that we should lose our tub to the rocks they implied beneath us, the captain ordered that the launch be turned round and that we should sail forth and attempt access further along.

'Captain, please, sir,' implored one of the men from the rear of the tub, I forget who. 'We shall take a care with the rowing if you let us.'

'You may take all the care you want, sir,' came the stubborn reply. 'If the boat cracks up we're left here to die – you know that as well as I do.'

There were muttered complaints but he was right, of course. It was not something that we could risk. And so we turned back to the water and away from the Reef for now. It was a disheartening afternoon and the capture of a boobie from the sky and its dispersal between us eighteen unlucky fools served as cold comfort.

Day 32: 29 May

ON THIS DAY WE FINALLY managed to steer our small craft through the reefs and arrive safely at a shore, which the captain suggested was off the tip of New Holland. The excitement that led us there was tempered only by Mr Bligh's constant reminder that we should keep our wits about us, for it had been only a few short weeks since we had nearly all lost our lives to the natives of the Friendly Islands, although to my mind it felt as if it had been many months longer than that.

As our tub settled on the sand we scrambled out of it at a pace and were delighted to find our feet making touch at last with solid ground. We did not run and dance, extending our limbs and acting like a bunch of Bedlamites as we had once before; we were too weak for that, our heads too dizzy, our stomachs too empty, our spirits too low. Instead we lay down for a time – the sun was upon us for once – stripped our clothes off to dry and stretched our limbs, without fear for once of kicking another fellow in the face or punching him in the eye. As I lay there, I swore that this would be the contentment of the grave, but then I pushed the idea far from my mind, aware how close I was to that very place and how far I would have to travel yet to escape it.

When some time had passed and we felt our energies a little restored, the captain split us into two groups, one to search for food and water – anything that might sustain us – and the other to begin some necessary repairs to our boat.

'The island looks deserted, lads,' he warned us – I was one of the selected foragers, and happy to be so – 'but take care and keep your wits about you. The savages might be in hiding if they saw us coming, and if they are you can believe that they will out-number every one of us tenfold.'

'Aye, sir,' we said as we walked off through the trees to see what we might find. Our party was six or seven, I think; I can recall that Thomas Hall was with me, and Surgeon Ledward, and the gunner William Peckover, but if there were others I cannot remember for sure who they were. The experience of walking was a delight to me. To my surprise, I found myself both tired as I stepped along, despite the fact that I had spent so many weeks sitting in the cramped environment of the tub, and energized. I thought that to increase my pace would see me either collapse in a fit of exhaustion or break into a run that might never end. It was a curious sensation and one that I could not comprehend.

'Over here, lads,' said Peckover, and his call coincided with my ears picking up the most glorious sound known to man – the splash of water running in a stream. We made our way through more thickets and, sure enough, here was a place, no more than a dozen feet in square, but enough to satisfy us. The water was cold and invigorating and we fell to it like dogs lapping at a puddle. I found my own head dipping low into it and enjoyed the sensation of the non-salted water as it engulfed me. When we were sated – and I know not how long that took – we looked at one another and laughed helplessly.

'We shall be heroes,' said Surgeon Ledward, shaking his head as he glanced around. 'An endless supply for every man.'

One sentence was enough to provide a break and we fell to drinking again; this time I swore that I could feel the water making its way through my gut and into my belly and I wondered for a moment whether I might drink so much that I would pop that suffering organ, but I cared not and drank my fill.

'Lads, take a look,' said Thomas Hall, standing up a little uncertainly as he nodded towards the stretch of rocks that sprang from the ground and seemed to be dotted with shells about their surface. 'Could it be what I think?' The rest of us knew not what he thought, but it wasn't long before he reached for one – the half of the shell that was attached to the rock held its place and he pulled the other forward – and ripped it open, revealing a shiny pale oyster inside. 'Oh my stars,' he said with a sigh of delight, a sigh that sounded like the one I had heard myself make on every occasion when I did the unspeakables with Kaikala, a sigh of utter satisfaction and contentment. He pulled the mollusc from its cave, popped it into his mouth and closed his eyes with delirium at the taste of it. Within a very few moments we were all at it, grasping and opening and pulling and eating. Looking around, I saw there were thousands of the creatures and could not wait to return to the beach to tell the men.

Even better, on our return we stumbled across some wild thickets filled with red and black berries – tens of thousands, I should have said – and we set about them like a pack of animals, caring little for how the thorns pricked at our fingers. We ate until our bellies were full and our tongues discoloured and our mouths and lips misshapen by the acidity of the fruit. And every bite was like deliverance.

When we finally returned to the beach to tell the others of our

429

find, I was starting to feel ill inside and a throbbing had begun behind my eyes that threatened to pop my head open and send my brain falling to the beach in a mush. I clutched my stomach, groaning, and wondered whether it might have been a sensible idea not to eat so much so quickly after such a long period of starvation. I pictured the oysters and the berries mingling within myself and, as I reached the captain and he stared at my black- and red-seared lips, it was all I could do to maintain my stance.

'Turnstile,' he said, staring at me with surprise in his eyes as he tried to make sense of my appearance. From the side of my eyes I could see that he had managed to start a small fire with wood and kindling, the crafty fellow. 'What the devil did you find out there?'

I opened my mouth to tell him, but before I could utter a word I saw that there was little need, for the contents of my dinner spewed forth from my stomach, rejected like a eunuch at a brothel, and on to the sand between the captain – who danced nimbly out of the way – and myself, whereupon I stared at the colourful mess before blinking my eyes as if in a drunken stupor and collapsing backwards to pass out.

It was a fine afternoon. One of the best I can recall from that whole cursed voyage.

Day 33: 30 May

I MUST NOW RECOUNT something that sounds like a vulgarity but might, I believe, be of interest to those who should ever find themselves in a similar position. For several hours of this morn- ing I found myself enduring the most uncommon case of the squits that I have ever known. It felt as if every oyster and every berry I had eaten the day before was in revolt against their temporary tenancy of my digestive system and seeking immediate egress. And in the war that they waged against my bowels, they were most definitely the winners. I could barely walk, I was in so much pain, and no sooner had I completed a movement that suggested I was done with the nasty business for a while than the great heaves came on me again and I was to be discovered in a thicket, bent over double and straining to relieve myself.

It gave me some satisfaction that many of the other men were in a similar condition that day and it was obvious to all this was so whenever one of our party made a dash from the shore to the trees in seek of a little privacy. Some, including Mr Fryer, were quite pale at the continuation of it and others seemed hardly to suffer at all. The captain himself, who had suffered a similar misery on Otaheite, which had inflamed his temper something terrible, seemed entirely impervious to the effects of this food and, indeed, he took humour in it, passing several remarks that I for one found to be both out of character for him and in questionable taste.

We had established that this island was of no great size but had proved uncommon generous in the spoils that it offered. There were no savages there to bang their stones together and threaten to do the same to our heads either, and that was a clear advantage. In truth, I think many of our number would have cheerfully stayed there, in this place the captain named Restoration Island on account of our arrival there coinciding with the date of the Restoration of King Charles II to the Throne, but the captain was having none of it. He was a terrible man for insisting on getting us home.

And so we spent this day filling our stomachs again – even those of us for whom the dining was a sure route to the bushes – and collecting as many oysters and berries as we could find to store in the captain's crate for the next part of our journey. We took all the flagons and coconut shells we could lay hands on and filled them with fresh water from the spring; indeed, by the time we were ready to depart, our provisions appeared to our eyes to be of healthy proportions, although in retrospect I realize that in truth they were scarcely enough to feed a couple of men for a couple of days, let alone eighteen men for who-knew-what length of time. It was simply the fact that the crate was full again that excited us. We little thought that on the morrow we would be down to our daily morsels and thimblefuls of waters if we were to make any attempt at survival.

'Get a good sleep tonight, lads,' said the captain as we settled down on the beach for a decent rest. 'We need your energies restored to their natural levels if we are to make Timor. Or as near to them as we can muster.'

I fell asleep that night watching the sun descend to the horizon and I stretched out a yawn, sure that the next part of our voyage would be successful and healthy. We had made it this far, after all, against all the odds and with the loss of only one life. Surely we could not fail now.

Day 34: 31 May

THE CAPTAIN LED US in prayers before we set sail this day and I was fierce surprised of it, for it had never been a regular part of our daily rituals. He offered up some thanks to the Saviour for allowing us to get this far unharmed – tell that to John Norton, I couldn't help but think – and beseeched Him to take pity on our troublesome tub and allow us to reach our destination safely and quickly. Every man jack of us uttered 'Amen' at the end but, in truth, I do not think that we were a spiritual lot. Sailors, I have found, rarely are. They care more for superstitions and ideas of magic.

We set sail in early afternoon when the sun was high and we

did it with a heavy heart, for we knew not when we would set foot on land again. However, to our surprise – although apparently not to Captain Bligh's – we found ourselves passing a number of islands along the way and, as evening fell and we had reached no further towards open seas, the captain determined that it would be a sensible thing for us to beach at one of them, which he said he thought might be an island called Fair Cape, and rest again for the night. We did so and there was a sense of anticlimax about it, for we did not attack the shore with our usual delight and mania, nor did we instantly go in search of food and water, although the captain allowed us to eat our fill as long as we committed to refilling our crate the following morning before departing again.

We agreed readily to this and spent a happy evening on the beach, where Robert Lamb revealed a previously unrealized talent for singing. He entertained us with several songs of a bawdy nature regarding the adventures of a tart by the name of Melody Blunt, who appeared to have neither morals nor choosiness about her conquests, and we all laughed heartily – even the captain, who tended to shy away from vulgarities – and afterwards I slept soundly with images of Miss Melody Blunt in my mind. However, not for the first time since leaving the *Bounty* I found that I was with the motions again and remembered what a terrible curse they could be.

Day 35: 1 June

W E SET SAIL AGAIN after a morning spent foraging in the thickets for any food that might later offer nourishment, three separate groups travelling in three separate directions, but only one was successful and when they returned to the camp with armfuls of berries their mouths were red and stained dark with juices and I knew that they had indulged themselves just as much as I had done a few days previously. We loaded ourselves back into the tub and set sail northwest by west-northwest and Mr Fryer and Peter Linkletter steered us quickly and carefully through the reefs, avoiding any trouble with the rocks below and delivering us out into wider waters without incident. I had a moment of great joy when, observing some fish passing by our stern and in towards the reefs, I plunged both hands together into the water and then pulled them up just as suddenly, and to my surprise a great white fish leapt, startled, out of the surf and found itself landing not in the water again but on the deck of our launch. Great delight was taken by all at this, for there was nothing like a fish to make a tasty supper, and the captain clapped me on the back to congratulate me and the men called me a fine fellow indeed and I began to think that perhaps I was forgiven for losing the spear during our voyage.

The waters were peaceful that afternoon and my thoughts turned back to Otaheite and the men who had driven us from the safety of the *Bounty* to the danger of the tub. It had been more than a month now since we had set forth on our adventures and I wondered how life had treated Mr Christian and his ilk during the same period. They would have returned to the island immediately, that was for sure, but whether they had been able to stay there was a different matter entirely. After all, they would assume that should we survive we would return home to England and the admirals would send another ship to hunt them down. It was my guess that the pirates would take the women they wanted and find another island near by. There were so many hundreds of them dotted around that part of the ocean that it would have been no great hardship for them to locate a remote one, difficult to access, and set up their new homes there, perhaps sinking the *Bounty* entirely so that they might never be spotted.

On the other hand, they might have stayed on Otaheite, safe in the assumption that the nineteen men who had once been their fellow sailors and friends would have died quickly, drowned in those southern Pacific waters, and that the truth of their cowardice and depravity would never emerge. Despite the differences I had with many of those men and officers, it saddened me to think that they would be happy to see me dead.

As evening fell, a great commotion came upon the launch when David Nelson, William Cole and William Purcell – the three men who had united to become the successful group of food-finders earlier in the day – began to complain of great pains in their stomachs and a pounding in their heads behind their eyes. Surgeon Ledward examined them and we each of us watched as he held their wrists between thumb and forefinger and pressed the flat of his palm to their bellies and nether regions. He approached the captain immediately and they spoke in hushed tones that I believe only Mr Elphinstone and I had access to.

'They are poisoned, sir,' said the surgeon. 'You saw them when they returned from their foraging. They have eaten too many of the berries. I suggest that they were poisonous berries.'

'Good God,' replied the captain, stroking his beard and looking worried at the thought of it. 'You think they will be taken from us?'

'Probably not,' he answered, shaking his head. 'I do think they will have a day or two of the most appalling pains, though. It will not go easy for them.'

'Let us avoid the use of the word *poison*, then,' insisted Mr Bligh. 'It will do our morale no good and will not change the present conditions.' He stood up then and made his way down the launch to our three stricken fellows. 'It seems that you have eaten more than your fill of berries while on Fair Cape, and our bellies are not ready for such abuse. You have naught to worry about, though. Like all things, these pains will pass.'

William Purcell seemed less than happy about this diagnosis and gave out a great cry of agony even as he clutched his stomach

435

and pulled his knees up closer towards his chest, but the captain merely nodded at him as if this was the end of the matter and returned to his seat.

That night was filled with the groaning of the three men and as the light grew dim and we were surrounded by darkness I confess I had murderous thoughts towards them, for, uncharitable of me as it was, I confess they fair gave me the chills every time they let out another cry of agony.

Day 36: 2 June

DESPITE THE FACT that I had spent eighteen months in company with the ship's master, Mr Fryer, I had enjoyed little conversation with him. He had been welcoming of me on my first arrival on the *Bounty* – indeed, after Mr Hall, who I had considered a weaselly thing, he was the first member of the ship's crew I had chanced upon, outside the captain's cabin on that fine day before Christmas 1787 – but since then had rarely so much as acknowledged my presence, so caught up was he with his duties on board the ship and his attempts to keep a civil relationship with Mr Bligh.

I was most surprised, then, to wake this day after an afternoon snooze to find my head using his knees as a pillow and he not in the least offended by it.

'Begging your pardon, sir,' I said, sitting up in a mortification and rubbing the sleep from my eyes. 'I don't know how that came about. A man will do strange things in his sleep, that's for sure.'

'Think nothing of it, lad,' he replied with a shrug, as if the matter meant not a jot to him. 'You got some sleep and revived your energies, that's what counts.'

'Aye, sir,' I said, pulling myself together and stretching my body as much as I could as I lay my back against the side of the tub beside him. I looked forward at the faces of William Cole and David Nelson as they rowed the launch; I swear I could see a translucence to their skin and their eyes had never looked more haunted or black.

'Who is this Mr Lewis, might I ask?' said Mr Fryer after a few moments had passed.

I confess I could have jumped overboard in surprise. 'Mr Lewis?' I said, quite forgetting my place. 'What do you know of him?'

'Nothing at all,' he replied. 'But you spoke of him in your sleep, that's all.'

I narrowed my eyes and felt a slight pain in my stomach, but as that part of my body had been in a constant spasm of agony for more than a month I gave it scarce consideration. 'I spoke of Mr Lewis?' I asked. 'And what did I say?'

'Nothing intelligible,' he said. 'Was he just a fancy of your dream? You cried out for him to unhand you, that was all. You said you would never go back.'

I nodded my head and stayed silent, considering it. I could recall nothing of my reverie. 'Aye,' I said finally. 'He was just a fancy, nothing more. I was unaware that I spoke in my sleep.'

'We all do from time to time,' he replied. 'I remember my dear wife Mary telling me that I had a tendency to talk about owls at the darkest part of the night.'

'Owls, sir?'

'Yes. It's a curious thing as I have no interest in owls whatsoever. But there we are. It's part of the games that the mind plays on us.'

I agreed that it was and looked out at the sea, smothering a yawn that might have sent me back to my reveries had we not been engaged in conversation. I threw Mr Fryer a look and noted how his beard had become red at the edges but grey at the tip. I was unsure how old he was – in his late thirties, I would have suggested – but our time at sea had done him no favours, as he appeared to be ageing before my very eyes.

'Sir,' I said after a long silence, a question that I had long wanted to ask him coming into my head. 'Sir, might I ask you something?'

'You might,' he said, turning towards me.

'It's just that I don't know whether you'll be pleased with the question, that's all. But I have a mind to know the answer.'

He gave me a smile and indicated the wide expanse of ocean that surrounded us. 'Turnstile,' he said, 'we maintain the farce of rank aboard a vessel like this in order that we might reach our destination safely. But looking around, don't you feel a certain equality of status with your fellow sailors? We might drown together at any moment and, if we do, we each of us will end up in the same place.'

'Aye, sir,' I replied, for there was no denying that true remark. 'Then, I shall ask it. I have wondered how it is that you came to be here.'

'Here, on this launch?' he asked, raising an eyebrow. 'Have you lost your senses, boy? We were put here by the traitors—'

'No,' I said, interrupting him and shaking my head. 'You misunderstand me, sir. I mean how is it that you joined the captain in the tub and didn't stay with Mr Christian? Otaheite was a fine place, sir, we all know that. And there were great delights to be had there. And if you don't mind my saying so, Mr Fryer, it has always seemed to me that you and the captain were not exactly brothers-at-arms.'

He laughed a little at this phrase and I smiled too, pleased that he was not angered with me for the sauce of it, but finally he gave a little shrug and lowered his voice as he answered me.

'You might well ask it,' he said. 'I dare say many of the men wonder at it. And you're right in thinking that the captain and I have had our . . . disagreements during the voyage.'

'I'm a great admirer of the captain, sir,' said I quickly. 'As I hope you know. And I'd never say a word against him. But I did think at times he treated you fierce hard.'

'Thank you, Turnstile,' he said, acknowledging this. 'It's thoughtful of you to say, especially since your loyalties are so clearly with Mr Bligh. Your devotion to him is well known by every man on board this tub and every man on Otaheite.'

I was surprised by this; I had never expected that others saw me as such a loyal character or even thought of it. Still, it gave me a warm sensation inside and I was glad of it.

'The truth of it is,' he continued, 'that I have not always been as well disposed towards the captain as I might have been. I have considered him cantankerous and rude, pig-headed and even simple-minded at times.'

'Mr Fryer!'

'We are talking as equals, are we not? We may speak as we find?'

'Aye, sir, but to say such a thing—'

'Is simply the truth of my feeling towards him. I have observed a man so weighed down by bitterness at his lack of rank – I refer of course to his lack of status as captain and his actual insignia as lieutenant – that he has allowed it to cloud his judgement at times. This sense of inferiority was well played upon by Mr Christian throughout our voyage. I could see that, but there was little I could do to resolve it. The captain envied Mr Christian's birth, his status, his privilege. Even, perhaps, his prettiness.'

My mouth fell open in surprise. I had never heard any man on board speak so freely.

'I will admit that I never saw the mutiny coming, but I do think the captain at times behaved in ways that incited the men un-necessarily. Insisting that they sleep on board the ship towards the end of our stay on the island, for example, was low of him. There was no call for it and it only made the men realize what they would be missing when they left. They had formed friendships and love affairs; to rip them away from that without consideration was ill-judged. I expected a great deal of trouble on our homeward trip, but not this.' He gestured around us both. 'Not this, Turnstile, never this.'

'Then, why . . . ?' I asked, hesitating as I tried to choose my words carefully. 'Then, why did you come with us?' I continued. 'Why did you not stay with the mutineers?'

'Because they were scoundrels, that's why,' he explained. 'And I took an oath of allegiance to the king when I joined the navy, as well as an oath to uphold the orders of my commanding officer. For the last eighteen months Mr William Bligh has been my commanding officer and, that being the case, I will obey him until the last drop of blood has left my body and the last breath has left my soul. It is called duty, John Jacob Turnstile. Duty, loyalty and good service. It is the best traditions of the English navy, the traditions in which my father and his father before him and his father before him served. It is the tradition in which I would want my own son to serve. There is nothing that Mr Bligh could have said or done to turn me agin' him. He is in charge, he is the king's man. It's as simple as that.'

I nodded, satisfied with the reply. It was not what I had expected of him, but it gave me a clearer idea of who the man was.

'And besides,' he said a few moments later, 'I wanted to go home and see my wife again. Duty, loyalty and good service are one thing, lad, but love is another. Perhaps you'll discover that for yourself one day.'

I smiled and took on the reddenings at the idea of it. I wondered whether these were traits I could hope for in my own future, whatever that may hold, however long or short it might be. Duty, loyalty and good service.

And love.

Day 37: 3 June

A S THE RAINS POURED DOWN on our heads, Surgeon Ledward
found himself in the intolerable position of having to attend
to himself, for he suffered the most hideous cramps in his
stomach and bowels, and on noting the whiteness of his face I
confess that I said a prayer to the Saviour that He might relieve
him of his suffering and allow him his reward. It was not to be,
however, for the poor man continued to feel the twin pressures of
fatigue and starvation and held his body tight to himself, uttering
cries from time to time that elicited both great sympathy and great
irritation from his fellow passengers.

The captain went to his side at one point but, not being trained
in the medical arts, could do little to help his condition; instead
he lay down very low beside him and talked to him in his ear. I
could not hear what was said – none of us could – but perhaps it
did some good, because his rolling and crying came to an end
soon enough and before long he was just another soul in the
boat, struggling to maintain both his spirits and his life against
the oppressive forces of rain, sea and debasement.

We came close to some more reefs in the afternoon, and then
to a series of small uninhabited islands, narrow enough that a
healthy man might have trod his way from one side to the other
in a morning. We landed briefly at several of these in the hope of
finding more food, and Mr Bligh himself collected an armful
of oysters, but they were so small they would have scarce
comprised one man's breakfast, let alone dinner for eighteen.

On the second island we found traces of turtle life but, to our
disappointment, no turtles. We combed the thickets and beaches

for them, but either they were too wise to be discovered or had blended as chameleons might into the glades, and once again we left with naught. By nightfall we were in our tub once again and setting forth for what the captain called the island of Timor but what we had named We-knew-not-where.

'Oh, for an hour of Michael Byrn now,' came a voice from the centre of the launch as we moved quietly through the night waters. I nodded my head in agreement, for a little music from our ship's fiddle-player would surely have lifted our spirits a deal; even the memory of our nightly dancing to invigorate our blood-streams was a happy one.

'Mr Byrn is a pirate and a mutineer,' snapped Captain Bligh in reply. 'And I'll not have his name uttered on this launch.'

'Aye, but he could give "Nancy o' the Gales" a good seeing-to,' said Mr Hall a little sorrowfully, and I could not help but recall that evening when he had been selected to dance to that very song and I had made the careless choice of Mr Heywood, the scut, as his molly. It all seemed so long ago now. A different lifetime. When I had been a mere lad.

'I don't care to hear of it,' said the captain, and I could tell by his tone that in other circumstances he would have shouted this out, but that on this night he was too fatigued to strain his voice. 'If another man wants to give voice to song, then so be it,' he added. 'But let us know of no treason-makers and let us not have that song.'

No one bothered. We had scarcely the energy.

Day 38: 4 June

FLETCHER CHRISTIAN, the miserable swine, had allowed Mr Bligh to bring his log with him when he was forcibly evicted from his rightful command, and the captain spent a good part of every evening scratching away on it with a pencil. Some nights he wrote for a long time, on others he wrote briefly, but I swear that a day did not pass on our voyage that some mention of our progress did not get taken down.

'Because we shall eventually return home,' he told me with a half-smile when I enquired as to why he bothered with it. 'And when we do, I believe that we shall have completed a most remarkable piece of navigation. I write the log as a record of all that has taken place since our exit from the *Bounty*, and also to make notes of the islands and reefs and shorelines we have spotted along the way. It's my duty, you see, as a seafaring man.'

'Do you write about me in there, sir?' I asked.

He let out a short laugh and shook his head. 'It is not a melodrama, Master Turnstile,' he said. 'It is a record of places and sights, the flora and fauna, the longitude and latitude of places that might be of interest to future travelling men. It is not my personal diary.'

'Do you mean to make a book of it?' I asked him then.

'A book?' he said, frowning a little and considering it. 'I had never considered such a thing. I imagine it might be a record for the admirals, not for the populace. Do you think it would be of interest to the general reader?'

I gave a small shrug, for what knew I of readers, I who had only read two books in my lifetime and both of them concerned with the land of China? 'I imagine you might ask Mr Zéla about that,' I suggested. 'The French gentleman, I mean. Him what got me into this messy business in the first place.'

'Ah, Matthieu, yes,' he said, nodding his head. 'Although truthfully, Master Turnstile, I think it was rather more your own fault that you ended up in your position on board our ship and not his, don't you?'

'Perhaps,' I admitted.

'But you might be right,' he said, writing a little more. 'The admiralty might see fit to publish my report so that the decent men and ladies of England would know exactly the character of officers such as Fletcher Christian and Peter Heywood. Their names will live in infamy after this, Turnstile, you mark me.' I didn't doubt it for a moment and told him so, suggesting that his memories would make worthy reading. The captain smiled at me and gave a gentle half-laugh. 'Turnstile, have you taken too much o' the sun?'

'No, sir. Why?'

'You're uncommon lively today.'

'It's my character, sir,' I replied, a little offended by the comment. 'Haven't you noticed it?'

Making no reply, he looked around at the dots of islands we were passing on left and right as we made our way into the open ocean. 'The Endeavour Strait,' he told me. 'It is magnificent, isn't it? Our ordeal was almost worth it just to pass through here in such a vessel.'

'Aye, sir,' I said, glancing around, and in truth he was right. It was a pretty sight to behold and might have been prettier had I not been staring at water without cessation for more than a month since.

Day 39: 5 June

A ND HERE WAS THE TORMENT OF IT. We had been sailing for thirty-eight days already and stopped at islands, when we could find them, for rest and sustenance, but I knew only too well from the maps I had studied day after day for a year in the captain's cabin that, when we passed through the Endeavour Strait, then there was nowhere left for us to go but onwards to Timor, and that was at least a week away from us. We would have to maintain our provisions and survive both hunger and drought until we next saw land, but when we did – *if* we did – our journey would be over and we would be saved.

There was a look of resignation on the faces of many of the men on this day. Some, such as Peter Linkletter and George Simpson – who had good days and bad days as far as his sanity was concerned – looked afeared of what was to come, and I do believe that the slightest expression of doubt voiced by any of the other men would have been the cause of consternation. Others, such as Robert Lamb, appeared almost excited by the challenge ahead, confident in the knowledge that, whatever happened, we would not have to endure this hardship for much longer. And then there were men like Captain Bligh and Mr Fryer, who wore their usual expressions – of forbearance – and looked ever outward for salvation. In my head I had the fears of the first group; in my soul, the bravery of the second; and in my heart, a desire to be like the third, for it was they who would ensure our survival, or so I believed.

As the captain provided our dinner that night from the crate, he was met with sighs and signs of a certain amount of disappointment from the men.

'You know where we stand,' he said, shaking his head. 'You know what is ahead of us this last week or more. We must eat only enough to keep mind and body functioning. We have no alternative if we are to survive.'

The men agreed, of course we did, but it made things no easier. This was our final challenge. And it began today, on our thirty-ninth day.

Day 40: 6 June

I HAD A LIGHT-HEADED FEELING throughout the day, as if my mind was not fully my own. After rowing for two hours, I stood up and had to grab the shoulders of two men or I would have fallen over, and they were unhappy about it and told me so. I tried to consult with Surgeon Ledward on the issue, but he was in a sleep that came and went and when he was conscious he did not seem himself at all, so I left him alone.

Other than that I can recall little of the day except a few grumblings from the men when the captain cancelled the middle meal of the day and offered us breakfast and supper only, and scant feedings at either of them. There was little that he could do. He wanted us to survive.

The rain was miserable too, I remember that much.

Day 41: 7 June

I WAS ILL AGAIN THIS DAY and every time I looked upwards towards the heavens I found that I had to grip something on either side of me to keep some semblance of reality. One of my eyes – my left, as I recall – took on a shading whereby I could not rightly say that I saw through it. I blinked away at it furiously but it made no difference and when I reported this to the captain he said it was the fact of my hunger playing tricks with my body. He sought agreement from Surgeon Ledward on this score, but that man merely nodded and said it was so and turned away from us, a rare thing to do to the captain. He appeared to me to be suffering from the depressions, though, and so was left alone on account of it.

'Perhaps when you awaken tomorrow it will be better,' the captain remarked, which comment only served to irritate me and not help a jot.

'And perhaps I'll be blind in both eyes,' I suggested. 'Must I wait until tomorrow to find out?'

'Well, what would you have me do, Turnstile?' he asked, equally irritated. 'Our focus must be on survival, nothing else.'

Swearing an oath under my breath, I stepped away from him and returned to my seat, which in my absence had been invaded a little by three separate men, who caused me to lash out at them verbally before they would agree to move. I felt as if the days were growing lengthier somehow and my tolerance levels for the torment we were suffering were decreasing with every minute. In the past there had always been the hope of an island, a place where we could rest and eat and where we knew we would not drown. Now there was nothing but ocean and it was a fierce lonely place to be. The captain said he knew not when we would spot Timor, perhaps a week yet, and I wondered whether we would all survive the voyage. Indeed, we were fortunate to have lost only one man so far – John Norton – although there were at least half a dozen souls in the tub who seemed to me to be destined for their reward in a very short time, should salvation not come to us.

In truth, I felt as if I was one of them.

Day 42: 8 June

THERE WAS MUCH CONSTERNATION today over the condition of Surgeon Ledward, who appeared to be sinking very fast, and as a consequence of it the captain gave him a larger ration of food and water than the rest of us received and we made no complaint on it. To my dismay I was left seated near him for much of the day and I didn't care for it, for I was sure he was going to expire directly in front of me and that would be a terrible omen for my own survival. It transpired I was being overly pessimistic and he remained with us throughout the day, as did others – Lawrence LeBogue among them – who were suffering nearly as badly themselves.

Mr Hall and I spent two hours side by side rowing the launch, and when we were relieved and replaced by William Peckover and the captain we took a seat together near the fore of the tub. I noticed then that the cook had a curious smile pasted across his phizzy and I demanded to know the reason for it, for I was sure that he was making a farce of me in his head.

'Keep your britches on, lad,' he said, a fine statement to make considering that those same britches were already in a terrible state of disrepair, with shreds and rips throughout. 'I were just thinking back, that was all. To when you first stepped on board the *Bounty*. How green you were then.'

'Aye, it's true,' I admitted, nodding my head. 'But then I had never been on board a ship before let alone one of His Majesty's frigates. You'll forgive me if I didn't fully know my way around.'

'You learned it quick enough, I'll give you that,' he said.

'And you were friendly to me when I arrived,' I replied. 'Unlike Mr Samuel, the old weasel: he made me feel inferior from the moment I stepped aboard. Told me that every man jack on the ship was above me and ordered me about like nobody's business.'

'I never cared for him,' said Mr Hall, curling his lip in distaste. 'It didn't surprise me in the least when he took up with Mr Christian and his pirates. He had an air of disloyalty about him from the start. I dare say he's making merry with half the mollies of Otaheite by this time,' he added with a sigh.

'He were an ugly sod,' I remarked. 'They wouldn't let him near them.'

'And you, Turnip,' he said. 'Do you miss the island?'

'I miss the sustenance,' I replied. 'I miss the feeling of food in my belly and a decent place to sleep at night. I miss the confidence of knowing that I would wake up alive in the morning.'

'And your young molly?'

'And her,' I admitted. 'A little, anyway. Even though she betrayed me for the scut Mr Heywood. But, still and all, she were fun at the time. Aye, I miss her.'

I found myself growing surprisingly misty-eyed in my good eye as I said this – my bad one was still covered by a misty haze that showed no sign of leaving me.

'There'll be others,' he said. 'When you're back in England, I mean. You'll fall in love again.'

I nodded and agreed that I would, but I wasn't so sure. There was no guarantee, after all, that I would ever see England again, let alone find love there. But we had to remain optimistic. It was either that or take a plunge in the ocean and not bother to come back up for air.

The evening time brought more rain and more stomach pangs. At one point they stabbed so hard that I cried out and was told to silence myself by the others, but by God the pain was so bad that I thought I was done for.

Day 43: 9 June

WE SUFFERED TERRIBLY through this day with rain and gales, starvation and a lack of water, and though finally we moved into calmer waters I felt my spirits at as low an ebb as I could ever recall them being. It was then, while seated quietly by the side of the tub, that the captain sat down beside me and began to speak in a quiet voice.

'We were at Kealakekua Bay in Hawaii at the time,' he told me, without any preamble. 'On board the *Resolution*. We had been there for some time and it was clear to all that tensions between ourselves and the savages were mounting. Things had started well, of course. Captain Cook was nothing if not able to impress a native chief. But they had dissipated terribly. I always believed the captain was too soft with the natives. He had too great a belief in their basic good.'

I sat up a little, surprised he had chosen this particular evening to relate the story, but pleased that he had. Perhaps he had seen how low my own spirits were.

'On this particular day,' he continued, 'an incident occurred, small in itself, but, added to a series of smaller insults over recent days, it was enough to push us over the edge. When we were anchored in warmer climes the captain preferred to leave the cutters and launches from the ship in the water and one of these, the large cutter, was stolen by the savages. It was unacceptable, of course, and when he heard of it the captain stated that the bay was to be blockaded until the cutter was returned to us. He sent out two crafts; a fellow by the name of John Williamson was in charge of the launch, and I myself captained the small cutter.'

'You, sir?' I asked, wide-eyed. 'You went to retrieve the stolen boat?'

'Aye, in a way. And had they surrendered it peacefully there would have been fewer consequences. But as we approached the bay it became clear that there was no peace in store for us. The natives were dotted along the tops of the cliffs, adopting war-like stances and wearing the type of garb they felt would protect them from our cutlasses and muskets. They were prepared for battle, that was clear to us all.'

'But why, Captain?' I asked him. 'Had they turned against you?'

'I believe so,' he replied. 'At first all had been well, but they did not recognize our right to their land or their produce. They were becoming belligerent about it. We had no choice but to show our strength.'

'What rights, sir?' I asked, confused.

'Our rights as emissaries of the king, Turnstile,' he said, staring at me as if I was the worst kind of fool. 'Isn't that clear? They wanted us to leave them in peace. Savages! Ordering Englishmen away!'

'From their land.'

'But you're missing the point,' he insisted, as if the idea was quite a simple one. 'It was no longer their land when we arrived. We claimed it. Anyway, as we approached, it became increasingly clear that there would be trouble and it was then that I noticed a large canoe of perhaps twenty savages setting forth from the bay, bound, no doubt, for the *Resolution*. They were eager, I'll give them that, for they rowed at such a pace that I had to put the fear of God into all my own rowers in order to make them change direction and row westward to cut them off. When we were close enough we raised our muskets and fired at them and, with grace and justice on our side, managed to pick off some of the rowers instantly. The rest, a cowardly bunch, dived into the water and the canoe capsized immediately, and those savages who had not been fatally injured swam back to shore. It was an early victory for us, to show strength, and had they recognized this perhaps things would not have continued.

'The next thing I knew, Captain Cook himself, along with four or five other men, was sailing towards us in a cutter. We held our position until he reached us and he was in a fury, a terrible fury.

' "There will be no more bloodshed," he informed me, as if I had been the author of the misadventure. "I am going on shore and I shall take the king hostage, bring him back to the *Resolution* and detain him there until all our boats and belongings have been returned to us."

' "But, Captain," ' I said, appalled by the idea, "Is that wise? When we have just—"

' "You may join me, Mr Bligh," he said through gritted teeth. "Or you may return to the *Resolution*. Which is it to be?"

'Well, needless to say, I leapt from the cutter into the launch and we were quickly on shore and the captain, marching ahead, made directly for the home of the island's high priest, with whom he had already established good relations, and informed him that we meant no harm to any of his people, only that we would not be the victims of a theft, not while we had breath in our bodies. He informed him of his plan to take the king with him back to the *Resolution*, but said that he would merely be detained as our guest, not a captive, and it was up to the priest to ensure that matters were brought to a speedy and happy solution.

'Without waiting for a reply, the captain then made his way for to village, even as some of our men were landing in the bay, armed with muskets. I heard the roar of canons from our ship and assumed that more canoes were leaving the bay and aiming towards them and one of the officers had taken the decision to blow them out of the waters. I considered this very sensible and said as much, and the captain turned on me in a fury and said, "Damn and blast it, this is how an incident becomes a catastrophe. Every shot that is fired destroys our reputations and lessens our relationship with these people. Don't you see that?" I told him that of course he was right, but it was good to show the savages who were their masters, and I presume he agreed with me, for he said nothing, simply continued on his way. I later learned that the other canoes, those that had not been damaged by the canon-fire, turned back towards Kealakekua, no doubt seeking vengeance for their fallen colleagues.

'We arrived at King Terreeaboo's house and the captain waited outside. When the king appeared, flanked by his two sons, Captain Cook extended an invitation to him to join him for dinner in his own quarters on the *Resolution*, and the king happily agreed. He was an aged fellow, Turnstile, and had to be helped back to the shore by his two sons, and none of them were aware that we had greater plans in mind. They considered it a simple act of hospitality, such as they had received from us on many occasions in the past.

'When we arrived on shore, the canoeists had returned and it was obvious that a great drama was about to unfold. Word spread immediately to the king's sons that both my launch and the *Resolution* itself had fired on the savages, killing some, and immediately a great cry went up, and in the mêlée the king fell and landed heavily on the beach.

'At this, events turned beyond control. The natives surrounded us and began throwing stones, knocking several of our men over, and our muskets were drawn and we had no choice but to fire at them. The captain was shouting something at me but I couldn't hear it, and I shot several of the savages dead even as they approached me. I turned to look at Captain Cook, delighted by my kill, and he was running towards me, no doubt to con-gratulate me, and, as he did, one of the savages ran at him from behind bearing a great boulder, which he crashed down on the great man's head. In a moment, he had fallen to the beach, but he rolled over immediately to defend himself. Before he could, another savage was upon him with a dagger, the cowardly swine, and he sank it deep into the captain's neck before dragging him a little forward and holding his head under the water. I made moves towards him, but a crowd of twenty or more savages were running towards my sailors and me. We were outnumbered five to one and had no choice but to turn and flee. We were fortunate that we managed to make our way back to our launch with no other injury than a rain of stones about our heads, but even as we sailed away I saw the captain, that brave man, rise once more to defend himself, clamber over some rocks, and then one last group of men descended on him with great stones and beat him to death.'

He became very silent after telling me this and his voice hesitated.

'It was murder, a terrible crime,' he said finally. 'But it is a fact of our lives, the end that any of us can come to if we accept the king's shilling. The question is how courageously we fall. And we avenged ourselves on those fellows most bloodily, of course. They lived only a short time to regret their deeds.'

I sat back and thought on it. It was not quite as I had expected the story to be, but he had told it now, he had done what I had asked, and there seemed little left for either of us to say. I couldn't help but wonder about his part in the drama, and perhaps he felt a little of that too in his retelling of the dreadful tale, but if he held regrets he made no mention of them. Finally he stood up and relieved one of the rowers, taking the oars in his great hands and urging his companion to row, to row faster, ever faster, that we might make our destination all the sooner.

That night, it should be told, we fair swept through the waters.

454

Day 44: 10 June

D<small>AVID</small> N<small>ELSON</small> and Lawrence LeBogue recovered a little today and it became clear that they would not be receiving their reward immediately. They sat up and ingested a little bread and water – more than their share, on the captain's orders – and seemed much improved.

The captain himself fell ill late in the day, suffering from an abnormality of the stomach, and was greatly aggrieved and not to be spoken to for much of the evening. For the first time in our voyage he curled up like a baby, hugging his body to himself for warmth, though with little success as it became impossible to do so when the rain soaked our clothes.

Later we saw some gannets and boobies, which gave us hope that we were near Timor, but the horizon offered nothing as yet and we had scant choice but to sail on.

Day 45: 11 June

B<small>Y THIS MORNING</small> the captain had recovered somewhat but he looked a miserable creature, as we all did. Our faces seemed sunken and hollowed-out, the limbs of many men appeared either to have contracted or become swollen intolerably by our cramped conditions, and we were sleeping for large parts of the day. I recall thinking that my life now consisted of only two things: rowing our launch or lying asleep. Conversation had died, argument had diffused, hope simmered gently.

When implored by the men to gauge the distance, Captain Bligh insisted that it would not be long now and we should be alert, every man jack of us, for the sight of land in case we had drifted too far off our course, that it would take keen eyes to discover it, but many of us had difficulties with this proposition, for our sight was lowly. My left eye had improved a little, but the shadow remained behind it and, although I had no glass to prove it, I doubted that I was the pretty lad I had been when I had left Portsmouth, or even Otaheite.

It was at this stage that my spirits sank again. Forty-five days we had been at sea and, while I yet lived, it was a miserable existence. I longed for freedom, for land to run upon, a fine meal to eat. I found myself regretting painfully the fact that I had chosen loyalty to the captain over a life of ease and sensual pleasure on the island. I found my anger bubbling and when I looked towards Mr Bligh I wondered what manner of man was he anyway, and why I had followed him when I was heading towards certain death.

I longed for food and water.

I was desperate for it.

Day 46: 12 June

I SLEPT.

I dreamed of the Portsmouth streets, empty and desolate, the winds blowing, the fruit stalls fallen over. I saw myself running towards Mr Lewis's establishment, desperate to see him, flinging open the doors and charging up the stairs to where my bunk and those of my brothers lay, but they were empty and the sheets pulled away. I looked around. I was alone.

I woke.

I sat by the oars with someone rowing beside me, who I knew not. I extended my arms and pulled them back in, dragging the water with me. I watched the horizon. I ran my tongue along my lips, hoping to find some moisture there. The sun burned down on me. I rowed and perhaps could have rowed until I died, only the captain told me my time had come and I slid away and found a small piece of the tub to call my own.

And I slept.

I saw the *Bounty* and happy days on it. I pictured sitting at the captain's table in his pantry with a fine meal before me, the captain and Mr Fryer on either side of me. The Frenchman, Mr Zéla, seated opposite. Captain Cook telling a story about an adventure he had enjoyed on the *Endeavour*. And then him pointing a fork at Mr Bligh and making an accusatory remark, at which point—

I woke.

I looked towards the horizon. Nothing. I stared at the sailors. None of us spoke. Mr Bligh divided a morsel of bread into eighteen and when he handed me mine I started to laugh, a queer sort of laughter, though, for there was no humour in it. I looked at the piece of bread; no bigger than my thumbnail, it was intended to last me for the day. I don't know what made me do it, but I rested my arm over the side of the tub, the bread held twixt thumb and forefinger, and released it to the water. Mr Elphinstone opened his eyes when he saw me do it, but made no signal; then he closed them again. I watched as the morsel bobbed for a moment or two on the surface of the water and then, to my surprise, a fish appeared and swallowed my breakfast, my lunch, my supper, before plunging down into the depths again.

It made no difference. There was no point eating any more.

Death was before me.

I could feel it.

457

Day 47: 13 June

SLEEP.
Hunger.
Rowing.
Hunger.
Thirst.
Hunger.
Nothing more.

Day 48: 14 June

THE CAPTAIN PLACED the bread in my mouth.

'Eat, Turnstile,' he said. 'You must eat.'

I locked my lips together. I no longer wanted it. I wanted him to leave me alone, to let me go.

'Get away,' I said, forgetting my station and pushing his hand away.

'Mr Fryer, hold his mouth open.'

A pair of unfamiliar fingers pressed my lips, separating them. I allowed it. My tongue extended and I tasted their salt. Then the bread, which I chewed although it made me ill to do so. Then a taste of water.

'Captain, that's your—'

'Quiet, Mr Fryer,' he whispered. 'The lad is going. I'll not have that.'

'But you are as important—'

'Quiet, sir,' he said beneath his breath.

I opened my eyes for a moment and there was brightness, the sun pouring down. I blinked and it was night. The rains seemed to have stopped and the gales too, or I could not feel them any more anyway. I could feel naught. My arms and legs were as light as feathers. The pangs in my belly had vanished too. In a moment of clarity I felt that my reward was due, that the Saviour was calling me home. Beneath my head there seemed to be a pillow, but how? I pressed my skull down a little and met with the solidity of bone. Looking up I saw Mr Bligh; my head rested in his lap, his hand was slowly combing my hair with his fingers. I smiled at him and for a moment he caught my eyes and smiled back.

'Stay awake, John Jacob,' he said and his voice was half-gone now too. He wasn't whispering; there was simply no way that he could speak any louder. 'We will survive. We will all survive.'

'He wants me back,' I said.

'Who does?'

'The Saviour,' I replied.

'Not yet, he doesn't, lad.'

'Mr Lewis, then. Him as what brought me up. He's calling to me.'

'He'll never have a hold of you again, boy. I'll see to that myself.'

I nodded and let out a deep and painful sigh.

'Stay with me, lad,' he said more forcefully. 'I . . . I command you to stay with me!'

I tried to smile, even as my head turned. I felt a dizziness in my skull and the world turned very dark and then very white. I could feel the very breath in my body seeping away. I exhaled once and waited – interested – to feel whether my soul would allow my body to inhale once again. It did, but it was deep and painful and I tried to swallow and willed myself to stop. To allow the end to come.

And then it did. The world turned a pale yellow, as if I was entering the sunlight, and I had a curious feeling that, if I tried to stand and run and dance a jig on the deck of the *Bounty* again, I could do so. That my strength would return. And this is it, I thought then, accepting the freedom of it.

This is the moment of my death.

And then came a tiny sound . . . I can hear it still . . . a voice . . . raised . . . a little . . . saying, 'Captain, Captain, look!'

'Captain, look yonder!'

'We've done it.'

'Captain, we've done it.'

And one very distant voice, low, resigned, grateful.

'Aye, lads, we have. We are saved.'

Part V

The Return

1

THE FIRST THING I FELT when I opened my eyes was hunger. The second was the sensation that I had been asleep for quite some time, and I immediately groaned, remembering where I was, in that blasted tub, with nothing to eat or drink and the life draining out of me. But as the mist cleared from my eyes and I started to focus on my surroundings, I realized that I was not in the launch any longer, but lying atop a bunk. There was a clean sheet stretched across my body and the air did not smell like it did at sea; it was fresher and warmer and there was no salt threatening to stop up your throat and give you the conniptions. A pleasant breeze was fluttering over my face and I turned my head slowly to see a woman seated beside me, waving a great fan up and down in a slow fashion to provide me with coolness.

I licked my lips and my tongue almost stuck to my upper gums, so dry were they, and I felt a great need for water. Not knowing what else to do to attract the lady's attention – for she was engrossed in thoughts of her own and scarcely paying me any attention at all – I searched deep down within myself for something approaching sound, and within a few seconds a groan escaped my mouth, such as might come from a grizzly bear or a calf moments after it has first found its feet.

The lady's eyes flickered towards me and she gave a great start.

'Oh!' she cried. 'You're awake.'

'Aye,' said I, my voice emerging gravelly from my throat, so that I hardly sounded like myself at all. 'Where am I? Have I earned my reward?'

'Your reward?' she asked, laughing and shaking her head as if I had no other business there than to make a farce for her. 'Dear me, no, lad. This is no heaven, I assure you.'

'Then, where . . . ?' I began, but before I could get any more words out of my mouth I felt a great sinking feeling, and the room went dark and when I opened my eyes again I was sure that several hours had passed, although the lady was still there, fanning me. This time when she looked in my direction she did not seem quite so surprised.

'Good afternoon, Master Turnstile,' she said. 'You're looking better already. You could do with some water, I dare say?'

'My name,' I whispered. 'How do you know it?'

I lost interest in the answer immediately, for she was pouring a cup of water from a tall earthenware jug so cold that a perspiration was trickling down its side. I looked at it and thought I might cry, but shook my head.

'I can't,' I said. 'Just a thimbleful. We must ration it.'

'There is no need,' she replied, smiling. 'We have water aplenty. Please do not worry about that any more.'

I took the cup from her and stared at it for a moment. A whole cup of water. It seemed amazing to me, the finest gift I had ever received. I put it to my lips and attempted to drink it all in one go, but she took it from me and shook her head.

'Slowly, Master Turnstile,' she said. 'You do not want to make yourself ill. *More* ill,' she added, correcting herself.

I attempted to sit up a little at that and as I did so I realized that, beneath my sheet, I lay in the altogether and was already half exposed to the lady. I immediately pulled the blanket to my shoulders and took on the reddenings.

'No need to be shy,' she said, looking away for a moment. 'I have been nursing you this last week. You're no mystery to me now, I'm afraid.'

I frowned but had scarcely the energy to acknowledge the shame of it, so simply looked away from her eyes to examine my surroundings. I was no longer at sea, that was for sure. I was in a room of some sort, whose walls appeared to be constructed from bamboo. The ground beneath us was solid, the bunk I lay in as soft as any I could recall, and from outside came the sound of movement and men's voices.

'Where am I?' I asked, feeling the surprise of tears behind my eyes, for this was a great shock to me altogether, although not an unpleasant one.

'Timor,' she replied. 'You have heard of it?'

'The captain . . .' I muttered, as memories of our voyage returned to me slowly. 'He talked of it. Do you mean . . . ?' I could scarcely believe that what I was about to suggest was a possibility. 'Do you mean that we arrived safely?' I asked. 'We are not drowned?'

'Of course you are not drowned,' she said. 'Or eaten by fish. Yes, you arrived. I have it that you spent forty-eight days at sea since the act of piracy. It's a remarkable achievement.'

'We survived,' I said, astonished by the fact of it. 'The captain said we would.'

'Your captain is a remarkable man,' she said.

I blinked and stared at her for a moment, a sudden worry entering my mind, and sat up so that my bits and pieces were almost on display, but I cared not. 'And he's alive too?' I asked. 'Tell me quickly: the captain, Mr Bligh, he is alive?'

'Yes, yes,' she said, placing a cool hand on the bare skin of my shoulder to comfort me. 'Now, lie down, lad. It will do you no good to expend your energies yet. You must recover first.'

'And he is well?'

'He was not well when you first came to our shores,' she admitted. 'Like all of you, he was very ill. One of the worst, in fact. But he recovered quickly. He has great . . . spirit, that is for sure. And resentment.'

'Resentment?'

She narrowed her eyes for a moment, as if unsure whether to

continue or not, but finally she shook her head and dismissed the thought. 'He is alive and you are alive and you are safe here. This is a Dutch settlement of civilized Christian men and women. We have taken care of you.'

'And I thank you for it,' I replied, lying back and feeling relieved now by the news. 'I was very ill?'

'Very,' she said. 'We thought we had lost you at one point. On that first day, you were very low. We gave you water and forced some fruit into you, but you rejected most of it. The second day, you rallied. The third you woke for a moment and sat up, startled, and spoke to me.'

'I did not!' I cried in surprise. 'I have no recall of it.'

'It was a delirium, that was all. You shouted "I'll not go back to you" and "I must save my brothers".'

'I said that, did I?' I asked quietly.

'Yes. But your brothers are safe. They are recovering too.'

I frowned and considered that remark. 'My brothers?' I asked. 'You know them, then?'

'Of course,' she said. 'You must focus, lad: you are failing to understand me. Your brothers. The men who sailed in the launch with you. After the mutiny.'

'Ah, them,' I said, accepting it. 'I see. You think I referred to them.'

'Didn't you?'

'Aye,' I said with a shrug, wondering whether I did or not. 'And what else then?'

'After that, you became low again and for a few days we knew not whether we might keep you in this world. But then yesterday I observed colour in your cheeks and you awoke.'

'I awoke yesterday?' I asked.

'We spoke. I gave you water and you wanted to ration it.'

I could scarce believe it. 'That was yesterday?' I asked. 'It feels like no more than a few minutes ago.'

'And now today you are much recovered,' she admitted. 'You are restored to us once again and the worst is behind you.'

'So I will live?'

'I believe so.'

'Well, I'm glad of it,' I said, shaking my head in astonishment at all that had happened. I felt a great weariness come over me and told her that I needed sleep again. She smiled in a very kindly way and said that was a good idea, that my body needed restoration, and she would see to it that I was fed and watered and kept clean and given all the sleep that I needed until I could stand and run again and make for home.

Home, I thought. I had forgotten that.

And as I drifted off once again, as my mind slipped from that most comfortable of rooms into another place, a place of dreams and memory, I swear that I heard a familiar voice speaking to the lady and enquiring after my health and her replying that there was nothing more to worry about, that it might take a few days yet, but I was an eager young pup and would not allow a little hunger and thirst to overtake me.

'Good, good,' said the voice, the captain's. 'For I will need him and his memory for what lies ahead.'

And after that, it was sleep again.

In August, some six weeks after we arrived at Timor, the crew of the *Bounty*'s launch were given passage on a Dutch ship, the *Resource*, towards Java, from where trade ships were departing for Europe and would give us safe passage home. I was fortunate in that I had almost two weeks in which to recover, during which time I took exercise and reinstated a healthy diet, which daily improved my physique and banished my pallor.

Not all were as fortunate as I, however.

It grieves me to report that, in the period between our tub crew sighting land and the day that I opened my eyes again, we lost five of our fellows, men who had survived the forty-eight days at sea but who were all but dead by the time we reached Timor. Peter Linkletter, the quartermaster, survived no more than an hour or two after we reached land and it seems that he never knew that we had arrived safety; in truth, he had been half-dead for two or three days by then and had been merely waiting for the Saviour to take notice of him and finish the job. By nightfall of that day we had lost Robert Lamb too, the ship's butcher, who had become terrible ill, as I recall, during the last week in the tub but who had collapsed in a seizure soon after stepping on to dry land.

The captain spoke with great regret of the loss of the *Bounty*'s botanist, David Nelson, who could not be revived with food or water and was called home on the second day after our arrival. I believe it vexed Mr Bligh in particular to lose him, as he was the last link to the breadfruit of Otaheite, a man who had felt as passionately about our mission as the captain himself, and one the captain hoped would speak up for him when we returned to England.

Following the ordinary sailing men who did not survive long was Mr Elphinstone, that poor fellow; he became the only warranted officer to die. Like all of us he had been in terrible dis-repair when we reached Timor, but whereas I had been fortunate to gather my senses and rally my health, he had loss all strength and had passed a couple of days later.

And then, finally, the day after I awoke, we lost Thomas Hall, the cook, and I felt a great sadness at it, for he had been un-common kind to me while we were on board the ship, and if he made our dinners with as much care as a dog or a filthy pig has for taste or hygiene, he made them all the same and I thought him a fine fellow and a friend as well. Mr Hall's funeral was the only one that I had the ability to attend and the pressure of our situation, the gradual comprehension of what we had suffered and endured, and the fact that I awoke to so much death, left me in a terrible condition and I wept like a bairn when we put him in the ground. The captain had to take me away to my bunk lest I made a holy show of myself.

'I'm sorry, sir,' said I, drying my eyes as I sat there, feeling as if a single kind word from him would bring more and more tears – more than tears, great whelps of unhappiness and misery pouring from my eyes.

'Don't be sorry, lad,' he said. 'We have been a crew of men, these last seven weeks. Aye, and these last two years. Why should you not weep for your fallen comrades?'

'But why did I survive?' I asked. 'Why did the Saviour choose to—?'

'Ask not that question,' he said sharply, silencing me immediately. 'The Good Lord makes His choices of who shall stay and who shall be called home. It is not for us to question Him.'

'But I thought I was dead, sir,' I told him, the great grief rising again. 'Those last days in the tub. I felt it around me. I felt that my life was at an end, that for me there would be no future.'

'I thought so too, lad,' he said, with scarce a thought for how such a line might affect me. 'Indeed, I was sure that you had passed at one point a few hours before we reached land and I took it mighty hard, mighty hard indeed. But you have strength that you did not know you had. You have built it up, lad, can't you see that? During our time together? You have become a man.'

I did not feel like a man as I sat there, weeping on his shoulder, but he allowed me to do it, that gentle man, and didn't make me feel a nance for it, and when I was finished he said that that was enough tears, I had got them out, and there were to be no more or he'd know the reason why.

And I said, 'Aye, sir,' and I didn't cry again.

Thirteen men from the original crew of nineteen who had been deposed from their rightful home aboard the *Bounty* boarded the *Resource* for safe passage to Java; we had lost a third of our number: the five recent casualties and, earlier, John Norton, who was lost to us when his head was smashed by savages on that first island we visited. A time that seemed like many years before.

I felt sure there would be great excitement among the men, a feeling that we were a band who would never be parted after our adventures, but to my surprise the atmosphere on board that ship was very low indeed. I noted a great muttering of resentment from the other fellows towards the captain, despite the fact that he had steered us successfully from the middle of the ocean to a place where we would surely be delivered home safely, but gratitude came there none and it appeared that the moment had arrived for recrimination.

An almighty row broke out one evening between the captain and Mr Fryer – the argument that they had been heading towards for the last two years – and things were said that should never have been said. Mr Fryer accused the captain of causing the mutiny himself by his behaviour towards the men: taking back privileges that he had honoured them with, treating them as if they were his personal chattel, and skipping between moods, from extreme cheer to dour low spirits, like a bride before her wedding day. The captain would have none of it and replied that Mr Fryer had never been the master that he had hoped for. He said that when he was a dozen years younger than Mr Fryer he himself had been Captain Cook's master and had done it at the age of twenty and one. What kind of an officer, he asked, does not have a captaincy by that age?

'You, sir, are not a captain,' countered Mr Fryer, flying an arrow through the captain's Achilles heel. 'You have the same rank as I, sir, a lieutenant.'

'But I have command, sir, I have command!' screamed the captain, his face red with a fury. 'A command that you shall never have.'

'I would not want one such as yours,' he shouted in reply. 'And as for being Captain Cook's master?' He shook his head and, to his shame, spat on the ground beneath his feet. 'An honest man would take note of his own deeds on that dark day.'

That was enough – more than enough – for Mr Bligh, who I thought would seek a cutlass and disembowel Mr Fryer on the spot, but instead he merely swore at him and ran towards him, their faces separated by no more than a kiss, although Mr Fryer held his ground bravely, and the captain denounced him for a coward and a charlatan and asked him why, if he thought so low of him, had he not joined his friend Mr Christian and returned to his despicable ways on the island of Otaheite.

'Fletcher Christian is no friend of mine,' roared Mr Fryer. 'Did I not leave the ship with him? Did I not sit by your side every league of the sea from there to here? And you dare accuse me of—'

'I'll accuse you of whatever in hell I want to accuse you of,' shouted the captain. 'I call you a coward, sir, do you hear me, and I'll see you hang for your behaviour and your insubordination.'

A great cry went up among the men now and two of them, William Purcell and John Hallett, rushed to the master's side and began to roar at the captain, accusing him of leading us to this unhappy day and insisting that their voices would be heard when we returned to England. That was enough for Mr Bligh, who called out to the master-at-arms of the *Resource* and, would you believe it, within a very few hours all three of those men – Fryer, Purcell and Hallett – were under arrest and sitting in chains and solitude down below, all the better, according to the captain, for them to consider their behaviour to date.

It was a dark atmosphere on board and for the first time I wondered whether we – and, really, I mean the captain – would be considered heroes when we returned to England as I had always assumed.

Or whether we would be viewed as something different entirely.

We arrived in Java with all our moods in disarray and I knew not what course this story of ours would take, whether men would

471

continue to mutiny and fight until we reached England, where wiser heads could separate us all and provide a fitting ending.

The head of the settlement in Java informed the captain that two ships were set for England over the weeks that followed; the first, a Dutch ship called the *Vlijt*, was to sail in a few days' time, the second not for another week after that. These were trade ships and not designed for passengers, although the second could take the bulk of the crew. Having been informed that the *Vlijt* could manage no more than three berths, the captain selected his clerk, Mr Samuel, and me to join him.

'Sir, I protest,' said Mr Fryer, who had been released from his manacles in the meantime but continued to remain under charges. 'As second-in-command, I should travel with you on the first craft.'

'You have not been second-in-command since your in-subordination,' replied the captain quietly, in a tone that suggested he did not care to argue any more, that soon enough this drama would cease. 'And if you still consider yourself an officer of the king, then I suggest you take charge of those men I leave in your care. We shall meet up soon enough in England, I warrant.'

'Aye, sir,' said Mr Fryer, narrowing his eyes. 'We shall indeed.'

'I said as much, did I not?' snapped the captain, and to my eyes they were a pair of infants who needed thrashing.

All the surviving crew came to the port to say their goodbyes to us, however, and the captain made a point of shaking every man's hand, including Mr Fryer's, and wishing them Godspeed and safe passage back to England, before stepping up the gangway with his books and his writing folders and disappearing from our view. He was followed by Mr Samuel a few moments later, which left me on my own, preparing to say my goodbyes to these men I had known for so long and who had fought with me during our forty-eight-day ordeal, and who had survived alongside me.

'Goodbye, men,' I said and I swear that it was a difficult thing for me not to be moved by the experience, for I felt an uncommon affection for every one of them. 'We have seen some times, have we not?'

'We have, lad,' said William Peckover, whose eyes were glassy too. 'I'll shake your hand before you go.'

I nodded and shook it, shook every man's, and each one said, 'Good luck to you, Turnip,' or 'We'll see you in England, Turnip,' and seemed sorry to see me go. It felt curious that our adventures were at an end.

'Goodbye, Mr Fryer, sir,' said I as I stepped towards the gangway and he walked with me a little way, out of the hearing of the other men. 'Might I be so bold as to say it has been a pleasure to serve with you, sir. I have a great deal of respect for you.' I swallowed nervously, for it was a bold comment.

'And I thank you for it, John Jacob,' he said, addressing me by my Christian names for once. 'You are looking forward to returning home?'

'I'm trying not to think too deeply on it, sir.'

'You will be there before us, of course. I would ask you . . .' He hesitated and bit his lip for a moment, considering his words carefully. 'Master Turnstile,' he said, 'when you return to England, there will be many questions asked and many cases to be answered. You have a loyalty to the captain, of course you do. I do myself if the damn fool would only recognize it.'

'Sir—,' I began, but he cut me off.

'I don't say it to blacken his name, lad,' he said. 'I say it because it is so. All I would ask of you is that you answer with honesty and decency any questions that are sent your way. Your loyalties, you see, are not to the captain, nor to me, nor even to the king. But to yourself. You may not even understand the value of the things you have seen and heard, but if you report fairly and truthfully, then there is no more that any man can ask of you. Neither the captain nor I. Nor even Mr Christian and his band of ruffians. Do you understand that?'

'Aye, sir,' I said, and I did and promised that it would be so.

'Then, I'll shake your hand,' he said, 'and wish you a safe journey home.'

I stretched my hand out and he looked at it for a moment but seemed to think better of it and reached forward, gathering me into his arms, and held me there for a moment. 'You have been a fine sailing companion,' he said quietly into my ear. 'And would make a very fine sailor. You should think on it.'

'Me, sir?' I asked, stepping away and raising an eyebrow.

'Aye, you, sir,' he said. 'Think on it, won't you?'

And with that he turned away and led his men back towards the settlement, where they would stay until it was time for their own ship to depart.

And so our final voyage began, the journey that was to take us home.

The captain had no official responsibilities on board and, although he was happy to lend any assistance that was required of him, he became little more than a highly ranked passenger. Most evenings he ate alone in his cabin, but from time to time he joined the officers and captain of the *Vlijt* for the evening meal. I sensed that he did not enjoy this, however, for our hosts looked at him in wonderment, questioning how a captain of one of His Majesty's frigates could possibly have lost his ship.

I believe this was a question that he too was asking himself throughout the journey home.

For my part, I had little to do either. The captain of the *Vlijt* had his own servant-lad to take care of him, so I helped Captain Bligh when he needed something, but that was not often, and I found myself increasingly bored and prone to daydreams as our journey continued. I had food in my belly, of course, and was well hydrated, but there was none of the drama on board this ship of trade that there had been on the *Bounty* and even the weather remained clement throughout most of our journey. In truth, I rather missed the excitement of it.

Captain Bligh tended to his notebooks during this time and continued to write his account of our voyage and the mutiny, the better to prepare himself for what Mr Fryer had referred to as the 'serious questions' that would greet us on our return. He also wrote long letters to Sir Joseph Banks, to the admirals of the navy, and to his wife Betsey, although why he bothered when he would see them before they could be delivered was a mystery to me.

Before setting forth, he had made a list of all the mutineers, along with descriptions of their physical appearance and character, and these were in turn distributed to various ports; he hoped that this would be the start of their capture, but I was less certain that this would happen.

And then, on the morning of 13th March 1790, a full two years and three months after we had left Spithead, our ship brought us to England. She brought us home.

Lieutenant William Bligh, a captain without a ship.

And John Jacob Turnstile, a young man now of sixteen, with nowhere to call his own.

2

THE STREETS OF PORTSMOUTH had always seemed very wide to me as a child. The town had appeared enormous, as if the entire world was contained therein. The people had felt like the only people of any significance. But walking along those narrow paths again I couldn't help but be struck by how small they were, or perhaps how much broader my horizons had grown. I was not the same lad who had left there on that cold December morning in 1787. I could feel the difference immediately.

Some time had passed since we had returned to England and, although I had duties in London that I was shortly to attend to, I found that I had a week at my disposal and decided to return to the place of my birth and my rearing and see it once again.

Arriving there, my stomach twisted and turned with a certain apprehension at the idea of seeing Mr Lewis again, although I did not fear him as much as I once had. Throughout much of my voyage on the *Bounty* I had been planning an escape, attempting to find any place where I might run off to and avoid returning to his dark gaze. And now I was here of my own volition. I felt strong inside when I considered it, but nevertheless I was nervous too.

I made my way along the streets and my feet took me to the very spot where my adventures had begun. The bookstore where the Frenchman, Mr Zéla, had conversed with me while I had sought a way to steal his pocket-watch. The fruit and vegetable stalls still stood, the people were the same, but they did not leap atop me now or seek to rip me limb from limb; rather, they called out to me that their apples and walnuts were the best in the land, the finest I could find if I travelled from Land's End to John O'Groats, and would I not buy some off them? I was better dressed than I had been before, that was the crux of it. And my hair had been trimmed short and neat. The navy had issued me with a fine pair of britches and a couple of chemises and I looked for all the world like a proper young gentleman.

'Care to buy a handkerchief, sir?' asked a voice behind me. I turned round and who did I see, only Floss Mackey, her as I had sold 'kerchiefs to myself in my earlier days. I would steal them from a gentleman and she would pick the monogram away for a farthing so I could sell them on for a penny. 'They're very fine 'kerchiefs, sir,' she added. 'You won't find better.'

'But don't you know me, Floss?' I asked, offering her a smile, and she frowned and looked a little nervous, as if I was about to accuse her of something untoward and summon a blue to hear the charge.

'No, sir,' she said quickly. 'And if you think there's anything wrong with these items, then you're under no obligation to purchase and I shall bid you good day.'

'Floss, it's me, John Jacob Turnstile. Don't you remember me?'

She stared at me for a moment and then her mouth dropped open as her eyes grew wide, and I thought she was about to take a stumble out of surprise. 'It never is,' she said.

'As sure as eggs is eggs,' I confirmed.

She shook her head then and reached forward with a laugh, feeling the quality of the material in my outfit. 'John Jacob Turnstile,' she said. 'I thought you were dead.'

'I am very much alive.'

'And in the peak of good health, by the looks of it,' she said, smiling a little as she did so. 'You ran away to sea. That's what I was told. You took passage with a trading ship.'

'It was no trading ship,' I replied. 'It was one of King George's frigates. But, yes, I set sail. I have only just returned.'

'Go on,' she said, smiling and looking me up and down. 'And how you've grown too! All tall and handsome and dark-skinned. I wouldn't have known you. Where was it, then?'

'An island called Otaheite,' I told her. 'In the Pacific Ocean.'

'I've not heard of it, duck,' she said. 'But it's done you the world of good. You were right to get out of here – nothing for the likes of you here. You were made for something more than picking pockets, if I'm not very much mistaken.'

'That was a long time ago,' I said, nodding, already ashamed by my past. 'It's not something I am planning for my future.'

'Oh no? Too good for it now, are you?' she asked, a trace of bitterness creeping into her voice. 'And what are you made for, then? Here! There was a great commotion after you went, you know. That man of yours was looking for you everywhere.'

'Mr Lewis?' I asked nervously.

'Yes, him whose house you resided in.'

'That's him.'

'I remember there was a din with a blue about it; he heard that you'd gone and they'd had something to do with it. He wanted compensation for the loss of you. But they said that he had no rights over you, it wasn't as if he was your father or nothing, and so he had to be on his way. He wasn't happy about it, I can tell you. He spoke about nothing else for months. He forgot about it after a time, of course: you're not as special as you might think you are, John Jacob Turnstile . . .'

'I never thought that—'

'But he was fierce angry. I'd stay away from him if I was you.'

'He lives, then?' I asked.

'Very much so.'

'I'm only here to reacquaint myself with Portsmouth,' I said quickly. 'I don't intend staying.'

She offered a few casual insults at this, her suggestion being that I thought myself too good for Portsmouth now, but she was wrong on that. I didn't think anything of the sort. I simply had other plans in mind. I had had an idea regarding my future.

Later that afternoon, I was in a different area of the town, eating lunch in a hostelry paid for with my own money, and I watched as a young lad, perhaps nine or ten years old, hovered outside a milliner's store opposite me. He was a pretty fellow, blond hair and blue eyes, if a trifle skinny, and I was on to his game immediately, for he had that air that I knew only too well of one who is waiting for the moment to pounce.

A gentleman and lady were at the store, and she was trying on hats, and even from my vantage point I could see a wallet peeping out of the pocket of his greatcoat. I could have swiped it in an instant and no one would have been any the wiser, but the lad was not dextrous and the way he was behaving I thought that he would be captured in a moment and the blues would be called. I was about to rise and make my way towards him to prevent him from making a terrible mistake, but another reached him first.

A man had approached from the opposite side of the street – he must have been standing out of sight, to the left of the window where I was seated – and he marched across and grabbed the lad by the wrist, then pulled him away into a dark corner beneath an awning, where he proceeded to remonstrate with the boy, not because he was a young thief, but rather because he was not doing a good job of it.

I felt the food turn in my belly as I watched the scene play out before me. Much as I wanted to turn away and run as fast as my pins could carry me, I was transfixed.

And perhaps something in my gaze was so intense that it made him stop chastising the lad for a moment and hesitate, as if he knew he was being watched.

Then he turned his head in my direction and narrowed his eyes and our gaze met.

And for the first time in two and a half years, I was staring directly into the eyes of Mr Lewis. And he was staring directly back at me.

Times had changed. Had we met within a few months of my original disappearance, then maybe he would have marched straight across to me, grabbed me roughly by the arms and dragged me to a dark alley somewhere to beat me until the blood poured from my ears. He might even have killed me. Or perhaps he would have locked me upstairs in his establishment and made me work for him every minute of the day until my debt was cleared. It is impossible to know. What I do know is that we had both changed sufficiently – or, rather, I had changed in size and confidence – that he did none of those things. Instead, he whispered into the young lad's ear while keeping a close eye on me at all times and sent him on his way, then leaned back against the wall as if he had not a care in the world and, with a half-smile on his face, waited for me to finish my lunch and emerge.

He looked much as I remembered him – I would have known him immediately anywhere – but perhaps he was a little more grey around the temples than he had been in 1787 and a little darker around the eyes. He was still the same uncivilized brute that he ever was, though, giving no thought to scratching his nether regions in the middle of the street, where ladies might be walking past him at any moment.

I looked down at the remains of my lunch and knew there was no point in continuing it. My appetite was far away. I hesitated, unsure what to do next, but I had little choice. There was nowhere for me to go other than through the door, and no possibility of escape. I would have to face him.

He offered a deep bow when I finally emerged, twirling his hand before me as if I was visiting royalty. 'Why, Master Turnstile,' said he, 'as I live and breathe. I had more hope of running into King George as I came out to work today than into your good self. But I am certainly glad to see you again.'

'Good afternoon, sir,' I replied, swallowing a little and not approaching him too closely. 'I'm pleased that my appearance is gratifying to you, although to suggest that the activities you are engaged upon constitute work is a nasty subversion of meaning, is it not?'

'Oh, hark at you!' He laughed, shaking his head. 'What kind of language is this you are using, might I ask? I heard that you were gone to sea to make your fortune, not sent to the 'varsity to make a nance of yourself.'

'Whatever I am,' I said quietly, 'I am what you made me.'

'Aye, lad,' he replied, stepping closer now and leading me forward towards a harbour seat, where fewer people were gathered and we could speak with more privacy. 'I made you, that's for sure. I was your creator. But then you abandoned me, thankless child.'

'I thought it was my parents who made me, Mr Lewis,' I

answered. 'And that you merely collected me off the street.'

'I remember your parents,' he said, sitting down, and I sat beside him, although keeping such a distance between us that a third man might have taken a place there. 'Your father was a drunkard and your mother a whore. Have I never told you that?'

'No, sir,' I said, looking down for a moment and sighing. I should have simply left him there alone but I did not have it within me. There were things that needed saying.

'Well, that's what they were,' he continued. 'And being as they were, I would think you only too happy to have been brought up by one such as I. Did I not give you food in your belly?'

'Aye, sir, and plenty besides.'

'Did I not give you a bed at night?'

'Aye, sir, and plenty besides.'

He narrowed his eyes a little and cocked his head to one side. 'And did you have no gratitude for that, boy? Did you not feel there was a debt of honour between us?'

'I recall spending my days walking these streets, gathering up possessions that I had no business taking, and bringing them back for your coffers,' I said sharply. 'And I remember earning you much more through those other pastimes in which you were so active.'

'In which *I* was active, boy?' he asked with a laugh. 'Now, that's fine and rich, that is. Why, there were never a lad so active in that as thyself, that is my recollection.'

I set my jaw harshly and felt my hands curl into fists; he saw it too but seemed nonplussed.

'And what is that for, boy?' he asked. 'Do you mean to hit me? Do you mean to start a commotion? There are blues all over here: do you not think that they will haul you off to the gaol if you attack me? Perhaps that would be the best for all concerned. Were you not destined for there, after all, when you were stolen from me?'

'One cannot be robbed of that which one does not own,' I

481

countered, and something in that line made him see red, for he leaned forward suddenly and took the top of my chemise in his hand.

'I did own you, boy,' he said. 'I owned you body and soul. You have cost me these last two and a half years and I will see recompense.'

'You will not,' I answered, pulling away from him now but feeling less confident than before. The hold he had over me was reasserting itself.

'You will come back with me and pay your debt or I swear that you will live to regret it. You're a bonny lad yet: you have a few years work left in you.'

I leapt out of my seat and swallowed hard, trying to keep the emotion out of my voice.

'I am leaving Portsmouth,' I said. 'I intend to—'

'You are going nowhere,' he replied, standing too and taking my arm. 'You are coming with me.'

His grip on my arm was pincer-like and I let out a howl, but as he would not release me I had no choice but to stamp on his foot, and this I did, before taking off at a pace.

'You cannot escape me, boy,' he called after me, laughing. 'I own Portsmouth and everyone in it. Do you not know that by now?'

I ran until I could no longer hear his laughter and found myself on a strange street – perhaps things had changed since I had last been here – and stopped, gasping for breath. I knew not what it was: the familiarity of the situation, the knowledge of how cruel Mr Lewis could be, the servitude I had felt towards him all my life. I found that, despite everything that had happened to me, my feet were taking me back towards his establishment, and for a moment I believed it was the only place where I could possibly live, that it was – for want of a better word – home.

I wasn't quite looking where I was going, however, for who did I run into only a blue emerging from the station.

'Watch where you're going, lad,' he said roughly but not

unkindly, and I apologized to him and he stopped before going on his way. 'Are you all right?' he asked me. 'You look distraught.'

'I believe I am,' I replied. 'I find myself with a difficulty.'

'And you find yourself outside a police station. Is that by chance or design?'

I looked up at the symbol of authority that hung outside and I knew what I had to do. Perhaps it was too late to save myself, perhaps my soul was lost for ever, but there were others, like the blond lad I had seen outside the milliner's. There were others I could help.

'Might I step inside, sir?' I asked, my confidence growing again, knowing there was only one way through this matter. 'There is a crime that I think bears reporting.'

'Then, you must follow me, lad,' he replied, turning back and leading the way.

And I did. I followed him inside and I sat down and spent the afternoon telling him all. I held nothing back, despite my shame, despite how he looked at me. I told him the truth of who I was and what I had done, and when I was finished he sat back with another blue and shook his head.

'You are to be commended for coming to see us,' he said finally. 'I know not what to say to you other than that. And now, if you please, I believe this Mr Lewis of yours deserves a visit, don't you?'

I watched from the end of the street that evening when the blues broke down the door of Mr Lewis's establishment, charged upstairs and took the men who were there into their broughams and the boys into their care. The whole event took no more than a half-hour and the street was in chaos as men and women came out of their doors, fire-torches in hand, to witness the commotion. None of the lads seemed sorry to go; I recognized one or two of the younger ones, who had been even younger still when I had lived there. I did not know where the blues might be taking them but felt sure that, wherever it was, they would have a better existence than they did at Mr Lewis's.

All the adults on the premises were arrested. However, there was one person missing: Mr Lewis himself. The blues made their way from house to house, enquiring of the neighbours whether they had seen him, but answer came there none, and soon they boarded up the front door so that no man might enter and then they took their leave.

A few hours later, close to midnight, I left the small room I was staying in and wandered down towards the harbour and looked out into the distance at the ships anchored in distant Spithead. I was sure I could see movement on some of them and wondered where they might be headed towards, and in whose company, with what mission. To my surprise, I felt a curious longing for it and finally understood how the captain had felt when we were anchored on Otaheite and he would look out towards the *Bounty* with yearning in his heart. It surprised me to feel this way, but I felt it nonetheless, and wondered what to do with such a strong emotion.

I turned to make my way back to my bed and walked along a street that was surprisingly busy with carriages for that time of night; the gentlemen who were coming from their clubs cared naught for the speed at which they travelled and one or two of them nearly crushed me, which would have been a cruel end to my tale after so much adventure.

'Turnstile.'

I swung round at the name and there he was behind me, Mr Lewis, a look of venom in his eyes.

'You,' I said, startled.

'Aye, me,' he said, advancing towards me. 'Thought you'd seen the last of me, did you?'

'No, sir,' I cried, stepping back.

'First you abscond, boy, when you are my chattel. Then you

return to set the blues on me? Rob me of my business, would you? Steal my lads away from me?'

'They are not your lads,' I insisted, feeling bold enough to answer him back now. 'They belong to no man.'

'They belong to me, just like you do,' he said, and the hatred in his voice was more than I had ever heard before. 'You're no more than a thief, John Jacob Turnstile, and I'll have you for it.'

He looked around for a moment – the street was empty – and took a long blade from within his jacket. My eyes opened wide at the sight of the knife.

'Mr Lewis,' I began, imploring him, but he took a lunge at me and it was all that I could do to escape a stabbing. 'Mr Lewis, please!'

'This is your last night on earth, boy,' he snarled, changing direction now, and I jumped back, facing the road, and he stepped into the gap between me and it. 'Aye, and this your last moment.'

He lifted the knife and, aware that I had no more than a second or two before it descended into my body, I jumped towards him, causing him a moment of sudden surprise, and he took a couple of steps back into the road.

'What the—?' he began. They were his last words.

Could I have warned him? Or did I mean it to happen? I do not know. The carriage came round the corner and ran him over before he even knew what was taking place; I dare say he felt a moment's terror and then nothing. I watched in horror as the carriage drove on and then pulled to a stop, and the voice of the driver called back, but I slipped into the shadows as he reached the broken body on the cobbles and checked pointlessly for signs of life.

As he ran down the street in search of a blue, I turned round and went home.

That business was over now.

3

I T WAS LATE OCTOBER before we thirteen survivors of the *Bounty's* launch were called before Admiral Barrington to witness the court martial of Lieutenant William Bligh on charges connected with the loss of His Majesty's frigate *Bounty*.

When I received word that I was to attend, I was immediately taken with a great consternation, for it seemed to me that the captain was being unduly charged, but I was reassured by the officers at the Admiralty that this was the typical way in which such matters were resolved. The argument that had taken place between the captain and Mr Fryer appeared to have ended as well, for the two men seemed to be in support of each other and did not contradict each other on any matter of evidence.

Like the other survivors, I was called to the stand, and took it nervously, for I feared I could become trapped into saying something I did not mean. However, my questioners appeared to think me of little importance and I was up and down those steps within the space of a half-hour of the clock. The judges considered matters for a very short time, the captain was acquitted and he walked from the courtroom a hero.

In the months since our return, the English people appeared to have become fascinated by the story of the mutiny on the *Bounty* and, in those early days at least, Captain Bligh was highly thought of by the populace for his success in steering our tiny tub back to safety. The king himself commended him and Mr Bligh was finally awarded that one title which had evaded him prior to our adventures – that of captain – and his further advance through the naval ranks was assured.

Later that year another frigate, the *Pandora*, under the command of a Captain Edward Edwards, was sent to Otaheite in search of the mutineers and I was astonished to read the names in the newspaper of those who had been captured: Michael Byrn, the fiddle-player; James Morrison, the bo'sun; the carpenter's mates Charles Norman and Thomas McIntosh; the ABs Thomas Ellison, John Millward, Richard Skinner, John Sumner, and Thomas Burkett; the midshipman George Stewart; the cook's assistant, William Muspratt; the armourer Joseph Coleman; and the cooper Henry Hilbrant.

And one other: the scut, Mr Peter Heywood.

Mr Fletcher Christian, the dandy, was never discovered.

But if I was surprised by this and the news that they were to return to England to stand trial under charges of mutiny, it was as nothing compared with the news that followed soon after that. The *Pandora* had come to damage and had sunk on the voyage home and four of those miserable prisoners – Skinner, Sumner, Stewart and Hilbrant – had perished as the ship went down. The rest were transported in various launches by the captain and crew of the drowned frigate to Timor, following the same route that we ourselves had been forced to follow, and onward to England.

If there was ever a time to think that the Saviour was playing games in the world, then this was it.

The trials that followed were of great public interest, of course, and the captain testified against some of the men, but only six – Morrison, Ellison, Muspratt, Millward, Burkett and Mr Heywood – were convicted; the rest were seen as loyalists detained by mutineers.

And after earnest entreaties on the parts of their families, Mr Heywood, along with Morrison and Muspratt, were pardoned by the king and set free.

The others – Thomas Ellison, who would never after all marry his Flora-Jane Richardson, Thomas Burkett, who had arrested the captain in his own cabin on that fateful night, and John Millward

– were all sentenced to death and they were duly hanged by the neck, a warning to others of the penalties of mutiny.

And thereafter the story of HMS *Bounty* was laid to rest.

4

NOT UNTIL TWENTY-SIX YEARS LATER, shortly before my own forty-fourth birthday, did my mind fully return to the events of those turbulent two and a half years. The cause for my recollections was the funeral of one of my oldest and dearest friends, Captain William Bligh, the hero of the *Bounty*, in Lambeth parish church, not long before Christmas 1817.

I had wondered whether I might see some of my old shipmates at the funeral, but most had died by then, or were away on foreign voyages, and there was no one left to represent the *Bounty* other than myself. In truth, attendance was sparse despite the great service the captain had offered over his lifetime: he had served under the great Admiral Nelson at the Battle of Copenhagen and acquitted himself valiantly there. He became Governor-General of New South Wales for a period and was considered a great hero in those Antipodean parts. He became a Rear-Admiral, and latterly Vice-Admiral of the Blue, one of the highest rankings in the forces. However, memories of the mutiny never faded and for some he was the villain of the piece, a characterization that could scarcely be further from the truth.

Mr Bligh was not perfect, few of us are, but he was worth a thousand Fletcher Christians and I would stake my life on that.

After the interment I found myself alone at Lambeth, for my wife had been unable to attend due to the impending birth of our eighth child, who would be born three weeks later. (Our third child, and second son, was named for my friend and his own god-father, William.) Unwilling yet to return home – for the memories of those years were pervading my mind deeply and causing me a curious mixture of regret, disappointment and delight – I wandered over to a local hostelry and ordered a pint of ale before retiring to a windowed corner to reflect upon the events of my life.

I scarcely noticed the gentleman approaching me, but his deep voice swept me out of my thoughts when first he spoke.

'Captain Turnstile,' he said.

I looked up but didn't recognize him immediately. 'Good after-noon, sir,' I said.

'I wonder if I might join you for a moment?'

'Of course,' I said, indicating the bench opposite.

He was a well-dressed gentleman with a fine speaking voice, and although I would have preferred solitude it was clear that he recognized me and wanted discourse and I was happy enough to offer it. However, he remained silent for a few moments when he sat, placing his own ale before him, smiling a little at me.

'I wonder that you don't recognize me,' he said.

'I do apologize, sir,' I replied. 'We have met before, then?'

'Once,' he said. 'Many years ago. Perhaps if I was to leave my pocket-watch hanging in sight, it might stir your recollection?'

I frowned, considering what he meant by those words, before their meaning struck me and my eyes opened wide in surprise. 'Mr Zéla,' I said, for indeed it was the French gentleman whose watch I had stolen all those years before and who had seen to it that I was spared the gaol and transported instead to the deck of the *Bounty*.

'Matthieu, please,' he said with a smile.

'I can scarcely believe it,' I replied, shaking my head. 'The years have been kind to you,' I added, for although he must have been in his seventies by then, he could have passed for a man twenty years his junior.

'I hear that quite frequently,' he replied. 'But I try not to focus on it. Why tempt fate, that's my motto.'

'And you're here,' I said, still amazed. 'You were at—'

'Admiral Bligh's funeral? Yes, I was at the rear of the church. I noticed you when you were leaving. I wanted to say hello to you once again. It's been many years.'

'Indeed it has,' I said. 'And I'm pleased to see you. You are living in London?'

'I move around a little,' he replied. 'I have many interests across the world. I must say, however, that I was pleased to see you here. I have followed your career with great interest.'

'I have two people to thank for that career,' I admitted. 'You, for sending me on board that ship in the first place, and William, for making me his protégé.'

'You and he remained friends all these years, then?'

'Oh, yes,' I said. 'When I returned to England, Mr Zéla . . . Matthieu . . . I was lost. I considered returning to my life in Portsmouth, but there was nothing there for me any more. After the captain was acquitted and promoted, he invited me on to his next command as an AB.'

'Your adventures had not turned you against the sea, then?'

'I thought they would,' I admitted. 'Indeed, during those forty-eight days on the launch, I swore time and again that if I survived, then I would never even bathe again, let alone sail. But perhaps that experience changed me for the better. William offered, I considered and accepted, and after that—'

'The rest, as they say, is history.'

'I only served with him one more time,' I pointed out. 'On that next voyage. After that I struck out on my own. I was fortunate to discover a talent for chart-making as well as a natural ability, I suppose, at the sea, and was promoted for my troubles. Before I knew it I was a master's mate, and then a master.'

'And now you are a captain,' he said with pride in his voice. 'And if the rumours are to believed, your career will not end there?'

490

'I know nothing of that, sir,' I said, blushing slightly, although I will admit that my ambition had not yet been fully satisfied. 'That will be for greater men than I to decide.'

'And they will, my friend,' he replied with certainty in his voice. 'I have no doubt that they will. I am indeed proud of you, John Jacob.'

I smiled. 'And I'm glad of it,' I said. 'But not as much as William was, I think. He accompanied me to the Admiralty on the day that I received my captaincy papers. We dined with friends afterwards and he paid me a fine tribute over the toasts, which moved me tremendously. He spoke of loyalty. And duty. And honour. The traits, I think, that defined his own life.' I felt my eyes fill with tears as I recalled that happy evening and the way that William had spoken of me.

'He thought of you as a son, I expect,' said Mr Zéla.

'Perhaps,' I admitted. 'Something like that anyway. I know that I shall never forget him.'

'And the island? Tahiti. You think of it often?'

'We called it Otaheite, Matthieu,' I said, correcting him. 'And, yes, I think of it often. I think of the men we left behind. The mutineers who were never discovered. I feel no anger towards them any more, though. They were strange days. And men behave curiously in such climates. I reserve any enmity I feel for Fletcher Christian.'

'Ah,' said Mr Zéla, nodding thoughtfully. 'Of course. The real villain of the piece.'

'The worst of all villains.'

'And you think that he will be remembered as such?'

I raised an eyebrow. 'But of course,' I said. 'Did he not turn on his own captain? Take a ship that was not his own? Break the solemn oath of his office?'

'I wonder will history recall these things,' he said.

'But I am certain it will,' I replied. 'Anyway, he is surely dead by now. So much time has passed. His villainy has ended and his infamy assured.'

Mr Zéla gave a slight smile but remained silent for some time. When he spoke again, he was thinking not of the days of Bligh and Christian, but of my own life.

'And you, John Jacob,' he said, 'you have lived a happy life?'

'Aye, and a fulfilling one,' I replied. 'And much left to look forward to, I hope. I have a loving wife, a brood of happy, healthy children. A career that satisfies me greatly. I wonder what else I could want from the world?'

'I remember when you were a lad,' he said. 'On that morning when we met by the bookstalls in Portsmouth. We had a conversation, the two of us, do you recall it?'

I threw my mind back thirty years and frowned a little as I remembered the boy I had once been. 'Not entirely,' I replied. 'It was so long ago.'

'You said that you had a mind for book-writing,' he told me. 'And that you would like to set your mind to that task one day. There was something about China, if I recall correctly.'

I let out a great laugh and remembered it cheerfully. 'I was a fanciful lad,' I said, shaking my head in amusement.

'So it never came to pass, then? You never wrote?'

'No, sir,' I admitted. 'I sailed instead.'

'Well, there is still time,' he replied, smiling. 'Perhaps you will yet.'

'I think not,' I said. 'I do not have a mind for making up stories.'

'Then, perhaps you could simply recall your own. In the future, there may be those who would be glad to read of your adventures. There may be some who will want to know the truth of that time and those years you spent on your first expedition.' He glanced at his pocket-watch then, a much finer specimen than the one he had owned back on the day we had first met. 'I would so much like to stay and talk,' he said, 'but unfortunately my nephew and I have business in London and we are taking a carriage there within the hour.'

I glanced over in the direction he had indicated at a young, dark-haired lad of about sixteen or seventeen – very much with the look of Mr Zéla – who was sitting near by patiently awaiting his uncle.

'I may write to you?' I asked, rising now to shake his hand. 'I should like to continue our conversation.'

'Of course. I shall send my address to you via the Admiralty.' He hesitated and held my hand tightly as he stared deeply into my eyes. 'I am very happy, Mr Turnstile, that your life was a successful one. Perhaps I did something good that day on the docks of Spithead.'

'I know you did, sir,' I told him. 'I know not what course my life might have taken otherwise.'

He smiled and nodded but said nothing more, sweeping out of the hostelry with his nephew in tow. I watched from the window as he marched down the street and out of sight; I never saw or heard from him again. Whether his address was lost or never sent, I do not know.

The conversation between Mr Zéla and me played out in my mind for days afterwards. I considered what he had said about recording the events of my life, but I was soon back to sea and there was no time for that. A decade later, however, and I was back in London with my sailing days behind me. A sea battle had left me deprived of my left leg, and although my life was not threatened I was forced at the age of fifty-five to return to a quieter life, one that involved the solace of grandchildren and the satisfaction of a place upon the Admiralty board, selecting officers, choosing captains, assigning great tasks to worthy men.

But of course my time was a little more free than it had been before and so I returned to that day, and that conversation, and I sat down with pen and paper and wrote a simple sentence at the top of it:

There was once a gentleman, a tall fellow with an air of superiority about him, who made it his business to come down to the marketplace in Portsmouth on the first Sunday of every month in order to replenish his library.

And, with that, I began my recollections, which now feel as if they have finally come to an end. My hope is that the captain's true character has emerged in these pages, as has that of the villain Fletcher Christian, and that when the generations who follow have cause to think of those two men, as they surely must, then the accolades will be placed correctly.

And as for me . . . I have lived a long and happy life, a life that was blessed by a chance encounter with one man that led to a position of willing duty to another. I had many more adventures in the decades that followed – adventures that would fill many thousands of pages, but which my pen is now too drained to write of – but in truth there were none that exceeded in excitement or wonder the ones spent on our mission to and from the island of Otaheite when I was a boy.

But those days are past now. I must still look towards the future.

Acknowledgements

The following books were of great help to me during the writing of this novel:

Caroline Alexander, *The Bounty* (HarperCollins, 2003)

William Bligh & Edward Christian, *The Bounty Mutiny* (Penguin Classics, 2001)

ICB Dear & Peter Kemp, *The Oxford Companion to the Sea*, 2nd ed. (Oxford University Press, 2005)

Greg Dening, *Mr Bligh's Bad Language* (Cambridge University Press, 1992)

Richard Hough, *Captain James Cook* (Hodder Headline, 1994)

Richard Hough, *Captain Bligh & Mister Christian* (Hutchinson, 1972)

John Toohey, *Captain Bligh's Portable Nightmare* (Fourth Estate, 1999)

The transcripts of the various trials that were held in relation to the *Bounty* mutiny were also extremely useful in assembling my story of what took place on board the ship.